Bodies of Light

SARAH MOSS was educated at Oxford University and is currently an Associate Professor of Creative Writing at the University of Warwick. She is the author of two novels: *Cold Earth* (Granta 2009) and *Night Waking* (Granta 2011), which was selected for the Fiction Uncovered Award 2011. She is also the co-author of *Chocolate: A Global History*. She spent 2009–10 as a visiting lecturer at the University of Iceland, and wrote an account of her time there in *Names for the Sea: Strangers in Iceland* (Granta 2012), which was shortlisted for the RSL Ondaatje Prize 2013.

'A tale that holds up a mirror to the female psyche' *The Times*

'Moss has an eye for striking phrases . . . [Her] period detail is superb and her characterisation convincing. A thoroughly satisfying novel' *A Life in Books*

'Compelling' *Big Issue in the North*

'An unsettlingly brilliant, compellingly uncomfortable novel . . . Moss's perception is delicate and pin-sharp' *Marylebone Journal*

'A poignant, well-written tale' *Sunday Times*

Also by Sarah Moss from Granta Books

FICTION

Cold Earth

Night Waking

NON-FICTION

Names for the Sea

Bodies of Light

Sarah Moss

GRANTA

Granta Publications, 12 Addison Avenue, London W11 4QR
First published in Great Britain by Granta Books 2014
This paperback edition published by Granta Books 2015

A CIP catalogue record for this book
is available from the British Library.

3 5 7 9 10 8 6 4

ISBN 978 1 84708 909 0

Typeset by M Rules

Printed and bound by CPI Group (UK) Ltd, Croydon, CR0 4YY

'We have clinical terms for disturbed, but not for *disturbing* persons.'

R.D. Laing and A. Esterson, *Sanity, Madness and the Family* (Harmondsworth: Penguin, 1964)

1

ANNUNCIATION

Alfred Moberley, 1856

Oil on canvas, 72 × 68

Signed and dated '56

Provenance: John Dalby, Manchester, after 1860; James Dunne (dealer, London) 1872; Sir Frederick Dorley, 1874; bequeathed to the National Gallery, 1918

A woman sits at a desk. Her right hand, holding a pen, rests in a pool of candlelight on the green morocco. Gold embossed edging crosses the light like a path through a forest clearing, and Moberley has painted the flame's glow reflected in her silver inkstand, and on her face. There is no ring on the hand, no glimmer around her throat, where a round grey neckline interrupts the pale skin, the hollow between her collarbones. The dress is an absence of light, although usually he enjoyed clothes, the colours and textures of fabrics and skin. Her hair fades into the darkness around her, concealing the arrangement at the back of the head. She looks up, towards the top of the white wall behind the desk, the expression on her face as if someone up there has just knocked on the door. A servant, perhaps, come with some trivial question about dinner or laundry, although in reality the one girl she employed would have been in bed for some time. We know from her letters that Elizabeth Sanderson Moberley believed in early hours, at least for other people. Moberley has caught the look on a face before politeness, the moment between saying 'come in' and assuming the correct mien. Whoever it is, up there, one has the impression that the Madonna would rather he had not come.

Anyone else, James Street recalled him saying later, any other artist living or dead, would have painted the angel. Moberley was not interested in apparitions but in absences, in what is no longer there. Hauntings, reverberations, shadows; the real stories, he reiterated, begin after the event. He did not admit what recent examination of the canvas reveals: that he did begin to paint Gabriel, aflame, inhuman, and then thought better of it. Street records him working on the Annunciation *late one night after a party, swearing by candlelight in the studio which arched into the darkness above him like a church. He always preferred to rise early to paint.*

*

'Elizabeth is in the drawing room,' Mary tells him. 'Mamma has been having another little chat.'

She skips off, jumping on the red tiles in the hall and avoiding the blue, leaving the front door open. At the other end of the hall, the door into the garden is open, and as he reaches to put his hat on the hatstand a breeze lifts the letters on the tray and the front door slams. He likes that, the way houses breathe, the way things move. The door on his left opens and Elizabeth looks around it. He feels his face smiling. Most women, these days, can't peer around doors, can't slip into a room. His friend William claims that his sisters have to squash each other's crinolines to get through their bedroom doors this summer, that they've had to give up lying on sofas after lunch because their skirts would be half-way up the walls. His mind produces an image, from the sofa's foot, of Will's younger sister Louisa in this position.

'It's you,' says Elizabeth. She stands on tiptoe to brush his cheek with hers. He takes her hands as she steps back, admires the coil of her hair, the curve of her breast under the cream and blue sprigged cotton. She smells of lavender and fresh ironing. She is all his.

'Is that Alfred?' calls Mrs Sanderson.

'I'm just going to show him the roses, Mamma.' She pulls him down the hall and into the garden, where he stands blinking, owlish, in the sun. He has walked from his office and was pleased to be in the hall where the tiled floor and the deep porch shading the fanlight mean that it is always cool. Another pulse of sweat seeps inside his clothes.

'I'll bring you a drink in a minute,' she says. 'Mary's been making something she calls lemon cup. Mamma was cross because she picked all the mint.' She stands in front of him, her shadow a cameo rippled by the grass. She puts her hand on his sleeve. 'Have you made an agreement? Is it ours?'

He draws swirls on the back of her hand with his fingertip, barely touching. A shiver passes over her shoulders. Good.

'I'm going to sign the papers tomorrow. You're quite sure about it?'

Her glance tells him not to be foolish.

'You know it will be empty? It won't feel like this house.'

She turns, so she has taken his arm, and they walk towards the shade of the willow tree, her skirt brushing against his trousers.

'I want space,' she says. 'I don't want lots of things. I want to be able to cross a room without having to go around anything. And I don't want curtains. Or carpets. Let's leave the floors quite bare.'

'Will you accept a bed?' He puts his arm around her waist. Their shadows merge, and are consumed by the shadow leaves of the willow. 'A table? Or are we to sleep and eat on the bare floors too?'

She pushes his arm away. 'You know perfectly well that Grandmamma is giving me her desk. And her old bed. Make a table for us. You have time.' She glances at him, gauging something. 'And I decided about the honeymoon. I'd like to go to your cousin in Wales.'

He nods, wishes there were somewhere to sit down, rest his feet. She's right, about Wales; he knows that if they went to her uncle in Cambridge he would find himself going about with Henley instead of attending to her. There will be other times for that. She's wrong about him having time to make a table, but he will do it anyway, for her, for them, for the house. Tables and beds, he thinks, eating and fucking: life.

Lord, bring me to true penitence for these and other sins that my blindness hides from me. Help me to see Your will and always in all things to submit to You. Use me, please God, to bring Alfred into the light and let us walk together at last in grace and righteousness towards Your Kingdom at our end. Amen. She rocks back onto her toes and rises to her feet in one movement. God is with her, His presence laid over her shoulders like a shawl warmed at the fire. She goes to the window, holds back the curtain. Her candle flickers in the breath of summer night, sending shadows leaping on the trellis-papered walls. There is still light in the west, behind the willow tree. The elm, as tall as the house, rustles, its leaves black against the uncertain darkness of the city sky. She hears the beat of a horse walking down the road, the rumble of wheels: no haste. In the new house, she thinks, she probably won't hear people coming and going. There will be the two beech trees, left from the woodland that stood before the new houses were built. They will plant fruit trees; Mamma has always said that it is foolish to cultivate flowers and spend money on garden produce. Apples, a Cox's Pippin like the one behind the coach-house here, and a quince because Alfred enjoyed the jelly she made last year. Plums. Mary can come and help to pick them. She bites her lip. During the day, the prospect of leaving Mary is tolerable, sometimes welcome. There is no point in giving garden space to potatoes and onions, cheap in the shops at all seasons, but she will grow peas and lettuces. Do cucumbers require a cold frame? Well, she thinks, and why should I, why should Mrs Alfred Moberley, not purchase a cold frame if the fancy takes her? She lets the curtain drop and goes to her bed, composes herself. The sheets are chill. She will put Grandmamma's desk in the small bedroom. A woman in the drawing room, Mamma says, is assumed to welcome inter-ruption. Go upstairs when you intend business, and shut the door. (Mamma herself keeps a desk in the corner of her bed-room; only Papa, she says, feels able to present himself there, and after twenty-five years he knows better than to do so.) Alfred won't show her his designs for the new hangings for Grandmamma's bed. A surprise, he says, for your first night in the house, and his eyebrows lift with his smile. She looks away. Mamma has spoken about that, too.

Her new dress, her wedding dress, as Mary enjoys annoying Mamma by calling it, is pebble-grey, cut from a length of rough silk that was her Christmas present from Alfred. You want nothing smooth, he said, nothing shiny, but perhaps you will this once accept silk? Spun by worms in the mountains of China? He showed her a sketch of the dress he'd made in his mind and she looked up at him, startled. The women he likes to paint are draped, enfolded, interesting to behold no doubt but hardly attired for church, or work. She had feared an impractical design, an unserviceable fabric. He has paid attention *to her*, he has thought of how she presents herself. The dress is like all her dresses, cut as are the gowns of working women to lie flat around her, to swing clear of the gutters and disintegrating middens she must cross in the course of her work. It is not intelligent, she says, to trail one's clothes on the ground, even at home, and it makes work for the servants to no rational end. It is not reasonable to use fabric enough for a platoon of tents to swathe one small woman, and besides one would be too hot. So the dress is plain, neat, referring to the present fashion in its pointed waist, pleated bodice and open, falling sleeves. ('They will trail in my dinner,' she had said, 'Mamma would not approve.' 'But I will approve,' he said, 'and it will be I who sees you every day.') And around the hem and the triangular 'angel' sleeves and the demure neckline is a swirl, a blossoming, of embroidery, fruit and leaves and flowers, buds and tendrils and full-blown blooms, grapes and strawberries and round fruit with crowns called pomegranates. Embroidered in grey also, he said. Nothing showy, no contrast. No beading. When the dress is made, he said, give it to me and I will send it with proper designs to a workshop I know. And after we are married, you will sit to me and I will paint you in it.

Someone – Mary – has laid the dress out on her bed while she was taking her bath. She drops her dressing gown and finds clean drawers, a shift, the thin stockings Papa gave her yesterday ('no need to tell your Mamma'), a pair of stays, chemise, petticoat. Her black shoes look wrong with the dress and that is a pity. No, that is something that should be beneath her attention. She shakes her head, her hair wet on her back, and puts on the first layer of clothes. 'Mary,' she calls, 'Mary, I'm ready for you to help.'

*

6

It is traditional, he knows, for the bride to be late, but he does not think that Elizabeth will be, or that Mrs Sanderson would permit any such affectation. He is there early, with Edmund, sitting in the choir stalls where they can see people come in. He knew, of course, that Elizabeth was inviting the women from her Welfare Society. She did ask him. A challenge, a test. Yes, he said, they are better Christians than most of my friends. And did not say that Christianity was no condition of his friendship. In time, he thinks, as she learns his world, she will see beyond her parents' limits. He will show her beauty, pleasure; north light falling through high windows onto white marble limbs, human voices in duet filling the opera house like waves taking a beach, glasses of red wine by candlelight; glories of which she has been deprived all her life, and she will open like a flower in the warmth of his knowledge. The welfare women have arrived early too, in a flurry of babies and muddy boots and bulging bags. Shopping, on a Sunday? (They have no other day, Elizabeth answers in his head, they are in the factories six days a week, and yes, the sellers they frequent do and must do business on the Lord's Day. There is no rest, Alfred, for the poor.) They settle like birds on a field, restive, an eye cocked for predators. This is not their customary habitat. A baby cries, the cat-like wail of the newborn, and its mother takes out her breast and feeds it. In the church. He wonders, not for the first time, if Leonardo da Vinci had a nursing model, and whether Charlotte, who is visibly pregnant and not, to his knowledge, married, would be willing to go on modelling with her baby. Suckling, he thinks, would keep it still. And of course, in time, there will be his own – Edmund elbows him. His parents are taking their seats, and the Sandersons are at the door.

*

7

The aisle seems longer than usual, longer than when she came in yesterday for a moment's quiet reflection. The stained glass, the green hills behind the Cross and the blue sea under the fishers of men, glow on the west wall. Yellow sunlight makes banners of dust shimmer under the windows above the apse. There are lilies on the altar. Faces turn. They are only the women from the club, and Mamma and Mary and Alfred's parents. No-one who hasn't seen her dozens of times before. Her hands sweat in the grey kid gloves. A hairpin presses behind her ear and she can feel a wisp of hair on her neck that ought not to be there. 'All well?' murmurs Papa. And if not, she thinks, if not? She takes his arm, forgets to hold up the white roses in her other hand. Alfred rises and stands at the top of the chancel steps, facing the congregation as if he were the priest. She lifts her head and begins to walk. All shall be well. She will make it so.

She has, she reminds him, travelled by train before. She went with Mamma to hear Mrs Henshaw speak about her work in Liverpool, and Papa has taken her several times – three times – to visit the Director in Altrincham. Even so, he thinks, observing the set of her shoulders under her cape and the way she's holding her face up, as if to catch a faint scent, she is alarmed. It is possible that she has read recent reports of robberies on this very line, but given where she walks, often alone, almost daily, he doubts that she fears crime. What, then? He sighs, holds the carriage door for her and offers his arm to help her up the stair. She steps up, holding her skirts in both hands so he sees the lace figure on her stockings. There are many reasons why a young woman might be despondent on the first morning of her wedding journey.

'You are facing backwards,' he tells her.

She continues to look out of the window. 'Perhaps I prefer to see where I have come from.'

'Than where you are going? Elizabeth, that is hardly encouraging.'

She glances into the carriage, to her feet, and then returns to watching the porters lifting trunks onto a barrow and a lady in pink silk and a veil in animated conversation with a man who is listening too intently to be her husband. 'Of course. A wife should be encouraging. Forgive me.'

He sits opposite her, where he will catch the first glimpse of the sea and will be able to see the engine when the track bends, a pleasure he has not yet analysed. 'You are angry with me,' he suggests.

'Alfred, even in marriage my feelings will not always be about you. I am leaving my home and naturally my spirits are affected. Did you not bring your newspaper?'

He did, not without doubts about the etiquette of reading on their first day alone together. He pulls it from his valise, opens it before him like a screen and begins to read. He has lost track of what has happened in Italy and fears, from his father's conversation yesterday, that there have been events about which the well-informed may be expected to hold opinions. Elizabeth – now apparently intent on two small boys kicking a ball of paper across the platform – probably is so informed. Her right hand finds the ring on her left hand through her glove and begins to prod it as one might a sore tooth.

'We can have it remade,' he says. 'If it is uncomfortable.'

She looks up, questioning.

'The ring,' he says.

'That will not be necessary.'

Her right hand folds over her left, like someone taking the

hand of a fretful child to cross a road. Like charity, he thinks, let not your left hand know what the right is doing. Or something. He lays aside his newspaper, takes out his drawing pad and begins to sketch her hands.

The train whistles and jerks forward. Alfred exclaims as his pencil skids. It is a condition of admission to her club that the women do not use such language, whatever they may permit themselves elsewhere. The tiles on the station wall begin to hurry past. She can still see the two boys, who, Mamma would observe, would better occupy themselves in learning a trade. Mary has offered to help Beatrice at the club this week, and Mamma has said that she may, that it is time she was seeing for herself the world in which she lives. Mary, Mamma said after witnessing her delight in Elizabeth's embroidered dress, has for some time shown a care for inessentials that she should, at fourteen, be outgrowing. The station clock dwindles at the end of the platform. It is Monday; Mamma will be on her way to the new school in Salford, so she can make her weekly report to the subscribers. There is some concern about the punishment book, that Miss Helston has not understood the strength of the committee's views about physical chastisement. Violence, Mamma says, teaches only violence; we must all learn not to depend upon others to control our impulses. A viaduct carries the train over the shameful tenements of Hulme. People sleep under the viaduct, not just drunken men and street women but children who have nowhere else to go. Their childhood does not last many nights under the arches. She recalls Mamma's methods of teaching self-control. I am going to tie this band around your wrist, Elizabeth, so that every time you see it you will remember this fault, and you will know that I am remembering it too. We will remove it on

10

Sunday if it has done its work. Mary, I think that before we go out you must put this stone in your boot and lace it tight, so that each step will remind you how you have disappointed us. Mamma collects the stones in the park, keeps them on the hall table in a basket woven by one of her rescued women. Really, Mamma, says Mary, soon you will be giving us hair shirts to wear. Would it not relieve your feelings simply to box my ears? As soon as Mamma's attention is diverted she removes her boot, even in the street, and takes the stone out. Mary has learnt, however, to keep the stone and pretend when they come home that it has been there all the time; Mamma's methods are not exactly violent but she does believe in the salutary effects of pain. Elizabeth fears she will miss Mamma's guidance in such matters. She must be vigilant with herself, more vigilant than has been her habit.

She crosses her feet. Alfred, who has not asked if he may, is drawing her. She ought to do something, read or sew or write a letter. Mamma gave her Mrs Henshaw's new book about women and work so that she could make use of this journey. They are coming to the edge of the city now, and the sky is clearer overhead. There are hills in the distance; she summons the schoolroom atlas to her mind. England's spine, rising above the Trent and running to the Clyde. She has never climbed a hill, or been to Scotland or, until now, Wales. The leaves on a stand of trees fidget on their branches. He is not, she thinks, drawing her face. His hands move fast, the fingers slim for someone of such heavy build. She remembers his weight on her in the dark, in the hotel room with its unfamiliar shapes and outlines, the sheets starched and rougher than the ones at home. I hope you slept well, Madam, said the maid bringing the morning tea, grinning. I hope you did too, she replied smiling, her peignoir fastened high at the throat. As if

11

she could not, if she chose, employ coarser innuendo than this girl has ever heard in the backstairs. She had known what to expect, and the reality was surprising only in its literality. He really did put that, there. He would do it again.

'Alfred,' she says, 'did you hear of the girl who, on her wedding night, left her husband in the drawing room while she went upstairs and chloroformed herself? And left a note on the pillow that said, "Mamma says you are to do whatever you like"?'

His pencil stops in mid-air. 'That does not sound encouraging either.' He looks at her. 'Are you wishing your Mamma had supplied you with chloroform?'

They are crossing fields now, the flatness of Cheshire. 'You know that I am not.'

His drawing begins again.

It has been dark for some hours by the time he sees the lights of Pennard House. There have been high hedges outlined against the summer night, and the coconut smell of gorse as the cart's wheels brush the edge of the road. A while ago, he put his arm around her, and although she continues to sit upright, her spine countering the bumps and jolts as if she were in gimbals, she has not pushed him away.

She puts down the hood of her cape. 'Someone has waited up for us.'

'Mrs Brant. The housekeeper. There will be bara brith and tea.'

Her head turns toward the light on the hill. 'They keep many servants?'

She is not accustomed to servants. Mrs Sanderson keeps a cook and one girl, believing that there is no reason why healthy adults cannot dress themselves and light their own fires. Just as well, considering his income.

12

'No-one will come into your bedroom until you have left it in the morning. This is country life. And there will be country food.'

Fresh eggs in the morning, and maybe bacon from the farm. Home-made bread and new butter. He is hoping that, when the honeymoon is over, Elizabeth will prove a better manager in this regard than he has been in bachelor life.

'I am hungry,' she admits.

He finds himself hesitating on his side of the connecting door. There is, after all, a single bed in the dressing room, and it has been made up, as if Mrs Brant expects him to use it. It is late. Elizabeth is tired. He bends his ear to the keyhole. Ridiculous, he tells himself, you are being ridiculous. He hears water being poured, the heavy jug settling on the marble washstand. The tinkle of scooped water running back into the basin. She is washing her face. She will have her nightdress on. He will knock.

'Alfred?' she says. There is a pause, footsteps over the bare boards. The door opens. 'I didn't know that husbands knocked.'

He shrugs. 'I seem to. I thought you might –' He looks her up and down. Bare feet under a white linen garment more like a shroud than a bridal nightgown, hanging loose from the shoulders. Her hair falling down her back, her face damp and pale. She looks rather a lot like Temple-Smith's Lazarus, only clean-shaven.

'You should come in,' she says. 'We are married now.'

There is indeed bacon, and Mrs Brant, aproned at the iron stove that runs the width of the kitchen.

'Good morning,' she says. 'Are you rested now, and ready

for your breakfast? And Mrs Moberley?' She glances towards the stairs.

He sits at the scrubbed deal table, its grain warm as skin, as a woman's thigh, under his fingertips. Cousin Frances, he guesses, will have risen hours ago. 'I will be very happy to see you both,' she had written, 'and I know you will forgive me if I go about my business in the usual way. You and Mrs Moberley will want to be walking and sketching, I don't doubt, and I will look forward to hearing your adventures when you come in. There is much to be doing in my garden in June.'

'My wife will be down very soon,' he says. The blush rises over his ears.

Mrs Brant twinkles at him. 'First time you've said it?'

'I didn't think it would sound so strange.'

He has practised to himself. My wife. Edward, allow me to introduce Mrs Moberley. Not his mother.

She puts the teapot in front of him. 'You'll get used to it.'

She turns back to the bacon, takes an egg from the bowl on the counter and cracks it into the pan. Another egg. Her back blocks his view, but he hears the crackle of hot fat. She must be thinking of her own wedding, of the first time she heard Mr Brant – dead, he thinks, some years – say 'my wife'.

'How long does it take?'

'Less than you think.' She lifts the edge of his egg with her wooden spatula and lowers it again. 'It's always surprising, how people get used to things. Even being at war, my husband used to say. Though I've always thought new babies take longer than you'd think to get used to. And people dying. That can stay a surprise for years. Do you know if your wife will be wanting eggs?'

'No,' he says. 'I have breakfasted with her only once.'

*

14

She understands now why people in Manchester speak of fresh eggs as if they were falling stars. Mere greed, Mamma says, when there are families not one mile from here who have not seen an egg of any kind these five years. The yolks are deep orange, almost red, and the whites crisp with bacon fat. She uses her fork to wipe the plate with a piece of bread that has oats on the top and some kind of seed in the crumb.

'Is it your cousin in the garden?' she asks. 'In a print dress and a straw bonnet?' A bonnet of the sort last seen in the city when Mamma was a girl.

'Frances is very fond of her garden. If you're finished, we could go out and meet her?'

She has spent several evenings with his parents, and she knows that they approve of her. Not given to extravagance. Steady and genteel, when one hears of young artists making the most extraordinary alliances. A restraining influence. They must have been afraid that he would marry one of his models. Will it take more than respectability to win Cousin Frances' approbation? She brushes down her skirt. At least Cousin Frances – Miss Moberley? – is plainly dressed.

It's colder outside than she expected, with a wind that blows her skirts hard against her legs, but between the trees and the sky she can see the sea. White waves surge and fall on the blue, and there is a ship with towers of square white sails like papers pegged up to dry.

'Later, might we walk to the shore?' she asks.

She has seen the sea before, of course. At Liverpool and once, as a child with Papa, in Morecambe, though as far as she remembers the tide was so very far out that the ocean itself was just another grown-up story, like the earth going around the sun or the clouds being made of water.

'You could take your paints,' she suggests. And then he can sit down somewhere and occupy himself.

'But I would rather walk with you,' he says. 'I'm sure Mrs Brant would make us a picnic lunch.'

Cousin Frances hasn't heard them crossing the grass. He coughs, and then touches her arm.

'Alfred!' She is older than Elizabeth expected, white hair tucked under the bonnet, although she stands tall and holds the gardening fork shoulder high, as another old lady might hold a spindle. 'And you are Elizabeth. Welcome, my dear.'

She kisses Alfred's cheek and takes Elizabeth's cold hand. 'And how do you find married life?'

I am never alone, Elizabeth thinks, and so far there is nothing to do. 'It is most kind of you to invite us here,' she says. 'I have never been in Wales before.'

Cousin Frances pats her hand. 'I hope we will give you happy memories.'

They walk to the sea down a green lane, where the trees meet over their heads to form a tunnel of bright leaves. Alfred shows her bluebells and wild garlic edging the path, and points out violets under the brambles. The gorse is furred with yellow bloom and dark blades of thorn and gives off an unfamiliar scent. There is birdsong but no visible birds, as if the day sings to itself. In Manchester, there will be brown fog, and heat. At home, Mary will probably be in the garden, reading under the willow tree whose weeping branches screen her from all but the closest inspection. Mamma will have shut herself in her room. There will be boiled meat and potatoes for lunch, the smell hanging in the air for hours after the meal has been eaten. They round a curve, and the sea is there. Flat rocks make a continuation of the lane onto the beach, into the water, as if inviting her to keep walking into the sea. Sunlight flashes from the waves. Pebbles, grey and pink, freckle the sand. Brown seaweed scribbles the high-water mark. She lifts her skirts and runs, stands on the rocks in the sun with the water leaping at her feet. He puts down the picnic basket and watches her, the ribbons of her hat fluttering in the wind, skirts flapping, face smiling at the sky. She turns to see herself being watched.

'Come on,' she calls. 'I should think we could paddle, couldn't we, being married?'

He joins her, takes her hand. 'We could swim, if we wanted to. Being married.'

They find a flat rock on the sand, warm to the touch, and clamber up to sit on it. She opens the picnic basket; no wonder it was heavy. There is a pie with glazed pastry leaves on the top in a blue-rimmed white enamel pie-dish, a lettuce, what must be salt in a twist of blue paper. Two bottles of beer – she has never drunk beer, Mamma does not approve – a fruit like a yellow plum, but with a warm, downy skin from which she almost recoils, as if it were alive, and more bara brith, raisin bread, buttered and folded. Two plates, two knives, two forks, two napkins. Cutlery coupled by her marriage. It is too bright, really, to sit in the sun. Alfred lies back on the rock.

'The tide's rising,' he says.

She needs a spoon to serve the pie and there isn't one. She opens the crust with a knife. 'Does that matter?'

He lifts his head. 'Of course it matters. We're below the tide-line. It will come up and up and past our rock and we'll be stranded here for twelve hours until it goes down again.'

He lays his head down again, stretches out his arms until his hand brushes her back. They are perhaps ten feet from the tide-line.

'We could paddle again.'

'We could stay here and eat apricots and watch the light on the sea. You could recite to me while I draw you.'

Meat filling, flecked with green herbs, falls out of the pie as she tries to transfer some to his plate. 'I can't recite. Mamma says rote learning is the enemy of women's education. Well, I can repeat German irregular nouns. Or conjugate French verbs. All of them. But nobody ever made me chant the names of the monarchs in chronological order and Mamma won't buy those ladies' anthologies of verse. She says we should read poetry or not, but not chop it into bits to patronise undeveloped intellects.'

He salts his lettuce. She serves herself pie, less than she gave him. Mamma considers pastry unwholesome.

'And do you agree with her?' he asks.

She takes some lettuce. 'Yes.'

She wakes in the night. There is no clock in the room, which doesn't matter, really, since neither Mrs Brant nor Cousin Frances showed any sign of thinking anything of her late rising yesterday. She could, she supposes, rise after eight and breakfast on bacon and eggs for the rest of her life now, if she wanted to. She shivers at the idea. Careful not to move the blankets too much, she turns over, straightens her legs. Alfred sighs, and resumes his slow breathing. Moonlight comes under and through the gap between the curtains, which are made of a shrunken cotton print with a lining too heavy for the fabric. The house is silent in a way that home has never been, the silence of old stone walls and fields lying dark outside, stretching to the sea. She wonders how the sea would look in the dark. She turns her head. She can smell the pomade Alfred puts in his hair, and the laundry-soap on his nightshirt which is different from her own. In time, she supposes, sharing a bed, using the same laundry, the same soap, they will smell the same. Mr and Mrs Moberley. The back of his neck is as thickly furred as his chest; she had not known, Mamma had not told her, that men had hair all over, like apes.

She wants to go to the window and look out at the trees and the sky. They heard owls earlier, and she has never seen an owl. Her foot itches, and Alfred seems to have trodden sand from the beach into the sheets. She will be sharing her bed for years.

Alfred has made the new hangings for Grandmamma's bed. He asked her, flowers and fruits, flowers and birds? He has been working on a design for a wallpaper where there are bees in blooming honeysuckle. Could it not be plain, she asked, white or cream to show the carving on the endposts? Oh you Quaker, he said, that an artist should marry such taste! Tell me, Elizabeth, would you prefer the pictures on the walls plain to show the frames? The new hangings, he says, will be a surprise for her when they arrive at the house. Their house. He is having the walls painted and papered. Some rooms will be as bare as she could hope for until they can afford the right materials, but it is important that he has drawing and dining rooms where potential clients can be entertained. That, he says, is one reason for buying the house. She has not reminded him that is it Papa who bought the house. He will expect her to provide dinners for these people and to preside at his table. He has given her a book about housekeeping, as if he thinks Mamma's teaching will not be sufficient guide.

'Elizabeth?' he murmurs.

'Shh. It's the middle of the night.' She pats him as she used to pat Mary, years ago when they shared a room and Mary had nightmares.

'I know. You're awake.'

'The moonlight woke me,' she says. It's slanting the other way now, over the black-painted floorboards towards the looped skirts of the wash-stand.

He sits up. His hair is tousled and there is the imprint of the rumpled pillowcase on his left cheek. 'Do you want to go outside? See it properly?'

Does she? 'What, in our nightclothes? Alfred, what about your Cousin Frances? And Mrs Brant, doesn't she sleep here?'

'No.' He pushes back the bedclothes. His legs, sticking out from his nightshirt, remind her again of apes, apes in white cotton. 'It wouldn't surprise me if Cousin Frances is out there herself, chatting to her roses or some such.'

He pulls back the curtain. 'Glorious. Look at it. Come with me.'

She looks away as he steps into his trousers, draws the sheets back up to her neck. Mamma had insisted that they omit the promise to obey from the wedding service. You must be free to do what is right, she told Elizabeth, and we know that Alfred cannot, at least at the beginning, guide you in matters of the spirit. You must lead him towards God. But with this freedom comes the responsibility not to resist for mere wilfulness or self-indulgence. Earn your liberty in great matters through obedience where only your own interests are concerned. Mamma had not foreseen injunctions to go into the sea in her drawers and shift, or to go out in her nightgown in the middle of the night. She rolls onto her side and stands up, neatly, displaying only her ankles. 'Pass me my cape,' she says.

*

20

I will stop noticing this, she thinks. This will be the road down which I walk every day, and I won't see how tall the trees are, how the chestnut leaves filter the sky. I won't notice the way the builders have gone to the trouble of patterning the bricks on those chimneys, the cabling in yellow, or the stone pineapples on those gateposts. That gaslight will shine in our bedroom window at night, but the hedge will grow, over the years, and the wisteria will cover the trellis. The carriage stops and Alfred, whose head has been lolling, sits up.

'Welcome home,' he says.

She climbs down before he or the coachman can help her, opens the wrought-iron gate and crunches over the gravel path to the front door. She has no key. She resists the urge to rattle the door, yank the handle until she forces her way in. Alfred is still paying the coachman. She goes around the corner, to where the conservatory fills the space between the twin bays of the dining room and drawing room. Alfred was too late to redesign the stained glass panels over the windows. That door, she knows, should and will be locked too, but she tries it anyway, and keeps going towards the back door, past the kitchen's high windows. The door has been painted a shade of dark green gloss that she doesn't like, and she can't get in here either. Footsteps cross the gravel behind her.

'It's easier with a key,' he says, offering one. 'Front door. The others are inside.'

She takes it and goes ahead of him along the drive, through the gap in the hedge and back up the steps into the tiled porch. Bigger than the porch at home, wide enough for several people with umbrellas or, she supposes, two women in crinolines to stand side by side. The key won't turn. Her hands are shaking. She doesn't want help. He stays on the step behind her. The brass knocker rattles as she pushes through.

Inside, in the square hall with its teak floor, sprung, the builder said, for dancing – not that there is room for dancing – she stops. The rooms around her are empty, waiting. Waiting for their lives to begin. The builders have been here, she thinks, they have eaten sandwiches out of paper packets and drunk from bottles of beer in my drawing room, gone up and down my stairs in their dusty boots, whistled in my bedroom. Only Adam and Eve had a truly new home.

'May I come in?' he asks, head around the front door.

She turns. 'I'm sorry. It's your house. But you've spent time here and I saw it only once.'

He comes in, decides against trying to take her hand. She veers away from him, into the drawing room.

'Oh.'

She knew, of course, that he had already papered and painted it. It is like being trapped in a forest, a forest at dusk in the autumn. Withering vines congregate, their pale tendrils reach and twist, and there's a suggestion of eyes, of pointed noses, in the shape of the spaces between dark leaves. The picture rail – how can they hang pictures against such a paper? – is mud-brown, like raw clay, not a colour she has ever seen in a house before, and the wall above it even darker, like peat, like open graves. Even the ceiling is coloured, the colour of puddles in a dirt road.

He comes in. 'I'm working on some curtains,' he says. 'Do you like it?'

The sunlit garden shimmers in the window, its greens too dappled, too bright, for the underground room.

'It's rather dark,' she says. 'Even in July.'

'We'll light a fire in winter. And there will be velvet curtains and candle-light.'

And we will feel, she thinks, like foxes in the undergrowth, except that foxes' earths are not also shop-fronts.

'You don't like it.'

He is her husband. This is her home. In time, perhaps, he will learn, she will teach him, to value a simpler life. 'I am unused to it,' she says. 'You know how simple are Mamma's tastes. I have not been brought up to appreciate this richness. Such display.' He reaches for her hand. 'Show me the dining room.'

He watches her walking ahead of him, head high, making the best of it.

'My dear, this is my work, you know. Our livelihood.'

She stands, floodlit by sunshine, in the bay window. His table is there, made from the fallen walnut tree that his father had saved for him these five years. His carpentry, he knows, is not his best work, but the workshop foreman helped him with the joints. No lion's claw feet, no legs curved as though bowed by rickets, but, thinking of his honeysuckle paper, he has carved a flower and a bee on one of the two supporting columns, as a kind of signature. There are not, yet, any chairs.

Her shoulders lift as she takes a breath, prepares to speak, pauses, her hand resting on the table's gleaming top. She tries again.

'I like this one. This seems easier. More comfortable.'

She can imagine herself reading or sewing in here, without feeling that she is on a stage. There is pale apple-blossom, leaves and twigs on the walls, and twice in each drop a small, brown bird.

'The paper will seem quieter when the room is furnished,' he says. 'And I thought we would have muslin curtains, for summer, and maybe velvet in the leaf colour for winter.'

'Yes,' she says. 'Yes, Alfred, I would like that.'

She comes to him, touches his jacket. 'And I like your bee, your worker bee. Have the hangings for the bed come?'

They go up the uncarpeted stairs, her skirts brushing the barleycorn banister spindles. There are carved acorns on the newel posts.

Returning to the club feels like going out for the first time after a sickness. The ring on her hand keeps catching her eye, like one of the bands Mamma used to tie around her wrist. She knows the women will want to hear about her honeymoon. She turns into the courtyard, and does not raise her handkerchief to her face although the smell, in this heat, is worse than ever. People live here, and breathe this air, and drink this water. She remembers the bluebells in Wales.

'Lizzie!'

It's Mary, waiting with some of the mothers on the hall's doorstep. Her black skirt is smeared with dust and her face is red and damp under her straw hat. They embrace, Mary's cheek cooler than her own.

'Mamma sent you alone?'

Mary takes her hand. 'She brought me. She's gone to the school, and to see Mrs Hayter at the infirmary. She said she'd come back before three o'clock. Oh, Lizzie, I do miss you. Mamma is such hard work. Can't I come and live with you?'

Elizabeth strokes Mary's unravelling plait. 'No, darling. For all the reasons you know. But you may come to tea, if Mamma says so. Alfred likes there to be cake and sandwiches. And he will see you home afterwards.'

Because Elizabeth and Alfred are both busy with their work. Because Mary's education is not complete. Because

Papa would miss her too much. But mostly because Mamma would not allow it, because Mamma has not finished with Mary yet.

Elizabeth unlocks the door. 'Do come in,' she says. 'Mrs Brown, Mrs Hampson. Mrs Jenkin, how is baby today? And Mrs Murphy, quite well again? I am afraid you have got very thin.'

Mary is lighting the stove, filling the kettles from the bottles of water that Elizabeth has delivered three times a week. She knows what goes into the river.

'Please sit down. Here, Mrs Murphy, have the low chair.'

Mrs Murphy, who lost her third baby just before Elizabeth's wedding, leans back and lets her head loll against the chair's wooden rail. Her eyes are sunken. She used to mend her clothes, but now a bare knee pokes through a rent in her skirt. She's wearing men's shoes, one unlaced, and her red hair is matted at the back of her head. Mrs Jenkin, cradling her own child, meets Elizabeth's gaze and shakes her head.

'Tea, Mrs Murphy? A biscuit?'

Mary sets out needles, thread and thimbles. She opens the drawers where they keep cut patterns ready for sewing, not adult outerwear, which is beyond the capacity of these women, but children's clothes and undergarments which are much more important to decency. Streetwalkers often have nothing to wear under their dresses. Women from the club may go in cast-off rags but they have what Mary calls 'secure foundations'. Elizabeth pushes aside the memory of some of her own secure foundations weighted by stones on a Welsh beach. She takes a book from the shelf under the window, 'Sermons for Mothers'. If she reads long enough, there will be little time for personal questions.

'Find the biscuit barrel, Mary,' says Elizabeth. 'Did you piece no clothes last week, Mrs Jenkin?'

'So Mrs Moberley, you will write to the subscribers?'

Something tightens, a pain. Perhaps it will be all right. She forbade herself to check before she left the house, having done so on rising and after breakfast. Checking changes nothing. But now – she drinks some more of her tea – now she really does need to use the necessary. Or at least it would be prudent to do so before setting out home.

'Mrs Moberley?'

'Oh yes, of course. Sorry.'

The others exchange smiles. The new bride with her new name. Let them think so. She shifts a little in her seat. Does something trickle? Her breasts have been sore. It is only a week. Perhaps two. The human body is not a railway clock. She has been late before.

She won't check again, not until she really does need to ease herself. They have put flagstones on the new pavement, in time for autumn. If she can avoid all the cracks – no, if she steps on every crack. If she can count to twenty before that cart passes. There would be expense. Papa will probably help with the doctor's fee and there is Mary's old crib still in the attic at home, and goodness knows she and Mary are practised enough at the making of infant clothes, but there will – would – need to be a monthly nurse. And a layette, and indeed furniture for the nurse. And for a nursery. It is foolish to say that they cannot afford to have a child. Alfred's income is ten times that of the most secure families in her club, most of whom include at least four children. But she cannot, at the moment, see how they are to afford it.

She could take an omnibus from here but it would cost

money. She will carry on walking. She crosses the road, returns the sweeper's greeting. Mamma has always said that the women's accounts of birth are exaggerated, soldiers' tales that grow with each telling. They do not have the habit of self-discipline, she says, and of course they do not have proper attendance. In many circumstances, if we permitted ourselves to scream and cry we would convince ourselves and our companions that our situation was insufferable; we do not do this when we scald our hand – Mary had just done so, and had cried – and we do not do this when we are unwell. Poor women do not have your upbringing, your discipline, and rich women have been taught that they are frail, sickly things who cannot rise from the chaise longue without mishap. If you find yourself in this condition, Elizabeth, continue about your usual business, take at least as much exercise as is your habit, be sure to eat only moderately and I am sure that you, like me, will experience no discomfort beyond the capacities of a rational mind to support. Many of those country women who are accustomed to outdoor work, their health undermined neither by city air and city food nor by luxury and indulgence, pass through these times without distress, and their children are almost invariably born strong and well.

Her feet are sore. When she gets home, perhaps she will make tea and sit in the garden, just for a few minutes. She is not sure her mind is as rational as Mamma's.

He wakes, as usual, at dawn. There are still no curtains in their bedroom; he's made sketches, a lighter version of the bed-hangings, but it will, he acknowledges, be some time, some months, until he is in a position to have them made. Mamma offers her old ones, Elizabeth says, but he distrusts the interim solution, has seen too many clients hang this picture here for

27

now, until they find time to call upon the framer, and have it still there, in the same terrible frame, three years later. If he lets Elizabeth hang that chintz he will see it every morning for the rest of his life.

The leaves of the beeches are beginning to turn, to spin with the murmur of wind. Later, someone will need to rake them from the lawn, or when autumn comes they will cover it like wet paper. Beeches, he supposes, naturally cohabit with other beeches, not with cut grass and rose bushes. The garden is going to be a perpetual battle to impose human ideas of order on a space that, left to itself, would perhaps revert to woodland, to the forest that must once have covered this place. He wouldn't mind living in the woods. Elizabeth has been speaking of fruit and vegetables. He must find a man to come and rake the lawn, and trim the hedge. He must allow some money to pay such a man. He should get up and do some more work on the designs for Mrs Chamberlin. He eases the covers off, not to wake her, but she's far away. Her breathing doesn't change. He doesn't want to wake her but he touches her hand and there's no movement, no murmur. Does she worry about money? He slides his feet into his slippers and steps carefully across the boards. It may be amusing to have no furniture now, the summer of their honeymoon, but he is beginning to see that it will be less of a joke in winter, that the contrast between the public and private spaces of this house may come to seem like a comment on the relative importance of his work and their marriage. She has not said so, not yet. After all, she spends much of her own time away from the house, working in the slums. She knows, better than he, how rich their poverty really is. She is not a woman whose spirits are troubled by curtains. Is she?

*

She is sewing. Something white, no larger than a table napkin but considerably more complicated, a three-dimensional geometry in fine cotton. She often speaks while sewing; it must require less thought, less devotion, than painting. More like carpentry. Perhaps he will learn sometime. It might be useful to be able to make his own tapestries. He looks again at the *Manchester Times* in his hands. The light is fading. Even with the window behind her, it must be getting harder to see the white stitches on the white ground. She holds her work up in front of her, pulls it a little, frowns.

'Of what do you think,' he asks, 'while you sew?'

She makes another stitch, draws the thread out across the leaves in the window.

'On this occasion, of dying and the world beyond.' She looks up, smiles at him. 'But that is not a practice. More often, probably, my mind runs on what to have for dinner that will not necessitate a shopping expedition, whether I might not have served my women better with a different reading, or a different response to the reading, and if there is anything I might venture to say to Mamma about Mary. The usual ephemera of the mind at rest.'

'But today you think of death?' He folds the newspaper away.

'Today I heard that one of the women has lost her son. He was ten. An accident in the factory. They could not stop the bleeding.'

The leaves stir at the window. A bird crosses the square of paper-coloured sky.

'Oh, Elizabeth. Will you visit?'

She puts down her sewing. It must, at last, be too dark. 'In a few days. I will attend the funeral.'

Her head is drooping. Her hands, for once, at rest.

'Elizabeth? Would you sit for me? The portrait?'

He has asked her before. She has been too busy, too tired. Perhaps next week. Does he not have other things to paint?

'Now?'

He stands up, holds out his hand. 'Just a beginning. Just to find a pose. The new armchair?'

She puts the sewing in the basket at her feet. 'Very well. Although I am tired. But I won't sit idle in an armchair. At my desk or not at all.'

It's a beginning. He can always persuade her to move later, when she is accustomed to the idea of posing, to his gaze and the barrier of the canvas between them. He follows her up the stairs, where dark is gathering in the corners of the landing.

'But wear your dress,' he says. 'Please. Your wedding dress.'

'It's late, Alfred. I have had a tiring day. I'll wear it for you next time.'

He lights the candle for her, kneels to arrange her skirts.

'Do you do this for your models? Move their clothes?'

She knows that his models do not always have clothes. She has known this from the day she met him, in the gallery, with her Mamma speaking of the unbound female form, free of whalebone and steel.

'As Vermeer arranged his flowers and fruit, no doubt.'

'They are as flowers and fruit to you? Charlotte?'

Charlotte had her baby last week, and modelled until the end.

'When they pose for me, they are patterns of light and form, shapes and colours. You know this.'

Yes. He does not want a pretty face or a well-turned limb, but a strong contrast, an 'interesting angle'. He does not look at them as he looks at her. He stands up, steps back.

'Stay like that. Stay still.'

It reminds her of the schoolroom. When we fidget like that, Elizabeth, it is because we are attending to our gross bodies. You are thinking of your hair, or the skin on your finger, or the strap of your bodice, and when our minds are occupied by such things they are closed to light and grace. You must learn to keep your mind on higher things. Mamma had made canvas mittens which she had to tie over Mary's hands to teach Mary to stop twisting her hair around her fore-finger.

She holds her head still. 'You won't object if I write? There is little point in allowing me to sit at my desk if I may not work.'

He is sketching. 'Just keep still this one evening? Later, you may write.'

She needs to write to the subscribers, all twenty-two, asking for more money because the women have asked her to buy primers and writing materials for the club. She needs to copy out the minutes of the last meeting. She needs, she remembers, to complete the household accounts, because Alfred will want to see them on Friday. He frowns, apparently at her waist. As well he might. A yawn comes upon her. She has never been so tired. If she is at home in the afternoons, she has to walk around the garden to keep herself awake, to write and sew standing up.

He has stopped drawing. He expected her to be uncomfortable, anticipated painting her discomfort. He knows that she sits to him in defeat, not, as with his models, because it is her job, nor, as with his two commissioned portraits, because she wishes to see herself through his eyes, but because he is her husband and he asks it. He wants to paint her defeat. But there is something else, in the angle of her chin and in the way she looks at the pages on which he has asked her not to write,

31

a charge as well as a surrender, as if she has a secret. An unhappy secret.

'Elizabeth, are you quite well?'

She turns her head, meets his gaze.

'Quite well, thank you. But I would like to go to bed soon. When you have finished.'

It will take some weeks to finish, he thinks. And by the end, he will know what she does not say.

2

JENNY, SLEEPING

Alfred Moberley, 1857

Oil on canvas, 58 × 64

Signed and dated '57

Provenance: Moberley family; donated to Falmouth
Polytechnic Institute by Alethea Moberley Cavendish,
1898

*One shoe has come off, and lies on its side on the carpet, black against the
blurred geometry of blue and green. The other hangs from her foot, about
to fall, its shadow spilt under her chair. There is sunlight coming through
the muslin curtain to the right, and a blur of blossom on the wall behind
her. Jenny's body is a curve of navy, because she's curled up in the chair,
feet hanging over one arm and her head rolled back against the other. Some
of her dark hair is caught back, but it's slipping down over her pale face
and her neck, giving the impression that the painting has a black-and-white
centre fading into the swirled colours of the wallpaper and Persian rug at
the edges of the canvas. One arm dangles, tanned, and there's a white
bandage on the hand. She's sleeping – her eyes are closed, and it's not a
posture a woman would adopt deliberately – but she looks uncomfortable,
as if she's been thrown into the chair or is trying to get a night's sleep in
a railway carriage.*

It has been suggested that the model was the Moberleys' housekeeper,

*of whom no other images exist. There is no record of the circumstances
of this painting, and the identification of the model is merely conjectural;
as far as we know, there was no other Jenny in Moberley's circle at this
time.*

*

She has been moving around for some time, slow footsteps
across the room and the boards creaking as they do. She hasn't
stayed in bed all night for weeks, going downstairs – he thinks
to eat – sitting in her armchair reading when she's too uncomfortable lying down. She stalks his sleep like a ghost, as if, restless
herself, she can't bear his peace. If they had another bed, he
would have slept there. He turns over, pulls the blankets around
his ears. She steps on the loose floorboard by the window, and
he hears a whimper in her slow exhalation. He sits up.

'Elizabeth?'

She is leaning forward, bracing her arms on the window-
sill, her bulk outlined against the night sky. There are still no
curtains.

'I think you should fetch Mamma. Now.'

He does hurry. But he doesn't run. First babies, Mrs
Sanderson has said, take a long time; even if Elizabeth feels
that there is urgency, they should remember that there is not,
that this sense of haste is among the erroneous impressions of
a first labour. A natural labour, she said, waving away the
cream jug he offered at the tea table, proceeds without drama
and haste. It is permitting agitation that causes complications.
And Elizabeth will not be harmed, his mother-in-law said, by
a period of time alone while you summon attendance; there
is most certainly no call for any woman to keep a midwife in
the house as fine ladies like to do. He remembers his wife's face
tightening as she closed her eyes and leant on the banister, and

34

his footsteps on the frosty pavement change tempo. Even so, this moment, this walk, is one of life's rare aporia, a moment of pause before everything is changed. The night air stings his nose and chest. There is a tracery of rime on the flagstones, a feathering that reminds him of Street's peacock curtains. High cloud drifts across the stars, and the city around him lies quiet, windows blank as closed eyes, trees and hedges stone-still.

The smudged charcoal black of the sky turns pallid grey. He should go to the office as usual, Mrs Sanderson says. It is not even time to call the doctor yet; Elizabeth has, as her mother feared she would, announced her crisis hours before it was necessary to do so. Working women go about their business for the first hours of labour, as did Mrs Sanderson herself. She will remain in the house and send for him at the correct time. No, she thinks it best if he does not see Elizabeth before he leaves. Elizabeth has allowed herself to become unsettled and it will be better for her and the baby if she is not indulged. Upstairs, there are footsteps, and a moan.

'Excuse me,' she says. 'I must endeavour to bring her to reason. I had hoped she would show more strength of mind. Go to work, Alfred. You can do nothing here and you will have need of all you can earn.'

Even so, he finds himself irresolute in the hall, his feet poised to leave and yet his weight balanced to stay. Can it be wrong to indulge a woman who is in pain? Genesis itself, surely, gives permission to labouring women to cry out, enduring such trial as can be justified only by the Fall of Man. Perhaps he should stay. To do what? He has a client, a very wealthy client, coming to the office to discuss a decorative scheme for his new house, including a ball-room. Mrs Sanderson is right, they need the money. The baby will need the money. And he knows nothing about birth. As Elizabeth herself would no doubt observe, these things are best handled by women. He opens the door slowly and eases it shut behind him. The sun has come out. Dew sparkles on the grass and there are snowdrops bright against the flower bed Elizabeth has dug by the front gate. A good day, he thinks, to be born.

The baby is crying, its rage spreading like smoke through the house, curling under the ceiling. She has lost her blotting paper. Probably Alfred has taken it. She waves the letter in the air, back and forth as if signalling to someone. There is no-one. The air is cold; after the last coal bill, she doesn't light fires during the day, not until Alfred comes home. She addresses the envelope. Three done, eighteen to do. The baby cries. She seals her letter and begins the next one. Her breasts tingle and begin to leak. Below, blood wells. The baby has left her permeable, seeping. Violated. *Dear Lady Heathcote*, she writes, *I write on behalf of the women of the Manchester Welfare Society to express our deepest gratitude for your contribution to our funds.* When she has finished this one and the next one, she will see what there is for her lunch, and feed the baby. It cries. It is taking the baby a long time to learn that screaming for what we want does not bring gratification.

'You don't think the grey too dark, Mr Moberley?'

'It will be dramatic. The gold in the curtains will shine across the room, and the lilies seem almost to glow. Your friends will be astonished. But you must keep the furniture very plain. Effects like this depend upon simplicity.'

As she turns to him, her scent wavers in the warmth of the fire. A log crackles. The clock on the mantle begins to chime.

'Will you stay for tea, Mr Moberley? I expect my husband would like to join us.'

Her figured skirts sway over the carpet as she crosses the room to ring the bell, an aura of silk rippling behind her. Elizabeth does not wear damask, does not rustle, does not lay claim to the space around her. He's never seen Mrs Dalby's feet. He doubts very much that John Dalby would admit to having enough time to take tea with the designer; Dalby's newly made fortune – railway stocks – somehow requires his constant attention.

'That would be delightful, Mrs Dalby.'

A servant in a white frilled cap and apron brings a tray with a round-bellied silver teapot nestling on a lace doily, and two cups and saucers with lace of their own. She's followed by a younger girl bearing a laden china cake-stand and something under a silver dome. He lays his sketches in the space between a group of pot plants and a herd of silver-framed daguerrotypes on the cloth covering the grand piano. He has much to teach Mrs Dalby. She pours his tea, both hands to raise the teapot, and then lifts the silver dome. He has an urge to hit it with a teaspoon, as a kind of tuning fork.

'I ordered anchovy toast for you. Gentlemen often prefer it to cake.'

He sits down with her and lifts his cup, a cup so thin he could crush it between finger and thumb.

'But I, Mrs Dalby, have a taste for sweetness.'

She laughs. Her fire sends a flickering light over her silks and her curled hair. After tea, she will play the piano for him, and at Easter, her husband will write him a large cheque, enough to pay the winter's bills and commission the weaving of the carpet for his and Lizzie's bedroom.

She hears Alfred's feet coming up the gravel path and hurries to pick up the baby. By the time his key is in the door, she is sitting in the rocking chair. She takes out her breast but the baby is too busy screaming to nurse. In her dreams, its mouth grows, lion-sized and then cavernous, chasing her and devouring her, and when she wakes she must offer it her breast. The baby's gums are like blades in her nipples. He comes up the stairs. His face is pink and he looks sleek, well fed. The baby's hand against her breast is cold; perhaps that is why it cries. He kisses her cheek and strokes the baby's face with his finger. It turns to his hand, mouth first, desperate, as if her breast were not waiting. He smells of the world outside, of smoke and sky and pavements.

'Has she cried all day?' he asks. 'Poor Ally.'

The baby is called Alethea, a compromise between his stubborn fancy for a Greek name and her insistence on one that stated moral ambition on the child's behalf. Penelope, indeed. Who would want a daughter named for a rich pagan woman remembered only for undoing her knitting? Martha, she says, Mamma suggests Martha. But Martha, he said, was a sanctimonious charwoman. A worker, she said, a woman worker rewarded for diligence and humility. Alethea, truth-teller. The truth shall set you free.

His finger grazes her breast and he pulls back, as if at the touch of a snake. 'And, of course, poor Lizzie also,' he adds, too late.

'She always cries all day,' she says. 'And most of the night. Will you take her?'

'One moment.'

He's wearing his smart work clothes, the clothes he wears to seem prosperous. The baby likes to vomit, spewing out, wasting, the milk that she makes and transfers with such pain and trouble. The baby has crusts on its scalp and she begins to pick them off and drop them between the floorboards, where

Alfred won't see and she won't have to clear them up. Some of its fine down comes too. A little blood seeps from one place. She rubs it with her finger and brushes the baby's cheek with her nipple, which is cracked and will bleed again when the baby sucks; the blood in the baby's vomit, the doctor has assured her, comes from her breast and not its stomach. This problem is common and her blood does the baby no harm. The baby cries, and does not feed. She puts her breast back in her bodice, and Alfred comes and takes the baby.

'Poor baby.' He pats its back, and it tries to suck his cheek. 'Poor little Ally-baba. Lizzie, is she cold? She feels cold.'

Elizabeth stands up.

'She is well wrapped,' she says. 'Hot rooms are unhealthy. I'll light the fire downstairs now you're back.'

On the stairs, for a few moments until Alfred brings it to join her in the dining room, she is free of the baby.

Although it's not as he would have designed it, he likes the office. The stone blocks and ornate pediments, the flourishes of carved acanthus leaves and pineapples, remind him some-times fleetingly, by sunlight, of Cambridge. Inside, through the heavy door whose key he sometimes catches himself fingering as he walks home, back to Elizabeth, there is dark red carpet on the wide boards and fires in the marble fireplaces. All three of the designers' offices are at the back, high up, where the north light flows through windows taller than Alfred. Clients are kept on the ground floor, sometimes peering up to the half-landing where they keep a silver epergne designed by James Street himself full of hot-house flowers. It's best, Street says, to maintain an air of mystery around the process of creation. It's like making sausages, buyers prefer to believe there is a secret, transformative process in the detail.

And maybe there is. He has been thinking for a few days about rowan trees, the pattern of shining leaves and dark berries, the regular intervals and angles at which the leaves grow, and the clustering of berries. He cannot think of anything else in the natural world that has quite that colour, that deep orange red. In a woman's dress, it would be called 'flame-coloured' – Mrs Dalby has an evening dress of almost that shade – but even the endless variety of fire does not include the depth of ripe rowan berries. In the north, rowan trees are thought to ward off fairies. Or maybe to encourage them, he can't remember, but anyway the association with folk belief pleases him. He will probably need to use a cream background, but he intends to try blue first, the very pale blue of a tentative spring sky, a colour he might, in another context, call 'robin's egg'. (When did he last see a robin's egg? He cannot remember ever doing so; perhaps the colour he has in mind is quite foreign to robins.) And the leaves a strong, summer green – he remembers the hedges in Wales – a brave foil for his flaming berries. He lets himself in and hurries up the stairs, already, in his mind, mixing paint for the pencil sketch he carries in his pocket.

Mamma has said that she should not attend the club while she is nursing the baby. Mary, Mamma says, can attend to it. The responsibility will do Mary good. It is Elizabeth's part now to care for her child. Mamma does not approve of nursemaids, who drug infants to keep them quiet, risk smothering them by sleeping in the same bed to avoid rising at night, and later teach rough speech and superstition. If a woman cannot care for her own child, if its education and moral progress are not her first concern in life, she is not worthy of motherhood. It is no wonder so many girls go astray when their upbringing, their very salvation, is left to the care of poor, uneducated servants while their mothers amuse themselves in idleness, attending better to their gowns and lapdogs than the immortal souls with which they are entrusted. Elizabeth looks at the baby, which is crying in its crib. Of course it has a soul, but the idea seems unlikely. The baby, so far, screams, sucks her blood and milk with gums that feel razor-sharp, or, occasionally, for entirely unpredictable lengths of time that make her afraid to start anything for fear of what she might do to the baby when it awakes and forces her to stop, sleeps. It seems more like an animal than a person, and not even a pet, which would purr or wag its tail to show pleasure, but an insect. A venomous insect. A reptile, except that reptiles, she believes, are usually silent. She understands exactly why nursemaids drug babies. The baby is still crying. She can hear Tess, the 'daily girl' Alfred has insisted on employing, moving dishes around in the kitchen downstairs. She will go down and ask for a cup of tea, and if the baby is still crying when she comes back it will be four hours since last time and she will feed it. Again.

He was right about the blue. It jars in the chord of green and orange. He's drawn the leaves in movement, as if a wind stirs on the wall, and he's working on the light on the berries. There's a murmur of voices next door, Street talking to RDS, and in a few minutes he needs to go downstairs and talk to Philip Sidford about his dining room, where the rowan design would go rather well. He could try a deep terracotta paint above the picture-rail, a few shades darker than the berries. He adds more burnt umber, more yellow. Someone knocks at his door.

'Yes?' His tone says what he means. No, *go away*.

She puts her head around the door. They are not alike,

these sisters, not in colouring or figure, but there is something about her face that gives him a sudden view of Elizabeth as she must have been ten years ago.

'Mary?'

She comes around the door, wearing one of the dark, skimpy dresses advocated by his mother-in-law, her hair in a tail down her back.

'Do you mind very much? I'm sorry, I didn't know how else to see you. Mamma thinks I'm helping at the school.'

School?

'Oh, you know, Alfred. St Catherine's. It's only around the corner.'

He doesn't know. He doesn't walk that way, where the streets are filthy, unpaved, and pick-pockets stand in dark corners.

'But you're not,' he prompts.

'I'll go in a minute. I'm worried about Elizabeth. And Ally. I don't think Elizabeth likes her very much.'

'Mary!'

She shifts her weight, ducks her head. 'Sorry. I shouldn't say it like that. I mean, I think Lizzie's not quite herself. I think she is unhappy, and I am afraid the baby is also unhappy. Ally cries all the time.'

He rinses his brush. He will need to go downstairs in a minute and he would like to get Mary out of the building before his clients come in.

'She won't light the fire when I'm out,' he says. 'I have told her we have money enough to keep the baby warm.'

Mary rubs her skirt between her fingers. 'Mamma doesn't approve of people cosseting themselves. Or anyone else, actually.'

She sees him glance at the clock. 'I'll go now. Sorry.'

42

She vanishes, as if she were one of the spirits against which the rowan affords protection. Or not. He gathers his papers, waits until he hears the front door and then follows her down the stairs.

Mr Sidford has asked him to visit his new house out in Bowden, and to bring samples to show Mrs Sidford. Mr Sidford was enthusiastic about the rowans, which Street asked Alfred to fetch from his room, murmuring something about genius and artistry. His wife, Mr Sidford said, would enjoy the idea of ordering something so new there is no sample available. Alfred walks fast, fuelled by success, by the prospect of more clients and more commissions and, of course, more money. He was right to buy a house he couldn't afford to furnish, right to believe in the firm, in his work, in himself. After the rowans, he will think some more about water lilies, perhaps with a nosing fish in alternate repeats of the main pattern. Street has recently bought a Japanese print showing goldfish in a pond, by someone who can convey spreading rings of water. But he wants a lily paper, dense with leaves and bright with petals. Nothing too watery.

It's been raining. There are still puddles, and his trousers are spattered with mud from the road, but he waited, delayed leaving work until the sun should come out, and here it is. The trees along the road, still human-sized, are coming into full, blue-green leaf, and the horse-chestnuts hold candelabra of pink and white flowers, like airborne hyacinths. Babies are said to like looking at trees; perhaps he will bring Alethea along here. Or take her to the park, to the Queen's Gardens which are only five minutes from the house. Later, she will play there with her hoop and skipping rope, will hide in the bushes and feed the birds. In his mind, there is a perambulator as well as a three- or four-year-old Ally. He's doing well enough, now, to begin a proper family.

For the first time, she is glad that Tess is in the kitchen. She woke up thinking of knives, took only porridge for her breakfast because even a butter-knife seemed a bad idea. She is still thinking of knives. The baby is still crying. For shame, Elizabeth, says Mamma, think of the club women, who care for four or eight children in a dwelling smaller than this drawing room, who have only a fire for cooking and that only when there is money for coal, who work all day as well as rising at night with their infants. You disappoint me, Mamma says. That I should see a daughter of mine a sloven and a coward! Mamma is right, has always been right. She is weak. She is slovenly. The baby has defeated her. If she goes out, she is afraid she will buy laudanum, and if she stays in the house, there are knives. And fire, and the staircase. And windows high under the gable. The baby cries. She cannot pick it up because of the windows and the staircase, and she cannot walk away because of the knives and the laudanum. So she stands there, in the doorway, and the baby cries. The baby drives her to evil thoughts. Its perpetual screaming calls her towards damnation. Before the baby came, she was full of light.

'Madam?'

She doesn't look up. Tess doesn't need to see what's in her eyes.

'Madam? Are you ill?'

She pushes her shoulders back. Imagine that there is a string from the crown of your head to the ceiling, Mamma used to say.

'A little tired, Tess. Thank you. I believe I will take the baby for an airing.'

She crosses the room and lifts the baby. It is wet, and smells. She holds it at arms' length. It screams.

'Tess, would you be so kind as to change her? Perhaps just this once?'

Tess is staring at her. 'Of course, Madam.'

'There you are,' Tess says to the baby. She clasps it as if it weren't urine-soaked and, somewhere under there, caked in excrement. 'There you are, baby. Come along, my tiny maid, and we'll make you all nice and clean, shall we?'

Tess leaves, and there is silence. She breathes, in, out, and there is still silence. She can hear the beech leaves rustling in the wind, and wheels along the road outside. It is, she thinks, Thursday. There is sunshine. She will take the baby to the club. It is Mamma's day for the Dispensary. The women will like to see it. Most of them appear to like babies. She used to think that she herself liked babies.

Alfred bought a perambulator, an expensive one. He says there is more money now, that they can afford to live well, can certainly afford to make it possible for her to take the baby out. They could, he suggested, pay for a nursemaid, if she would like. She would not like. She may be a sloven and a coward but she is not – yet – so utterly abandoned as to hand over their child to a stranger, to abdicate the responsibility with which she finds herself entrusted. Yes, she agreed, she is finding these weeks hard, but does he think he is married to someone who will not endure what is hard? Does he think her weak, imagine that a little money will tempt her to the foolish emulation of fine ladies? She hopes she has strength enough to value her eternal soul over a few weeks' ease. He will not, she thinks, mention the subject again. She objected also to the perambulator, for the price of which the club women could feed their families for many weeks. If Alfred wishes to help infants, she remarked, the money would be better spent on coals and soup for dozens than unnecessary extravagance for one. But the one, he said, is mine, and so I like to spend my money on her. The baby, of course, enjoys the perambulator. It desists from crying there as it will not in her arms, or at her breast, or in its crib. Tess returns with the baby, silent but for hiccups.

'Put it in the perambulator, please,' she says, and watches Tess carry it down the stairs and lower it onto the nest of blankets as if it were a crystal vase, a tiara being placed on its silken cushion. 'Thank you, Tess, that will do.'

She closes the door behind her before bumping the perambulator down the stairs onto the gravel, where the wheels sink and she has to brace her arms and her knees to plough a path to the gate. The baby begins to cry again, but it seems quieter outdoors, even here. Perhaps she will go east, to the factory district, where there is noise enough to silence even this infant. Mamma is always telling her to take more exercise.

He is at Mrs Dalby's tea-table again. She invited him to come and see the dining room, which is, at last, finished.

'I cannot believe it is mine,' she says. 'Do you know, Mr Moberley' – she lays a hand, smaller and paler than Elizabeth's, on his sleeve – 'do you know, I come in here every morning, all alone, and I stand here and look and look, and think that this is my very own and I can come in here and adore your beautiful work any time I please? It seems almost too beautiful to use, a sacrilege to bring people in here wearing brash colours and introduce odours of food and scent and a babble of conversation. Of course everyone admires it greatly – I have been giving out your name to half Cheshire – but I cannot think that they all understand it as you have taught me to do. Oh, Mr Moberley, I cannot tell you how much I enjoy it!'

Flattery, he thinks, the artist's opiate. Silly words from a silly woman. But he worked hard on this room, dreamt of it as he walked the streets and lay through Elizabeth's restless nights, and woke with the colours clear in his mind. And he was right. The golden lilies shine out from their curving leaves, and the butter-yellow at the top of the wall echoes the flowers' light, while the sage green, darker than Mrs Dalby wanted, frames her and her new, plain, table and chairs. The long windows face west, and he would like to see the room, as he has imagined it, at sunset and twilight. She shows her ignorance by worshipping here in the mornings, if that is indeed what she does. Nevertheless, she says that now she is embarrassed by the rest of the house, that she longs for each room to be as striking as her new dining room, and that Mr Dalby has said that she may instruct him to send sketches for the drawing room (this, he thinks, is the one with the piano and the daguerrotypes). And so here he is, taking tea, this time with iced queen cakes instead of anchovy toast.

'You see?' she says. 'I remembered, and sent Jane specially to Daniels, didn't I, Jane?'

Jane, capped and aproned as last time, bobs her head. 'Yes, Madam. First thing, to be sure of getting them.'

'So you see you must stay and eat them with me.'

There is no fire this time, but sunlight strained by lace curtains which veil a pleasant view of the garden. He can see fronds of the honeysuckle that frames the window undulating at the edges of the machine-made lace, which is not as clean as it might be. That will go, along with the doilies and the cloth draping the piano for no good reason, and most of the occasional tables whose sole purpose seems to be the elevation of dusty plants in silver pots embossed with cherubim and roses. Will he be allowed to change the fireplace?

47

She sees him looking. 'I am almost ashamed to see your gaze on my house, now I know the transformations of which you are capable! But you must tell me exactly what to do, what I must buy and what I must throw away, and you will find me quite perfectly submissive. Lemon or milk?'

Good Christ, he thinks. Her dress is cut low, half an inch too low for daytime wear, and she must be so tightly laced she can hardly breathe. He could span her waist with his hands. If you unlace a woman like that, does she spring back into shape like a released sponge, her lungs whistling as they re-inflate? Elizabeth says that corseted women become weaker and weaker as their bodies come to depend on whalebone rather than their own muscles, until they can barely stand without support. Perhaps Mrs Dalby would instead subside like a dress when it is taken off and lie there immobile. Quite perfectly submissive.

He meets her eyes. 'Lemon, please.'

'And do take a cake.'

He does. They are good. He and Elizabeth could afford to buy cakes from Daniels now, but Lizzie wouldn't consider such a thing. Decent women make their own, except that she doesn't. Cakes ruin the digestion, and anyway she is too busy caring for the baby and writing to benefactors. He looks around, imagining the room stripped and bare to plaster and wood. Some of the dreadful oils in ornate, gilded frames look like family portraits, but perhaps, with tact, they can be relegated to the stairs. And then he will start again. There is enough light for the water-lily paper. Perhaps the Dalbys could be persuaded to put in a pond on the terrace outside, with real water lilies. This tea-table, with its bulbous legs and lion's paw feet, could be replaced by something in pale oak, maybe with a small joke, a tiny frog or a dragon-fly, carved into one leg.

Dragon-flies. Dragon-fly curtains? Iridescence, the brightest of blues, the whirr of wings, the diagonal bodies. The floor needs to stay bare, but could there be a tapestry on the end wall, weeping willows and a shady pond, lilies and dragon-flies?

'I can see that you are thinking, Mr Moberley. Are you inspired?'

He finishes his tea, misses the saucer as he replaces the cup. Like making sausages, Street says.

'Perhaps I am. Mrs Dalby, would you be so very kind as to excuse me? I believe I have the beginnings of an idea for you. And I will return next week?'

She rises, as if drawn by strings.

'But of course, Mr Moberley. Fly at once! Next Thursday, perhaps, and Jane will go to Daniels again?'

He bows. 'You are too kind, Mrs Dalby. I thank you.'

The perambulator limits her to streets she wouldn't usually frequent. The wheels are narrow, designed, really, for nursemaids to push around London parks, and certainly not for the mire of Manchester's working districts. So she can't go to the club, or to visit the Poor Schools, or to the infirmary, where anyway Mamma says she must not take the baby. In any case, Mamma says, taking such a costly thing through streets where the people have never been able to give their children a hot meal would be in the worst possible taste, not to mention placing temptation in the way of the indigent. It is indeed a shame and a sin to fear a fellow-creature, but if Elizabeth and Alfred will insist on flaunting their wealth then there are places she should no longer set foot. Elizabeth does not fear, now less than ever, because anyone who wanted to knife her would only save her the endless conversation with her own mind about doing it herself, and anyone willing to take the baby would likewise realise a situation for which she longs but about which she can do nothing herself. Just make it go away, she finds herself praying now, although she has hardly tried to pray since the baby was born. Take back the baby, give me back my old life and Lord, I will do anything that you ask of me. But she knows what the Lord asks of her, because of what she has. And she knows she has that for which thousands of women across the land pray nightly: a kind husband, a pleasant house and a healthy infant. She is an ungrateful child, unworthy of her blessings. You should be on your knees on the stones, says Mamma, giving thanks and imploring forgiveness for your ingratitude. We will kneel together now and ask God to give you penitence.

But he doesn't. The baby has parted her from God.

She walks the streets, the perambulator and her sober clothes her guarantee of safe passage. Men proposition her still, and she replies, as Mamma taught her ten years ago, 'May the Lord have mercy upon your soul.' A prayer unlikely to be answered, but sufficiently disconcerting to allow time to walk away. She walks the omnibus route, which is paved, telling off the shops like beads on a rosary. Ribbons, hats, meat (enamel trays set to catch the blood). An iron-monger, the window festooned with iron chains as if they were paper chains at Christmas time. What do people in Chorlton want with so many iron chains? The cobbler, with lasts of people's feet displayed like the meat around the corner. The fruiterer, where unripe plums show fingerprints on their dusty bloom. The baby cries. Another butcher, a haberdasher, a flower-stall. She keeps walking, her hair wet with perspiration under her black straw hat. The perambulator has a canopy, but since the baby cries all the time anyway she doesn't bother to raise it. Let the child have something to cry about. She crosses the road, not because there is anything she wants on the other side, and keeps walking. The shadows have tilted as the afternoon wears on. Sometimes she thinks she can almost hear the slow drip of passing seconds, each dead moment like the wait for a raindrop to cross a window. Heat rises from the flagstones and flies crawl, crow-black, on the dung in the road, and congregate on the baby's blanket. It must have soiled itself again.

She keeps walking. Traffic thickens, the rumbling of wheels on stone rises like the noise of the spinning machines outside a factory. The perambulator opens a way for her, like a plough through the crowd of men in hats and dark broadcloth, women in bright prints, some buoyed like boats by their crinolines, parasols their sails. The shop windows here are bigger and cleaner, so the sun glares off them as from a mirror. She is thirsty, always thirsty.

'Miss Sanderson?'

A harlot. Frayed pink silk, crusted around the hem, torn at the breast. A black eye under a grazed forehead, a bruise on the chin, but even so –

'Jenny? You?'

Jenny was – is – the daughter of one of her women. Jenny used to attend the school.

'I heard you married.' Jenny peers into the perambulator. 'Oh, there's a fly on her! Poor baby.'

If Elizabeth had a penny for each time someone says 'poor baby' she could have bought a sewing machine for the club by now. No-one says poor Elizabeth, tired and thirsty and bored beyond despair.

'Jenny, has someone hurt you? Your face . . .'

Jenny laughs. 'Not just my face, love. How old is she? What did you call her? I heard you was expecting. And you ain't Miss Sanderson any more.'

'Mrs Moberley. About three months. Her name's Alethea. Jenny, what happened?'

''S pretty. Nothing. Lost me job. Did you have a hard time with her?'

'So you need work? I can help you, you know.'

Jenny could come to the house. If Alfred can invite his clients, why should she not invite hers?

Jenny leans over and strokes the baby's hair. The baby cries more quietly and looks at her. 'I doubt it. Not now, you can't.'

Elizabeth digs in her bag. Alfred likes her to carry his card in case she talks to someone who might want to employ the firm, which she doesn't, ever. 'Here. It's my husband's card but that's my address. Come and visit. You can play with the baby if you like.'

He hears Alethea first, because the room that's too small to be called his studio is beside what, despite the lack of nurse, they call the nursery. He waits, brush poised; Elizabeth will go. There is no movement downstairs, where he believes her to be sewing. He washes in more of the background. Ally's crying rises a tone. The nights are lengthening again. He won't have natural light for much longer and he doesn't like doing this part by candlelight. He dips the brush again and holds it, dripping, over his pot of water. When she was first born, the baby's cries sounded like the mewling of a cat and he didn't understand how Elizabeth could hear them from another floor, but Ally's got better at making herself heard. She sounds angry, has the same outraged tone as Mrs Dalby when her bell isn't answered. He smiles to himself and gets up. Ally baby, Princess Al. He'll take her down to Lizzie, save Lizzie the stairs.

It's much darker in Ally's east-facing room, and at first he can't see her. He walks blindly towards the crib, and finds that she has rolled over and is lying with her face pressed against its wooden bars, apparently unable to reverse her achievement and roll back.

'Poor baby.' He picks her up, though he knows Elizabeth thinks she should not be taken out of the crib once she's been put down for the night. She rubs her wet face on his neck and he pats her back as the crying subsides. He stands, swaying from one foot to the other like someone not dancing at a ball, and catches the milky scent of his daughter's hair. 'Poor baby. Papa's princess Ally. Shh. There now. Papa's sweet one.' I sound, he thinks, like a nursemaid. No wonder they are said to be stupid. 'There, baby. Hush now.' He begins to hum, a waltz, and the baby softens in his arms. No need to disturb Elizabeth. He can do this.

He has just picked up his brush again when the doorbell rings. This time he hears her footsteps cross the dining room and hall. There is a murmur from the next room but no cries, and the front door and women's voices. She had not mentioned visitors this evening; it must be one of the committee members. He has a few more minutes of fading light.

But he works on, and then, by candlelight after all, on. Even the stillness of water lilies is not static, and he wants a sense of their tugged movement, of the shining drops and pools of water on their already shiny leaves, and maybe a suggestion also of the life stirring underneath. At last one of his candles gutters, and then another quietly goes out, and when he looks up the room is dark and the sky outside streaked in the west, behind the beech trees. He stands up and stretches, his shoulders cracking. Ally is still quiet. Elizabeth had a visitor, he recalls, but there are no voices. She must have left without him hearing. Has Lizzie gone to bed? He crosses the room, avoiding creaky boards, and peers over the banisters. There's light under the dining room door, so he goes down. Elizabeth is sitting in her usual chair, reading the Bible, but opposite her, in his usual chair, is a sleeping woman, her hair over her face. The hair is streaked and crusted with some dark substance – blood? – and, as he comes into the room, he sees that there is blood down her pink dress, whose hem is torn and spattered with mud almost to the knee. He can't see her face clearly, covered with hair and dim in the candlelight, but something looks wrong. Elizabeth turns a page.

'Ah, Lizzie?'

'Her name's Jenny.' She doesn't look up. 'She's the daughter of one of my club women and she's going to stay with us for a few days. Someone's hurt her, badly, and she's very tired.'

'Lizzie?'

She looks up now. 'What?'

'Ah, Lizzie, what are we going to do with her?'

She puts her Bible down. 'You are not going to do anything. I'm going to sit here with her until she wakes, and then I'm going to draw a bath for her and find her some decent clothes and probably call a doctor to attend to her injuries.'

He stands there, his water lilies still in his mind, his baby daughter sleeping overhead, his tiredness. If he offers to help, she will probably send him out into the night to find a doctor willing to attend an unwashed street-walker, or give up his bed to the woman. It will do you no harm, Alfred, to know the merest taste of what tens of thousands of people within two miles of here suffer every hour.

'Good night, then,' he says.

'Good night, Alfred.'

When he wakes, the room filling with grey light and the baby crying in the nursery, she's not there. He pushes the covers back; it's cold, and this winter, whether Elizabeth likes it or not, if he has to interview and appoint a girl himself, they are going to have a servant who will wake them with tea and light a fire before he has to get out of bed. Charlotte has recently called on him, hoping for work because her baby's father has left her and gone to London. He sent her away, being of no use as a model now with her breasts and stomach stretched and hanging like empty bags. With her own infant sent out to nurse, she could care for Ally as well as helping Lizzie around the house. He leans over the banister, barefoot in his night-shirt, and shouts.

'Elizabeth? Lizzie? Where the devil are you?'

The house is silent, and Ally is still crying. She holds up her arms as he approaches. He picks her up; she's wet through as well as hungry. Poor baby. He wraps her in a blanket, not to soil his nightshirt, and joggles her on his shoulder.

'Elizabeth! Come here!'

She doesn't. He puts the howling infant down on his own bed while he puts on his dressing gown and slippers, and then carries her downstairs, into the cavernous chill of the hall. There's no-one in the drawing room, the dining room, the kitchen. No-one answers his bellow down the cellar stairs (not that he really expected her to be down there). Ally is still crying. A man who can make a table must surely be able to change a baby's clothes. They return to the nursery, where he puts Ally back in the crib while he finds a pile of clean diapers under Elizabeth's rocking chair and some very small garments in a cupboard. The garments have strings and it is not entirely clear to him which of the baby's limbs goes through which hole, but the point is only that she should be comfortable. He opens up the blanket. The baby's outer layer is easy to remove. Under it is something that will need to go over her head. He tries; it gets stuck around her eyes and the crying becomes hysterical. Poor baby. Where in God's name is her mother? He will be late to the office. He vanquishes the small jumper, and the next thing has ties down the side and the thing under that buttons. She doesn't seem to object to the removal of her socks, leggings and diaper, and now he's calm enough to observe the folds of the diaper before he drops it on the floor. A triangle, of course, folded again. A man who can drape a woman to resemble the goddess Athene has no reason to fear the arrangement of cloth. He overcomes his anxiety about the pin. Ally's legs, red in the cold, lift as she gulps air, and the hollow in her ribcage deepens as she prepares another howl. A tear runs over her temple and he blots it with his sleeve before it reaches her ear. Poor baby. There is nothing he can do for her hunger. He pushes her feet into a clean pair of leggings, threads a damp starfish hand through each hole in one of the things with ties. He tries stretching the neck of the jumper and easing it over her head held wide in his fingers, which seems to work. He doesn't bother with the top layer, a fine cotton garment that adds nothing to her warmth, drops the wet things on the floor and folds the blanket around her again. He feels better, but there's no sign that she does. Where the bloody hell is Elizabeth?

He hears feet on the gravel as he carries Ally downstairs, both of them dressed and more than ready for breakfast, but it's only Tess. Mrs Moberley, she points out, always does breakfast. Mrs Moberley likes Tess to arrive at half-past eight, which it is. He doesn't want any breakfast, he says, but he does need to go to the office. Here's the baby. He believes Mrs Moberley was called early to attend to one of her charity women in some kind of trouble. She must have been unexpectedly detained and will surely be home soon. Tess is please to send for him, here, at this address, if his wife has not returned by midday. The baby, he supposes, will have to wait; if Elizabeth does not return this morning he will call on Mrs Sanderson, who will know what is to be done.

He sits at his desk. He's writing to the printer about the lily paper, trying to describe the colours he wants ready for his next visit, but the ink has dried and he's watching the fire, the first fire of autumn. Elizabeth cannot be allowed to go on like this. Especially with the two new commissions, they have money coming in, enough to make the cold rooms and lack of servants affectation rather than prudence. And in any case, if Elizabeth will not consent to a nursemaid he will himself make an arrangement with Charlotte, and someone – perhaps her mother – must speak to Lizzie about her obligation at least to feed the child. He intends to have the comfort he can afford whether she wishes it or not, and he does not intend that his child shall starve for lack of the most basic care. He unfolds the note that arrived an hour ago and re-reads it. *Dear Alfred, there is not the slightest cause for alarm. I had merely escorted Jenny to Dr Davenport, knowing that he will see pauper patients out of charity before beginning his day's work; there are yet men who grudge neither their time nor their sleep where there is unrelieved suffering. It being Thursday, I will not expect you until late. Elizabeth.*

And so it has come to this. He will indeed take tea with Mrs Dalby.

There are éclairs this time, and the fire is lit again. He lays out his water-lily sketches on the piano, sweeping aside the daguerrotypes and setting the pot plants on the floor, and she leans close against him to see them. She's wearing scent again. Diamonds on fine gold drop from the pink holes in her ear-lobes, curtained by shining hair, and again she's laced so tightly that he could touch his fingertips around her waist.

He can, in fact, touch his fingertips around her waist.

She laughs and doesn't move.

'Have you been wanting to do that for a long time?'

'Perhaps I have,' he says.

She takes his hand and raises it to her breast, to the bare skin above her bodice.

'Perhaps, Mr Moberley, there are other things you have been wanting to do?'

'Perhaps, Mrs Dalby, there are.'

He stays to dinner, to discuss the lily pond with Mr Dalby. Four courses, three wines. It's dark before he leaves, too late for the omnibus so he has to take a cab. He walks up the gravel path as quietly as he can, hoping Elizabeth will be asleep, hoping that he will be able to leave early and go to the office and think there about what he has done. About Mrs Dalby, Emilia, who smells of powder and violets, whose flesh is so soft it seems as if his hands might pass right through her. He eases the front door open, leaves his coat and hat on the newel post to avoid opening the coat-cupboard, whose door squeaks. He creeps upstairs. There's light in his and Lizzie's bedroom. He peers around Ally's door, holds his breath to hear her breathing, but there's someone else there too, a huddled shape on the floor that raises its head.

'Sir? It's me sir, Jenny. Mrs Moberley said I could sleep here. I'll tend the baby if she wakes in the night.'

He withdraws. A whore in Ally's room, sleeping with his infant daughter? He goes into his own room and shuts the door. Elizabeth is in bed, reading the Bible.

'Lizzie,' he says. 'Lizzie, get that woman out of here,

tomorrow morning. I'm going to take Alethea and sleep down-stairs with her, and I want that street-harlot gone when I come home tomorrow. Do you understand?'

She lowers her book. 'That street-harlot is a fifteen-year-old girl who has been despoiled and beaten by gentlemen, Alfred. Two gentlemen at once, in fact, on Tuesday. And they have left her in such a condition that even if I were to do as you ask and return her to the streets, she would be unable to continue with the trade that for the last six months has kept her from star-vation. I should say that the very least she is owed by the gentlemen of the middle class is a few days' food and lodging. Would you like me to tell you what has been done to her, Alfred, by men like you?'

'Elizabeth!'

'Men against whom she has no protection in law, and who continue, perhaps this very night, to abuse her sisters in the same way, without fear of justice or even loss of reputation. Men who have learnt that the streets are populated with girls to whom they may do whatever pleases their depraved incli-nations. And it is she from whom you would protect your daughter? She and not they?'

He sits beside her, stretches a tentative hand towards her arm. She is shaking.

'Alfred, if you throw Jenny back onto the streets, I will leave this house with her.'

And Ally, he thinks, will you take Ally?

'I said nothing about throwing onto the streets. I don't want her sleeping with Alethea.'

'She asked to. She likes babies. She's never slept a night alone in her life. She's little more than a child herself.'

'A child? After six months on the streets?'

Elizabeth pulls up her legs and rests her chin on her knees.

Her hair is in a plait down her back and he remembers that first night in Wales.

'There are children younger than her. And yes, they are children, though they have been robbed of their childhoods.'

He tries to imagine what Street would say about this, or Edmund or RDS. My wife has invited a street-walker to stay for a few days. A whore is sleeping on my daughter's bedroom floor.

'You must find her somewhere else tomorrow. And I'm not happy about her sleeping with Ally. I shall take the crib downstairs with me and pass the night on the day-bed.'

Jenny has gone when he comes home the next day. But two days later he comes back to find Elizabeth and Alethea out somewhere – the perambulator is not in the hall – and Jenny once again asleep on his chair, wearing one of Lizzie's dresses. There's sun on the apple-blossom wallpaper and one of her shoes has fallen onto his Persian rug, so her pale face, dark hair and navy dress stand out against the light and soft colour of his dining room. Her hand is still bandaged; Lizzie says she tried – and failed – to protect other parts of her body from broken glass. He fetches paper and pastels from upstairs and settles at the table to make a sketch.

3

STUDY IN GREY
Aubrey West, 1866
Oil on canvas, 192 × 127
Signed 'ABW' and dated 1866
Provenance: Sir Frederick Dorley, 1867; wedding present
to Eliza Morton, 1881; James Dunne (dealer) 1891; Mrs
Jane Kingsley (New York) after 1897; Kingsley family

Two girls in one chair, wearing the same dresses and shoes. Their skirts
merge as if there's one grey muslin creature with four feet in black san-
dals, two pairs of folded hands and two heads, one taller and darker than
the other. The chair, upholstered in grey velvet, has a wing back against
which the children lean, one head in each corner. Their hair is unbound,
standing out around their shoulders. The smaller one's legs stick straight
forward. The corner of a grand piano and a violet-grey wall stand behind
them. There's no visible source for the daylight that infuses the picture, like
one of those cloudy English skies that could be any time of year, any time
of day. They stare out at the viewer. He hasn't tried to disguise their
boredom.

*

Ally peers over the banisters, pressing her chin against the
wood. The mahogany looks warm but it's been polished to ice,

and her bare feet are cold. She pulls the sleeves of her night-dress over her hands and tries to see if she can open her mouth while her chin is on the handrail. She moves her jaw from side to side, as if she's part of the wood trying to wriggle free. The candles in the hall below are lit. Papa won't have gaslight, because of the colour. She leans over a bit further, purses her lips and blows a thin stream of air to make the flame below her falter. It's hard to aim. She hears Papa's laugh from behind the dining room door, and the voices rise around him like a swirl of birds disturbed.

'Have they gone through?' May is holding both handles of their open bedroom door and leaning back to swing from it.

'Shh. Not yet. They're still talking.'

'They're never going to get up. Never ever.'

'Shh. What, do you think they'll be still there in the morning? Jenny will go in to sweep and they'll be still sitting there in their evening dress?'

May stops swinging. 'Yes. Drinking wine from the red glasses and laughing. And we'll go down for breakfast and they'll still be there, and at lunchtime.'

'Tess will change the dishes and they won't notice!' Ally says. 'Papa will say, do take some porridge, Mrs Sidford. And they'll still be talking. We might as well go back to bed.'

May frowns. 'You said we could take some of the dessert when it comes out. You said so. You said there'd be candied plums and Turkish delight.'

Ally stands up straight, as if there were a hook attaching her head to the ceiling. 'We show our character in accepting disappointment,' she says. 'All right. Let's wait a bit longer. I'll be Aubrey and you be RDS and we're meeting the ghost in Venice.'

'Can I be the ghost?'

'No. You'll forget to wail in a whisper.'

'I won't. I can remember. I learnt last time.'

Ally remembers. Stealing from the dessert is a really bad idea, the kind of thing children do in the books Aubrey gives her that doesn't work if you try it in real life.

'All right. You be the ghost. But let's go back in our room and shut the door. We'll hear if they ever leave the table.'

Aubrey's Venetian ghost has been one of their favourite games this autumn. Sometimes Papa lets them use some of the props in the studio, and then Ally likes to dress up like the princess in Aubrey's copy of the portrait of Luisa d'Urbino, wrapping the red velvet around her shoulders and winding the paste necklaces around her head, because Aubrey said the ghost was richly dressed and dripping with jewels. Usually they have to make do with an ordinary ghost in a nightdress. Aubrey and RDS stayed in a hotel for their first few days in Venice, but it was expensive and there were fleas, so they went looking for lodgings. It was a hot day and there were reflections in the canals which RDS wanted to paint, but Aubrey made him keep going, working their way down a list of addresses that a kind lady had given him. Most of the rooms were already taken, because lots of people like to go to Venice to see the water and the pictures and the beautiful churches and palaces. (Yes, Papa said, one day, when you are older. If Mamma says we may.) At last, late in the afternoon when they were tired and hot and the shadows of the palaces had reached over all the reflections, they knocked on a door where the lady said yes, she still had a room, right up at the top under the roof. Aubrey and RDS went through the wooden door and found themselves in a cold, stone hall, more like a barn than part of someone's house, with its own little canal so that the people who lived there could bring their boats right into their house. The lady took them through another door and up and up a stone staircase, worn so much that it was slippery and hard to climb even on that bright day. Up and up they went, higher and higher, the stairs narrowing until Aubrey hardly dared to look down, although the lady's back stayed straight, straight as Mamma's, as her black skirts swept the stairs. There were doors on each landing, leading, Aubrey guessed, into marble halls with fireplaces as big as Mamma's pantry, where windows the size of the dining room wall were hung with tattered velvet curtains. The lady didn't take them into any of those, but up and up until the stairs ended in an arched doorway. There was hardly room for the three of them to stand outside it, so Aubrey waited on the stairs, still afraid to look down. She took a huge, iron key, as big as that ladle, and they followed her in. Light blinded them after the dim staircase, northern light pouring through the roof-lights. She'd said it was one room, and there were no internal walls, but the attic covered the whole of the top floor. They had to duck around the roof beams, the biggest tree-trunks Aubrey had ever seen, big enough to build the Venetian galleons that used to go right down the Mediterranean to Africa and the Holy Land. When Aubrey stood in a gable to look out, on the other side of the roof-light he saw a nest of squabs – baby pigeons, May – in a chimney pot on the other side of the glass, which hadn't been washed since those galleons bestrode the world (that's Shakespeare, Ally, and one day we'll read it together). Behind the squabs were waves of red-tiled roofs, and in the distance the cupola of San Giorgio Maggiore. They would have taken the place anyway, but it also happened to be clean, equipped with two beds and a perfectly acceptable selection of furniture and a small stove where they could heat water and cook. The lady said that their washing could be done by her household and that there was an excellent trattoria around the corner where they could arrange meals for a good price. A place of their own in Venice! Aubrey could have kissed her, even more so when she said – as they signed the agreement – that some people claimed to have seen a ghost up there, a grand lady of two hundred years ago. She personally saw no reason why grand ladies would frequent garrets in life or afterwards, but in any case the ghost lady was quite harmless and rather pretty. She hoped the English gentlemen would not be afraid?

Aubrey found himself waiting for the ghost, especially in the evenings when he and RDS sat at the table by candlelight, writing their journals and letters and talking over the day. Sometimes when he woke in the night he would catch himself straining to see across the apartment, where there was always something creaking or fluttering. The attic got very hot during the day and, since the windows didn't open, they propped open the door at the top of the stairs at night. Perhaps the ghost would come that way? She didn't, of course. He knew she wouldn't, because ghosts don't exist. Not, at least, in rainy and sensible England. And then one day, in the morning, in broad daylight, RDS had gone out early to paint and Aubrey was puttering around, having slept late and woken with a headache as grown-ups sometimes will. He was trying to tidy his clothes away when he thought he saw someone move at the other side of the apartment, right away by the gable. Yes, May, where the squabs were. Damn headache, he thought, but the figure was still there, and when he looked up he saw a dress of deep blue silk, the darkest colour on a peacock's tail, with great skirts like a sail and a deep, square neckline. He couldn't see her face clearly – it was blurred, somehow, in the morning light, although the dress was as clear as you are now – but there were pearls in her dark hair and a winged cap of the peacock silk and lace. He wasn't afraid. She paced the room, like someone troubled or much preoccupied, with her hands folded as if in prayer, or perhaps just because her sleeves were tight and that's how women held themselves in those days. Aubrey stood there like a fool with certain articles – yes, Ally, that's a polite way of saying underclothes – hanging in his hands. Goodness knows what the ghost lady would have thought of those but she didn't seem to see him. And then she was gone, pfff, just like that, and he sat down on the bed and wondered if he was dreaming, or even a little mad. And maybe he was, because they never saw her again, and he's still not sure RDS really believes him. We do, said Ally, we believe you, don't we, May?

'A new dawn is shining, over the sea. A new day is stealing o'er river and lea.' Papa holds the last note until his voice cracks. His singing is so dreadful that although he sings this song almost every morning, Ally couldn't guess how the tune is meant to go. She pulls the blanket over her head.

'Light comes to the cities, it comes to the hills. It shines on our railways, and on England's mills. Girls, must I sing another verse?'

He tugs on Ally's blankets. He's opened the curtains and it's too bright. 'Come on, Princess Al. Were you holding court all night again, up here while we were dining? Time to get up.'

May is sitting up and looking around as if she's never seen their bedroom before. It has the Briar Rose paper that Papa designed just for them, as if to stop princes getting through in the night, and a silky rug that Mamma says is really far too good for the nursery, on which they sometimes fly to Arabia or the North Pole. Over the table, Mamma has hung a text in a large black frame to which Papa objects. It breaks up the briar pattern and dominates the wall. Ally knows it by heart now, from Matthew 6, just after the Lord's Prayer.

> *But thou, when thou fastest, anoint thine head, and wash thy*
> *   face;*
> *That thou appear not unto men to fast, but unto thy Father*
> *   which is in secret: and thy Father, which seeth in secret,*
> *   shall reward thee openly.*
> *Lay not up for yourselves treasures upon earth, where moth and rust*
> *   doth corrupt, and where thieves break through and steal:*
> *But lay up for yourselves treasures in heaven, where neither moth*
> *   nor rust doth corrupt, and where thieves do not break*
> *   through nor steal:*
> *For where your treasure is, there will your heart be also.*
> *The light of the body is the eye: if therefore thine eye be single,*
> *   thy whole body shall be full of light.*
> *But if thine eye be evil, thy whole body shall be full of darkness.*
> *   If therefore the light that is in thee be darkness, how great*
> *   is that darkness!*

She reads it through again, moving her lips. How would she know, if her body were full of darkness? The last few leaves are still clinging to the beech outside the window. Ally hears Mamma opening the wardrobe door in her bedroom.

'I'll pour the water for you,' says Papa. 'Downstairs in ten minutes, please.'

Ally sits up and watches Papa pour steaming water from the jug into their basin, which has roses on the inside. You haven't washed your hands properly if they haven't both touched the roses.

'Come on, lazybones. I want to see both of you standing up before I leave the room.'

67

Sometimes May curls up again after he's left, and is late to breakfast so that she has to go to bed without supper. Ally stands up and gets first wash.

'May, we try to eat without making a noise,' says Mamma. 'Jam or butter on your toast?'

'Jam,' says May.

'Jam?'

'Jam, please, Mamma.'

'That's better.'

Mamma makes the jam, with plums from the garden, and lets Ally and May help. They have to dribble it from a tea-spoon into a saucer of cold water to see if it's set.

'I will be visiting the Home this morning.' Mamma passes May's toast. 'Ally, you may accompany me. There is, I regret to say, a little girl only a year older than you newly arrived.'

'What about me?' asks May.

Papa puts down his newspaper. 'Ten? A ten-year-old?'

Mamma nods, once, as if there is nothing to say.

Papa shakes out and folds the paper. 'And you want to intro-duce Ally to this child?'

'Catherine needs a playmate. The women are making too much of her.'

'Find Catherine someone of her own class, then. Ally has no need of such a friend.'

Mamma draws herself up a little taller. 'Ally needs to under-stand the world around her. She needs to be prepared to make herself useful.'

'You're too young,' Ally tells May. It is the first time Mamma has suggested taking Ally to the Home.

'Later, perhaps,' says Papa. 'Although there are other avenues she may wish to tread, and will be more still in ten years' time. For now, she is a child and will remain so. I must go to the office.'

'Children must learn.' It is one of Mamma's favourite sayings, that and 'children must be taught'. Aunt Mary says that both Mamma and Grandmamma like to say 'must'. 'I will not have my girls believing that everyone lives as they do.'

'And I will not have them dragged into the gutter when they should be playing. Ally, you are not to go out with Mamma today.'

'Alethea, you will do as I tell you. It is time you began to become familiar with the Home.'

Ally looks from one to the other. The porridge in her mouth is too thick to swallow.

Papa stands up. 'Very well. Alethea, do you wish to go with Mamma to a dirty place where bad women stay or will you stay here, help Jenny and play with May?'

Mamma sets down her coffee cup.

'"Bad women", Alfred? Because they are bought by good men, I presume? And you suggest that I preside over dirt?'

Ally can't speak. She separates her mouthful of porridge with her tongue and gulps a bit and then another bit. She may be going to be sick. She looks at Mamma, who has fixed her gaze on the amputated rose-bushes in the flower bed outside.

'Well?'

Her throat closes. She can't swallow the last bit. They both look at her. Mamma will be angry. She digs her fingernails into her palm.

'I think I'd rather do as Mamma wishes, please, Papa.'

Papa leaves. A moment later they hear the front door bang.

'On reflection, I believe I will take both of you.' Mamma

refills her coffee cup from the tall silver pot. 'There are some sights it is never too early to see.'

They walk. Exercise is the best preventative for the nerves from which inactive women often suffer, and good habits must be formed early. It's cold, but there's blue sky above the trees. Ally tries to walk on Mamma's shadow. There are horse-chestnuts, waxy in their green and white shells, all over the pavement.

'Hurry along, May. We did not come out to gather chest-nuts.'

May tries to put one in her pocket, but the prickles stick out too far.

'Ow,' she says.

'That's what happens when you dawdle and pick up unnec-essary rubbish,' says Mamma. 'Do come along.'

Ally takes May's hand and they scurry after Mamma, away from the big houses and trees, down the street where they sometimes go with Jenny to buy groceries and on, along a road where Ally's never been before.

'Are we going near Papa's office?' she asks.

Papa took her to the office once, and Aubrey gave her tea and cake while Papa went off to talk to somebody important.

'Not as far from it as he would like to think,' answers Mamma.

Ally should not have mentioned Papa after what happened at breakfast.

'My legs are tired,' May murmurs.

'Shh,' says Ally, though she too is beginning to think that her toes will wear through her boots if they don't stop soon. Mamma strides along, her skirt swinging, hands held in a muffler that makes her walk as if she's carrying something precious. The shops they are passing now are different from the ones nearer home. All the buildings are smaller, as if they are walking through a shrinking world. Soon the streets will be the right size for Ally, and then for May, like their friend Alice's playhouse, and then for Ally's big doll Rosamunda that Aubrey gave her at Christmas, and then for the finger-sized fairy dolls he gave May. Mamma will crush mouse-carriages with every step. The paint is flaking off these shop-fronts, and the windows have thick grime around the edges that fades into the middle like breath on cold glass. They seem to sell the same kinds of things as everywhere else; meat, vegetables, clothes or hot pies. There is more to step around on the pavement, and sometimes clots of rag or dirty clothes in doorways. She hasn't seen any grass or trees since the very beginning.

'I don't like it here,' says May.

Mamma stops. 'What did you say, May?'

May looks at the ground and grinds the dusty pavement with her boot. 'Nothing, Mamma.'

'You don't like it. Nor do the thousands of little children who live here. They would like to have your house and your nice toys and good hot meals. They would like to sleep in your clean bed and wake up to see your bedroom roses, and wash in your pretty basin.'

May's eyes widen. Ally squeezes her hand, imagining dirty fingers reaching for Rosamunda and hair lying in elf-locks on her pillow.

'Now, come along, and you'll see how those little children have to live.'

They fall into step again. May is blinking back tears. Ally leans in to whisper. 'She sounds like the three bears. Who's been sleeping in my bed?'

71

'She won't let them in, will she?'

'Papa wouldn't let her,' says Ally. 'He made the rose paper for us.'

Somewhere, hidden in these dwarf buildings, are the children who deserve what Papa gives to Ally and May.

They are flying on the silk carpet when Aubrey calls, on their way to America. Papa has been reading to them about the pioneers, who are crossing hundreds and hundreds of miles of prairie, further than Ally can imagine, in wagons made of wood and canvas and pulled by horses. Children travel in the wagons too, and camp outside with their parents at night, under the stars. Wolves howl in the moonlight and there are often cyclones and hurricanes, but the pioneers keep going towards the West where there will be farms in the mountains and rich forest running down to the sea. Ally and May have borrowed the globe from Mamma's office and they have it on the floor beside them as they cross the Atlantic. May is looking down to see a whale spouting in the sea below and Ally has just seen the coast of New England in the distance when they hear the doorbell. Papa is visiting one of his clients, Mrs Dalby, who has a lily pond that the girls might see one day, and Mamma is at her Home, so they will not be called downstairs to be polite to visitors.

'I can see dolphins too!' says May.

'Not near whales,' says Ally. 'Some whales eat dolphins.'

'My dolphins are running away, and I can see them leaping and leaping over the waves.'

'*Swimming* away.' Ally's getting hungry. It's possible that Mamma will have told Jenny to wait tea until she comes home.

'And this whale doesn't eat dolphins, anyway. This is a friendly whale.'

'Not too friendly. I see a whaling ship coming.'

Papa has a book about whaling ships sailing in the Arctic. Ally hasn't read much of it but she likes the pictures.

'May, are you hungry?'

'No,' says May. 'My whale is at the very bottom of the sea and there are more whales for it to play with.'

'You can't see the bottom of the sea from a flying carpet.'

There are footsteps on the stairs. Tea-time? A knock at the door. No-one knocks at the nursery door.

'Good afternoon,' says Aubrey. 'May I come in?'

May runs into him and hugs his legs. 'Play with us.'

'Stay for tea,' says Ally.

'We're on the magic carpet.' May takes his hand and tows him across the room. 'We're going to America to see buffalo and pioneers.'

Aubrey sits down. 'I like buffalo. Where are you now?'

He takes them over the coast of Labrador and then across Hudson's Bay, where they see fur-trappers paddling canoes down icy rivers and circles of wigwams with smoke rising straight up in the frosty air. As they come down over New England, the seasons turn back and there are whole hill-sides of bright leaves, copper like the beeches in the garden but also red like the maple tree at the arboretum and brown as the chestnut leaves will be in a few weeks. The leaves in the garden are wet and slippery, already rotting down into the compost that Mamma will use for next year's plants, but in New England the sun shines white in a blue sky and there are children playing American games outside schools with American flags fluttering from the roofs. We could land, says Aubrey, and buy some clam chowder and pumpkin pie, if you like. Clams are a sort of shellfish, May, and I believe pumpkin pie is sweet, made with a kind of spiced custard. Mamma once said that Aubrey takes too much interest in food.

'Vegetable custard?' asks Ally.

'Maybe not. Very well, we'll keep going.'

They check the globe, and begin to rise over the foothills of the Alleghenies, where there are farms and orchards sparkling with red apples. It gets colder as the air thins and they cuddle up to Aubrey, poking four chilly feet inside his tweed jacket. There is snow on the mountain-tops, and the tracks of a family of bears, who are, Ally, just looking for somewhere to hibernate, and then Jenny rings the bell in the dining room. Tea-time, at last. It's only bread-and-butter and a pot of weak China tea because Mamma was not expecting guests and Jenny doesn't count Aubrey, so they drink the tea with spoons to be clam chowder and Aubrey makes a pile of bread, sprinkles it with sugar from the sugar-bowl and slices it like pumpkin pie, and then he takes out his drawing pad and the dining room inkwell and sketches some pen-and-ink buffalo for May, who turns out to have something more like a crocodile than an ox in mind. After Jenny has taken the tea-things, he makes up the fire in the grate and lights it with matches from his pocket; Mamma, he says, would not want them to be cold. Dusk falls outside and the streetlights flare, picking out leaves still hanging off branches blackened by rain. Ally and May climb into Aubrey's lap in Papa's big chair by the fire, and he tells them a story about two little Venetian girls who go to school every morning in a gondola, nosing its way through the mist rising from the Grand Canal in the wintry dawn.

May is trying to spread her junket round her bowl with the back of a spoon. You have to finish what's on your plate but you're not allowed to scrape up food. Papa pushes his bowl away. He hasn't finished his junket and he hasn't even tried a prune. Ally swallows. The only good thing about junket is that it goes down easily.

'Girls, we have something to tell you,' he says.

Ally's spoon bounces on her junket like a smack on a bare leg. Papa doesn't look as if it's anything bad. Maybe they are all going to accompany him to London next week?

'You know,' says Mamma, 'that you two will need to be able to earn your own livings. And you know that by the time you are grown up there will be many more opportunities for women?'

'Yes, Mamma.'

'Miss Johnson and Miss Leigh are starting a new school for girls, to make sure that some at least are prepared for true work of their own. A place where girls can learn Latin and mathematics as well as French and music. And it is in Didsbury. You will be able to walk there.'

'There will be other girls for you to play with,' says Papa. 'And Miss Johnson has persuaded Mr Stott to sell her one of his fields so that the girls will have a place to run and play games and make gardens. You know that Mamma is too busy with the Home and her other work to go on teaching you at home.'

'I could teach myself.' Ally pulls the spoon out of the junket, which is harder than you would expect and makes an improper sound. 'I've hardly started reading your books, Papa. Aubrey would teach us.'

'It's time for you to go to school,' says Mamma. 'You will be taught there what you must learn to be a useful and independent woman. Let us hear no more about it.'

May looks at Ally. Her eyes have filled. Ally pushes the spoon back into the junket. 'But isn't May too little?'

'No,' says Mamma. 'I would hardly send her if she were.

Now stop playing with your food, Alethea. Remember the children you saw only last week and give thanks that you have it.'

Jenny takes them to school on the first day. Mamma is at the Home and Papa visiting a client. It's raining and Ally's new skirt gets splashed with mud.

'We'll go down the back roads once we know our way,' Jenny says. 'It'll be cleaner so, and quieter. But we don't want to go wrong and be late your first day.'

'We could just go to the park instead.' May jumps over a puddle, but not quite far enough.

'Oh May, you've splashed mud on your skirt, you naughty girl. No. You're lucky to be going to school and learning. There'll be other girls there to be your friends.'

'I like playing with Ally. And Aubrey's our friend.'

Ally realised yesterday that they would see less of Aubrey, who often calls in the afternoons when they will be at school. She hopes Papa has told him what is happening, and also that they will, Jenny says, be home by four o'clock most days.

'What about lunch?' she asks.

'There's a cook at the school, your Mamma says. I dare say there'll be puddings.'

May skips. Mamma doesn't allow puddings at lunch unless Papa is home. Sweet things are unwholesome for growing girls, promoting habits of self-indulgence and vitiated appetites.

The school is just a house, on a road of similar houses. They are smaller than home, though in the same style: red brick and stained glass. Papa has recently started to design stained glass. Jenny stops outside the front gate and makes them stand still while she tucks wisps of hair back into May's plait and tells

Ally to re-tie her bootlaces and do it properly this time. Then they walk up a flagged path with the stumps of pruned roses dripping beside it. May grabs Ally's hand and stands behind her as Jenny rings the bell.

Jenny goes away and a servant girl in a black dress and white apron takes their wet coats and shows them into the front parlour. There are polished floorboards, walls painted the colour Papa calls sage, with white woodwork and framed prints that Ally can't see properly from the doorway. She feels May, behind her, tightening her grip on Ally's skirt. There are plants on bamboo plant-stands in the bay window, and the room is full of girls. Eleven, twelve, thirteen of them. They were all talking and now they have stopped and they are looking at May and Ally. Ally looks back. The front door has closed behind them or she would grab May and run back out onto the street. An older girl in a print dress comes towards her.

'I'm Kate Crenshaw. You must be the new girls?'

Ally coughs. Her voice isn't working. 'I'm Ally.' She's squeaking. She tries again. 'I'm Alethea Moberley. This is my sister May. I'm nine and she's six.'

Kate Crenshaw bends down to May's level. 'Hello, May. You'll soon get to know us all. You're the very youngest so we'll all look after you.'

May rubs her forehead against Ally's arm.

'We've never been to school before,' Ally explains. 'She's shy.'

Kate Crenshaw goes around the room and tells Ally everyone's names. Ally forgets to listen. They are nearly all taller than her. Kate and one of the others are already wearing their hair up and skirts almost down to their boots and waists tighter than Mamma would approve. There's a coal fire in the grate and no screen. She's too hot. She puts her arm around May.

77

'We are waiting for first bell,' Kate tells her. 'Then we go into the schoolrooms. I expect Miss Johnson will send for you. She is strict, you should mind your manners.'

A bell rings, louder than the dinner bell at home, and the girls pour out of the room. Ally follows, leading May. Some are going up the carpeted stairs and others to the end of the hall.

'Come up with us,' says a girl about Ally's height. 'It's the big ones downstairs.'

They go into the room above the one where they started, also sage-green and also with bare boards and a small fire. A grid of nine desks, three by three, faces a table at the front where a woman sits behind a pile of books.

'Come in, girls, and sit down quietly.'

She has dark hair in a low knot, and is wearing a navy silk gown with ruffles that Mamma would consider extravagant. Remember the poor women who have not clothes enough to keep warm and no money for coals.

'Alethea?' says the woman. 'And May? Come here, please.'

Ally has to pull May. The woman smiles.

'I'm Miss Johnson. We're very glad to have you here and I hope you'll be happy with us. May, I know this is daunting but if you can stand up straight and let go of your sister you will feel better.'

She waits. May raises her head but her eyes are screwed closed and she doesn't let go of Ally's hand.

'Very well. Now, I will give out these books and then you and I can have a talk and see where you should start.'

The other girls have sat down at the first six desks. Miss Johnson gives each girl one of the blue, cloth-bound books.

'Study chapter four, please, girls. Alethea and May, let us come into this corner and speak quietly.'

Miss Johnson tells Ally some sums and asks her to solve them in her head. She can do the first ones but she can't divide any number greater than 144, which is the top of the multi-plication tables Mamma makes her recite as they walk. Miss Johnson gives Ally a copy of *A Midsummer Night's Dream*, which Aubrey read to them until Mamma told him it was unsuitable, and asks her to read one of Titania's speeches and then explain what it means. She asks Ally to recite the Kings and Queens, starting at the beginning, and tell her what she knows about each of them. Ally knows about Alfred and the cakes and the princes in the tower and remembers a lot more than she thought she knew about the Reformation and the Dissolution of the Monasteries because RDS talks about them when he and Papa are planning stained glass. She knows a little about the Cavaliers and Roundheads but more about their clothes than why they were fighting, and after that she knows about the French Revolution from listening to Aubrey read bits of *A Tale of Two Cities*, but Miss Johnson says she was asked about the rulers of England, not France. Miss Johnson says she will set a composition for Ally to write at home. She gives Ally one of the blue books and tells her to go and sit down and read chapter four, and then May takes hold of Ally's dress and holds tight so she can't walk.

'May, let go of Alethea,' says Miss Johnson.

Ally tries to uncurl May's fingers and May starts to cry.

'May, stop that. You're not a baby in the nursery any more.' May wants to go home.

'She is shy,' Ally says. 'We have always been at home.'

'Alethea, when I want your opinions I will ask for them. Now do as you are told and sit down.'

Ally tugs her skirt from May's grasp and walks away. May howls. Miss Johnson stands up.

'May, if this continues it is clear that you are a baby and not ready to be in school. I will have to send for your Mamma and tell her that you are unable to behave like a schoolgirl and she will have to take you back home until you are older. I imagine she will be displeased. Would you like me to do that or are you going to stop that infantile noise?'

Ally isn't sure that May will be able to see past her immediate need to go home to think of Mamma's anger if she does. Last time May wouldn't stop crying, Mamma tied up her mouth for the rest of the day. She watches May bite her lips together. Strangled noises are still coming out.

'Good,' says Miss Johnson. 'Now, sit down at the back and compose yourself. If you can keep silence for this lesson, May, I will talk to you while the others have their break. Otherwise, I will send for your Mamma. Do you understand?'

May nods and walks unsteadily to a desk. She won't meet Ally's gaze.

Ally writes her composition about the Dissolution of the Monasteries and how Henry VIII freed English spirits from the slavery of Papism. Miss Johnson marks it 11/20, but writes 'very good' at the bottom. Ally has to write out 'dissolution' ten times in her best writing, with both 's's, but Kate Crenshaw says that 11/20 is a good mark and that Ally should not only be pleased but should not tell the other girls in her class because they will be jealous. Ally tries harder with the next one. The blue books are called *The Boys' History of Great Britain, volume four* and they are about the reign of Elizabeth I, James I and the Gunpowder Plot and Charles I. Miss Johnson asks the girls to write one composition supporting Mary Queen of Scots and one supporting Elizabeth. Ally and Aubrey talk about it, and then Ally writes her pieces while Aubrey tries to explain multiplication to May, using marbles on the magic carpet. Look, he says, here are three marbles and here are another three and here are another three. How many marbles? May counts them herself. Nine. And they are pretty. She can see tiny flames inside them. Yes, says Aubrey, the glass reflects the fire. How many groups of three are there? May looks at him. There are nine, she says. Aubrey rearranges them. How many threes?

Ally knows that Mary was wrong, but she likes her as she does not like bossy, red-haired Elizabeth. Mary could have had a nicer time by pretending to agree with Elizabeth but she wouldn't. She writes about Mary living by her conscience. The fire flickers yellow in the hearth and she can see wisps of smoke curling off the coals and diving up the chimney.

'Aubrey?' she says. 'Aubrey, what if your conscience tells you to do something wrong?'

Aubrey looks up from the marbles. May begins to arrange them into a snake.

'I think you should ask your Mamma. But I suppose that if you know something is wrong, it's not your conscience telling you to do it.'

Ally draws a treble clef on her blotting paper. Everyone has to learn music at school, although Mamma considers it a trivial pursuit. 'What if you think it's right at the time but later people say you were wrong?'

Aubrey shrugs. 'Human error? Or maybe the later people are wrong.'

She puts the pencil down. 'How can something be right and then wrong?'

May's snake begins to slither, one fire-lit marble at a time.

'Because most things seem right to some people in some places and times and wrong to others in other places and

81

times. I expect the Romans thought they were doing the right thing when they crucified Jesus. Controlling superstition, like Henry VIII burning heretics.'

'Anyway,' May says. 'If Jesus hadn't been killed he wouldn't have redeemed us, would he? So he had to be crucified, which means that someone had to crucify him. So they were sort of doing the right thing. Is it tea-time yet?'

Ally and Aubrey are still looking at May. They look at each other. May's snake moves on, more like a caterpillar.

'Soon,' says Aubrey. 'I brought a cake from the baker. I thought it would make a nice treat after a day at school. Your Mamma is out late on Wednesdays, isn't she?'

Ally's compositions get 12/20 and another 'very good'. Miss Johnson asks her to arrange the flowers on the table where the girls eat their cold luncheon every day. No puddings, because Miss Johnson shares Mamma's views about girls and their appetites, but more butter on the bread than they are allowed at home and sometimes cocoa to drink instead of tea. Ally gets all her sums right and moves on to the next section of *Mathematics for Schoolboys*. If 2,640 tiles are required to cover one side of a roof and there are 23 new houses, each of whose roofs have two sides, how many tiles should the builder order? There are 12 men on an expedition, each requiring 3 ounces of tea per week. Their journey is 437 miles long and they expect to cover 11 miles each day. How much tea should be purchased? The numbers fall into place, right or wrong, easily checked, easy to see where she made a mistake. She can look at the table, set for guests, and calculate the number of pieces of cutlery. If each fork weighs half an ounce, how many pounds of silver are on the table? She, too, tries to teach May: here are eight spoons. If we divide them between four places, how many spoons does each person have? May looks at the setting and wonders why anyone would need two teaspoons at dinner. Miss Johnson does not approve of corporal punishment for girls, so May spends half of her morning breaks standing in the corner, face to the wall, hands on her head, while Miss Johnson at the desk behind her reads the girls' work. The other girls save their biscuits for her and give her first turn at the skipping games they play on fine days. Nebuchanezzar, King of the Jews, bought his wife a pair of shoes. Ally usually trips before the counting even begins.

It's still fully dark. Ally reaches out to move the curtain. The streetlights are burning and the road is silent. A wind leans on the leafless trees. Ally turns her pillow over and settles back. She was sent to bed at the same time as May last night, for crying. It is her tenth birthday, and Saturday, a half holiday. After school, Mamma will take her to the Welfare Club to give Sunday books to the children, and Grandmamma is coming to tea. Aunt Mary has sent presents, and if Ally and May behave perfectly, but *perfectly*, for Grandmamma, they may stay up to the first part of dinner with Aubrey and RDS. If Grandmamma makes one little complaint about them to Mamma, they will be sent to bed the moment Grandmamma leaves and Ally's birthday cake, with its pink sugar icing, will be given to children who are grateful for their pleasures. Mamma counts on them not to shame her.

Papa sings 'For She's a Jolly Good Fellow' instead of 'Dawn is Shining' when he comes to wake them. Jenny has put a vase containing one hothouse flower and some ferns from the garden at her place, and there is her birthday letter from Mamma.

'Read it in a quiet moment,' says Mamma. 'And we will have a talk tomorrow.'

Last year's letter said that Ally was nervous, emotional and easily swayed, and that she should not allow her behaviour to be guided by feeling but remember always to assert her reason. Mamma would help her with early hours, plain food and plenty of exercise. Ally looks at the letter, plump in its cream envelope. She hopes Mamma wrote it before scolding her yesterday.

They do not behave perfectly.

As soon as Ally and Mamma return from the Club, before Ally has even taken her coat off, Jenny calls May down and tells both of them to go out into the garden and play until it's time to come in to wash and dress for tea. Jenny wants to be sure that everything she tidies will stay tidy until Grandmamma sees it.

'I will see to my desk,' Mamma tells Jenny. 'And we must cover the painting on Mr Moberley's easel.'

Mamma's desk always looks orderly to Ally, certainly better than the table in the nursery where Ally and May work on their home-lessons, which May had to tidy this morning. Papa is making an oil painting about a lady saint who is tied up and being hurt under her clothes. Ally would prefer not to have seen it herself, although Papa says the interesting part is that the important thing, the event of the picture, is not visible. It's a picture about what you can't see, Papa says, but Mamma is probably right that Grandmamma will see perfectly well.

It's been raining since dawn. The lawn squelches underfoot and only Ally has her galoshes on.

'Shall we go back in and ask for mine?' May stands on the gravel, puddling the grass with one foot.

Ally looks at the front door, their wet footprints on the red tiles of the porch. 'I think they'd probably get cross. We'll have to change our shoes for tea anyway. Just try to stay off the grass.'

She looks around. Only the rhododendrons still have leaves, on which raindrops gather like the mercury Papa showed her when the thermometer broke. There are slanting dark patches on the house's brickwork, where the wind has swept rain against the walls, and the clematis around the conservatory is hung with drips. A magpie hops under the beech tree. Foolish superstition, Mamma says, but even so Ally finds herself casting around for another one to make two for joy. Maybe she can save this one until she sees another and count them as a pair, like carrying numbers in arithmetic. Carrying magpies.

May pulls her hand, muffled in wet gloves. 'Let's go look for the foxes. It'll be drier under there.'

May used to be afraid of foxes. She used to dream that foxes lived in the garden and slithered into the house at night, snapping their sharp teeth and clacking their claws across the floorboards while everyone else slept. May's foxes slunk under her bed and hid, ready to pounce if she moved or spoke. Aubrey found out when he read Aesop's Fables to them and May froze in his lap at the fox, and the next day he told them about a family of foxes who did indeed live under the rhododendrons. Mr Fox went out at night, not to creep into houses but to find food for Mrs Fox and the baby foxes. The Foxes had been living here since before the houses were built, back when it was still woodland teeming with little creatures. But now he had to go a long way, right out into the countryside, and meanwhile Mrs Fox had a terrible time with those four babies, who wouldn't play quietly in the den but were forever rushing out onto the lawn to frolic in the moonlight. The fox family were thinking of moving out to the mountains – yes, the mountains where Papa and Aubrey went walking last summer – to give the babies more space and purer air, and so Mr Fox wouldn't have so far to go every day. May's night foxes went away after that, and in summer she built a twig house for the Fox babies to play in under the bushes, but she hasn't mentioned them for weeks.

The rhododendrons have grown, and Ally, forcing a way under their canopy, scratches her face and streaks her sleeves on the wet bark. Even May has to crouch, but the mulch underfoot is only springy with damp and few raindrops find a way through the leaves. Ally tries to straighten her back and gets a trickle of water down her neck.

'It's a cave,' says May. 'And we're outlaws in the forest. We have to keep very still and quiet while the enemy goes by.'

'They've been searching for us for weeks,' says Ally. 'But we're safe here. We slipped through a crevice in the rocks. We can't light a fire until they're gone, but we've gathered nuts and berries and at dawn, before they were up, we caught some fish to cook later. We can stay here for a few days if we need to, and gather our strength for the journey ahead.'

They make a sleeping area, and build a fire-place and a fire. Ally twists leaves into cups which they use to catch rainwater. Twice, they hear footsteps passing through the forest outside, and once there is a burst of song and uncouth laughter from the direction of the river. They wrap wild roots in leaves to bake in the fire. And then Jenny comes, poking the leaves aside with an umbrella. What on earth are they doing, hiding here when they know Grandmamma is visiting? How do they think poor Mamma is feeling? Jenny has tramped all over the garden, muddied her shoes and stockings and got soaked to the bone, and was about to tell Mamma that they had run off into the street. They are to come inside – through the back door – and change their clothes at once, and she would not be in their shoes for anything once Grandmamma has gone and Mamma is able to think again. And gracious, May, look at your boots! You'll be cleaning those yourself, to start with. Ally, you haven't been sitting in the mud, you bad girl. What were you thinking? Your poor Mamma! Such naughty girls.

Jenny drags May out by her hands and slaps her face, hard, one side and then the other, as she emerges. Ally follows of her own accord, crawling in her haste, and is slapped before she can stand up. Jenny is not from our sort of people, says Mamma, and so naturally she acts in anger sometimes. I am sure you deserve it. Ally holds a cold wet hand against her cheek.

'Inside with you at once.' Jenny takes their hands and begins to pull them across the wet grass. 'There'll be no birthday cake for you.'

Ally has to pack up her cake for the Sunday School children at St John's. Aunt Mary's presents, foaming with tissue and ribbons from London shops, go to the Children's Hospital. Grandmamma told Mamma that her girls' disobedience and bad manners are most distressing, a predictable consequence of sending them to a school where worldly ambitions are encouraged and mere learning valued more than the precepts of Christ. Mamma has attended more to depraved street-women than to the salvation of the souls for which she is responsible to God. Mamma, says Jenny, coming to close the curtains and shut the door at five o'clock, had to leave the room to be sick. How could Ally and May do that to their own Mamma? No-one wants to hear a sound from this room until tomorrow morning. They are lucky to have such a gentle

Mamma, for most children would be whipped until they couldn't sit down for such behaviour.

But someone does want to hear them. After they hear the guests arrive, there are careful footsteps up the stairs and their bedroom door-handle turns.

'Ally?'

It's Aubrey.

'We're not asleep,' she says. 'We were naughty.'

Aubrey comes in and shuts the door behind him. 'I heard.'

May wriggles over in her bed and pats the covers. He sits down. 'Your Papa told me to have a long look at his painting in the studio. Since he showed it to me yesterday, I think he knows I'm paying you a call. Happy birthday, Ally.'

She lies back on her pillow. 'It's not.'

'No, I suppose not. Might these help?'

He takes a package – two packages – from under his jacket. 'RDS has something as well. He'll try to slip up later, when your Mamma's left the table. And Papa says I may take you out to tea next Saturday. So don't despair, Princess Al.'

She saves the parcels to open tomorrow. She doesn't feel like having presents at the moment. If she were to hand them over to Mamma in the morning, for the poor children, Mamma might understand that she never meant to be bad. But then Mamma would want to know when Aubrey had given them to her and she would be angry with Aubrey and Papa. May's breathing changes, but Ally gazes into the dark, listening to the voices from downstairs. They were told to go into the garden, so that wasn't where she went wrong. Jenny would have been angry if they had played on the lawn and left footprints and got wet, but perhaps Mamma would have forgiven that if they had come in and changed before Grandmamma arrived. Or maybe it was all right to go under the rhododendron but they should have taken better care of their clothes and shoes. Wherever she went wrong, Mamma has seen again that she is bad. She does not deserve Aubrey's gifts.

Aubrey takes them to Daniel's. The girls at school talk about the tearoom but Ally and May have never been. Mamma is spending the afternoon at the Children's Hospital and Ally is fairly sure that neither Papa nor Aubrey has mentioned this outing to her. They go on the omnibus, right into the middle of the city near Papa's work, to the square by the Royal Exchange where there is a fountain. For the first time in weeks, it's not raining, and the flagstones are dusty under their best shoes. Ally leans back against Aubrey to look right up to the top of the Exchange, tall as a mountain – though she hasn't seen a mountain – against the grey sky. Pigeons roost, small as pebbles, on its ledges. Men in dark coats hurry up and down the stairs, intent as ants. Papa has explained what happens in there, more than once, and Ally thought she understood at the time but it hasn't stayed in her mind. People buy and sell things that aren't there.

May skips across the flags, probably playing some kind of private hopscotch. Water blows out of the fountain and throws a dark pattern across the stones. There aren't many women here, only a few bundled beggars under the arcade towards which Aubrey is leading them and a pair in long dresses and hats passing the other side of the square. Ally would like to stay and watch.

'Come on,' says Aubrey. 'Are you going to have meringues or éclairs? And you can drink French chocolate instead of tea if you like.'

May, arrested on one leg on a small stone, looks up and

begins to stride towards him, taking steps so big that she can hardly keep her balance. Aubrey, his coat blowing open in the wind, holds out his hand and she leaps, catches it and throws herself against him, laughing.

'May,' says Ally. 'Don't make such an exhibition of yourself.'

Aubrey and May begin to whirl around in Exchange Square, holding hands and leaning back as they spin.

'That's what I do, Princess Al,' calls Aubrey. 'That's the artist's job, to make an exhibition of himself. And of his friends.'

On the way home, Aubrey leans forward from the seat behind theirs.

'Ally and May, I have a favour to ask of you. A great favour.'

They sit forward and twist round, so their three faces make a triangle, joggling along by the grimy windows.

'Of us?' asks Ally. She's not sure if he's joking, if he's going to ask them to fly him to Timbuktu on the silk carpet or invite him to the baby foxes' birthday party.

'I would like to paint you.'

'Paint us?' says May. 'What, you mean like the Picts?'

The Picts, Papa told them, were the original English people, before anyone started to come from Rome or France or even Denmark and the Low Countries. Papa likes the Picts. They painted their bare bodies blue to alarm the Roman soldiers, but it didn't work in the end.

'Paint a picture of you,' says Aubrey. 'You remember I painted a picture of Jenny? A bit like that.'

Aubrey's picture of Jenny, in Ally's opinion, is actually a picture of a dress and a piano. Aubrey paints the way Papa talks about painting, as if it doesn't matter who's making the shapes.

'What do you want us to wear?' she asks.

Aubrey smiles at her. 'I thought grey. And I'd like to sit you on that grey chair Papa bought at the auction. I've asked your Papa and he said yes.'

'What about Mamma?' asks May.

'She said sitting still would be a good discipline. Especially for you, May. As long as it doesn't interfere with your school-work.'

So the next week, Ally and May come home from school, wash their hands, change into the grey dresses that Aubrey had already had made for them and go into the drawing room to sit in the grey chair. Papa has allowed Aubrey to hang grey silk over the wallpaper. They sit. May had thought that Aubrey would talk and tell them stories while he painted, but he doesn't, and when May asks Ally what Kate Crenshaw said about Charlotte Hays bringing her doll into school he frowns and asks her to keep still.

'We'll play when I've finished,' he says. 'And I brought you a treat for your supper, to say thank you.'

Ally goes through the multiplication table in her head, right up to twelve twelves. Then she goes through the prime numbers. There are fewer as you go up because of course the prime numbers themselves have multiples, but there are, Miss Johnson says, an infinite number, which means that Ally will never come to the end of thinking about them, especially when she's grown up and can hold bigger numbers in her head.

'Please sit still, May,' says Aubrey. 'I know it's dull but I need you to keep still now. Be a statue for me.'

Mamma's letter told Ally that Mamma is pleased to see her doing well in her lessons, and that Mamma hopes that if Ally keeps working hard, she will be able to make a career and achieve her independence as a woman. But Ally thinks too much of herself, and must remember that the only true work alleviates all those horrors of poverty and suffering with which Ally should be becoming familiar. Mamma is troubled to see signs of nervousness and self-indulgence in Ally's disposition, and she is afraid that if these tendencies are not curbed, all Ally's work will be in vain because a nervous, silly woman is entirely useless and exists merely to feed on the labours and efforts of others. Ally must learn self-discipline as Mamma herself learnt it.

Then Mamma stroked Ally's hair. Mamma told Ally that she wanted Ally to prove to herself and to Mamma that she could choose to pain herself and could bear the pain she had chosen without complaint, without nervous fuss. Mamma took a candle from her desk and lit it at the fire. She told Ally to roll up her sleeve above the elbow, because we do not flaunt what we choose to endure but hold it in our deepest, silent selves. *Thy Father which seeth in secret himself shall reward thee openly.*

Ally's foot is stiff. Aubrey seems to be looking at May. Very slowly, she points the foot and straightens it again. Without moving her head, she turns her eyes towards the garden. The angle makes her eyes hurt but she can see a blackbird on next door's chimney pot, and then another bird coming to join it. Dusk is coming. She thinks it might be raining out there.

4

PERSEPHONE AND DIS

Alfred Moberley, 1872

Oil on canvas, 103 × 134

Signed and dated '72

Provenance: James Dunne (dealer) 1874; John Dalby
(Manchester) 1875; by family descent to William Dalby;
Crouch and Sanderson (dealers) 1949; Victoria Gallery
1950

Persephone was a fashionable subject in Moberley's circle at this time, but Moberley's is an ambivalent and complicated version, using his older daughter's adolescent awkwardness to convey the liminality of the central figure. His Persephone is going down into Hell, glancing back over her shoulder at the mother – viewer, artist – outside the frame. There is no fruit nor flowers here, no horns of plenty, and Moberley is, unusually, more interested in the landscape of the underworld than in the female figure. There are shapes in the cave into which her feet are leading her, dark figures in the darkness which not all viewers will see. The autumn world from which she turns is already decaying. Three leaf skeletons, fine as veins, drift in the foreground, and the trees hang bare, windless, dripping. No birds sing. There's nothing to stay for, and her gaze is empty, perhaps not reaching for the last glimpse but realising that her mother Dis has already gone.

*

It's hot. One of the men climbed on a chair and opened the windows before Mrs Butler started speaking, when people began pushing down the rows to reach the last few empty seats. Ally turns her head, her hat brushing Mamma's shoulder. There are people standing three deep at the back, women as well as men, their skirts overlapping like badly arranged flowers.

Mamma dips her head to whisper. 'Listen to her, Ally.'

Ally is listening. Mrs Butler has been describing the state of affairs in Paris, from where she is newly returned. The *Police des Moeurs* (police of morals, Ally thinks, except that '*moeurs*' also means 'customs'; does this ambiguity tell her something about the French?) sweep the streets nightly, rounding up everyone who might be a prostitute, which means every woman who cannot prove that she is not a prostitute. The police, plain-clothes and mostly demobilised soldiers, have quotas to fulfil. Even the presence of one's husband is not sufficient evidence of virtue, and several prominent women of good name and unimpeachable reputation have found themselves detained as they crossed the pavement between a theatre or a dance and their waiting carriages. Mrs Butler tells her audience about a young mother whose baby became sick while her husband, a railway man, was away at work in another town. The baby became sicker. The mother decided that she must go for the doctor, even if it meant leaving her child alone in its crib for half an hour, but as she ran through the streets she was caught by the police, tied up and bundled into a cart with all the other women out that evening and taken away to St Lazare, where the women are subject to forcible examinations, allegedly so that they can be diagnosed and treated for venereal disease to stop them infecting the gentlemen of Paris. Although this woman submitted immediately in order to get back to her child, she was not released for five days. The baby died, alone, hungry, helpless. The *agents des moeurs* must make their daily number of arrests. When there are not enough women outside, the police begin to break down doors at night in the poorer streets, looking for anyone who cannot prove that she has a legal means of support. How is anyone to prove such a thing at three o'clock in the morning? It is not infrequent for the seamstresses and shop-workers of Paris to jump out of their upper-floor bedroom windows when they hear the police at their doors.

Mrs Butler lifts her hands to her audience. Her reputation for beauty is justified, and Mamma will surely pass comment on the extravagance of her dress later. This is the effect of setting legal controls on prostitution. Women lose even those poor liberties they possess at the moment. The French police now have a licence to seize any woman off the street and subject her to the most degrading and distressing of procedures, and any woman outside without her husband may be treated as guilty until proven innocent by the least innocent of means. Can they imagine, Ally and Mamma, the crowd of flower skirts at the back, the few men whose dark clothes blot the bobbing hats and brushstroke skirts of the seated audience, what would happen if someone proposed such a law relating to men? If men found that leaving their homes meant subjecting themselves to arrest, imprisonment and physical violation? If this new Act, the Contagious Diseases Act, is allowed to sully the statute books of England, the shame of France will find its twin here, in England. The most elementary rights of the British subject, *habeas corpus* itself, will be withdrawn from half the population, merely for the crime of being female. Will they,

Ally and Mamma and all the bright women, join her and rise against this stain on Britannia's honour?

A shiver runs over Ally's shoulders and the audience rises to its feet, as if about to march out down the streets of Manchester and across the nation to London, to where the men of Parliament in their black coats toy with women's lives and bodies in the somnolence that follows their lunchtime port. Even Mamma is applauding, though her face remains set.

It takes a long time to leave the hall. Voices rise around them, the ascending chatter of massed women. Skirts rub and twist around each other, a dance of silk and cotton around the regiment of scuffed wooden chairs. Mamma keeps meeting acquaintances and stopping, blocking the flow which has to eddy and find another channel behind her. Ally stands pressed against Mamma's navy serge, keeping herself as small as she can. Her need to leave, to move, to get out of the stifling of clothes and bodies, presses hard against her throat and chest, up through her hands which want to shove and shove and force a way out into the wind and rain flickering against the barred windows. She pushes her shoulders back. She can't get enough air into her lungs. She holds herself, muscle tightening over bone. Holds herself down.

Prostitutes are women who sell their bodies to men. Mamma has not been specific about what the men do with the women's bodies, or how a body can be sold or bought separately from the soul that inhabits it. Prostitutes look like everyone else, so whatever is done to their bodies has no visible or permanent effect. The men, Mamma says, make the women sick, and then want to humiliate and imprison them for being sick. She does not say why men would want women to be sick and humiliated. Ally does not ask. The Contagious Diseases Act has made it illegal for sick women to sell themselves to men, although not for men to buy sick women. The only way to check whether a woman is sick is to examine her. The examination is carried out in a police station, where women are strapped down. Any decent woman would rather die than endure such a thing. Since there is no way of distinguishing women who sell themselves from women who happen to be out in the evening, the result of the new Act is that any woman who ventures outside her home in an area where the Act is in force – to attend a Welfare Club, for example, or to buy food for her family after finishing her day's work – may be subjected to forcible examination by the police. The colours around Ally shiver and blur, as if someone has spilt water on a painting.

Rain drums on the umbrella and drops onto Ally's shoulder. Rain does not drive Mamma onto the omnibuses, and Ally isn't tall enough to hold an umbrella above other people's heads. Mamma's grip is tight around Ally's forearm as they thread the crowd; it's lunchtime and the streets are thronged with factory workers, women with shawls over their heads and men in caps. Everyone's looking down so Ally can't see faces, only waterlogged hems and pushing shoulders. She hangs on to Mamma. May has gone to spend the afternoon with her friend Emily, where she says there is a room full of toys, including a dolls' house as big as a chest of drawers with four storeys and a turning staircase. May says they have a special tea brought to the nursery, sandwiches with the crusts cut off and fruit cake every day. Ally is too old for toys. She will go home and take tea and bread-and-butter with Mamma and then, she supposes, sit in her room and study Monday's lessons until May comes home.

Mamma looses her arm. The streets are quieter here.

'So what did you think of Mrs Butler, Ally?'

Ally steps over a puddle. 'She's very beautiful.'

Mamma's face tightens.

'I mean, Mamma, that it must be hard for a woman of such wealth and powers of attraction to devote herself to the work of rescue. Her temptations must be great.'

Mamma nods. 'She is a strong soul. I am sure she has temptations, but I doubt that worldly display and luxury have much appeal to Josephine Butler.'

If that were so, Ally thinks, Mrs Butler would dress more like Mamma.

'What would you say then are her temptations, Mamma?'

Mamma's stride slows a little. 'I cannot say. We have not spoken of such things. But I would guess that when she sees such sights as she must encounter almost daily, and hears the stories of girls no older than you sunk almost beyond the reach of light, and runs again and again against the scorn and stubbornness of the men who rule this land, despair must beckon. In Paris, Ally, she found girls locked by the police in a windowless cellar, bound into strait-jackets and left for days in the dark with a little bread and water but without the use of their hands, and no access to a convenience of any kind. For the sin of trying to resist an examination. And when she presented the Chief of Police with her account he told her that such women are accustomed to live in filth and that she degraded herself by visiting them. It takes a great spirit to see and hear such things and continue to work in hope and charity, Ally. She is an example to all of us, and one I hope to see you follow.'

Water is seeping into Ally's left shoe. 'Yes, Mamma,' she says. She does not ask what kind of examination it was that the girls did not want to take; she is beginning to understand.

*

Someone screams, and she's sitting up, her heartbeat hammering in her head. Her breathing has stopped. Her nightdress is wet around the neck and under the arms. The door opens and she tries to pull in air to scream again. May's sitting up too, looking at her.

'Alethea. Stop this at once.' Mamma, with a candle. 'Are you ill?'

'There were men.' Ally's voice is high. 'In the dark. Coming at me.'

Mamma turns. 'May, lie down and go back to sleep. There is nothing wrong. Ally, get up and come with me.'

Ally stands up. The men are still there, in her head. Mamma takes her shoulder and steers her onto the landing and then into the nursery. She sets the candle on the table and sits in the armchair. Ally stands in front of her.

'Are you unwell, Ally?' Mamma's cool hand reaches up to her forehead. 'You have no fever.'

'No, Mamma.'

'So what is the reason for that hysterical noise?'

'None, Mamma. I had a bad dream.' Ally begins to shake. 'I was asleep when I screamed, Mamma.'

'And now you tremble.'

Ally tries to stop but she can't. Her jaw hurts with the effort.

'I'm sorry, Mamma.'

'You must try to control these tendencies, Alethea. Nerves and hysteria show a weak and foolish disposition. You will run mad. I trust you understand that there is nothing romantic, nothing worthy of attention, in this behaviour?'

'Yes, Mamma.'

'Go back to bed. We will consider some ways of reminding you to control yourself in the morning.'

Mamma stays in the nursery, with the candle, while Ally

stumbles back into the bedroom and trips over something on the floor. It takes her a long time to get warm again, and longer to go back to sleep. A reasonable person, she knows, would not fear Mamma's reminders. A strong mind would rejoice in its improvement; her dismay at the prospect only confirms her need for greater discipline.

'Miss Johnson wants to see you.' Charlotte Evans stands in front of her, one red ringlet pulled forward over her shoulder. Charlotte Evans is grinning; she thinks Ally is in trouble.

Ally notes her place and closes Emerson's *Essays*, which she does sort of understand. She thinks about the way Mamma says 'thank you' to tell Jenny to go away now and stands up.

'Thank you, Charlotte. That will do.'

Charlotte tosses the ringlet and skips away, button boots frisking under her flounced skirts. Enough cotton there to dress a window, Ally thinks, if anyone wanted curtains in such colours which they wouldn't.

She has come to like the school building. The smaller rooms hold more light than at home and there is a sense of purpose and business in the rhythms of feet on the stairs, pens on paper, voices among the flowers in the sitting room. Ally had not noticed until she started to spend her days here that the rooms at home are mostly empty, that wherever she is there is a vacant room next door, above and often below. She passes May, skipping with her friends in a scribble of flying skirts and hair, and greets Cook on her way past the kitchen. Miss Johnson's school is doing well now and there are hot lunches for the girls every day. Ally cannot think of anything she has done to justify Charlotte's smirking. Her marks are always good, and she is now ahead of all but Miss Johnson's 'college group', the oldest girls who are bound for the new Women's College at London

University. Miss Johnson subscribes to the campaigns for a Cambridge college for women; there is hope that by the time Ally is old enough she will be able to take a Cambridge degree.

She runs up the stairs, her shadow flickering over the shadow banisters on the wall. Miss Johnson's door is open and sunlight lightens her dark green walls, the colour of gentlemen's clubs and leather armchairs.

'Good afternoon,' says Ally.

She isn't in trouble. Miss Johnson looks up from her papers and smiles.

'Alethea. Come in and sit down.'

Ally crosses the polished boards and sits on the Chesterfield, legs crossed at the ankle. Miss Johnson comes around the occasional table, of whose ornate legs Papa would disapprove, and sits beside her. Beside her! Ally waits.

'Alethea, your Mamma paid me a call yesterday. Has she discussed this with you?'

Ally's insides feel as if they're falling faster than the rest of her. 'No.'

'You surprise me. She has not spoken to you about the campaign for women doctors?'

Ally looks up. This is not, then, about her hysterical tendencies. She runs her finger gently over a sore place on her leg. Blisters, Mamma says, are a traditional prescription for weak nerves, and where the weakness persists the blistering must be repeated.

'Because examinations at the hands of male doctors degrade women and lead to the diminution of exactly those sensibilities that protect female purity, and because many modest women suffer unspeakable pain and inconvenience for years rather than consult a man about certain troubles, especially those following a mismanaged labour?'

Miss Johnson sits up. 'Gracious me, Ally, where on earth did you learn such things?'

Ally pleats her fingers. 'Mamma. And her rescue home. She took me to hear Mrs Butler.' The fringe on Miss Johnson's rug is tangled. Ally would like to kneel on the floor and comb it out straight.

'Mrs Butler? I see.' Miss Johnson gazes out of the window. A cloud the colour of a bruise looms in the east. 'And you are thirteen?'

Ally nods. 'And a half. Some of the girls in Mamma's Home are younger than me.'

'Yes, I suppose they are. Even so.'

There is a pause. The cloud, Ally decides, is moving so slowly that it won't reach this part of Didsbury until afternoon school has begun.

'Has your Mamma spoken to you of her hopes for your future work?'

'We are to be useful, independent women whose lives are beneficial beyond our domestic circles.'

'Indeed.'

Ally looks up. 'Mamma has said I am to be a doctor?'

'It is her hope. You show the necessary aptitude and application. But Ally, it will not be easy. For a woman especially, I am afraid that a scholarly mind and a willingness to work hard is far from sufficient for this course.'

Ally swallows. 'I would like to be useful to my sex. I would like to be able to save women some of the humiliation and pain that is our lot.'

Miss Johnson touches Ally's hand. 'I am sure you would, my dear. It could hardly be otherwise. I do not doubt your readiness for this work. But there is strong opposition to women's medical education. It may be necessary for you to go to

America, or to France. It may not be possible for you ever to obtain the qualifications open to men. You are choosing not only to be a doctor but to be a pioneer, a fighter in the vanguard, and I fear that your energies would be absorbed at least as much by the battle as by your work as a healer. You are young, Ally. You need make no commitment, even in your own mind, but know that if you do as your Mamma wishes you are choosing perhaps the hardest of paths.'

A weight lifts from Ally's shoulders. Her head feels light, like the time Papa took her and May to Aubrey's exhibition and poured them each a small glass of champagne. Mamma believes in her. Mamma has a purpose for her. There is a way to justify herself.

'I can do it,' she says. 'I will do it.'

Miss Johnson smiles. 'Ally, you are not called to do anything for some years. You don't need to look like a young saint. All that we need consider now is the course of your studies for the next three years. Your Mamma wishes you to begin Latin and to study Anatomy and Chemistry along with Botany. You can join my college group for the Latin and you will attend Dr Hayter's popular lectures for the Sciences. I will chaperone you myself when I can, and otherwise we will have Polly escort you. I dare say she may prefer it to dusting.' Miss Johnson hesitates. 'Run along, Ally. After all, you are no younger than many boys who choose a vocation.'

Ally stands up. 'I am older, Miss Johnson, than many girls who have one forced upon them, in the factories as well as on the streets.'

'I know that. What does happen, Ally, is rarely a guide to what should happen. I will see you this afternoon for your first Latin lesson.'

*

Ally likes Latin. It seems more like Maths than like French, a language with an integral logic. English words are slippery, leaning on each other and on unspoken presences, on ghosts, for their meanings. Latin is so tightly woven that it barely needs punctuation, the relationships between words so clear that the order in which they come doesn't matter. Life would be easier if we spoke Latin.

Aubrey says that social life in Ancient Rome was at least as complicated as in nineteenth-century Manchester. He says that no language is proof against what is not said, that people lie and, more interestingly, keep silent, in every tongue on earth, including Greek which is even more highly inflected than Latin. Anyway, the ghosts in English are what makes it interesting, those Viking and Norman presences floating about in our sentences and our poetry. He has taken Ally out to tea, just the two of them this time. He says Ally looks like a girl who needs a treat, needs someone to indulge themselves in unnecessary expenditure on her behalf. She's looking thin, more like a factory girl than the blooming daughter of Manchester's foremost artist. He's quoting Papa's latest review, which has become something of a family joke; would Manchester's foremost artist care for a drop of milk in his tea, and could he perhaps find a moment to pay the butcher's bill? It's easy enough, these days, to find a time when May has been invited to a friend's house for the afternoon.

'I still prefer Latin,' Ally says. 'And Maths.'

Aubrey shrugs. 'Good. It will be useful to you, I suppose. Ah, now look at that!'

A waitress approaches; older, Ally thinks, than she is, but not older than the College Group. She moves smoothly over the deep carpet of the tearoom and she's carrying a tray supporting something that looks more like a geological feature than a cake. Other people, mostly women, mostly in drooping hats, turn as it passes.

'Croquembouche,' says Aubrey, as if hailing a long-lost friend.

Ally watches its progress. It reminds her of the cairns built by Ancient Britons as way-markers. 'You don't imagine we'll eat all that?'

Aubrey is smiling at it. 'We'll eat as much as we want. You can take the rest home, if you like. For May.'

Ally shakes her head. She doesn't, really, like cake all that much, certainly not as much as Aubrey thinks she does. Or maybe not as much as he does himself.

'Could we take it to the Rescue Home? It's not far. Almost on the way back.'

The cairn is being lowered onto the doily in the middle of the damask tablecloth. There are pastry pebbles glued together with what must be burnt caramel, dusted with powdered sugar. It smells of butter.

'Wherever you like, Princess Al. Let's enjoy eating it before we worry about the bak'd meats.'

Hamlet, Ally thinks. The funeral bak'd meats did coldly furnish forth the marriage tables. Aubrey read some of it to her and May one wet Saturday afternoon when May had a cold. She sips her tea while Aubrey removes the topmost pastry.

'For you, Princess Al. I ordered this specially as soon as you did me the honour of accepting my invitation.'

He bows to her.

'Aha! A smile. Lady, all my labours are repaid.'

She smiles properly. 'Stop it, Aubrey. And thank you. I'm sorry to be dull. This is a lovely treat and you're a kind friend to think of it.'

'Kindness nothing, my Lady Alethea. My heart leaps at the boon of your acceptance of my poor gift.'

She eyes the pastry. It looks impervious to spoons, likely to roll away if assailed with a fork.

'Tell you what,' says Aubrey. 'Pick it up. None of these good ladies have ever seen a croquembouche before, they don't know what to do with it. Show them how it's done in Paris.'

He thinks she won't. He thinks she's a little girl who will be frightened of getting it wrong. Holding his gaze, smiling a little, she picks up the pastry, bares her teeth and bites. Aubrey applauds silently from the other side of the shiny damask.

When they leave, he offers her his hand down the steps. She takes it and jumps.

'Ally!'

'What?'

He offers his arm. 'I thought you were being a grown-up lady today.'

She takes it. 'Inside, I was.'

They set off, sedately, the ribboned box containing the bottom half of the croquembouche hanging from Aubrey's other hand. There are tentative shadows on the pavement from a sky like watered silk.

'But on the streets you are a child?'

She withdraws her arm. 'On the streets no girl is a child, Aubrey. You know that.'

'Ally, is that what troubles you?'

She walks on. 'I don't know, Aubrey. There is much by which to be troubled, is there not? In our day and age? Especially for a woman.'

'As in any age.' He crooks his elbow for her again. She should stand alone, make her point, but her hand creeps back to his arm. She can feel muscle under the broadcloth. It must, in some ways, be pleasant to look forward to a future of being cared for by someone, having one's responsibilities limited to the provision of meals and mended socks. Being told not to bother one's head about the world beyond the front door.

'Do you know, Al, I often think that if I could choose any time to be born, and any place in the world to live, I would probably choose to be here and now? Think of the opportunities, the ships and railways, the Empire opening up at our feet, the new inventions and discoveries. Our cities with their teeming enterprises. The days in which a man lived and died where he was born, eating what his father and grandfather ate, sleeping where they slept, labouring as they laboured, obeying as they obeyed, are gone. Think of the world's goods and manufactures flowing into England, our arts and sciences flowing out! Children born into poverty, even the sons of some of your rescued women, can go out to India, Canada, perhaps even Australia, and come back independent and proud. There are troubles, but what richness also.'

She notes a splash of cream on her skirt, is briefly dizzied by the passage of paving stones under her feet. Is there any point?

'A man,' she says. 'Sons. Fathers and grandfathers, come to that.'

And women, she wants to say, women not even able to vote against the government that has made criminals of any member of their sex unable to prove her virtue without losing it in the process. Women whose choices are now, more than in the days Aubrey deplores, limited to prostitution within or beyond the law, unskilled labour for which they are paid less than men doing the same work, or teaching girls the largely pointless skills by which they are distracted from acquiring any knowledge that might give them power. If Aubrey can hear Mamma – as he has heard Mamma, often and long over the years – without learning to care for these matters, she cannot hope to rouse his mind. And he has not brought her out to hear a lecture.

'Ah, you are your mother's daughter still, Ally. With such champions, how could women fail? Come, there was no suffrage movement until our age, was there? Your time is surely coming.'

'Perhaps there was no need,' she says. 'Until the progress in which you rejoice. Perhaps women have lost where men have gained.'

'Your time is coming, Princess Al. How could it not, with such charming champions?'

He circles his hand in the air, scrapes his foot and bows like a Renaissance courtier. Mamma is right; men dismiss women's opinions because the woman expressing herself is pretty, or because she is plain, because she is young or old, single or married, because, in the end, all women's speech is considered to be merely personal. It must then be the duty of every rational woman to demonstrate with every word that she is reasonable, measured, objective, to prove herself and therefore her sex capable of speaking without emotion.

Aubrey tucks her arm against his waist. 'Now, will you take me to your Rescue Home, Princess Al? It will be my first visit. And then there is something I would like to show you at my studio, if you would do me the honour.'

Mamma's rescue home, Ally thinks. But for the first time, she wouldn't mind putting her name to it.

Aubrey is stiff and awkward at the Home, as if he thinks the women might seize him and eat him up. He offers the cakes to the Matron as soon as they are admitted and then turns to go. Ally holds his arm as she asks after Betty, who has had a fever.

'Might we visit Eva, Matron?'

Eva is sixteen, and will be leaving next week, to go into service on a farm in Cumbria. The Home has connections across the North; it is important that the women do not return to their old haunts, where familiar associates make it too easy for them to return to past habits.

Matron looks Aubrey up and down. Men, apart from the vicar, are not generally permitted in the Home.

'Eva is in the kitchen, Miss Ally. Mr West, I wonder if you would like to see our pictures? Mr Moberley has been very kind.'

Aubrey blows his hair off his brow when the door closes behind them. 'Goodness me, Al, I didn't reckon on an interview with the Matron. I'm glad she doesn't rule my life.'

Ally takes his arm again. 'Don't you think it might be a better life if she did, Aubrey? Anyway, she needs to be firm. She is also capable of great kindness.'

'You would send me to the reformatory, would you, you ungrateful baggage? I dare say you are right. Regular hours. Plain food. No more croquembouches. Now come and see my new toy, Princess Al.'

The sun comes out as they cross the city centre again, casting a shadow theatre on the pavement as people step out, singly and in pairs, from work to home, to the shops for necessary purchases or idle pleasure, to give and buy and sell. Skirts swing, boots stride or saunter, little button shoes step out, trousers scissor. Hats and caps glide or bob, and in the forest of walls and windows above the walkers' heads pigeons squabble and coo. Ally catches her reflection in plate glass windows: neat enough. Not bad. Too old, at least, to be Aubrey's daughter, which people used sometimes to assume. The stone buildings bathe in sunlight, bronze plaques gleaming as they pass through the office district. She's been to Aubrey's rooms once before, with Papa and May, when Aubrey had just sold a painting and was opening champagne and planning a trip to Paris.

'Here we are.'

His name beside the door. He unlocks it and stands back. 'Please.'

There are pigeon-holes for post at the bottom of stairs lit by a full-length window on the half-landing, as in Papa's office building, and a table bearing an ailing aspidistra below. A path of thick green carpet across broad oak boards. No letters for Aubrey. He follows her up the shallow stairs, directs her left at the top where he unlocks another door. She remembers this, a large mirror in a narrow hall, but now it has the same apple-blossom paper as the dining room at home, and a pale Persian carpet hanging on the end wall.

'Second left. You remember it?'

She must have been too young to notice rooms properly, or too interested in the champagne and biscuits. She remembers that there was room for her and May to run around, and that later they sat under a table together while Papa and Aubrey consulted maps and became excited. She does not remember the dais under the north-facing window, where, at the moment, there is a couch for a model to recline, or the pile of thin white cotton beside it. She does not remember the panel of Turkish tiles around the fireplace, although she does, now, vaguely recall the story of their acquisition. Usually, rooms seem to shrink as she grows, as she assumes full-scale, but she does not remember feeling so diminished by the height of this ceiling and the bareness of these walls. There is a statue, a half-size cast of a Greek woman, under the high west window, spreading her shadow across the floor, and spatters of paint, as if birds had roosted, in the centre of the room. Aubrey opens the alcove cupboard.

'Look, Ally. It's a camera. A kind of man-made eye.'

It looks like a box, a large leather and wood box, and it has three legs, like a telescope or a gun.

'Have you taken many photographs?' she asks, stroking the stitching and the polished wood.

'I've been practising. Between paintings. I'll show you, if you like. And Al, I wondered, could I take one of you? Because you're changing so fast now, we could have you, just as you are at the moment, to look at later when everything's different and you're all grown up. You're so pretty today. Would you? It's just like modelling for a painting. And we don't have to let anyone else see it if you don't like the result.'

She remembers her image in the shop windows, the transience of her reflected neatness, gone in the step of a foot, the shift of a cloud. She looks at the couch, at Aubrey with his fine hands and slight shoulders, his narrow waist. He smiles at her. 'Yes?'

'Yes,' she says.

'And you'll undress for me, just a little, as you do for your Papa?'

She shrugs. 'Yes, if you like me to.'

He helps her with her buttons, the hard ones in the middle of her back.

'Will there be corpses, do you think?' Polly turns to latch the gate behind her.

'Corpses?' Ally sees a spectral audience in her mind, a disintegrating parody of the frocks assembled for Mrs Butler. The daffodils in Miss Johnson's flower bed are in bud.

They set off together. She's taller than Polly.

'What's it called. Dissecting.'

'Oh. No, I shouldn't think so, Polly. Not in a public lecture. With ladies present.'

Were there women in the public dissection rooms of Edinburgh? On the table, of course, but in the audience? She has been reading the anatomy books Mamma gave her for Christmas, where all the women are shown with their legs spread wide and cut off, in cross-section at mid-thigh, even when it is the belly or thoracic cavity at issue.

'Oh. Well, that's all right.'

She glances sideways at Polly, whose carriage is better than her own. Ally is developing a stoop, Mamma says, and must take more exercise.

'You were hoping for corpses?'

'I were and I weren't. I expect we're just the same as animals, really, inside, and I seen enough of them. There were a shambles at the end of our street. Not much I don't know about innards.'

The illustrators of the books have sketched the open bellies – uteri – of women at all stages of pregnancy, have exposed foetuses from the three-month manikins that would be just right for May's longed-for dolls' house to the curiously compacted infants ripe for the outside world, squashed up so tightly it is a wonder they could live. The ones in the books, of course, did not live. The ovaries are like the twin branches of the beech tree at home, the uterus, cervix and vagina the trunk. No, that's upside down. Better to have the roots deep inside and the fruit making its way towards the light. Maybe. She shivers.

'You all right?'

'Yes, thank you, Polly.'

They have come to the crossing. Behind them are antimacassars, potted palm trees, monthly journals. Ahead, beyond the line of grimy shop windows, lies the country where raw sewage seeps into cellars, lice-infested people lie on piles of rag and more than half of babies born will die before their first birthdays.

They cross. The boy sweeping the crossing has boils on his head.

'Where do you live, Polly?'

'With Miss Johnson, of course. Got a room in the attic.'

'No, I meant before. When you were little.'

'Withington. My dad were a factory man. Overseer, actually. You?'

They step around a trail of unpleasantness across the pavement.

'He's an artist. And he designs rooms. Wallpapers and curtains.'

Polly's nose wrinkles. 'I suppose somebody's got to do it. Never thought about it before.'

Ally has passed the new university building often, and heard Papa on the subject of its mock-Gothic gargoyles and finials. Street bid for the job, sent in drawings showing what could be done with local bricks and a simple, modern design allowing for quiet corners as well as grand spaces, and was turned down in favour of this gloomy monstrosity. There is a museum somewhere in there to which both Papa and Aubrey have promised to take her and May, some day when they have time. Aubrey has more time than Papa.

There are broad steps leading up to a great wooden door in a stone archway. Ally and Polly pause, exchange glances. Men pass behind them.

'We are meant to be here,' says Ally.

She picks up her skirts – although the steps are shallow and her skirts still above her boots – and walks up. There's a small rectangular door cut into the big arched one. No knocker, so although she feels the need to be granted admission she turns the handle and opens it. Entering where she is not invited: she'll need all the practice she can get. She hears the scuffle of Polly's shoes on stone behind her and steps over the lintel. She's in a stone hall that rises above her like a church. A grid of encaustic tiles stretches from her dusty shoes away down a broad corridor, from which wooden stairs rise. Light filters down from narrow windows fifty feet up. Her feet want to turn and run, back into the light and the grimy bustle of the street outside.

'Miss Ally –' says Polly, and her voice echoes along the corridor.

There's a glass-windowed hutch, Ally sees, under the stairs, and a figure in it. She sets off. The window slides open and the porter, calling her 'Miss', gives directions; they came through the wrong door and may now go out and round or follow a set of instructions, up the stairs and left after the first door and right before the second and down the first flight of stairs on the left and then along the corridor and first on the right after the second set of doors, you can't miss it, Miss. She doesn't want to go back out, not now she's got this far, and the lecture doesn't start for another fifteen minutes.

'Come on,' she says to Polly. 'It will be an adventure.'

They walk quietly, but the scuffle of shoe leather on glazed clay hurtles between the stone walls. She thinks of the work in the thousands of tiles under her feet, the digging and tempering of the earth, the layering of fine and coarse clay, the design and preparation of motifs, the making of the slip. The hardest part of making tiles, Papa says, is to get them flat and keep them that way. The fires of the kiln will find and magnify the slightest weakness or error.

She's in the corridor again, walking, but this time she's alone. It's darker and the gaslights are lit, flaring against the pale stone. They are set too high on the walls, illuminating the lines between blocks but casting the tiles and those who walk them into darkness. Those, because there is another set of footfalls behind her own. As long as she doesn't look around, it could be an echo. Nervous people, she knows, are prone to foolish fears. She keeps walking, holds down her speed, and the other steps scuffle along behind her. There is a short flight of wooden stairs, with a brass handrail set into the wall. She goes down without looking at her feet, imagining herself hanging from a string like a puppet, as Mamma says a woman should. There are double swing doors. She pushes, not to check her pace. The door squeaks as it closes behind her. This corridor is lined with arched doorways, each with a name-plaque beside it and a sliding sign that says 'IN' or 'OUT'. Everyone is out. There are stone stairs ahead, up this time, and then the doors behind her squeak and the scuffling comes closer, fast. Cold hands close over her eyes.

'Alethea!'

Mamma. Candlelight. She's sitting up. Her cheek stings. May's sitting up too, her plait unfurling and the blankets pulled up around her knees.

'Alethea, you are hysterical. I will not tolerate this. Get up.'

She puts her hand to her cheek.

'I had to slap you to stop your screaming. Come with me.'

Mamma takes her arm and pulls her out of bed. Her legs

aren't quite working and when she stands up the room drains away from her sight and everything spins.

Cold. Shaking with cold. Wet hair, water in her eyes and nose, and someone sobbing.

'Stop that noise, May, or we will have to treat you for hysteria too.'

She tries to stand up but Mamma's hand is on her head, in her hair, pushing her down again. She fights, kicks against Mamma, gets her hands onto the washstand and pushes away from the basin, but Mamma is stronger. Her chest bursting and fear rigid through her body and Mamma's strength on her neck.

Cold water runs down her neck and soaks her nightdress. She tries to stop shaking.

'Better, Alethea, or do you feel as if you might faint again? Cold water is the best cure.'

She can't stop her teeth chattering. 'Better. Not again.'

Mamma reaches for her neck. 'Better?'

'Better, thank you, Mamma. I am sorry I fainted.'

Mamma stands up and looks down at her. Sit up straight. String upon the head.

'I am sorry your hysteria worsens. I had hoped you were learning to control it. I will not allow you to succumb to this weakness, Alethea. I think I must consult Dr Henry for you again.'

It was Dr Henry who prescribed the blistering.

'We cannot have you waking the household like this. You had better come downstairs.'

Mamma escorts her, face dripping, down the stairs, and then down again to the scullery where Jenny does the laundry. There's a red tiled floor, two Belfast sinks with tall brass taps and a mangle. A window at the top of the wall looks out at the feet of anyone coming along the drive, but it's still dark. She's shaking again.

'You will stay here until morning. This room, Ally, is luxury compared to the homes of many women and girls who endure uncomplainingly and without dreaming of their nerves privations of which you can scarcely conceive. You must and will learn not to indulge yourself. I will not have my daughter fancying fashionable ailments for herself.'

Ally steps into the scullery, her wet nightdress wrapping itself around her legs, and Mamma and the candle leave. All the cellar doors have bolts on the outside, but Mamma doesn't know her as well as she thinks she does: Ally wouldn't have left. She doesn't want to be hysterical.

May comes running up the stairs, and there are voices in the hall. Dr Henry, and Mamma. He asked Mamma if he might examine Ally and Ally started shaking again, but he wanted only to take her pulse and look in her mouth. She had to lie down and let Mamma raise her skirts a little, but only to show where the blisters had been. Then he and Mamma went back downstairs to talk.

'I listened,' says May, a little breathless. 'I only just got away before they came out.'

Ally looks up from the books she hasn't been reading.

'You know that's wrong. It's bad to eavesdrop.'

May stands on one leg and lifts the other in front of her, testing her balance. 'I think it's bad to half-drown someone for dreaming.'

They've had this conversation several times.

'It wasn't for dreaming, it was for screaming. And fainting like silly women who lace their corsets too tight.'

May lowers the leg, slowly, the way they practise in dance

class. 'You were asleep when you were screaming. And you weren't even wearing stays, you were in your nightie. And she slapped you when she says there isn't ever any good reason for violence.'

'It's what you have to do when people are hysterical. Like the blistering. It hurts but that's not why they do it, it's to make me better.'

'Anyway, I listened.' May stands normally, and starts running her finger around the spiral pattern on the doorknob. 'Do you want to know or are you so goody you don't want eaves-dropped information even about your own self?'

A breeze slithers through the chestnut leaves outside, pulsing with green. She ought to say no.

'No, I'm not. Tell me.'

Dr Henry told Mamma that most of his colleeks ('colleagues', says Ally, and tries to explain, *collegium* like college, but May doesn't want to know) would say that Ally was studying too much and that brain-work is a known cause of hysteria in young girls. As Mamma knows, he is not of that view, although it is not good for girls or boys to study to the exclusion of moral and physical development. But he is sure that Mamma always puts moral growth and health ahead of study, and so he sees no need to review Ally's schoolwork. He is of Mamma's view that hysteria is a disorder of over-indulgence, found only in idle, wealthy and usually unmarried women, often imitated by young girls wishing to gain attention. It is worth noting that factory girls and busy housewives who have no servants to do their work for them appear immune to nervous troubles. He is sure that Mamma does not allow her daughters to eat mustards, pickles, highly flavoured foods of any description, but advises that Ally should also be forbidden red meat, sweets and pastries and any kind of raw fruits. He

118

could not recommend tea, coffee or cocoa. She must go to bed early and rise early, perhaps to help Jenny with the housework since physical work is an excellent palliative for such ailments in young girls. Scrubbing floors would be a very good exercise for Ally. Unlike many of his colleeks, he does not recommend physical punishment for girls so afflicted, as tending to make them more excitable and highly strung (I wish Mamma would tell Jenny that, adds May, who has annoyed Jenny several times in the last week), but the cold water treatment is effective for reviving those in a faint and it is indeed sometimes necessary to slap or otherwise startle patients in the grip of a hysterical fit. The blisters, it is to be hoped, may have a deterrent as well as curative effect, and in general he would recommend that when Ally shows symptoms of weakness she is required to undertake more rather than less activity. His own daughters are set to wash sheets, rise early to sweep and lay fires, and scrub the floors when they give offence. We know who finds work for idle hands, Mrs Moberley, and Ally is coming to the difficult age now.

'But Mamma wants me to be a doctor. I can't be studying Anatomy and washing floors, can I?'

May shrugs. 'I'm just telling you what they said. I'd go and talk to Papa, if I were you. He won't want you scrubbing anything.'

Ally turns the page of her Latin grammar. 'No. I want Mamma to see that I can do it. That I'm not entirely weak.'

There is no more of Papa's singing in the mornings, not for Ally. She still has her bed in the room she shares with May, and still does her school work at the round table in the room that's no longer called 'the nursery', but Mamma has her make up a bed on the floor of the attic room next to Jenny's so that

Jenny can rouse her early in the morning without disturbing May. Mamma tells Papa that the doctor has said Ally must keep early hours if her health is to be preserved through her present fit of growing, and that May is sickening from the disruption of Ally's hysterical attacks. Just for a few weeks, it will be better to separate them, and better to keep Ally away from the rest of the family at night. Jenny has the doctor's instructions, and will be able to do anything that may be necessary. Mamma does not tell Papa that Ally has an alarm clock to wake her before Jenny rises, and a list of tasks she is to accomplish before breakfast: sweep the downstairs grates and lay the fires; clear, polish and light the stove; clean the family's boots and sweep or wash the floor of one room each day. May, too, has her daily tasks, dusting, mending and helping Jenny in the kitchen. Idleness is dangerous for growing girls. Every woman should know how to run her own home and it is a disgrace for healthy people to rely on others to meet their daily needs.

Ally misses her room, and her bed. The attic room has a skylight, crossed by occasional birds, but she can't see the trees any more, nor hear the footfalls, wheels and horses which tell her that there are people around, going to parties and coming home from work when her own house lies silent around her. She feels exposed sleeping on the floor, vulnerable as a wounded animal. Mamma wants the mattress in the middle of the room because it's hard to make a bed against a wall. The house's noises are different on this floor and she keeps hearing what can't really be things moving around in the eaves. Sometimes, when she wakes in the night, she wants to creep down just to listen to May's breathing for a while. Mamma would hear her on the stairs.

May feels sorry for her about the housework, has even

offered to help if Ally will wake her up, but Ally finds she doesn't mind. None of the tasks is difficult. Unlike pushing through algebra, unpicking Latin and her gradual mapping of the human body, Ally's progress around the house is manifest. The stove was cold and full of ash and is now clean and hot. There were muddy footprints on the linoleum floor inside the back door and now they are gone. She kneels on the floor with Papa's boots on yesterday's newspaper before her and the shoebrush in her hand, dust spreading over her apron, making a visible difference. She wakes before the alarm, before the first pallor of sunrise, and works harder, cleans the steps and the front porch as well as the hall, blacks and polishes the stove before lighting it, waxes the spindles as well as the banisters. She doesn't show Mamma, who would think she was asking for praise, but she is sure that privately Mamma notices and is pleased.

Papa's footsteps come up the stairs, heavier and faster than anyone else. Women, Ally thinks, even Mamma, even Jenny, move around their own homes like burglars.

He stands in the door, the bottoms of his trousers muddied and rain on his shoulders and hair and whiskers. He's alight with some discovery, the kind of new plan that usually means his meals have to be taken to the studio. Ally is memorising the names of the bones in the hand and May's writing out the subjunctive of 'avoir' on her old slate. Every time she writes it she erases it and starts again; they have worked out that if you write something fifteen times and say it over as you go to sleep, you will know it in the morning.

'My sweet girls, do they teach you to sew at that school of yours?'

Ally and May exchange glances.

121

'Fancy sewing is an extra,' Ally tells him.

'Ally's in College Group and I do Botany instead. Mamma says –'

He shakes his head. 'Yes, yes, Mamma says. A waste of time for frivolous adornment, I'm sure. I don't want you to make me a scalloped petticoat. I have people for that. Come into the studio.'

The schoolroom is cold and Ally's arms have stiffened. May stumbles as she stands up. It's already dark in the hall. There's a fire in Papa's studio and they both stand beside it. Warmth spreads across Ally's back like a benediction. There's a new painting on the easel, an oil portrait of a woman who came to dinner a few weeks ago. The woman has a copper-coloured dress and something red twisted through her dark hair. She's lounging in a chair with her feet up, gazing into a log fire whose light glimmers on the silk of her gown and her cabled hair, an easier pose than Ally has ever been given. Papa is rummaging through a pile of fabric on his table in the gloom at the other side of the room.

'I'll light some lamps. Look what Street's son sent. He's in Switzerland. Look, here.'

May's shoulders make a small sigh. Neither of them moves away from the fire.

'Girls, are you cold?'

'A little,' says Ally, as May says 'yes, very'.

He brings them an armful of fabric. 'Why don't you light the nursery fire?'

May rubs her cheek against his arm. 'Honestly, Papa, do you really think Mamma would allow us a fire? We have good warm shawls and flannel underthings and there are children in rags, in homes with holes in the walls, who do not complain when they have not fire.'

122

Ally picks up one of the garments over his arm. 'We don't really need one, Papa. We had fires in the winter. Mamma is not unjust; she has no fire by day either. It's warm enough when we don't sit still for too long. This is very pretty. How is it worn? Surely not underneath.'

Papa kisses May's hair and takes a spill from the fire to light the lamps. Yellow light blooms on the table, spreading over papers covered in Papa's beautiful italic writing and a variety of printed fonts with which he's been experimenting for the new poems, and over the folds of a cashmere scarf heaped like a relief map of a mountain range on the battered oak table top. Another glow blossoms in front of the lily curtains, pale starbursts whose intricate crimson and green background haunts the lamplight. Ally holds up the garment in her hands so May can see it, a cap-sleeved white cotton chemise, smocked at the neck to fall loosely, unshaped, to the hips. It looks like any shift, the kind of thing everyone wears under a corset or stays, except that the smocking is red and the yoke and sleeves are covered in bright flowers done in thick cotton thread, red and pink and yellow and blue.

'Could you do something like that?' Papa asks. 'I could send it off but they'd be pretending to make it simple, trying to be rustic, and I don't want anything fake. Could you try? If I drew a design on the fabric and gave you a sketch of the colours? It's for some cushions, a white room with window-boxes. Mrs Montgomery. She's just back from her own Alpine tour. It might not work. Our own poor peasantry is so long in the cities there's no vernacular embroidery left.'

May cocks her head.

'Coming from the common people,' Ally explains. 'Not from the elite, or from abroad. English is a vernacular tongue.'

May fingers the chemise and turns it over to see how the

123

stitches are held down at the back. Ally leans to see. Papa's right, it's not 'fancy', requires none of the feather-stitching, tucks, knotwork or cut-outs taught by Miss Frost to girls whose parents want to avoid idle hands without giving their daughters the keys to any useful form of knowledge. She and May, competent plain sewers of infant clothes and their own underwear, given time for trial and error, could do it. May, voluntary maker of dolls' clothes and patchwork balls for the children at the hospital, would enjoy it.

May crouches and holds her hands out to the fire. 'We could do it, Papa, but the problem is when. We have our chores and our schoolwork and days at school. There's only Saturday afternoons left and I usually go out to tea and Mamma takes Ally to the Home or the hospital. Even on Sundays Ally's usually studying. I'd like to try, I liked sewing and I always wanted to do embroidery, but it will take me a long time. If you need it soon you'll need to ask Mamma to let me off chores.'

'I can see about that. You'd rather be learning embroidery, wouldn't you, May-bird?' Papa tugs gently on Ally's plait. 'Princess Al?'

She rubs her toe along the edge of the hearthrug. Papa knows about people's work. He will understand. 'Honestly, Papa, May's the one who likes sewing. I've got all my college group work and the anatomy after school and my housework in the mornings.'

He takes his hand away. 'So you can't help your Papa in his work?'

She takes his arm. Something in her chest is pressing up against her throat. 'I would, Papa, truly, but I have no time. None. I rise early already. I have no leisure. I could tell you I would do it but I cannot tell when I would fulfil my promise.

124

It would be as if I were to ask you to draw anatomical diagrams for me as well as doing your own work.'

He removes her hand from his arm. "I cannot admit the comparison. Of course your Mamma has ambitions for you, but your little studies, Ally, are hardly the same thing as my work. You have no time to assist me? To lend me your talents? I am disappointed.'

'I'm sorry, Papa.'

He steps away from her, and then the thing in her throat rises up so she can't breathe. She hears her vocal cords roaring as she tries to suck in air, and the lilies and the cashmere scarf splinter and rearrange themselves and the kaleidoscope moves faster and she can't breathe and her heart has hardened to stone and is banging on her breastbone like a fist on a window and there are running footsteps and May screaming and she hides her face in her knees by the fire, away from Mamma's slapping hand. Mamma's voice says Alfred, she is insane, we have lost her. My daughter has lost her mind. This is it, madness.

Papa carries Ally to bed, her own bed in the shared bedroom, although now she can breathe again she could perfectly well walk. She is shaking and sweaty, can smell herself through her clothes. Dr Henry comes, but it's Jenny, not Mamma, who stands at the foot of the bed. He takes Ally's pulse and tells her to open her mouth. Papa comes in and stands looking at her almost as he did when she was a little girl and had influenza, when he brought her soup and stayed, sometimes, to talk about the mansion where he was making a library. Dr Henry says that Ally is to take a month off school, away from her anatomy lectures and extra Latin. The company of rescued women may be unsettling, for although they are forbidden to discuss their past lives with each other or anyone else, by definition these women have colourful histories and alarming manners. (This shows, she thinks, Dr Henry's limited experience; most of the women Ally knows have the same dreary story to tell, the story of being poor and getting poorer until only one's body is left.) Young women naturally become emotional in the presence of the gravely ill, so she should not visit the hospital either. Her hours must be fully occupied in a way that precludes, as far as possible, any reason for excitement. Housework is strongly recommended. Handicrafts would provide an excellent occupation, inculcating patience and application as well as keeping her busy. Her diet must be plain and low: oat gruel for breakfast, bread and butter with milk at lunch, bread and milk or a milk pudding at supper. She must keep very early hours and reading should be limited to devotional texts. Papa's eyebrows lift, but when Dr Henry asks to speak to him in another room the two men leave together. Their voices rumble from downstairs. Ally turns onto her side and curls away from Jenny's disapproval, closes her eyes although she knows Jenny knows that she's pretending. She has no idea what comes next, whether any of the future will be returned to her or if she's now someone else, a madwoman instead of a doctor-to-be. She keeps her eyes closed, although she knows this isn't a dream.

The front door opens and there is talking in the hall, Papa and Dr Henry and still no word from Mamma, and then the door closes and Papa's tread comes up the stairs again and across the landing.

'She's pretending to be asleep,' Jenny says. 'Ashamed of herself.'

Papa sits down on the bed. 'Thank you, Jenny. That will be all for now.'

The door closes. Something must begin. She opens her eyes.

'Princess Al. Everything too much?'

She doesn't turn over. 'I don't know what happened, Papa. I couldn't breathe. Was I mad?'

His fingers slip along her shoulder. 'You were unwell. No physical cause so the doctor thinks it's nerves. Not unusual at your age. We need to keep an eye on you, Princess Al.'

She can see the soft outline of his shadow on the rose paper. 'Where's Mamma?'

'Ah. Mamma was upset. She worries about these things.'

'She's angry. She thinks I'm mad. Weak-minded.'

His knuckles rub the back of her neck. 'We are both concerned for your nerves. Mamma sometimes has a rather – black and white view of the world. Have you noticed?'

She curls tighter. 'No. She tries to make it better.'

'I know that, Al. Listen, I'm going to have Jenny bring you some hot water to wash, and then you can come and have your lunch off a tray with me in the studio. It won't be bread and milk, we'd have you turning into a calf on Dr Henry's diet. And then for the next few days you can come and model for me, come and be Persephone for a while, and then we'll see where we are.'

He turns at the door. 'Try not to worry, Ally. Mamma's just disappointed.'

5

NAIADS UNDER THE WILLOW

Alfred Moberley, 1873

Oil on Canvas, 186 × 214

Signed and dated '73

Provenance: Sir Frederick Dorley, 1874; Christie's (London) 1902; Francois Chevalier (Paris) 1902; Musée d'Orsay after 1947

Still fascinated by sunlight and foliage, he has painted the shadows of a weeping willow in the river, the wavering of running water interwoven with the movement of leaves in air, and of light through leaves. Water and light flow left to right, without framing, teasing the viewer with what is out of sight downstream. The river runs over stones, silted and reflecting their earth colours in the beer-bottle translucence of the water. Reeds strain in the margins, combed by the current and bowed like wheat in the wind. Fronds of willow trail idle fingers on the surface, each carving a small wake, and there is a suspicion of fish under the darker branches. The naiads are almost an afterthought, two barefoot girls on the riverbank, right at the edge of the painting. Their loose white garments are dishevelled, slipping off the shoulder of the taller girl and kirtled up to show the calves of the smaller as she sits in the grass with her knees drawn up, her head turned away towards the water so the sun fingers her tumbling hair. The older one sits with her feet tucked under her, peeping from beneath the slim thighs outlined by a single layer of cloth. She's looking down into the water too, braced by one bare arm whose muscles continue through the exposed shoulder and into her neck. The hair on her nape is damp, curling, and we can see her spine and her shoulder-blades like wings above the sagging dress. Green, brown, gold flow across the canvas, starred by the white of their dresses and the marsh-flags on the other side of the river.

*

She should have stayed at home with Mamma. The hospital there has only a paved yard for the children to take the air. There is little wind, even here, and from the hill behind the village she can see by the dirty brown fog lying over it where the city lies, a pastel smudge on a watercolour landscape. There are thousands of children under that smudge whose lives could be saved by the clean spring-water in the stone jug beside the wicker hamper, and by the hay-scented air in Ally's lungs and the clear river where May is paddling, dipping the hem of her dress as she tries to catch fish in her fingers, as instructed by the farmer's son this morning. Many of the women in the Home have never seen a forest, wouldn't recognise the chamomile smell of sun-baked grass or the darkness of the secret folded places of marsh-flags. Mamma is with those women, teaching them and praying with them in the dust and the thick smell of drains – and no drains – in mid-summer. Ally turns back to her book; here, at least, is a promise she can keep. Troy burns. Aeneas loses Creusa, and returns to search a city where blood lies in congealing pools and the pleas of the dying whisper in the walls.

Aubrey rolls up his trousers and joins May in the water, holding her when she steps on a rolling stone and once almost catching a fish. May says she's cold and they climb out and lie together in the sun on the bank. Aubrey tells her a story, about a time he and Papa tried to row on a river in France. May picks up the needlework she left beside the picnic basket and begins to stitch again, filling the outlines of poppies with red silk. It must be the slowest possible mode of representation. Would Papa persist in painting if each eighth of an inch took him – Ally counts as May's hands glide – fifteen seconds? Would Aubrey? Aeneas, stateless, leads his son and father away from Troy, into the strange haunted spaces beyond the city walls. Providence their guide, she thinks, though Troy was no Eden. There are some ways in which the warring classical gods make more sense than the Christian one. It is very often hard to have faith that there is justice in life, and plain that much suffering is undeserved. How much easier to believe in gods who bicker, throw thunderbolts in fits of temper and betray their protégés after listening to others' lies. How much easier to believe that sometimes our gods desert us. As, indeed, Christ himself for a moment suspected: Why hast thou forsaken me? She prays: Lord, I believe. Help thou mine unbelief. The problem of suffering, of why the good die young, is only a test of faith, a test passed by Mamma and Mrs Butler and countless other good workers in the world.

'Time for lunch, Al.'

She looks around. They have spread the blanket in the dappled shade of the willow, and set out a whole ham on a plate, a round loaf, fat as a river-stone, a snake of cucumber naked on a gingham cloth. There are pimples in the glaze on the stoneware mustard-pot, and a pool of butter lies like stained glass in a square white dish. Papa is still busy at his easel, but Aubrey sits on the hamper with May at his feet, both looking as if they slaughtered the pig and milled the flour themselves.

'Moberley,' calls Aubrey. 'Lunch.'

Papa doesn't turn. 'In a minute.'

'I'm starving.' May rests her head against Aubrey's knee. 'We walked about twenty miles up that hill.'

Ally folds her notebook into the *Aeneid* to mark her place and picks up her dictionary and pencil. 'Five miles, at most. I'm not supposed to eat ham. Or mustard.'

'Have bread and water, then,' says May. 'Just as you like. No-one's going to tell Mamma. There are plums I picked from the orchard to have afterwards and you can not eat those as well, if you want.'

Aubrey tugs May's plait. 'Not everyone's such a cunning little fox as you, May-bird. If Ally wants to follow the rules you should respect her self-control. But Al, you are on holiday. Even the Church allows a little celebration from time to time, no?'

Ally sits on the opposite side of the blanket and tucks her skirts around her knees and feet. 'It's not about church. Dr Henry says such foods inflame the nerves. I won't risk not being allowed to do my work for a slice of ham. Would you cut me a piece of bread, Aubrey?'

May reaches to pass Aubrey the loaf. 'I'd have thought your nerves would be better here anyway. I'd have thought stopping your work for a week would do you more good than refusing nice food.'

'Papa's not stopping,' Ally points out. 'Nobody's telling Aubrey not to read and write. Anyway, I lost too long in the spring to stop now.'

Ally had three hysterical attacks in a week at the beginning of March, two of them in public. She humiliated Mamma and disgraced herself before the lecture audience, which included not only most of Mamma's associates but the wife of one of Papa's clients and two of Manchester's most prominent doctors, whose teaching she may be seeking in a year or two.

Mamma incurred the cost of a carriage home and Ally could not be permitted to leave the house for several weeks, weeks spent in housework and modelling for Papa, who required a difficult standing pose wearing a draped garment inadequate for warmth or, in Ally's view, modesty. Aubrey liked the painting so much that Papa gave it to him.

He balances the ham and its plate on his knees and begins to carve. May kneels beside him like a dog hoping for scraps.

'I'll take a plate to Papa,' says Ally. 'So he doesn't have to stop if he doesn't want to.'

But Papa comes to join them before May unwraps the plums from their linen cloth, casting himself down on the grass to lie propped on one elbow like a Roman senator at a feast. 'More ham, please, and lots of mustard. Is there any beer?'

May raises her eyebrows at him. 'Beer, Papa? Intoxicating liquor when there is work to be done? Papa, please may Aubrey take a photograph of me? He says he can work it outside.'

Papa rolls onto his back, arms folded behind his head. She doesn't think she's ever seen him lying down before. The pattern of leaf-shadow covers his face. 'Aubrey may do whatever he pleases. If he wants to play with machines, he has my blessing. It's just a fad, May. A summer game. What's actually there at any given moment doesn't tell you much.'

She leans over and balances a plate of ham on his stomach. 'I know, Papa. But it's interesting.'

Aubrey tickles May's neck with a willow leaf. 'The clever part, Moberley, is to know which moment does tell much. And then to command the technology to seize it.'

Papa places the ham at his side and sits up. There's grass in his hair. 'Just as you say. How's Aeneas, Al?'

'Sad,' says Ally. 'And careless. He seems to recover from the loss of his wife rather fast.'

'Other things to do, no doubt.' Papa's mouth is full of ham.

'Why does reading about Aeneas help you to be a doctor?' asks May.

'Because lots of the books are in Latin,' says Ally. Which is true, but only part of the truth. Because all the scientists can think in Latin. Because being a doctor means joining the world of people – men – who know the *Aeneid*. *Timeo Danaos et dona ferentes*.

Papa lies under the tree for a long time after Ally and May have packed away the half-eaten ham, rinsed the pool of butter into the river and offered the crusts of bread to two passing moorhens. Ally goes back to Virgil, working more slowly as she nears the Harpies, pretty girls from the shoulders up and foul monsters below. Aubrey and May wade across the river to pick marsh-flags, and then May bruises her foot on a stone and cries a little and they go off downstream, carrying Aubrey's camera and all its luggage, to find the right light for a photograph. Aeneas' ships hail the Strophades. The willow's shadow shifts across the grass and the buttercups at her feet cease to shine. Ally's back aches. She changes position so the sun lies on her shoulders, shifts the dictionary from her left to her right leg and goes on. The harpies snatch the feast from the tired men. They seem to materialise in the air, as if they don't quite come from anywhere, harsh voices heard before their shadows appear on the thyme-strewn hillside, endlessly greedy for what was never theirs. Disgusting ravening women. Ally's throat tightens and the willow begins to fragment. Not here, let it not happen here.

'Ally?'

She swallows. 'Yes, Papa?'

'Go and find the others, would you? It's getting late and I can't think it takes so long to seize one moment. I have letters to write.'

'Yes, Papa.'

She stands up, holding her breathing as slow as possible because once she starts to gasp she has lost, is mad again. Papa watches her. She starts to pick up her papers, mark her place.

'I'll look after those, Al. Take a little walk. Find your sister.'

She breathes in. 'Yes, Papa.'

'Call if you need me.'

She nods. Lord, have mercy on me, a miserable sinner. Out of the depths I have called unto thee. Why should God hear her and not the mothers of dying infants? She breathes out. The trick of light that casts straight sunbeams through trees is at work, as if she could take one in her hand. A moorhen calls from the water, and her thin shoes sink through the crispness of last year's leaves into the humus below. She hurries, as though Papa were really in haste to leave, as though he would be angry at being kept longer from his letters. Thin branches and tendrils of morning glory have grown over the path tentatively worn through the woods. Brambles tug at her skirts and draw beads of blood on her forearms. The river murmurs behind the trees. Birds scuffle in the bushes as she passes, and high over her head a raven calls a warning. The pain in her chest is melting. How far did they go? It must have been difficult to carry all Aubrey's equipment along here, and surely one sun-dappled clearing is as good as another for taking a photograph. She stops, listens: her own breathing, her heartbeat echoing between her breastbone and her ears, something scurrying through the leaves, and something else at shoulder-height rustling, pausing, rustling. A sigh of wind through the trees, lifting her hair from her hot face and rearranging the light around her, the muttered monologue of water over stone. And then May's laughter, high and wild as she has rarely heard it.

Ally walks on towards the sound, and sees a patch of black, Aubrey's jacket hanging from a branch, on the gold and green. She ducks under a branch, and more careful now balances to crush a nettle underfoot. Mamma has uses for nettles. Aubrey's camera stands like a scarecrow, like a witch, between the trees, but Aubrey is not behind it in the usual embrace. He's over there, under the tree where May lies on a blanket. It's a pose Ally recognises, on her side with the upper leg drawn up and the foot tucked behind the other calf, the lower hand behind her head and the upper arm stretched over, a position that accentuates the curve of thigh, hip and waist while tilting the breasts upward, for models who have such things. It's not as comfortable as it looks, putting pressure on the lower back and straining the raised arm. May's clothes are in a heap by the camera and she is stark naked, the arrangement of leaves and sun continuing across her legs and belly and bony chest, her hair fanned out onto the ground behind her. Aubrey squats beside her, adjusting the angle of her raised arm and the tilt of her face in the sun, placing a tendril with green leaves across her outspread hair. Titania, or maybe Puck. Ariel taking a moment's rest. You can see that her face and hands are a different colour from the rest of her, as if they are newly painted and have not yet dried. Quiet as a woodland animal, Ally turns back towards Papa, and the *Aeneid*.

Ally and May are allowed to walk to and from school alone now. Ally is almost seventeen. As Mamma told Papa, if she is to go and live in Edinburgh in two years' time, to travel alone on the train and make her own way to and from the medical school, she should be able to walk a mile unescorted. Papa, whose sister has probably never walked a mile alone in her life, acquiesced. He wanted to get back to his studio. They do not tell Papa that it is not going well for the seven women who were allowed to matriculate at Edinburgh, that many of the professors refuse to teach them and they have been assaulted by their fellow-students, followed home from the university and insulted. If Papa took an interest in such matters, he could read about them in the newspaper. Mamma has some hope that it will be possible for Ally to study in London when the time comes, but she is not optimistic; after Elizabeth Blackwell's triumph in not only qualifying as a doctor but joining the register, the Medical Council is acting quickly to prevent any further women being able to practise legally. There is always America, where there are women's medical colleges in Boston and New York. Ally tries to imagine crossing the Atlantic, weeks in a tossing wooden box. It is unlikely that Mamma would consider the expense of a private cabin to be justifiable. There are not slums in America like the ones here. Several charities are now working in the city to send the most deserving and hard-working slum boys to America, where they can learn farm-work and grow up to have land of their own. Some British women are studying in Paris and Geneva.

May tugs her hand. 'Ally, you're not listening to me.'

May's been talking about her friends at school, about who said what to whom in relation to Clarice's new dress.

'Sorry. I just can't see why they care all that much what someone else wears.'

May gives a skip, as if her impatience is too strong for speech. 'Because we're all frivolous and trivial, of course, and we'd rather think about the width of a ribbon than the salvation of the poor. Honestly, Al, do you think Mrs Butler appears like that without giving thought to her dress? Because I can tell you she doesn't. It is possible to be good and pretty. But not without trying.'

Ally glances down at her own clothes. Mamma has forbidden corsets entirely, so she is shapeless under her coat. The jacket is an old one of Mamma's, altered not very well by Jenny. You can see where the tucks have been let out of the skirt she's had for several years, and her blouse has an unfashionably floppy collar and ink-stains on the sleeves. Under the coat, jacket, blouse, petticoat and chemise, her body has failed to assume the form she sees in Papa's friends' paintings, or in classical statuary, even though Mamma says that trussing up the female body is a taste unique to modern Europe and that the beauty of Greek and Roman women derived from fresh air and exercise. Mamma does not read Greek or Latin.

'You know how much I admire Mrs Butler. But she has money as well as taste and leisure. And a lovely face to begin with. How could I aspire to that as well as to being a doctor? My patients won't care about my dress.'

May looks her up and down as they walk. 'They might. I mean, doctors need to look as if they're doing well, don't they? Who wants a doctor who can't afford shoe-leather?'

Who knows what a female doctor should wear? Miss Nightingale is insisting on uniforms for her nurses, ostensibly so they look professional but mostly, Ally guesses, to stop them being taken for prostitutes who are the only women usually seen around military encampments. There are hosts of women, in the Bible as well as in sermons, who are condemned because they care more for their clothes than for their salvation. One can also be condemned for the opposite offence. She feels again the tightening of the world around her, the impossibility of everything.

'Bother,' says May. 'Frost's here.'

They are at the gate, too late to take a turn around the corner. The Reverend Frost is on the doorstep, poised as if to leave.

'He's an interesting man,' says Ally. Which is true, but just now she wants tea, and then a couple of hours in peace to prepare for a Latin unseen and a mathematics test tomorrow.

'His work ought to be interesting but he makes it sound duller than mending socks. Anyway, he won't want to talk to us. He likes fallen women, we're too respectable. Smile!' May assumes a demure expression.

Reverend Frost is the new vicar of St Catherine's parish, recently come from Oxford. He slept one night in the poorhouse when he first arrived, to help him understand the lives of those he serves, and he's started offering soup to children who come to his Sunday School. It may be bodily hunger that brings them, but they will soon learn to understand that they do not live by bread alone. He says that Mamma knows his parishioners better than anyone, and he relies on her to help him avoid pauperism, to make sure that charity is expended on those capable of permanent improvement and not wasted on sustaining the undeserving poor in their slothful state. He's asked Mamma to lead a new group of Lady Visitors, who will make regular visits to parishioners' homes to offer advice and guidance on cleanliness, money-management and child-rearing. It would be an abuse of resources to devote charitable income and labour to households too mired in filth, gin and improper living to benefit from the lessons available to them.

Mamma is standing at the door. The Reverend Frost turns

to them, takes first Ally's hand and then May's in both his own.

'Good afternoon, Miss Moberley. And Miss May. You are both well, I trust?'

They murmur.

'Excellent. I was just saying to your Mamma that we have need of young ladies to help with a new sewing club. To read to the women, you know, and perhaps amuse little children while their mothers attend.'

Ally and May refrain from exchanging glances.

'We would be delighted.' May looks down, as if too shy to make eye-contact. 'We find ourselves very busy, you know, during our school term. My sister's health is not strong. But perhaps in the holidays, at Christmas . . .'

There are plans to spend Christmas with Aunt Mary in London.

'I will speak to my daughters,' says Mamma. 'I am sure they will oblige. Come in, girls. There is something I must tell you. Good afternoon, Mr Frost. You will surely find that you can depend upon May's assistance.'

He bows. The gate closes behind him.

Mamma holds open the front door for them, and begins to speak before they have hung up their coats. The door stands open, letting in hoof-beats and the clatter of wheels from the pavement outside, a man's laughter and a few leaves. Mamma, also, needs Ally and May to help her. She has written a piece for the *Manchester Times* about a little girl called Emily, and some people are saying that what she has written is not true, or that what she describes is an anomalous event that is not representative of common practice.

Emily came to the Rescue Home from the Lock Hospital,

where she spent the summer – while May and Ally were disporting themselves in the mountains – being treated for the most horrible of diseases. Emily is twelve. She has never known a father, and her mother was a factory worker who died of fluff in her lungs two years ago, leaving Emily in the care of an uncle who sold her to Mrs Crumpsall. They may recall Mrs Crumpsall's name? She claims to be a mid-wife but is known to procure girls for certain establishments serving gentlemen with particular tastes, or merely those who take the simplest approach to avoid being infected. Mrs Crumpsall, as she always does, personally verified Emily's intact state before accepting her; Emily was promised, and given, a meat pie for her co-operation with this process. Then Mrs Crumpsall bathed Emily, gave her new clothes and escorted her in a carriage across the city – the first time Emily had ridden in a carriage, or seen flowers growing in gar-dens – to a house in Knutsford, where there is, Mamma wrote, a room with thick carpet and double doors so that gentlemen may take their pleasure without fear of interfer-ence from those who might hear their young victims protest. Some gentlemen, indeed, take pleasure in the signs of girlish distress. And in that room Emily was ruined. Mrs Crumpsall was able to repair her parts once, but after losing her second virginity Emily was worth no more than any other woman and was left on the streets, there to manage as best she might until she found herself confined to the Lock Hospital. Mamma has written that there are thousands of Emilys every year in every city in Britain and that it is a disgrace to the nation that the men who buy children in this way commit no offence in law, that the guilt of adult women forced to sell themselves extends to twelve-year-olds compelled into acts they do not understand. Mamma has written that the age of consent must be raised to criminalise all who buy and sell little girls.

Gentlemen have written in response to Mamma's piece, and spoken about it at public meetings and even in Parliament. They have said that Mamma besmirches herself with such concerns, that no decent woman would wish to know anything about these matters. They have written that Mamma is unwell in her mind, that the editor should be ashamed of himself for allowing a woman so afflicted to cover a page of a serious newspaper. It is indecent to publish such sick fancies in a paper that enters the homes of Christian families; the proper place for Mamma and her stories must be the asylum. They express their concern and sympathy for Papa. Mamma knows, she says, that two of the gentlemen who have written these things are regular patrons of the house in Knutsford. Mamma believes that many of those gentlemen in Parliament who resist changing the law have their own very personal reasons for doing so. She has written again about Emily, about how Emily has been treated for her physical ailments but seems permanently affected in her mind. The women at the Home call her Satan's Child because of her terrible screaming fits, during which no-one can pacify her and she will make the most shocking allegations about those around her. She runs shrieking through the house and will, if unrestrained, smash windows and break furniture. It is feared that her future lies indeed in the asylum; sickness of the body may be cured, but there is a deeper taint of the mind that no medicine can address.

Now, so far Mamma has not spoken of this sequence of events to Ally and May because she did not wish them – Ally in particular – to be provoked or alarmed, and Mamma is pleased that no whisper of the scandal has reached them at school. (Ally remembers some whispering a few days ago, and that certain girls who used to play with May seem to have quarrelled with her recently.) But now Mamma needs Ally and May to help her prove that in English cities the virginity of children is indeed for sale. Ally is fair legal game for any man now, and treated as an adult should she break the law, but May is exactly the right age for this experiment. Will May do just as Mamma asks, without asking any questions or telling anyone about it, to help all the little girls like Emily whose health and futures are taken away from them as surely as if they were murdered and thrown into a ditch?

May drops her coat on the floor. Mamma's gaze is held by it, by the valleys in the grey wool and the mud smeared from May's boots. May is sorry to disappoint Mamma, but she cannot do this. As Mamma will recall with a moment's reflection, any association with such a scheme would be enough to destroy May's own future; if she is to make her own living, few respectable employers would countenance such a story, and if she is to marry, many families would summarily reject a girl with such experiences. Especially when there is already public interest in the matter, May declines to connect herself with such an undertaking.

Mamma's back stiffens, as if someone has tugged on the hook connecting her head to the ceiling, but she says only that May should hear the plan before refusing to help, that it is a sign of an intemperate disposition to make such a hasty rejection. Naturally she does not propose to expose May to any danger, and in fact is offended by the suggestion that May does not trust her Mamma's discretion; it is not the place of a mere girl to presume to judge such matters. The Reverend Frost himself will play the part of May's violator, so they may proceed with perfect confidence. Mamma asks May only to put

143

on the clothes of a beggar girl, to allow herself to be left in the care of Mrs Crumpsall, who will examine her but whose profit, after all, depends upon conducting this procedure with the utmost care, and to resist whatever restraint or compulsion Reverend Frost may pretend to require with only the strength one would expect of a street-child. In particular, May would be required to disguise her cultured voice until she found herself alone with the Reverend Frost.

Ally leans against the newel post, faintly reassured by the pain of its turned carving against her vertebrae. The fingernails of her right hand dig into the skin of her left palm. What if Mr Frost's honour, like that of so many outwardly respectable men, should turn out undependable? He would hardly be the first clergyman to take advantage of a young girl in a compromising position, and who would believe May, after the event? What if Mrs Crumpsall should receive a better offer for May from some other man? It is not as if her word is to be relied on. But Mamma is right, Ally herself is too old, too well-grown, to play such a part. It is exactly May's youth, her air of delicacy, that makes her desirable for such a role.

May shakes her head. She finds it extraordinary that Mamma, who has devoted so many years to campaigning against the forcible examination of young girls, would submit her own daughter to such a proceeding. It might be a different thing if May's own health depended on a medical examination, but merely to prove a point, to play a part, May will permit no such thing. As for allowing herself to be tied up, perhaps gagged, by a known procuress – May doubts that Mamma has Papa's sanction for this or any other part of the plan, and ventures to suggest that, were May to seek her Papa's advice, he would be unhappy with Mamma's proceedings. May meets Ally's eyes. In fact, she continues, unless she

144

is much mistaken, it is Papa's consent and not Mamma's that even under the present law would make such an arrangement legal; has Mamma not told them that a man's daughters may be bought or sold like any chattel but become criminals when they themselves profit from the transaction? That a mother has no authority in law? Mamma as well as Mr Frost and Mrs Crumpsall, May thinks, would find herself guilty of abduction. Were such a matter to come to the attention of the authorities.

Mamma draws herself up. The front door is still open, cold air snaking up the stairs.

'You think to threaten me? You choose to protect your own reputation from imaginary future slight rather than help to change the law and protect an entire generation from the most horrifying of assaults?'

May nods. 'I must, Mamma. Your proposal leaves me no choice. To ensure my own future work. Quite apart from the immediate danger, which I do not consider negligible, who would allow me to nurse, or teach, or go about among women and girls who aspire to virtue, if I were known to have done what you ask of me?'

Mamma's stance shifts. Ally thinks about running out into the afternoon, but she has nowhere to go. She wants Aubrey, or Papa.

'You would come to no harm, May.'

May shrugs. 'That seems far from certain to me, Mamma. You know that even the words "virginity" and "ruined" in connection with a girl's name are enough to destroy any hope of fulfilling work or respectable marriage. You need one of your parish girls for this, Mamma. Not me. Or Ally. And I am sure Papa would agree.'

May picks up her coat and turns to the coat cupboard.

Ally swallows. 'I'll do it, Mamma.'

Mamma looks at her. 'You are too old, Alethea. You would be said to be selling yourself like any other woman. And we cannot take the risk of hysterical fits in the course of the encounter. Very well, May. You had better dust the dining room before tea. You disappoint me.'

Mamma goes back into the drawing room, not where she usually spends time alone. Ally slides down the newel post, spine bumping over the turns, and sits on the bottom step.

May looks down at her. 'Are you well, Al?'

I thought she would kill you, Ally thinks. I thought she would wish you dead.

'Surprised. I thought she might – I don't know. I thought she would be very angry.' She would have been very angry, had it been Ally and not May who refused her request. But May is not weak, does not require moral training.

'No need for you to go round fainting on the stairs if she were. She'll find someone else. It's not as if she were lacking in girls with little to lose. I'm not one of them.'

Ally nods. 'May – wait. Do the girls at school know? What Mamma wrote?'

'What do you think, Ally?'

May goes into the kitchen, to help Jenny and find a duster, leaving Ally thinking about what she has to lose.

Mamma says no more about her experiment, though Papa seems to have stopped bringing home the *Manchester Times*. He's coming home late these days, usually after the girls have gone to bed and often after Mamma has turned out the lamps and locked up the house. Street has won the commission for Collingham Brown, a new department store being built on Deansgate. Papa has been to London and may soon be sent to

Paris to see the great shops there, where there are mirrored staircases and crystal candelabra, great fairy-tale palaces quite unlike the places where people buy things in Manchester. Collingham Brown is not to be extravagant or vulgar, but Papa has been told that at this stage, this early stage where he is being paid to imagine what might be, he should spare no expense in the pursuit of excellent taste. Later, there will be compromises, but now Mr Collingham wants to know what Street and Co. would do if they were without constraint. The painting on Papa's easel is swathed, half-finished, and the studio looks as if pieces of silk and watercolour sketches have rained across all flat surfaces. They are not to clean in there until further notice. Street comes over to work there with Papa sometimes, especially on Saturdays and sometimes also Sundays, although Mamma disapproves and provides only the cold lunch assembled by May and Ally so that Jenny can attend morning church.

Ally is working hard too. The wife of the Professor of Anatomy has formed the Manchester Association for the Higher Education of Women, and persuaded several of her husband's colleagues to offer lecture series, not just on English Poetry and Art History but also, this year, Mathematics, Chemistry and Philosophy. Miss Johnson herself escorts her College Group. The Cambridge Entrance Examinations are now open to women and Miss Emily Davies has informed Miss Johnson that she is presently in negotiation for premises for a Cambridge college for women. Professor Lewis's wife comes over to speak to Miss Johnson after one of her husband's lectures. The girls wait, restive as pent calves. Ally and Louisa have been intent for the last hour, making notes, fitting what Professor Lewis tells them into what they already know, and are leaving with knowledge they did not have this morning, the shape of their worlds a little changed, but the others have been twisting their hair, pleating the fabric of their skirts, thinking about the next meal or who they might marry or how to make up the fabric they bought last week. They murmur to each other, waiting to be released back into the world where what there is for tea and whether one has a cold matter more than the mechanism by which an orb of jelly translates light into perspective, distance, beauty, horror.

Ally has heard several sermons suggesting that science undermines faith, that the more scholars understand about the workings of the world the less they honour mystery. Her experience, so far, is quite opposite; whether humans evolved from apes or not, who could fail to be moved by the astonishing intricacy of the human eye? Is it not more remarkable that the mechanism is shared by birds and perhaps insects than it would be were it limited to those made in God's image? The minutely adjusted compromise of spine and skull that allows (most of) us to fit through our mothers' pelvises and then walk upright, the only-just-functional plumbing of ear, nose and throat, even the movement of food through the guts, the workings, dear God, of the human heart: the body proclaims the unplumbed immensity of God's care for his world, and there is so much still to be discovered. The brain is one grey mass, its appearance offering no clue to the forms of language, thought and dream, and yet it can be divided into areas governing different aspects of human, or animal, capacity. The application of electrical currents to the exposed brains of dogs causes muscle movement, allowing us to map the neural pathways of the brain, the flickering of electricity through the mammalian body. There are head injuries that deprive the sufferer of speech but leave him able to write, others that turn gentle men to violence and vice versa. It is almost possible to point to the physical location of character, of behaviour, if not of the mind itself. One day, there may be a surgical cure for evil, for melancholia. Or hysteria.

The women's silhouettes stand like upturned wine glasses against the light from the high window, and then Miss Johnson turns and beckons Ally.

'Mrs Lewis would like to meet you, Alethea. I have been telling her of our hopes for you.'

Mrs Lewis wears violet silk and a bird's black wing in her violet hat. She holds out a gloved hand to Ally.

'I am so pleased to hear of your ambitions, my dear. I want you to know that we will all go on working for you. There are Women's Education Associations in every city now, you know, and we will prevail. It is the hope of my life to live to see women graduate, enter professional life and even vote. Think of it! I do not see how they can allow women to graduate and not to vote. You may be among the first enfranchised women in Britain, in Europe. You will live to see women enter Parliament.'

Ally shakes her head, thinking of Emily's story. Mamma has told her something about what Emily's customers like to do. In the darkness of their hearts, in their secret, double-doored rooms in the silent suburbs, men believe that women are less than human.

Mrs Lewis touches Ally's cheek. 'Promise me one thing, my dear. Promise me never to give up, never to despair. And I promise you that we will not stop working for you.'

Ally flinches from her gaze. There are things in her mind to which no-one should be exposed. If Mrs Lewis knew of her weakness, she would not offer such hope.

'Can you promise?'

She looks up. 'I will try. I can promise to try.'

Mrs Lewis nods. 'Go well, my dear. We are all behind you. Come to me at any time if I can help you in any way. We cannot allow any distractions, any trivial demands, to hobble you now, and I know too well how hard it is for a woman to insist on time for her work.'

Ally glances at Miss Johnson. 'Mamma wishes my success. She has work of her own.'

'It is a great advantage being at school,' Miss Johnson suggests. 'It is the girls trying to learn at home for whom I feel sorry. One is constantly required to break off to fetch a parcel or take tea with a visitor or wind wool for one's aunt. Girls are allowed a pastime, and if they wish for Botany or French rather than knitting lace or producing needlepoint that nobody wants, the eccentricity may be tolerated, but a girl at home is always at someone's beck and call. It is reserved for men to tell people to go away until a more convenient season.'

The other girls have broken into open chatter, and the volume from the group is rising. The women look away.

'I must go,' says Miss Johnson. 'We must not dishonour these halls with shrieking females. Come, Alethea. Good afternoon, Mrs Lewis.'

Ally walks with Louisa to the omnibus. It's starting to rain.

'Do you think Miss Johnson went to school?' Ally asks.

Louisa shrugs. 'Not that she's ever mentioned. She likes you, ask her.'

'She'll never take her degree, will she? Not now. Even if we do, and younger girls. She'll watch us all going off and doing things she couldn't do.'

Louisa draws her skirts aside as a muddy cart passes. 'That's why she's a teacher, isn't it? That's the whole point of the school.'

It hasn't occurred to Ally before that the women who work to bring about these changes won't themselves enjoy the results. Miss Johnson will not graduate. Professor Lewis's wife is too busy writing to subscribers, seeking support and running her house to attend any but her own husband's lectures, and since he could presumably tell her what he knows over dinner she must do this out of wifely loyalty more than for self-improvement. Even Dr Blackwell's father refused to allow his daughter to be paid for her work; saying it was well enough to practise medicine as a hobby, or from philanthropy, but a professional woman brings shame upon her family, impugns the husband and father whose purpose it is to provide for her.

That evening, Ally makes herself a timetable: home from school, fifteen minutes to wash, change and have tea, fifteen minutes to clear away and then three hours to work until supper. She must still do her chores. Mamma maintains that no-one is too important to prepare her own food and clean her own house. Ally's ambitions are no licence for arrogance, and, unlike housework, brain-work gives no protection against nervous weakness. After supper Mamma sees that Ally helps Jenny wash the dishes and clean the kitchen, and that she brushes and polishes everyone's boots, mends her own and May's clothes. Then Ally is sent to bed, back in their shared bedroom for now, but she has found that the gaslight outside sheds enough light that it is possible to read while sitting behind the curtain on the windowsill, and the light burns until dawn. Ally waits until May is asleep and then pulls the blankets off her own bed. She folds one around her waist, so it pads her seat as well as keeping her legs warm, and the other over her shoulders, on top of the shawl she puts over her head.

She cannot risk using ink, balancing on a window-sill in the dark, so she borrows a soft pencil from Papa's studio, dark enough that she can see her own writing in the half-light, and she works her way through everything Miss Johnson sets, everything that might be asked by the University Entrance examiners. She thinks of these people sometimes, these men, as she huddles there behind the curtain, men who dictate the thoughts of so many pupils and teachers, who can change the course of people's dreams and daylight reflections on a whim. She will beat them. She will join them. Staying awake is one way of preventing nightmares. She goes back to bed when she hears Mamma locking up, in case Mamma looks in on them, and sometimes sleeps a little then, waking again when the grandfather clock in the hall chimes two to read and work through the silent hours when the city seems almost to sleep around her until she can slip back to bed, sated, for another nap before it is time to lay the fires. It works. As long as she keeps to her timetable, there are no more hysterical attacks. Dr Henry was right. Keeping to strict hours and working hard enough staves off madness. She is doing well, just like Papa.

And then one night she sees Papa. She can set herself, now, to wake to the clock. Wind soughs through the trees outside and the curtain stirs in the draught. May sighs, shifts, and relaxes. Ally's nose is cold and she knows how the floor will feel to bare feet. She pushes back the blankets, wraps herself quickly and takes her Horace, notebook and pencil from the table. She knows, now, that at least some of the Romans thought of Rome as Papa does of Manchester, not the centre of civilised life but a dirty, busy place whose main intellectual function is to focus artists' minds on the quiet green spaces where they would rather be. In her mind she sees the hills outside Rome: vines ripen on sunlit terraces and olive trees bloom in a palette of ochre and grey. The shadows of white towers fall crisp across parched grass and in the distance, figures in white move across the hillside. One day, perhaps, she will go to Italy. But here there is a carriage coming along the street outside. It's rare for anyone to pass at this hour, and she cranes to see who else walks her small-hours world. Two horses, and four wheels, not a hansom cab. It stops outside the house. She drops her pencil. No-one gets out. The trees bend and sigh and still no-one gets out, and then she hears a woman laugh, and Papa's voice. She slips off the sill and crouches, eyes at window-level, to watch him open the door and step down. He turns and talks through the window, and a gloved hand comes out to rest on his arm, and then at last he takes the hand, pulls the glove down to kiss the knuckles, steps back and waves as the carriage drives off. He opens the gate carefully and walks up the drive, not along the gravel path, and then steps onto the grass to reach the front door. It closes behind him, and he comes up the stairs, more like a burglar than like the man of the house.

6

ERIS AND THE APPLE

Alfred Moberley, 1874

Oil on Canvas, 126 × 87

Signed and dated '74

Provenance: James Dunne (dealer) 1876; Albert
Chamberlain, 1878; Crouch and Sanderson (dealers)
1882; James family (Birmingham) after 1918; bought by
Birmingham City Art Gallery, 1971

*Not the Judgement of Paris, the three naked goddesses painted by so many,
but the moment before the squabble, the Goddess of Discord returning to the
wedding of Peleus and Thetis with the golden apple in her hand. Moberley
has eschewed the faux-classical settings favoured by RDS for such scenes:
no statuary, no Florentine approximations, laurel wreaths or olive boughs.
Who is to say, he wrote, where a wedding of the gods would take place?
The northern version of the story about the bad woman and her cursed fruit,
the evil godmother who appears unbidden and brings ill luck in the form of
the apple, whispers in the background. Eris wears a loose green garment,
perhaps medieval, pinned on the shoulder with a gold brooch heavy enough
to drag on the fabric and woven like Irish lace. There are rubies and pearls
in her ears, about her neck and in her dark hair. She stands outside a stone
archway set into an ivied wall, through which we can see the swirling skirts
of women dancing and the darker, vertical forms of men watching. One*

hand rests on the rough stone – the limestone of Moberley's northern child-
hood? – of the arch, her fingers soft against the pitted carving, and the other
is raised, weighing the golden apple as a boy might weigh a stone. There
is engraving, like the letters on a tombstone, on the apple's gleaming curve,
dull yellow under the low sky, but she's looking through the arch, at the cel-
ebration from which her own misbehaviour has excluded her.

*

Mamma and Papa are going to Paris. Papa has been invited to
exhibit at the Musée de la République and Mamma wishes to
meet the women working for reform of the *Police des Moeurs*.
The Contagious Diseases Act is now part of English law, and
all that Mamma and Mrs Butler feared is coming to pass.
Respectable women have killed themselves after forced examinations, girls who had not fallen have done so after being so
degraded in the police station that they have no modesty or
dignity left to lose. You are a good girl after all, the police
doctor in Chatham had said to a sixteen-year-old picked up on
her way home with a pint of porter for her father. Look, the
speculum made you bleed. They unfastened the straps holding
her ankles apart and her arms to the table and without both-
ering to pick up the clothes they'd torn off she walked to the
dock and kept walking over the edge. Sick prostitutes are guilty
of the crime of catching a disease with which it is perfectly
legal for a man to infect them. The law has entered the body
of every woman who happens to find herself in one of the
named port towns, where it is feared that prostitutes will bring
the British Navy to its knees with syphilis. Meanwhile, the work
of Florence Nightingale and her uniformed nurses has reduced
the death rate in the Crimea from thirty to ten percent.
Until her work took effect, more men were dying of cholera,
typhoid and infection than of wounds received in battle. Miss

Nightingale does not support the campaign for women doctors. There are monstrous regiments of women at every turn.

Papa has spoken of shutting up the house and sending Ally and May to stay with Aunt Mary in London while he and Mamma are away, but Ally is only weeks from taking her examinations. She will surely pass in any case, says Papa, and if she does not it is perfectly possible to take them again. If her passing depends on last-minute cramming she is probably not prepared anyway. Ally looks at the floor until the first horror of this remark has faded from her face.

'I know Mary,' says Mamma. 'The girls would do no work at all, Alfred, of any kind. I am afraid she is almost entirely given up to dissipation these days. When she does find a moment to write, I hear of nothing but dinners, concerts and clothes.'

Ally catches the twitch of a smile on May's face at the idea.

'What of the Home, Mamma?' she asks. 'I could visit and send you reports if I stayed here. The new Matron will be arriving, you know.'

Mamma nods. 'The girls are quite old enough, Alfred. There are women younger than Ally married and raising families. How do you think she will manage in Edinburgh if she cannot take responsibility for her own home for a fortnight? They will be at school every day. Miss Johnson will soon know if there are difficulties.'

'I could ask Aubrey to stop by,' says Papa. 'He doesn't seem especially busy at the moment. You'd like that, wouldn't you, Al?'

'I would. And Papa, I really can't miss school. Not now.'

I've come so far, she wants to say, I've worked so hard. But she mustn't sound hysterical.

*

Mamma summons her the night before they leave. The trunk stands like an expectant dog at the foot of the bed with Mamma's valise beside it, and her bedroom, stripped of brushes, slippers, hairpins, the usual impedimenta of sleeping and waking without which not even Mamma faces the world, looks as if its occupant had died. One day, she will close Mamma's eyes and draw a sheet over her face.

'Go carefully, Mamma.'

Mamma, seated on the bowed stool at her dressing table, back straight and hands folded as if for a portrait on her grey serge lap, frowns.

'Please don't fall prey to foolish alarms, Alethea. There is no more reason, and perhaps less, to expect disaster in Paris than in Manchester.'

Ally looks at her feet, touches her fingers to the side-seams of her skirt to stop herself twisting her hands.

'Yes, Mamma.'

Mamma takes an envelope from the table before her. 'Here is ten shillings, which must feed the three of you until my return. The larder is already well stocked so I will expect you to have change to give me. You will need to be able to manage a small budget next year, and so your Papa has instructed Aubrey that he is not to supply you with delicacies in our absence. I expect to find the house as I leave it, and you must not ask Jenny to perform any additional tasks for you. She is already too hard-worked for one whose life has been so wearing.'

'Yes, Mamma.'

'Papa worries, you know, about sending you off to Edinburgh on your own. He is reluctant to allow you to go. You might regard this time as a chance to prove to him that you can overcome your weakness.'

Ally shivers. 'Yes, Mamma. I will try.'

Mamma nods. 'Let us hope that you succeed.'

Mamma stands up, and Ally almost expects to see ripples of surprise in the mirror over the dressing table at the movement. Mamma lays a hand on Ally's shoulder and Ally fails to stop her body flinching. It knows Mamma's hands.

'You must conquer your nerves, Alethea. You will be about your chores in the morning so we will say goodbye now. I will look for your letters and hope for good reports.'

'Yes, Mamma. Goodbye, Mamma.'

She hesitates at the door, wanting to add something. What do people say when their mothers leave?

'Goodbye, Ally. Close the door behind you, please.'

May is in bed, reading by candlelight. Not *Pilgrim's Progress*, which is what Mamma has set her for nightly reading.

May sees her glance at the novel. 'It's good. Molly lent it to me. From her married sister. You'd hate it.'

Ally starts to undress. 'So would Mamma, I expect.'

May rearranges her pillow. *Pilgrim's Progress* is by her head, where she can pick it up if she hears Mamma coming. 'I wasn't intending to offer it to her. What did she say to you?'

Ally emerges from her chemise. 'She gave me ten shillings for food. They've told Aubrey not to bring cake.'

'I'm sure they have. Ten shillings?'

'It's more than –'

'I know, Al. More than many households within one mile of here can hope for in a month. I go about there too, you know.'

It's true. May has begun regularly to spend her Wednesday and Saturday afternoons at the children's and lying-in hospital, and sometimes to visit patients after they have been allowed home.

Ally buttons her nightdress. 'I'm sure we'll manage.'

May turns a page. 'We'll have to. Anyway, Aubrey said he'd bring a ham. He says it will last us days.'

'Papa told him not to.'

'Mamma told Papa to tell him not to. I know.'

Two days later, she hears Jenny's steps on the stairs in the morning, later than usual, almost time to wake May. She's done all the hearths, lit the range, and stopped herself boiling the water for Mamma's morning tea. The house feels different without Mamma, as if its anchor is dragging a little. She takes out yesterday's loaf for May's toast.

'Good morning, Jenny.'

'Morning. Miss Ally, I have to go away for a few days. I had a message from my sister last night.'

Her hands stop on the loaf and the knife.

'Your sister?'

Jenny sees her family once a month, on a Sunday afternoon, has done since Ally can remember.

'She's been taken bad. Needs me to look after her children. The little ones.'

Nobody looks after children like that, Ally wants to say. They run around the streets and get lured into charity schools and welfare clubs by the promise of soup.

She starts cutting bread. The loaf is dry; she and May don't eat enough to have fresh bread. 'How long will you be gone?'

Jenny draws herself up, as if she's already left, already stopped being a servant. 'Depends how soon my sister gets well. I should think I'd be back before your Mamma comes home. I can stop by, if you like, make sure you're managing in the kitchen.'

Ally cuts another slice, more than they will eat. 'Don't trouble, Jenny. After all, I'll have to manage for myself next year.

You'll be busy enough with the children, I expect.' She glances up. 'I'll write to Mamma, of course.'

Jenny shrugs. 'I suppose you will, Miss. She's always been kind to Anne. Sent her things for the babies.'

'Mamma is kind to everyone,' Ally says. Unlike herself, she knows. She feels as if she could this moment stab Jenny in her pillowy stomach with perfect equanimity. 'You are leaving this morning?'

'I'm afraid I must, Miss. She can't leave her bed.'

'Very well, Jenny. I hope you will let me know if there is anything we can do to help.'

She doesn't mean it. She's going to have to manage the house quite unassisted as well as going to school and studying, and she will not, *will not*, allow this alleged illness of Jenny's sister to jeopardise her entire future career.

'I'll do that. Goodbye, Miss. Mind you remember the grocer's order and the butcher's bill, and don't let Miss May leave the bluing bag in the wash-water again. Your Mamma won't want to come home and find her linen all blue.'

Dear God, laundry. They will have to do the laundry, a whole wash day. And the ironing.

'Goodbye, Jenny. I hope your sister recovers soon.'

'I'm sure you do, Miss.'

She goes straight up to wake May.

'Jenny's gone. She's gone away. And it's wash day tomorrow.'

'What?'

May sits up, hair over her face, breath sour with sleep. Ally explains.

May pushes back the hair , licks her dry lips. 'Funny how Anne gets ill two days after Mamma goes away.'

161

'People do get ill. Especially there.'

'Once in sixteen years in the only week we really can't spare her?'

'There have been other times we couldn't have spared her. When you were born. Papa's shingles. When we had measles. Grandmamma's dying.'

'Mamma was here then. She'd have gone to Anne's house with soup.'

They look at each other. No. They are not going to go and verify Jenny's story. What good would it do?

'We'll have to do the laundry,' Ally says again.

May gathers her hair on her neck. 'We could send it out, I suppose.'

'On ten shillings? Not as well as eating.'

May lets her hair drop. 'We could eat less. Let Aubrey feed us. He must have someone to do his laundry.'

'His landlady,' Ally says. 'I think she might wonder, don't you, if there are six petticoats and eighteen pairs of drawers along with Aubrey's linen.'

They are both thinking of Aubrey's linen. Ally shakes her head.

'I only meant that he would know where we could send it.'

'Mamma would be horrified. She has never sent it out.'

May pushes back the sheets. 'Mamma is not here. She need not know.'

'No, May. She trusts us. We must show her that we can do as she expects.'

'No-one,' says May, 'could do all that Mamma expects.'

She stays in the pupils' sitting room at lunchtime, going over her algebra again. Does one remove the buttons from Papa's linen before boiling? For how long should pillowcases be starched? She has never ironed the lace collars Papa gave to Mamma before; how does one know that the iron is not too hot? She gathers her wits. Algebra. Whatever happens to the laundry, she must not fail now. But Mamma must not return to find that she is indeed weak and idle, not competent to care even for herself and May. But she must keep working, must remain entirely focused on her studies. She works the sum again, and comes out with an answer different from her last. Bother. Start again, and concentrate this time.

The door opens. May. 'Oh, good. I thought you'd be here. Charlotte says I can go to her house for tea. I thought it would save us a meal.'

She puts down her pen. 'But what about the washing? I can't do it alone.'

May shrugs. 'We'll do it tomorrow. Or send it out. Don't worry about it, Ally, it's just washing.'

'It's not just washing, May. There's Mamma's lace collar and I've never done Papa's linen before and there's the starching and bluing and mangling and ironing, and what if it rains, we'll be out at school and we can't bring it in, and then we'd have to start all over again. And I still need to eat, even if you're out. It doesn't save anything, it just means more bread going stale and wasted.'

May turns the door handle, watching the latch advance and retreat. 'Al? You're sounding just a little bit nervous. People do laundry all the time.'

'Not while they're preparing for examinations they don't. Not unassisted. May, Mamma will be so angry if she comes home and we haven't done it, if the house is dirty and messy and there's no food.'

'Mamma's not back for two weeks, there's plenty of time to

do the washing. We can do it on Saturday afternoon if you prefer. When I get back from the hospital. And the house isn't messy.'

She slams her book on the table. 'It gets messy. And dirty. We can't do it on Saturday, May, we'd have to dry and iron it on Sunday. And we're making more washing every day, towels and dishcloths and sheets as well as what we're wearing. You can't just go out and leave me to deal with it.'

'I've arranged it with Charlotte now. They have nursery tea, with sandwiches. I can probably eat enough not to need supper. Her brother will see me home.'

'May –'

May goes. Ally wants to hold a candle-flame to her arm, to raise blisters on her thighs. She puts the flesh at the base of her thumb in her mouth and bites until blood comes, iron welling onto her tongue. It's only when she feels better that she remembers that a bite-mark on her hand tells everyone she's not sane.

It's not the first time she's been alone in the house. It can't be; Jenny goes out often, for shopping or to the post, and Mamma is rarely at home. But there's something about the silence, the house's lack of expectation, that weights her wrists and ankles like sleep. She feels as if she's moving underwater as she changes her shoes, hangs up her coat. She should wash her hands, Mamma likes them to wash their hands after school. May has left the soap in the water and it's turned to jelly, stringy like mucus on her hands. If she puts it where it should be, it will drip away through the wire basket. Perhaps she should sit it on blotting paper. The towel is damp. She goes into the dining room, where there may be blotting paper in the sideboard's left-hand drawer. Sunset is hours away, but gloom is already beginning to gather like dust in the corners. She traps her finger in the drawer handle. The blotting paper must be under the table brush, whose silver back is tarnished. There are crumbs in the drawer, and no blotting paper. She should polish the brush. Mamma won't like its tarnish. The silver-cloth is in the kitchen. She notices as she passes that the door of the coat-cupboard isn't properly shut, which is because Papa's mackintosh has slipped from its hanger and is blocking the hinge. She takes it out and hangs it properly, with the buttons fastened. The house creaks over her, the two floors and ten empty rooms above her head. What proportion of the cubic volume of the house does she occupy? (Archimedes in his bath, but surely the displacement of water is the kind of thing that thousands of people noticed and categorised merely as common sense before Archimedes wrote it down.) Not much, anyway. She closes the cupboard door and goes into the kitchen. A silver-cloth. May has left the butter out, and a buttery knife balanced on it. She puts the lid back on the butter-dish and carries it down to the pantry, comes back up and washes the knife, dries it, puts it away. The tea-strainer by the sink still contains used tea leaves, which should be spread out to dry ready to clean the carpets tomorrow. What was it? A silver-cloth. She must make a start on tomorrow's Latin, and look over her notes from last week in preparation for tomorrow's anatomy lecture. The table brush is tarnished. Mamma will be angry. She stands in the darkening kitchen, the silver-cloth in her hand, her Latin plucking at her mind.

Ally sorted the laundry and set it to soak last night, while May was asleep. She's always done this for Jenny: sheets, table-cloths, towels and napkins to soak in warm water and soda; tea-towels and dishcloths boiled in lime, rinsed and left in a fresh lime solution; underlinen, nightgowns, petticoats and

Papa's shirts soaking in cold water. There is blood on her own drawers and one of her petticoats, ink on most of Papa's cuffs and something that looks like red wine on his dress-shirt. She unpicks the bodice of Mamma's walking dress, which has indigo in the dye, from its black skirt. She will ask May, the better needle-woman, to sew them back together at the end. She understands now why Mamma has always insisted on plain clothes and regarded lace as a symptom of moral failure.

It's fully dark when she wakes, so dark she has to wait to hear the grandfather clock chime four times to know that it is indeed time to get up. Cold air snaps at her feet and legs as she fumbles for her slippers and makes her way downstairs. The first thing is to light the range and the copper. The match flares, conjuring a sphere of cast iron and orange flame around her hand. Holding her wrapper tight around her shivering body, she stirs the soaking clothes with the washing-stick. It will be best, she decided in the night, to wash the sheets and linens now and finish the third rinse before they go to school. They can do the bluing rinse, the cottons and Mamma's dress, which seems to have blood on the outside of the skirt as well as being much mired about the lower part, when they come home, and they will have to eat bread and butter, if there is time to eat at all. She goes upstairs to wake May, who was insisting even as she went to bed that they should 'get someone in' or 'send it all out'.

'It's frothing up again, May.'

May is meant to be skimming the dirty froth off the boiling cottons while Ally wrings out the sheets and towels, but she's drawing in the steam on the window with her finger and humming to herself. Not a hymn.

May makes one swoop with the skimmer, dropping the grey froth into the sink, and then tries to write her initials in what's left on the boiling tub. 'You can see how people end up going dirty, can't you?'

Ally braces herself to lift Papa and Mamma's double sheets. 'No.'

'Oh Al, you must. Imagine if you were old, or sick, or expecting, having to carry those sheets.'

Ally drops the sheets into the basket. She'll need May to help her fold them before she puts them through the wringer. 'Someone would help. People only get sicker and weaker when things are dirty. May, this is housework, not painting.'

May has been trying to make a circle of open water on the boiling froth. She yawns. 'I might have to go to bed soon, Al. I'm tired.'

Ally twists the rough water out of a towel, finding satisfaction in the sound of falling water and the way the cotton resists her hands. 'No you don't, May. I'm tired too. We're staying up until this is done.'

'You may. I said I thought it was a foolish idea, two girls doing a whole wash day after school. We should just have done our underthings and told Mamma we didn't have time for anything else.'

Ally twists a hand-towel, as if wringing its neck. 'May Moberley, are you mad? Tell Mamma we didn't have time?'

May shrugs. 'I'm not the mad one.'

She yawns again and puts down the skimmer. 'Anyway, I'm hungry. There are eggs, aren't there?'

'May, we can't start cooking. Don't be ridiculous. Even Jenny doesn't cook on wash days.'

'Jenny prepares meals the day before. Which you didn't.'

'Nor did you! You're the one who wants to eat.'

'Mamma left you in charge. I'm sure that includes cooking.'

Ally throws the remaining sheets, wet, into the basket. 'If you want to eat, there's bread. If you're tired, the sooner we finish this the sooner we can sleep.'

'I think Mamma will be disappointed, don't you, if I tell her you didn't cook and expected me to live on bread?'

Ally reaches towards the copper of boiling water and then takes up the skimmer instead and throws it at May. It misses and dents the plaster behind her.

'And if I tell her you had another hysteric fit and threw things at the kitchen wall? You might find yourself a patient in the asylum then, not a doctor.'

She lunges for May and trips over the basket.

'Fighting like a street-urchin. Violent as a madwoman,' says May. 'No self-control, Al.'

She takes the omnibus home from the university. It is wrong, she is indolent and self-indulgent and spendthrift and they will be going hungry before Mamma comes home, but by the time the last handkerchief was pegged on the rack in the basement grey light was seeping even there, and when she came up the stairs into the kitchen she heard birdsong in the garden and the rumble of wheels and beat of horses on the road. The range was still hot enough from boiling clothes to make tea; they must try to use less coal. There will be ironing to do tonight, at least the linen which, hanging in the kitchen, should be almost dry. Then she can move the small clothes up from the basement, where nothing really dries, even in summer, and hang them over the range. It is important, she remembers, not to cook kippers or bacon or anything fried, while the clothes are there. Kippers and bacon are both cheap. May spoke of eggs: perhaps an omelette would placate her, encourage her

168

not to tell stories to Mamma? The feather on the hat of the woman in front of her arches like a fountain almost into her lap. How do you clean hat-feathers? She looks around the omnibus: a cloak with satin ribbons, the lace trimming on a skirt peeping from below a coat with cord frogging, quilling framing a bonnet. The whole panoply of women's clothing is part of the conspiracy to waste women's time, to absorb them in petty hour-by-hour maintenance of themselves and their homes so that nothing can ever change. She recalls the 'freedom suit' worn by some American women described in a recent issue of the *Englishwoman's Magazine*. She and May mocked the short skirts and loose waists but they are right, those sisters across the sea, to start with clothing. And with medicine. Of course women cannot enter the professions as long as they are corseted too tightly to breathe, hobbled by narrow skirts and obliged to spend at least one full day a week tending to these disabling garments. As long as their insides are ripped and broken, secretly bleeding and leaking, and the only help on offer is at the hands of those who caused the damage. She rubs a clear space in the mist on the window. Almost home.

She can hear voices as she burrows in her bag for her keys, May and someone else. Aubrey.

He opens the door. 'Good evening, Princess Al. Are you very cold and wet? You should have taken a cab, Princess, on such a night as this.'

She gives him her hand. 'The omnibus was extravagance enough. I'm afraid you find us in disarray, Aubrey. I can't give you dinner. And the only tea is stale bread and butter.'

He takes her coat, shakes it and finds a hanger. A man who notices fabric. 'No, it's not. I brought fruit cake. And a game pie. Your Mamma told me not to feed you, so I thought it might help. And May's been telling me that you two were up all night at the washing? Poor child. She looks as tired as you do.'

She follows him into the kitchen. The sheets are still damp to the touch, but maybe not so damp that a hot iron won't finish the job. She fills the kettle and riddles the range. 'I can't play and chat tonight, Aubrey. There's all the ironing and Miss Johnson is going to go through last year's examination paper with me tomorrow. Where's May?'

'Resting. I put her to bed, poor little May-flower. We'll take her some tea, shall we? And then she can get up for supper.'

Ally leans against the flour cupboard and allows herself to close her eyes for a moment. 'If you like. I have to do the ironing.'

She will not make up May's tray. Aubrey pours tea into a cup from Mamma's best set and waits for Ally to fill the smallest milk-jug and offer the sugar-bowl. Mamma does not allow them to sugar their tea. He asks for a knife and plate and cuts a generous slice of fruit cake for May. 'Do you have flowers anywhere? My mother always used to put flowers on the tray when someone was ill.'

Ally opens the range to put the irons to heat.

'She's not ill. She was fine at school. And no, we don't have flowers. It's October.'

'Don't you want to go up and see her? Al, have you two quarrelled?'

Could May be ill? There have been fever patients at the hospital.

'If she asks for me, I'll go. When I've done the sheets.'

Aubrey takes off his jacket and unfastens his cuffs. Bright white cuffs, representing hours of soaking, scrubbing, rinsing.

'Come on. I'll help. It will be fun, I've never ironed anything before.'

May comes down to eat the game pie, her footsteps slow on the stairs. Her hair is loose and she's wearing a wrapper and Ally's shawl, a hand-made gift from one of the women in the Home, over her nightdress. Aubrey offers his arm, as though since playing tag at lunchtime she might have become too frail to walk from the bottom of the stairs to her place at the table in the dining room.

'We should write to your Mamma, Ally, if May isn't well tomorrow.'

May rubs her cheek against his arm. 'I'm sure I'm just over-tired, Aubrey. The sheets were rather heavy.'

Aubrey shakes his head, passes her a full plate. 'You should never have tried to lift them, May-flower. You're no strapping great washer-woman with arms like hams.'

She's trying to translate her thoughts into Latin, mostly as an experiment. The Examination will not require her to be able to discourse on black-leading, or the washing of woodwork or the removal of stains from chamber-pots. The Romans, she supposes, must have had words for these things, must have done them, but either they did not write them down or no-one considered such writing worth preserving. And it must be easier in a warmer climate, where there are not coal fires making soot and ash, and laundry can be dried outside without fear of brown fog. Hypocaust heating would be much cleaner than open fires. And all done by slaves anyway. Did the Romans have curtains? Builders have recently found the remains of a Roman villa while building the new station in the city centre. There would have been more wood, then,

171

for the hypocaust, but even so the climate of Manchester, Mancunium, must have seemed most unpleasant after Rome. Did they spend the winter huddled in their togas, complaining about being posted here to the north-western edge of civilisation? Will their ghosts walk the platforms of Oxford Street Station? This she can translate, at least apart from the platforms and the station. *Manes*, ghosts. Maybe she will pass. She has never been to Edinburgh. Hills, and the Firth of Forth glittering between tall stone buildings. Slums as bad as anything in Manchester, but filled with plaid-wrapped Gaelic-speakers dispossessed from their ancestral Highland homes, the lilt of mountain voices in their accents. Aubrey has begun to speak of making a painting trip in the Highlands. It doesn't matter, anyway; the point is to become a doctor, whatever her surroundings.

'How long have you been up, Al?'

She sits back on her haunches. 'About three hours. We need to go in half an hour.'

May reaches out to touch her shoulder. 'Won't you be ill?'

'Mamma will be angry if it's not done. If she gets back to find a dirty house.'

May sighs. 'Very well. Look, I'll make some breakfast for both of us. I promised to go to the Hospital this afternoon, some of the children are expecting me, but after that I'll help, I promise. Just tell me what you want me to do. And Al? I'm sorry about yesterday. What I said. It's just that it annoys me sometimes. How you must take everything so seriously.'

Ally dips her brush and goes back to scrubbing. 'Don't trouble yourself, May. We don't want to risk your being over-tired again. Just please don't make any mess.'

Mamma and Papa will be back on Monday. She's going to have to break the Sabbath, and to rely on May not telling

Mamma she has done so, but as long as May doesn't walk on any of her clean floors or light the fires in any of her clean grates or wipe her shoes on any of her beaten and brushed doormats, Mamma will, she hopes, find the house at least as clean as she left it. She wrote to tell Mamma of Jenny's sister's illness and Mamma replied that they should send soup for Anne and puddings for her children and that she expects them to rise to the challenge. She hoped Ally's preparations for the Examination are proceeding. She has learnt a great deal in Paris and will have much to discuss with her Committees when she is home.

Mamma and Papa's train is due at five, and they will take a hansom. Ally ought to be studying. May is downstairs, helping Jenny in the kitchen (Ally finds herself fretting that Jenny will mess up her kitchen, that Mamma will find crumbs on the floor and smears on the table and think Ally has allowed them to be there). *Higher Mathematics for Boys* is open on the table before her and the window ajar so rain-scented air trickles into the room. She wants to get up, wander into Papa's studio – cleaned as much as possible without rearranging anything – into her and May's bedroom, check again. She will not rise from her chair until she has worked the next three problems. Will not. She's checking the second one when there are wheels on the road, and they stop outside the gate. They are here. Her heart and stomach seem to drop into her pelvis. She feels colour scalding her cheeks, counts her breathing in and out. Her breath catches again at the idea of Mamma finding her in the throes of an attack. Hold it, hold it in. There is the rumble of Papa's voice, the click of the gate, decisive feet on the gravel. They are here, and she can't move at all, can't leave her chair. The grime in the embossed letters of *Higher*

Mathematics seems to pulsate on the worn red leather cover. Downstairs, she hears May and Jenny hurrying to the door, and voices in the hall. Her arms seem to have stiffened, but she forces them to push her back from the table, forces her legs under her and her back to stand. Her knees lock as she tries to cross the room. They will think her mad, after all her work. She pinches her thigh, hard and harder, makes a fist and pounds her own head, and the pain unlocks what was jammed, allows her to move again.

Mamma finds the lower drawers of May's bureau in disarray, stickiness on a shelf of the larder where a bag of sugar has leaked, a piece of cheese which was not properly covered and has dried out on the cold shelf, and rust in the handles of butter knives that were soaked in too deep water before washing. Worst of all, Ally ran out of money and has not restocked the larder. Mamma speaks to May about the drawers first and May speaks back; she and Ally have kept the house running and clean, eaten within their budget and kept up with their schoolwork. If Mamma doesn't like the state of May's bureau she doesn't need to look at it. Charlotte's Mamma was most surprised to hear that Papa and Mamma had thought it suitable to leave them at all, had offered to have her to stay until their return so that she would be properly attended. Mamma tells May not to be impudent and to tidy the bureau at once, and May flounces upstairs. Not, Ally suspects, to tidy the bureau, which she will probably do herself; even when she is not the immediate object of Mamma's anger, the spate of rage makes her feel sick. Mamma's fury is the weather in Ally's mind, more and less alarming but always there, always to be taken into account. It doesn't seem to be like that for May.

'Ally,' says Mamma. 'Come and sit here.'

She puts her mending in its basket and comes to the seat Mamma indicates, the stool beside Mamma's chair where she has always liked them to sit to be scolded. She hardly needs to say anything to Ally any more. Sitting there is enough to make her want to be dead. She has disappointed, again. Extravagance, sloppiness, laziness. It is not good enough, and does not promise well for her future. She must go now and clean the knives and shelves. Papa, Mamma believes, has brought her some trinket from Paris; whenever she wears it, she must remember these failings and strive to do better.

There is no point in Ally continuing to attend school after the Examination. Miss Johnson says that she should take a period of rest, that vacations are also part of the scholarly life. Dr Henry speaks of nervous exhaustion, and agrees with Mamma that regular work, real service not brain-work, is indicated, for idleness is known to exacerbate nervous trouble. Aubrey wants her to pose with May, one last one, he says, before she becomes a grown-up bluestocking too busy setting bones and cutting people open to spare time for such frivolity as modelling, but Papa, also, wants her to pose. May suggests that Papa and Aubrey paint the same scene from different angles, an idea not well received by either of them. And then Mrs Lewis, the Professor's wife, comes to tea on a day when Mamma is at the Home and offers to send – nay, insists on sending – Ally some-where. The seaside, she suggests. She cannot, alas, herself accompany her, not without bringing at least some of her chil-dren, which would obviate the point of Ally's resting, but she knows of an excellent boarding house at Morecambe where if Mamma could find a suitable escort ... ? Mamma, Ally explains, is most unlikely to do anything of the sort, and in any case since Ally will be unescorted in Edinburgh and, indeed, in her professional life, she should accustom herself to independence. And, grateful as she is for the suggestion, she cannot think that Mamma would sanction her leaving all her duties here, duties somewhat neglected while preparing for the Examination, for mere pleasure. Mrs Lewis replies, gazing out of the window into the improbable greenness of an English lawn in early summer, that Ally will likely find herself doing many things unsanctioned in the coming months and years. She will perhaps need to accustom herself to the disapproval of those around her, to independence of spirit as well as body. But if Ally does not like Morecambe, there is no more to be said.

Then Aunt Mary, who has been corresponding regularly with May for some time, encloses a letter for Mamma. Her children have been ordered to the seaside after measles and James cannot spare time from work to escort her (James being an art dealer, this seems improbable). She fears the trip cannot be counted a pleasure outing since the baby in particular still requires a great deal of care, but if Ally – and of course May if she might be excused from school – could be persuaded to join her in Broadstairs for a fortnight she would be most grateful. She knows that Ally is not yet too important to object to being asked for such a service!

May has taken care to present the letter at Sunday tea, when Papa is there, although Ally knows the last post for May came on Thursday. Ally watches May's face as Papa and Mamma begin to argue: she looks like someone who, looking down at her hand, already knows that she will win a card game. With Mamma distracted, May spoons jam onto her bread-and-butter. The child needs a change of air, says Papa. Anyone can see that she is pale and tired, quite unfit for a new regime of study. If she is to go away in the autumn – and he is still far from content with the prospect – she requires a holiday and a rest. Perhaps more recreation than Mary offers; he does not see how exhausted nerves are to be restored by acting as an unpaid nursemaid. Nonsense, says Mamma, fine fancies and indolence. Dr Henry – Papa is not interested in Dr Henry. If Mamma wishes a doctor's opinion on which to base her plans, he is happy to consult another man. Professor Lewis, for example, who in his time taught Dr Henry.

Ally pleats the tablecloth. 'Papa, please. I can remain here. There is much for me to do. Really. Just as Mamma wishes.'

May shakes her head. 'Al would agree to anything, Papa, rather than hear people be angry.'

It is a sign of Ally's being run down, Papa adds, that she is too enervated to wish to go. It is a sign of her good sense, replies Mamma. She knows that idleness is bad for her, and what needs cry out at the Home and the hospital. Papa stands up, about to return to his studio; the poor child has never been allowed an afternoon's idleness in her life. Rubbish, says Mamma, Aubrey is perpetually indulging them in foolish excursions and sweets, not to mention your taking them to the mountains.

Bile boils in Ally's stomach as her fingernails press into the skin of her palms. 'Please – Papa.'

May sets down her teacup. 'I, also, wish to make a change,' she says. 'I intend to leave Miss Johnson's this summer and join the Nursing School.'

Georgie lays his hand on Aunt Mary's green silk lap. Outside, orchards and circular barns – oast-houses, Aunt Mary says – shimmer against a blue sky. The south of England is another country.

'Mamma, when will you open the basket? I'm so hungry.'

Aunt Mary and Nurse, so far nameless, exchange smiles.

Georgie has eaten two pieces of bread-and-butter, one apple and one sponge drop since they left Charing Cross not two hours ago.

Aunt Mary consults the watch on a gold bracelet veiled by her lace cuff. 'We should wait another half hour, properly. Are you hungry, Ally?'

Her shoulders stiffen. What does Aunt Mary want her to say? Mamma does not like people to be hungry, to attend to bodily inclinations. 'Not very, Aunt. That is to say, I could eat.' Perhaps Aunt Mary wishes to eat but prefers Ally to be responsible for the abandonment of regular habits. 'Or wait. That is, half an hour does not signify.'

She feels her face redden. Aunt Mary looks at her, as if that wasn't the right answer.

George tugs on his mother's skirt. 'It does. I'm hungry.'

'Nurse?'

Nurse adjusts the blanket over the sleeping baby. 'I'm thinking, Madam, it would be as well to eat while Freddie sleeps. The movement often lulls a child, but then when it stops ... And there'll be Whitstable soon and then Margate and you need to keep your strength up, Madam.'

'Very well. Georgie, do you think you can open the hamper? Pull the pegs. Yes, like that. Well done. And pass me that cloth and let's see what Cook has given us.'

There is a cluster of stone houses, a church. There must, she knows, be poverty and suffering in these villages just as at home. Some of those thatched cottages will hold families of ten sharing two rooms. The school-house surrounded by trees will be owned and controlled by a landowner who determines the present and future lives of all on his land, and there is no Women's Association for the girls of rural Kent. But she wonders, all the same, how those for whom these surroundings are normal would see Manchester. The first apples gleam under dark leaves, and in a cherry orchard there are women and girls balancing on shaded ladders as they fill baskets with fruit. Birdsong in place of the clatter of machines, and the sun on their backs and wind in their hair instead of cotton in the lungs and sweat-soaked clothing. Ill-paid, of course. Merely seasonal labour, and their husbands and sons out fourteen hours a day as beasts of burden for the rich.

'Cold chicken, Ally? Mayonnaise sauce? Cook has done us rather well, I think. And goodness only knows what we'll find for dinner.'

Aunt Mary has taken rooms in the same house every summer since she was married. It is unfashionable, she says, with plasterwork like a vulgar wedding cake, and the appointments hopelessly dated, not in the least the kind of thing Ally's Papa could approve, but Mrs Hughes is the most delightful landlady and so good-natured about the children. And it would be foolish to go to the seaside and then pass one's time overlooking a busy road less attractive than the gardens at home. The trap crawls down a cobbled lane as densely thronged as Deansgate. The shops have paned windows instead of plate glass. Gulls shout across the roof-tops, and there is a smell of fish on the wind.

George stands up. 'Look, Cousin Ally, the sea!'

Nurse catches him before he falls on the baby. 'Do be careful, Master George.'

Ally steadies herself on the handle as she cranes to see it. She had not expected so much light, more light than water. In the middle distance, ships' masts etch the waves' horizontal strokes, and the wall curls around the harbour like a cat's tail. It is like a seascape and not so: a workplace, a habitat, and also a reach of sky and wind that reminds her of the Pennine Moors where Papa and Aubrey took her and May last summer. Heather, also, bows and ruffles under the wind's hand and there too she has seen shadow-clouds scud faster than sails across the planet's surface. She would like to go to sea.

'We will bathe tomorrow,' says Aunt Mary. 'I hope you brought a bathing dress?'

Her stomach falls. 'I have no bathing dress, Aunt Mary. Mamma – I will be very happy to watch you swim. Perhaps to take care of Freddie for you?'

Aunt Mary pats Ally's knee, her brown cotton knee with a bloom like a plum's from wear and washing. It is an old dress of Mamma's re-made by Jenny. 'I have Nurse for that, my dear. Bathing would do you good. We might belt one of my suits for you but no letting out would make it long enough for decency. We will see what the local shops can supply.'

A sliver of sea flickers like a silvered mirror between grey stone buildings. 'But I thought you needed me. For the children.'

Aunt Mary looks out of the window and then reaches to touch Ally's hair. Ally flinches. 'My dear, you are nervous. I wanted you for your company. It's a long time since you and May paid us a proper visit. And I thought the sea air would be a restorative after all your hard work.'

Ally feels herself blush. 'May wrote to you. She asked you to invite me. Out of charity.'

'My dear girl. Out of affection. Out of family feeling. And perhaps also because my sister is not so unlike your Grandmamma that I do not know what it is to grow up under her jurisdiction. I married young, you know, and without Grandmamma's approbation. I know that Elizabeth thinks me quite dissipated. I thought a little of my dissipation might bring you pleasure, and help to ready you for the work ahead. I admire you very much, all that you have achieved and all that you have set yourself. And I do not like to think of you subject to unnecessary privations.'

There are tears hot behind Ally's eyes. Aunt Mary's words make her feel as if her skin is being peeled back, as if her body's workings are laid bare. 'Mamma is a strong woman, Aunt Mary. She does not spare herself.'

'Nor did Grandmamma. And people who do not spare themselves rarely spare others. Let me spoil you a little, Niece. Allow those taut nerves a little slack.'

The tears spill. 'Don't, Aunt Mary. Please. Work is best for my nerves. Mamma says.' A sob rises. 'It is not safe to indulge myself.'

George, who has been sitting on Nurse's lap looking out for a donkey, turns round. 'Cousin Ally's crying.'

'Even grown-ups feel sad sometimes, Georgie-boy. Cousin Ally needs a good rest and she shall have one.'

Ally remembers the anatomy and chemistry books in her case. Aunt Mary can't stop her working.

There is shouting outside. Distress. Fear. The room scoured by white light. She pushes back the bedclothes and goes to the window. Sunrise over the rooftops, the surface of the sea glittering as if raindrops of light were splashing into it. *And before the throne there was a sea of glass like unto crystal.* She has always thought of the 'crystal sea' in Revelation as limpid, a transparent depth, but the prophet John, she thinks, was seeing this, a substance in perpetual motion and full of light, moving like liquid, reflecting sunshine like a solid. Glass is only melted sand, an act of transubstantiation. She leans forward; the shouting comes from a seagull chick standing on the gutter below her casement, ululating with need. Hunger, mothering? She withdraws, afraid that if it sees her so close it may throw itself over the edge, but finds herself scanning the sky for the chick's mother. She is sure birds are meant to have some arrangement, some parental taking of turns, to avoid giving their infants the impression of having been abandoned. Although probably the principle is to protect the species by deterring predators rather than to prevent the alarm of individual chicks. The chick is unconsoled. Enough, she thinks, pathos and foolishness. She looks at the books by her bed. No. She will go for a walk.

The house stands silent around her as she dresses. Unfamiliar with these floors, anxious to disturb no-one, she takes her boots in her hand, eases the handle as she closes her bedroom door. Aunt Mary insisted that she take the front room on the top floor, with Nurse and the boys across the landing, facing the back garden rather than the sea. It will be quieter for them, said Aunt Mary, and it is not as if the children will appreciate the view. Stairs always creak least on the outside edge, away from the banisters. Aunt Mary sleeps in the room below the children, opposite the parlour whose bay overhangs the promenade. She sidles down the last flight towards the front door, where she is pleased to see the key in the lock. Fragments of red and blue scatter the timber floor where the stained glass panels on each side of the door filter the morning.

'Oh! I didn't see you there, Miss. I mean, good morning, Miss. Were you wanting morning tea, Miss? Only I was told to take the trays at eight.'

The maid, not yet in her apron and cuffs, stands against the dining room door, holding it open with her hip because she has a bucket of rags and brushes in one hand and a long-handled broom in the other. Without Ally, Jenny must be exhausting herself sweeping the grates and floors at home. Mamma will not like Jenny to be overworked, will be blaming Ally for her pleasure-seeking.

'Your bucket is heavy. Would you like me to help you? With the grates, I mean. Or the floors.'

The maid looks away, as if Ally has made an indecent proposal.

'Only, I do it at home.' She hears herself, nervous, too fast. 'To help our – well, we don't call her a maid. Mamma dislikes servants. That is to say, not the people. She does not dislike servants themselves but the idea of servants.'

The maid bobs a kind of curtsey. 'Yes, Miss. Only if you'll excuse me, Miss.'

She must have used her foot to close the door behind her. Ally clenches her teeth, yanks her own hair. Fool. Idiot. They will laugh at her now, downstairs, this maid and the cook and probably the landlady herself. She is Mrs Dunne's poor relation, the clumsy niece who wants to clean other people's floors. They are probably already mocking her made-over clothes with the let-down hems and patched cuffs, her roughly made laced boots. Mamma says button boots are expensive and quickly worn, not serviceable for women who walk instead of lying in easy chairs and riding in carriages. Mamma, knowing herself right, is immune to the fear of others' laughter, never doubts that those who concern themselves with such matters as boot-fastenings are trivial souls with small hope of salvation. Mamma trusts Ally to teach herself the same high mind.

She holds the handle as the door latches behind her. A light wind lifts her hair – she forgot to take her hat and jacket from the stand in the hall – and blows sand around her stocking feet. She will not sit on the doorstep, to be found by the maid. She is no princess who cannot bear the stones beneath her feet. There is a flight of steps leading from the promenade down to the beach, where the sand is exactly the colour Aubrey paints the skin of dancing women. Seated on the last step, she is hidden from the land at her back, positioned on the cusp of England. A lighthouse, South Foreland, Aunt Mary said, stands guard on a hill behind the town, its lantern at rest. The harbour is a crooked arm sheltering boats, which lie on the water like birds with folded wings. Further out, there are four, five, six ships with sails held high, leaning against the wind, heading east. Holland, Denmark, the Baltic Sea, perhaps even the fjords of Norway where Aubrey painted last summer. She would like to send Aubrey a post-card, if she had money for stamps. The sand is warm under her feet and she picks up a handful and lets it run through her fingers. Like water. Small waves run silently to the shore. There are men doing something with fishing nets on the harbour wall but for now, here, she is alone, and she leans back against the steps and lifts her face to the sun.

7

DANCES IN GREY

Aubrey West, 1877

Oil on canvas, 91 × 165

Signed 'ABW' and dated 1877

Provenance: Aubrey West; bequeathed to Richard Dawnay Smith 1917; by family descent to present owners

West drew a series of figures in movement, pencil sketches, pastels, and three oil paintings in 1877, of which this is generally considered the best. The girl wears the garment he designed for his dancing models, a single layer of thin muslin, open at the back, gathered onto the shoulders and cut so long that to dance the girls must hold up the fabric in both hands and split the garment behind. Her nakedness shows clearly; he was interested in the relationship between the billowing, clinging muslin and the firmness of muscle and skin beneath and between. Her hair is dressed high on her head, not to obscure the muscles and tendons of the neck. She's plump, curls of hair slipping onto her neck as she moves, and she sweeps low, one leg bent as if to curtsey with the other outstretched to the side, both hands holding her muslin swathes high as an angel's wings so the back opens wide, framing the finials of her vertebrae, the dimples above her buttocks and the roundness of her behind, pendant as ripe apples. Her shadow stretches towards the viewer, foreshortened as if light falls on her from on high. The pose – not pose, the movement – opens her so there is the suggestion of a shadow between her spread legs. Nothing, quite, for committees to question, not explicitly. Nothing, he said, to shatter the illusions of Mr Ruskin, or at least not those illusions.

*

She uses tissue paper, lots of tissue paper, bought specially for this purpose with Mrs Lewis. Wrapping clothes in tissue is not the sort of thing the Moberleys do and she doesn't really know how, but that's not the point. May's packing will be properly done. She spreads a rustling sheet on May's bed, the red blanket showing pink through the white paper, and then lays out a pair of drawers. One sheet of paper for each garment? She folds the paper in, edges to middle, and then folds the drawers along the centre seam, following the curved line that makes no sense until you've finished sewing the whole thing. She finds herself making the overhanging edges of paper into points, as if she's wrapping a Christmas present. She lays the package in the trunk, its torn grey lining already overlaid by towels, and starts again, parcel after parcel, recognising some of her own darning on May's drawers and chemises. May wants to wear her hoopskirt to travel; madness, Mamma says, but then Ally has no idea how one would pack it. Corsets, stained under the arms, one of the strings broken and knotted. Wool stockings and, May has insisted, her one pair of silk. What is the point of having them if they are never to be worn? Yes, even on a Scottish island. There are bound to be parties, or entertainments of some kind. Even Dr Johnson asserts the Highland taste for dancing. (May is thinking, Ally thinks, of *Guy Mannering*, allowing herself a daydream of a young laird and a future as the lady of a castle by the sea.)

There is a button missing from one of May's black shoes, and a tear in her dressing-gown pocket, as if she's been

186

carrying stones around early in the mornings. Mamma says Grandmamma used to carry stones to put in her and Aunt Mary's shoes when they were naughty. Ally tries to imagine the ground May's feet will tread in these shoes: are there made roads, pavements, on the island? Will there be a garden, leaves whirling in the autumn winds? May will be living in the 'Big House', the house where the Cassinghams themselves stay when they are on Colsay, but Aubrey says it is more like a hunting lodge than an aristocrat's country residence, that May must not travel in expectation of richness and luxury. The poverty of the islanders, Lord Hugo has told him, is absolute. There is no money at all, no commerce, no exchange. They have what they catch from the sea and the cliffs and what they contrive out of the barest materials found, and live the simplest of lives, quite free from every pain and care of modern life. May will find them entirely innocent of the longing for material possessions and personal indulgence that leads so many of the poor to whom she is accustomed into discontent and, consequentially, crime. Her work will not be onerous; in such a small population, it is not to be expected that there will be more than half-a-dozen confinements in a year, so much of her time may be devoted to teaching the island women to care correctly for themselves and their infants before and after delivery, and there will also be much opportunity for the kind of visiting work to which she and Ally have been trained from girlhood. Lord Hugo's sister is of the view that the women have everything to learn about proper household ways and cleanliness. Ally puts aside May's jersey, which has a hole in the elbow, and hopes that May will show discretion in teaching the women to take care of their families' clothes.

She closes the lid of the trunk and carries the pile of mending downstairs. There is a smell of beeswax in the hall and the banister is a little tacky to her fingers. Usually she would at least suggest that May sees to her own darning, a token protest before doing it herself, but today she finds the idea of her own sewing against her sister's skin, between May and her outer, visible clothes, pleasing. The hall is unusually dark because the dining room door is closed, which is normally done only in winter to keep the heat of the fire in. Someone is in there. She pauses with her hand on the handle; silence, and then May's voice, low, and her giggle and then – ah – Aubrey. She finds herself knocking, as though she thinks her sister might need warning of the interruption of her tête-à-tête. Aubrey coughs, there is a scuffling sound, and then May opens the door, pink-cheeked. Her hair is coming down over one side of her face and her collar is disarranged.

'What?'

She sees the clothes over Ally's arm. 'Oh.'

Behind her, Aubrey straightens his lapels in the mirror over the sideboard.

'I've been packing for you,' Ally says. 'I need the mending basket so I can darn your clothes.

'Oh,' May says again. She looks down. 'Aubrey has been telling me about Colsay. He says I may hope to see the northern lights this winter.'

'If you would allow me to get the basket, I could mend your jersey before I set off to visit Mrs Lewis,' says Ally. 'Good morning, Aubrey.'

Mrs Lewis herself answers her ring, a blonde child peeping from behind her skirts. 'Ally! Come in, my dear. I have good news for you!'

She ushers Ally in, takes her wrap and brushes dust from her skirt. Ally looks away, not for the first time, from the thought that Mrs Lewis's children are to be envied. The child – Matthew? – staggers as Mrs Lewis's skirt swings around her feet.

'Sorry, my chicken.' She scoops him into her arms and he sits astride her hip, depressing her hoop so she bulges on the other side. It has occurred to Ally recently to wonder if Mrs Lewis is expecting again. 'You remember Ally, don't you?'

He puts his thumb in his mouth and leans his cheek on Mrs Lewis's plum satin shoulder. Did Mamma ever hold Ally like that? The poise of the perfectly curved head on the thin neck is beautiful, a triumph of physiology. His mother strokes his silken hair, drops a kiss on his crown.

'Come in, Ally, come and sit.'

She follows Mrs Lewis's trailing skirt down the hall, its progress jerky as an injured animal. Mrs Lewis is the most amiable person Ally knows, but the elegance of her dress is not matched by personal grace. The good news might be anything from a new lecture series to the admission of women to the British Medical Association.

There is a small wood fire crackling behind the fireguard in Mrs Lewis's sitting room, and two more children sitting on the hearthrug over a jigsaw puzzle. A pair of knitting needles skewer a ball of red wool lying on the sofa, which has a white trellis pattern on an impractically pale blue. Mrs Lewis picks up the knitting and pats the seat beside her for Ally.

'What do you think it is? Guess?' She clasps the yarn.

'I cannot tell. I can never guess what people will say.'

The girl on the rug looks round. 'Papa says we may have a puppy?'

'Certainly not. This concerns Ally. Though it will serve all of us in the end.'

Ally shakes her head. 'Tell me.'

'The University of London is to admit women to all degrees! What do you think of that? *And* the Association has raised enough for two scholarships for Manchester women. And, Alethea Moberley, I am empowered by the committee to offer one of them to you! There now.'

Ally looks at her.

'Do you not faint, or weep? Shall I not send Susan for the smelling salts?'

The room is the same, the curtains looped over their tasselled cords, firelight flickering under the tarnished brass hood, Susan's pinafore washed gold by its light.

'I? Do you mean that they include clinical training?'

Clinical training has been the barrier for so long. Ally has known that she will have to go to Paris or Geneva – only Mamma will not countenance Paris – or, for the last two years, Dublin, to qualify. And that the General Medical Council will not recognise her foreign qualification when she does.

Mrs Lewis nods. 'It had to happen, Ally. The Senate voted.'

Ally shakes her head. 'I know. But there have been so many reconsiderations and reversals. We have thought before that the battle was won.'

Mrs Lewis touches her shoulder. 'This battle is won. The war goes on. But you will be our General. Or Admiral, or Commander, or whoever it is who leads a battalion.'

Ally shrugs, and their eyes meet and they smile. 'Triumph,' says Mrs Lewis. 'Triumph, Ally. We have had and surely will have yet so much defeat, let us revel in this. It is not small. You cannot join the Royal Colleges, or the British Medical Association. We have much evidence that the great majority of your male colleagues regard you as an aberration against nature, a disgusting, unsexed creature and a danger to the public. But you will graduate, Ally. You will be Dr Moberley, and, most importantly, you will be able to save tens of thousands of women from the indignity and neglect of male doctors. I feel as if we ought to call for champagne! I think I will give a dinner to celebrate!'

Ally shakes her head. 'Wait, Mrs Lewis. Wait until it is sure.'

'Susan,' says Mrs Lewis. 'Run and bring me *The Times* from Papa's desk, would you? Tell him Mamma needs to show it to Miss Moberley.'

With a backward glance at her puzzle, Susan goes, leaving the door open behind her. The draught is almost pleasant.

'Even if the principle is secure,' Ally says, 'we do not know that I myself will succeed.'

'I know it. This is the beginning of everything.'

Ally shivers. They, women, are in no position to take any progress for granted. Failure waits always in the wings. 'We mustn't anticipate our success, Mrs Lewis. I thank you. And I will do all that I can. For all the women of the Association. But no champagne, not yet.'

On the doorstep, she finds herself trembling, although she's well wrapped and coming from the fireside. Her hands shake so much she can't fasten the clasp of her bag. It's been months since her last hysterical attack, before Easter. She leans against the column supporting the canopy of the Lewises' porch and counts her breaths, in two three four, out two three four. A cart rattles along the road. Two men go by, talking, not noticing her. A bird scurries in the privet hedge, disturbing the white reflections in the dark leaves, and she wants to run, to go straight from here to – to –. Not London, where she is meant to be going anyway. She does not envy May, bound in the opposite direction for Aubrey's island, a place from which it sounds almost impossible to disappear. Liverpool, maybe, a ship to America – where there are female doctors, and colleges for women, where many British women have gone for exactly those opportunities that lie now at her cold feet – no, to Australia, with its immeasurable interior, to the prairies of Canada, somewhere into which she can vanish, a place without expectation.

She begins to walk, easing the latch of the gate to avoid drawing attention to her delayed departure. Do men know this, the fear of failure? Do the men who are about to begin their medical training shake, and feel sick, and breathe hard because the more they succeed, the narrower the gates through which they pass, the more straitened lies the path ahead? You carry the hopes of many, says Mamma, says Miss Johnson, see that you do not fail us. At the crossing, a man lays his ungloved hand on her sleeve and makes an improper suggestion. 'May the Lord have mercy upon your soul,' she murmurs, shaking him off and averting her face. If she fails now, if her work over the next years is anything less than excellent, she betrays not only Mamma and Miss Johnson and Mrs Lewis and all the supporters, men and women, of the Women's Education Association whose money will be keeping her, but all those women who have been denied higher education in the past and, worse, all those who will be allowed it in the future only if the University of London's experiment in admitting them this year is a success. Her breath catches and the shop-fronts and the hurrying crowds around her waver as if through water. She cannot do this. She must.

She kneels on the tiled floor, a candle in its pewter holder beside her. Usually, she finishes with her own boots, which can be cleaned and polished less thoroughly than the others, but today she skips her own entirely, gives Papa's a perfunctory

192

brushing and, after cleaning the men's boots that Mamma finds most practical, takes up May's. Papa bought May button boots, because she asked him for them. Ally sits back, folds her legs under her and pushes her hand into May's boot, her fingers cramped where May's toes curl all day, her thumb lifted in May's instep. The heels are worn on the outer edges, because May walks with her feet turned out a little, and on the inside the insole is wearing through, the fabric roughening, under the ball of May's foot. Ally believes that her earliest memory is of May taking her first steps, towards Papa in the Princess Gardens around the corner. Then for a long time May was slow, unsteady, needed Ally to hold her hand and help her up when she fell down. Ally takes the shoe-brush in her other hand; the shoes are mired and so May must have made time, on her last day, for some welfare visits. She remembers May trotting at Mamma's side, forbidden to run and unable to walk fast enough to keep up, and later May learning the skipping games at school, her boots tapping and bouncing over the whirling rope. Games Ally was never asked to join. She scrubs dried mud – a faint odour, perhaps something worse than mud – from the toe-seam, spits on a cloth to rub dirt from the buttons, bends them back to clean underneath. There is no point in pretending that May would ever think to clean under her boot-buttons. She rubs a cotton rag in the hollow of grease in the tin and begins to work oil into May's boots, so that her feet at least will be cared for on Aubrey's island. May goes, she thinks, not because she is called to save pauper women but because Aubrey wants her to go. A true vocation would offer more comfort, better protection against the winter to come, than this shameless affection.

Mamma sent May up to bed soon after supper, reminding her how long tomorrow's journey will be, but when Ally comes upstairs with the smell of shoe-polish hanging on her hands, there is a line of lamplight under their bedroom door and rustling and bumping inside.

'May?'

She has opened the trunk Ally packed for her, unrolled the tissue packages.

'I can't find it,' she says. 'I put it in myself, after you finished, and now I can't find it.'

She pulls out her brushes, her new sponge and soap. 'It can't have gone. I must have lost it. I'm such a fool.'

May's hair has come loose from its night-time plait and her face is pale. Ally takes her cold hands. 'What, May? What is misplaced?'

'I wanted to wear it tomorrow but I put it in the valise instead so it couldn't get lost on the journey. But now I can't find it. He gave it to me only this morning.'

She clutches at Ally's fingers.

'He? Aubrey? May, what did he give you?'

Not a ring. Let it not be a ring. In any case, Mamma would not permit – although in some ways, a ring would make more sense of this journey than any other talisman. And better, perhaps, a ring than another form of jewellery, which would suggest an illegitimate understanding.

'A shawl. The most beautiful cashmere, Ally. You have never seen such a thing.'

The lamp flickers, golden light sweeping the briar rose paper.

'And you put it in the valise, and then took it out again?'

'I put it in. I took some of the tissue from something else and put the shawl under the top things, to keep it safe. And then when I went to make quite sure it was there, it was gone.'

The garments Ally mended, ironed, folded, enfolded, lie

194

tumbled around May's feet on the floor. May might, she thinks, have lifted them out, laid them on the bed. She squats to gather them, and under the edge of May's blankets, where they are hanging off her bed, is a fringe of pale tassels glowing against the bare boards. She scoops cool, slippery cloth, so heavy its weight slithers over her rough fingers.

'Here, May. It was under your feet all the time. I suppose you were too agitated to see it.'

It is a costly object, ashes-of-roses with threads of gold and the shadow of a leaf-pattern, as if the silk lay under a summer birch tree, dappling the pink with grey. The fringe is so light that her fingertips feel nothing when she reaches to touch it, soft as air. She doesn't want to wrap May in this thing.

'Where did Aubrey find it?' she asks.

May shrugs, holds out her hands for it. 'I didn't ask. Samarkand. Timbuktu.' She touches it to her face, turns to breathe its sandalwood scent. 'Thank you, Ally.'

May stands, holding Aubrey's gift, while Ally packs her case again, checks to make sure that nothing else has fallen or been misplaced and then, glancing at her sister, rearranges her bedclothes and turns down the sheet. 'Here, May. Get into bed before you freeze. Let me pack that for you. Unless you want to hold it all night.'

May holds it out. 'Thank you, Ally. I'm sorry.'

Ally lays out more paper, spreads the shawl across her own bed, folds, tucks, rolls, settles the package between May's petticoat and her chemise. May will probably take it out, anyway, on the train, and hold it close as a miser keeps his gold. *Lay not up for yourselves treasures upon earth . . . For where your treasure is, there will your heart be also.* May has turned away from her, pulled the blankets up around her shoulders. Ally blows out the lamp and climbs into her own bed, pushes her feet into the cold linen. *The light of the body is the eye: if therefore thine eye be single, thy whole body shall be full of light.* She remembers May's body full of light, her hair spread over the green leaves of the summer wood, and this morning, behind the closed door when Aubrey must have been giving her the shawl. *But if thine eye be evil, thy whole body shall be full of darkness.* The text is still on the wall.

It is strange to have other people around so early in the morning, and only Mamma not dressed. May has made Ally lace her tight, even though, as Ally pointed out, there will be no-one to do it for her at the hotel in Edinburgh or, very probably, on Colsay, not unless May thinks the housekeeper would stoop so far. It makes her feel better, she replied, for taking the train so far alone, even if it is just for one day. She stands in the hall beside her trunk and her valise, pale and neat, the shoes poking from under her skirt shiny with Ally's polish. Mamma, who is always properly attired, who appears from her room at night wearing a dressing gown different from her day-dresses only in fastening at the front, has a shawl falling open over her nightgown and hair unrolling from its plait to hang loose about her shoulders. Mamma takes May's hand in one of hers and touches her cheek with the other.

'You will faint on the journey, so tightly laced. You damage your health, May, and lay yourself open to distressing approaches when you flaunt yourself so. Ally, what do you mean by lacing her so, today of all days? And there is hardly time to change now. You will be ill, May, and you know what can happen to women alone on the trains, especially when they draw attention to themselves with conspicuous dress.'

May takes both Mamma's hands in hers. 'Hush, Mamma. See, I can still draw a deep breath. And Papa has bought a first-class ticket for me in a ladies' compartment, so I need not fear unwanted advances from anyone.'

'First class?'

First-class travel is wanton extravagance and a form of pride. Ladies' compartments are for women who fancy themselves irresistible and cannot trust to a modest and sober comportment to repel certain attentions. Papa comes down the stairs, fastening his cuffs.

'For May? Yes, Elizabeth, first class. Any man who could afford it would send a young daughter so. I still have half a mind to accompany her myself.' He puts his arm around May and kisses her. 'So far to go, May-bird.'

May leans against him for a moment and then stands tall. 'I prefer to go alone, Papa. I must begin to be responsible for myself, and it will be easier, I think, to make the journey alone than to feel myself young and in need of protection until the last possible moment.'

The gate clicks, and they hear footsteps up the path.

'My cab,' says May. She turns to Ally. They hold each other. Ally can feel the top of May's cruel corset through her clothes, and the wings of her shoulder blades, and then May is stepping back, opening the door, picking up her valise, and the cabman is lifting the trunk Ally packed for her. Stop, Ally thinks, come back. This is all wrong. May is being sacrificed to Mamma's ideals, sent too far to do something that is too hard.

Papa clears his throat. 'I'm coming with you to the station, May. See you safely onto the train.'

May nods. 'Goodbye, Mamma. I will write. Goodbye, Ally.'

Mamma reaches out to touch her face again. 'God bless you, May.'

When the door closes behind them, Mamma walks stiffly as far as the stairs and then sinks onto the bottom step and hides her face in her hands, her nightgown riding up to show bare white ankles and a bulging vein in her calf. Ally stands for a moment, her mind running ahead with May and Papa through the sleeping streets towards the city centre where even at this hour there will be market sellers and street sweepers afoot.

'Mamma?'

Mamma does not reply.

'Mamma? May I bring you something? A glass of water?'

Mamma shakes her head, her face still hidden. 'Nothing. There is nothing you can bring me.'

After a moment, Ally goes into the kitchen to light the range, and while she is there she hears Mamma tread slowly upstairs to her room, where she stays until it is time to go to the hospital committee meeting. Papa must have gone straight to the office from the station; he does not return that day.

Ally turns to lock the door behind her and feels as if she has left some great burden inside. The house must have been like this once before, for there were more than three years when she and Papa and Mamma and Jenny lived here before May came into the world. We expected you to be jealous, Papa has said, as children are when a new baby arrives, but you were only interested. When she cried, you would hang over the crib and sing to her and hold out your toys, even when Mamma told you to leave her alone. You begged to be allowed to push the perambulator and were merely indignant when your Grandpapa made one for your doll instead. Ally wonders, closing the gate, looking back at the house, if even then she was more relieved than dismayed to share Mamma with some-one else.

Mamma has become more exacting since May went away.

Even Jenny has been made to repeat work Mamma judges skimped, and Mamma has given away Ally's new hat because she considers it garish and unsuitable for work among those whose taste for display must be ardently discouraged. Food has become even plainer; no butter or gravy, nothing sweet – May loves sweets – only cold water or weak tea to drink. There is no reason but immoral indulgence, Mamma says, to encourage healthy people to eat beyond hunger when there are others sickened by famine at the gates. Papa dines elsewhere most nights and Aubrey has almost ceased to call. Ally waits at the crossing. She does not want to think about how Mamma's days will be when Ally has gone to London.

She is to live with Aunt Mary, at least at the beginning. They had expected Mamma to oppose the idea, as she has always opposed accepting Mary's invitations to the girls to pay extended visits during the school holidays, but when Papa suggested it she merely nodded. Ally and Papa exchanged glances, eyebrows raised.

'Really, Mamma? You do not object?'

Mamma shrugged. 'If Mary is willing to have you – and I gather you have already corresponded on the subject – it will save us having to find a boarding house for you. I suppose we will pay her your board, but I dare say she will not take what a landlady would ask.' Mamma had glanced up. 'I trust, of course, that you will find a more serious congregation than Mary appears to enjoy.'

Ally assented. Aunt Mary attends – occasionally – an Established church in her wealthy neighbourhood where the ladies go gorgeously dressed and the sermons would allow hearers to confuse Christ with a plump Tory vicar who prefers the poor to know their place and cannot speak the names of fallen women. She will, of course, find somewhere more congenial, but she does not think that it would cross Aunt Mary's mind to deny her freedom of conscience any more than she would deny her a preference for milk or lemon in her tea. Mamma is quite right to be shocked at her sister's light-mindedness; Ally had never imagined such attention to corporeal matters as she witnessed in Broadstairs, but a frivolous mind can in some ways make a pleasant companion.

Her skirts beat in the wind, the first of the equinoctial gales, and her hat-pin pulls in her hair. The lime trees' branches bounce above her head. On her storm-scoured island, May must be reduced to tying on her hats, a habit which she likes to claim defines the woman who puts her own ease ahead of respect for the milliner's art. Or perhaps even to the shawls that Aubrey says the island women pull over their heads in fair weather and foul, as if they followed Judaic sensibilities with regard to women's hair. Letters, Ally supposes, must inevitably take longer than one is accustomed to expect, longer even than Mamma's letters from Paris, for Aubrey says there is no regular ferry service, that the islanders cross the Sound as necessity dictates and weather permits. And then the post must make its way from the nearest town – Inversay? – to Glasgow and only then by train to Manchester. Probably the men who deliver the island post to Inversay will also collect what is sent from the world outside to the islanders. She has sent three so far, and perhaps May will receive all at once, as she has heard that the Canadian pioneers often do, reading in order as if their families' lives were a serial fiction. She will write again tonight. Would May still envy her living with Aunt Mary, May who despite her love of finery and taste for gracious living has gone so gladly to Colsay, where even she can expect neither? Ally catches herself shaking her head as she walks – nearly there now. May is much changed. God grant her useful work and a safe return, God give us grace to hold each other in sisterly love together as apart. And send news of her soon.

Rain is beginning to darken corners of the stone building as she rings the bell, the drops still beading on the cobbled road. All these valedictions fuel her desire to run away secretly one night. She is going and everyone else is staying – what more is there to say? But she has come to say it. Mrs Grant lets her in, exclaims over her wet coat, her lack of umbrella, the possible consequences of wet feet, and will she stay to tea, perhaps give the rain time to pass over. As a doctor, she supposes, at least if she finds herself in private practice, she will be required to deal with much of this, the splashing around the untimely visitor, the extra fluster caused by the anomaly of a woman making a professional rather than a social call. She soothes Mrs Grant and is permitted to pass through to the sewing room. A woman she doesn't recognise, a new arrival, kneels on the floor of the passage with her behind pumping as she scrubs the red tiles. Cleanliness, Mamma says, is both the foundation and the outward sign of the self-respect these women lack. There is a murmur of voices from within the room, falling silent at her knock.

The women rise and bid her good afternoon. She takes a piece from the mending basket, a worn stocking, and sits among them. The stocking, coarse to the touch as carriage upholstery, has been mended before by someone who has cobbled it into lumps, and the bad mend has been washed to a felt.

'And so you are to leave us, Miss? You and Miss May both?'

She nods. 'I for London and May into Scotland. I will be a doctor, Ruth, and take a university degree. There are new worlds opening to us.'

201

Ruth narrows her eyes to thread a fresh needle. 'To the likes of you, maybe, Miss. And I'm glad, for you and for others. But it'll take more than university degrees to make a new world for us, wouldn't you say?'

Miss Emma, replacing Mamma's favourite supervisor who married last month, puts down her own work. 'Enough, Ruth. I'm sure we're all very pleased for Miss Moberley. And, of course, sorry to see her go.' She nods to Ally.

'It's all right, Miss Emma. Ruth is right to say that at this moment such changes seem to offer little to her class. Ruth, listen. I want to be a doctor so I can treat women. So we need no longer choose between modesty and health. So there are healers who know what it is to inhabit a woman's body. Our opponents have said that no man would ever accept treatment at the hands of a woman doctor, and yet they require us to expose our most intimate parts to men. And I won't just treat ladies. I want to open a clinic like our Children's and Lying-In Hospital here, only for poor and working women with any kind of sickness, where they can come in the evenings and pay only what they can spare. Think how many you know who could have been saved by such a thing, Ruth.'

Ruth, reproved, nods without looking up.

'There's no doctor ever set foot in our court,' says another woman. Jane? Ally has not visited as often as she should recently. 'Think they'd get robbed, I dare say. Or muck on their clothes, or catch God knows what. Right an' all, so they would!'

The women laugh. But Ally will save them. Some of them, women like them. Their lives, if not their livelihoods or their living conditions or indeed the monstrous injustices that define them. She will.

*

There is no tender scene in the hall at dawn for Ally. Papa is at work and Mamma out when Jenny helps her carry her bags to the omnibus. Papa left an envelope on the table in the schoolroom, containing ten pounds, a promise to visit before Christmas and a PS: best not to tell Mamma about this money. She had expected one of Mamma's little talks, a warning about hysteria and mental weakness, the injunction to strive hour-by-hour for discipline and self-control, but, as has become her habit, Mamma went straight up to her room after supper and spoke little at breakfast, almost as if she had forgotten that Ally leaves today. She is fretting about May; perhaps Mamma will write to Ally, even visit London, when a letter has come and relieved her mind. May's silence may be a good sign, Aubrey says, that she has reached the island and the people there have what they need for the winter and find no necessity to brave the Sound in this season of storms, but even word from the Cassinghams to say that May arrived safely would be comforting. It may take longer, Aubrey says. You underestimate how far one can be from civilisation within the bounds of the Kingdom. If he spent more time, any time, in the courts of Hulme and Ordsall he would not say so.

She had not thought about how to convey her bags from the omnibus into the station, and has to endure the annoyance of other passengers as she drags them from the rack until a gentleman comes to her assistance and summons a porter, to whom, in her fluster, she gives all of the money put aside for buying sandwiches and tea along the way. She's not really hungry, anyway, and Aunt Mary is sure to offer a supper when she arrives. Second class, for Ally, and nothing but her unlaced waist and respectable demeanour to save her from the attentions of the man in the opposite seat, who in fact shows interest only in his newspaper. Her mind slows as the train pulls out, settled, now, by the inevitability of what she is doing. Here she is, sitting, idle, and yet even so in motion, achieving with every passing minute and yard greater proximity to London and her future life. She has, naturally, supplied herself with books, but there is no need to read, no need to do anything but watch as time and England pass by.

We will of course meet you from the train, Aunt Mary wrote. *Don't think of leaving the station alone, or* especially with anyone else, *whatever he or she may say.* Really, Mamma said, Mary must think you a half-wit. Or imagine that I have educated you in the dark. It is more likely that Aunt Mary doesn't trouble enough with newspapers to know that Mamma was the 'ESM' who first alerted the nation to the White Slave Trade in the *Manchester Gazette*, after her trip to Paris disclosed the presence of young English girls in the brothels of France and Belgium. Ally was spared no details of their experiences. She is careful to meet no-one's eye as she climbs down to the platform, to stand quietly while the porter brings her bags, although, she thinks, boldness, an air of assurance – beyond her at the moment – would surely be a better strategy. Only her shoulders tighten as a train screams behind her and smuts blow into her face. She is accustomed to crowds, of course, but she has never seen so many people under one roof. If it fell – look up, she thinks, it won't fall. The track curves away, back towards the North, and above it the canopied glass roof floats as if the wrought-iron pillars are anchoring rather than supporting it. She allows the porter to lead her down the platform, away from the train which has carried her so far, and the Great Hall opens around her like a library, like the pictures of Roman bathing houses only filled with light rather than water. A double staircase leads up to an ornate portico which would seem to indicate the presence of a Roman shrine, perhaps a sibyl entranced behind the heavy doors, but does in reality, the porter informs her, lead to the railway offices.

'I'll take you to the ladies' waiting room, Miss.'

This is where unwary girls, relieved by the absence of men, confide themselves to procuresses impersonating nuns and nurses. In Paris, Mamma found a seventeen-year-old who had answered an advertisement for a governess for an English family and been told on arrival that she must repay the cost of her ticket by attending to the wishes of certain gentlemen and that her clothes would be held in security until she did. The only children in the house were girls similarly employed. I will be a doctor, she reminds herself. I will care for such children. At twenty, a plain twenty, she is anyway almost too old to be of interest to the flesh-traders. She has no more money for the porter.

'Ally! There you are. My dear, I am so sorry to be late. Only the boys would come too and you know how it is trying to leave the house with children, first one thing and then another, their shoelace is broken or they have lost their hat and Nurse busy with the ironing. Are you very tired? We have given you one of the attic rooms, hard by the servants but we thought it would be quieter for your studying. Easier to keep the children from troubling you. And how is Elizabeth? I hope you've heard from May? I must say, I think her rather too young to go so far alone. Yes, my dear, I know that servant girls do it all the time, but May is not a servant girl and anyway they don't go off to little islands with no postal service where I dare say there are very few households anyway. Come, this way. We will be home very soon.'

Aunt Mary deals with the porter, somehow, without breaking a sentence. The leaf pattern of her print day-dress sits neatly about her, plain, unshowy, but, following her across the hall, Ally sees that the pattern is perfectly aligned at the seams and the skirt modestly swagged and gathered as only the most skilled seamstress could achieve. She is wearing a kind of jacket Ally has never seen before, forest green silk with a feather trim in a colour seen on no bird in nature, where her arms come through wide sleeves stitched low on the waist. It is not practical.

There is rain outside, and a hurrying forest of umbrellas. Carriages and hansoms line the pavement. Ally follows Aunt Mary's leaf-skirt, holding her bag close against her waist, and a man is opening a carriage door and helping them in.

'But my bags –' she says, stooping still.

The boys leap at her out of the gloom in the carriage. 'Cousin Ally! Was it an express train? How fast did it go? Did you see the driver? George wants to be an engine driver.'

They both make train noises.

'Cripley will see to your bags. Sit down, my dear. We will soon be home.'

She leans forward to look out, but the damp hats and tired faces could just as well be in Manchester and the windows don't let her see up towards facades and rooflines.

'We will show you some of the sights tomorrow, if you are not too tired. We are very near to the British Museum, you know. The boys are eager to take you. And we can walk to the Park. You will want to take the omnibus to the hospital. Cripley will escort you, at least at the beginning.'

She imagines herself appearing under escort, as though someone ready for the dissection room, for the pauper wards, were incapable of taking an omnibus.

'No, please, Aunt Mary. I must prove myself equal to the work.'

Aunt Mary pats her hand. 'We will see, my dear. I don't see what difference it makes how you get there. You know we allow ourselves the small easing of life in this house.'

'You make things hard for me,' says George. 'Like writing that letter to Uncle Matthew.'

Aunt Mary shakes her head at him. 'If you wrote letters more often, they would not be hard.'

Ally starts as he sticks his tongue out at his mother. Aunt Mary raises her hand – he will be slapped for insolence – but she only pretends to cuff him and they both laugh. They are in a quieter street now, and the houses made of a stone paler than in the North. She cannot see what is amusing.

Aunt Mary's house has a railed area and stone steps widening from a portico onto the pavement. It reminds Ally of the building where Aubrey lives, both being made with the plain lines and high ceilings of eighty years ago, but there will be no studio here, no statuary. And no velvet couch.

'You've never been to our new house, have you?' says George. 'You haven't seen our nursery or our rocking horse. You haven't been in our garden.'

'Hush, George. You can show Cousin Ally your toys tomorrow. You ought to go up to bed and she needs to rest and eat now.'

The carriage stops and George opens the door before Cripley can get down from the box – 'George, don't!' – and jumps onto the pavement, which is too far so that he rolls onto his back in the dust when he lands. He looks up at Aunt Mary, grinning. Ally has thought about living with Aunt Mary, but she had forgotten that she will also be living with Aunt Mary's children. And with Uncle James, whom she remembers only vaguely, dapper as a magpie and annoying Mamma by his enthusiasm for Papa's painting talk.

'You're quite sure you will be happy up here? Because there is the official spare room downstairs. Only it's next to the boys' room and whatever we tell them, I can't promise they wouldn't come in when you're working, and I know you may need to rest during the day if you have to work at night and they seem quite unable to learn to tread quietly and not bang doors. I'm just hoping it's one of the things they teach at public school or Oxford or something since otherwise I can't see how men ever learn not to knock things over all the time and thunder on the stairs.'

Ally, who has been looking out of the window at the garden in the square, through the waving leaves towards the windows opposite, turns back. 'Some of them don't learn. They wake the baby and then accuse their wives of nagging.' She remembers that they are speaking of Aunt Mary's sons and their putative households. Perhaps houses by then will have elevators instead of stairs, so much easier for the servants. She hopes there isn't some underfed child employed to carry coals all the way up here. 'But I'm sure George and Freddie will be perfect gentlemen. One wouldn't want to see children their age quite without spirit.'

Although less spirit would be entirely acceptable.

'Anyway, I like this room very much, Aunt Mary, and it's kind of you to think about these things. I will be very happy up here.'

'Are you quite sure? You'll tell me, won't you, if you find you'd be happier downstairs? It would be the easiest thing in the world to change around.'

Ally tries, and fails, to imagine herself saying such a thing. As if any rational being could be unhappy with a warm, clean room to herself.

'Of course. But I know I'll be perfectly comfortable here.'

Her need to be alone seems almost physical, an expanding presence that must soon push Aunt Mary out of the door.

'I do hope so. Now, Fanny will be bringing you some hot water – I'm afraid the bathroom is on our floor – and she'll help you dress. And this must be Cripley with your trunk.'

Ally, not used to the sounds of this house, to the constant rumble of London or the footsteps which may be coming from next door, or to the rain, still, on the windows and roof, only now hears dragging and puffing from the stairs. Jenny carried that case without complaint this morning. Home tugs her, far away and empty, now, as an eggshell. Does May also think of the smell of polish and turpentine in the hall, the way the morning light falls through the stained glass panels in the front door? Cripley and the case knock on the door. He dabs his forehead with a balled white handkerchief. He smells.

'Sorry, Madam, only it's not easy getting a thing like this up those stairs. I suppose it's full of books, Miss Moberley? Something heavy.'

She is making trouble already. Getting on the wrong side of the servants, who will spit in her food and scorch her clothes but still have to bring her hot water to wash herself and carry away her chamber pot and clean it.

'I'm so sorry, Mr Cripley. I should have unpacked it downstairs. I had enough trouble getting it down the stairs at home.'

Cripley snorts. You can see the phlegm going down his throat, as when a snake swallows a mouse.

'I should think you would, Miss.'

'Thank you, Cripley,' says Aunt Mary.

Alone, at last, for the first time since she woke thirteen hours ago, she sits on the bed. It yields, softer than the beds at home. She has not passed a night away from home since last summer. The room smells of the dried rose-petals in a dish on the bureau, of coal and the scented soap on the wash-stand. She would like to lie back, but if she does she will want to stay there, her deep reluctance to go downstairs and perform dinner reinforced by physical comfort. There are grey smudges on her fingers, and her skirt has brushed dirt onto the lace counterpane. More work, for someone. She tries to brush it off and only rubs it in. She attempts to stand up without touching the counterpane, wobbles and sinks back into the bed. Come now. Giggles, or maybe tears, rise in her throat. She sits for another moment. It's still raining, but the light has changed, as if the sky means to clear soon. There are more footsteps on the stairs; Fanny, bringing her hot water. She goes to the door to take the ewer and sends Fanny away. Aunt Mary must know that no daughter of Mamma's needs help to put her own clothes on, and anyway she does not want Fanny to see the darns and patches under her dress. Although, of course, all the servants will see everything when her clothes go to be washed.

It was the dissecting room she had feared most. For other things, there is preparation. One can learn anatomy from books, chemistry from demonstrations. The examination of patients is a skill gradually achieved, and one will learn with time and practice to understand each person's story, to see how the body's meanings relate to those of the tongue. But there is no rehearsing for this. One wakes as someone who has not taken a blade and cut human flesh and returns to bed as someone who has, and there is no going back.

There is an odour in the corridor. Not the kind of odour one might fear, butcher's shops and courtyard middens, but something that catches the back of the nose with a more urgent alarm, something quite alien to the human body. They wait in the students' sitting room, all eight having arrived early, all eight attired in shirtwaists and dark skirts. There are armchairs around the fire, all upholstered in the same fussy fleur de lys, and a rag rug on the red-tiled floor. The windows are too high to see through, and uncurtained. Mrs Elston, the secretary, has a fire kept in this room all day, and later there will be afternoon tea at the table and Mrs Elston passing the sugar and insisting that 'her girls' do not speak of their work until they have left the table. Work hard, Mrs Elston says, but when you are not working, think and speak of other things; the men students have their diversions and you need yours. The smell is embalming fluid, says Annie, whose father and brother are doctors, who seems to come from a house where it is possible to speak of these things. After the first shock, Annie says, it will be no worse than jointing a rabbit for the table. Ally's throat closes. Edith says that she does not eat meat, does not understand how anyone who works to heal bodies can feed themselves on dead flesh. To build our own muscle, says Annie, to make us strong for our work. Edith, whose wristbones are moulded like the feet on chairs Papa scorns, whose lank hair is the same yellow colour as her face, only shakes her head. The boiled egg and buttered toast lying at the bottom of Ally's stomach turn over, a curdled yellow mass. She remembers the bluish shine of the egg white, the mucus around the soft yolk. She is going to be sick, before they have even entered the room. No. Weakness, hysteria, nerves. Do male students vomit at the very idea? Well then.

She smoothes her skirt. 'We are all of us strong enough to

be here,' she says. 'We all know what we have overcome to be in this room, far greater obstacles than our colleagues. I am sure we will not gratify those who would deny us our place within these walls by faltering now.'

'I was not faltering,' Annie points out.

Edith brushes something from the hem of her skirt. 'Nor I. But man or woman, it is surely the better doctors who flinch from applying steel to human flesh. Who cannot see the body without a soul.'

'But the souls have left these bodies,' says Annie. 'So you need not flinch.'

It is five to eleven, time to put on their canvas aprons for the first time and enter the room in readiness for Professor Grebe. Ally stands up. 'Of course. But we must learn to flinch only inwardly. And to remember that our calling is not the care of souls.'

Afterwards, she is unreasonably relieved to find that there are no marks on her apron. She stands beside Annie, their sleeves rolled to the elbow, scrubbing their hands with yellow carbolic soap. There are grey scratches in the white enamel sink, and the steam is welcome to her nostrils scoured with chemical fumes. Annie uses the nail brush the way Jenny cleans dried mud from the porch steps at home.

'Don't tear your skin,' Ally warns. They have been told about open cuts and dissection.

Annie raises her eyebrows. 'Teach your grandmother,' she says, but she puts down the brush and holds her hands under the tap.

Ally shakes the water from her own hands. She doesn't, somehow, fancy the towel hanging near the basins where they have been told to put what is removed from the cadavers. 'So was it like –' Like jointing a rabbit. She glances towards the fallen shapes under their sheets. 'Like cooking?'

Annie gazes at her hands as she dries them.

'Not exactly. Shall we go for a breath of air, before lunch?'

Ally is not convinced that the atmosphere of Bloomsbury is 'fresh air', but there is a garden behind the School's house. She wraps her shawl around her shoulders and pulls it up under her coat collar. Annie pins on a hat with egret feathers reaching over her hair and pulls real kid gloves from the pockets of a fur-trimmed coat. Annie's heels tap along the hall to the back door. Annie carries herself like someone who expects attention. She holds open the door for Ally and they go out into the autumn. There is a tree in the middle of the lawn – plum? Mulberry? – and flower beds around the edges. Dead leaves swirl on the grass and crunch underfoot as Ally and Annie approach a circular bench around the tree's trunk.

Annie sits down. 'Do you know, almost as much as it felt strange to be slicing someone's belly it felt strange to be standing still so long? Now I understand why our cook is always complaining about her legs.'

Ally tries to gauge the correct space to leave between her skirts and Annie's. 'We will have to get used to it. Ward rounds, and surgery. The factory workers at home complain too. Rightly. There is nowhere they could sit.'

Annie leans back and lifts her arms above her head, raising her skirt to disclose those tapping buttoned boots. 'In the north? You sound northern.'

Annie has always lived in London, not very far from here. She is living with her parents. Her brother is in practice with her father and there is a sister married to another doctor. Another brother is away at school and there is a little sister still

213

in the schoolroom. Ally must to go tea one Saturday; Annie's Mamma likes to meet her friends.

Friends? She has known Annie less than a week. Annie is looking at her, expecting something. Thank you, she says, that would be pleasant.

'And you?' Annie asks. 'You have brothers and sisters?'

May tugs so hard inside Ally that she has to stop herself standing up and walking away. A brief note from Papa said that they had still had no word from her, that Mamma was not herself and he was thinking of writing to the Cassinghams. She pulls off a glove, cotton not kid, and begins to plait its three longest fingers.

'Oh,' Annie says. 'You have lost someone. I am sorry.'

Annie's gaze slides up Ally's grey skirt, her violet shawl, and for the first time Ally understands why someone might want to wear mourning. To show that there are questions that should not be asked. To show that one is incomplete.

The glove unfurls itself. 'No. But my sister has been away from us for a long time. She has not —' Not written. Not sent word. Not arrived? Not survived the train journey or the sea crossing or the cliff tops, or a fever she might have caught in the Glasgow hotel or from one of her patients?

'And you miss her, of course. Mamma often says how lucky we are that Harriet lives so close. Your sister married?'

Ally shakes her head. She must not cry. 'A nurse. She went away.' She swallows. She must think of something else to say, a diversion. She should not have come out here with Annie. But Annie, after one glance, looks away.

'Do you think Professor Grebe is really on our side?' she asks. 'Papa said he refused to sign the letter to *The Times* and said nothing in the Senate's discussions.'

In June, twenty-five of the country's senior doctors signed

a letter to *The Times* expressing their support for women doctors after Henry Maudsley published an article in the *Fortnightly Review* saying that it is well known among doctors that women become hysterical unless they have rest and seclusion during menstruation and therefore that simple biology prevents them following any kind of profession. Any kind except the oldest, May had said when Ally showed her this missive, and washing his clothes and cooking his meals. Even the most reasonable woman, he wrote and *Fortnightly Review* printed, is not sane for one week in every four, and in any case recent research has established once and for all that women's brains are smaller than men's, their intellectual capacities confined in the most elementary way. (And the gorilla, Miss Johnson wrote to the editor, has brains bigger than Dr Maudsley's, not to speak of the elephant and the whale; in any case it is not widely observed that the men with the most capacious skulls are the cleverest. But her letter was not published.)

'He teaches us,' Ally points out. 'He must think us capable of learning.'

'Or want the money.'

The leaves at their feet stir, although Ally feels no wind about her ankles.

'He's a professor!' she protests.

'Even professors must eat. And rumour has it that Grebe keeps another table across the city.'

Ally shakes her head. Medicine, she knows, is and must be messier than Latin and Mathematics, and God knows that where humans are concerned purity of any kind is a delusion, but for now she wants her new London life clean, wants a world in which she can't see people's secrets.

'Rumour is a foul beast. An eye for every feather and a mouth for every eye.' Another of Virgil's vile women.

Annie recognises the quotation. 'It was Dido, not Aeneas, who suffered. As usual. Tell me, Miss Moberley, do you think it possible that men and women will ever be considered equal? Or must we make our case on some other basis?'

Ally tries to rub dried mud off her boot with the other toes. 'The difficulty is whether it is possible to combine equality and difference, since we are evidently not the same. My mother likes to adduce the example of the American Negro, who has at least in some places begun to achieve formal if not practical equality despite the visible difference, but I doubt very much that the female Negro is regarded as equal to the male, much less to the white man. I do not set my sights on such abstractions; it is our place only to learn and practise medicine, to which we may aspire without also demanding suffrage.'

Annie smoothes her skirts. 'You do not see our work as part of the greater struggle?'

'Of course. But if we do not concentrate our energies upon our work, on proving that we can be unimpeachable physicians, we will undermine that struggle. And of course there are perfectly good conservative arguments for medical women. Our patients need not choose between modesty and treatment, and if the objection to women as birth attendants is their lack of education and training, it is a better answer to train women than to violate decency in the name of medicine. I sometimes wonder how many of our opponents would turn over their unmarried daughters to a male gynaecologist.'

'Oh, the great majority,' says Annie. 'And really, Miss Moberley, male doctors are not our enemy. My own Papa has an excellent practice among young women from some of London's best families. It is a matter of trust, of which we should all be worthy, men and women alike.'

She feels as if Annie has kicked her. She is no good at this, at feminine confidences. 'I apologise. I meant no offence. Forgive me, Miss Forrest. I spoke only from my own experience.'

Annie takes her hand and squeezes it. 'I know you did, my dear. And you have been much more in the world than I have. Only we must not get to thinking of the men as our adversaries. Tell me, have you thought of giving public lectures? You speak so well on these subjects.'

A shudder slithers down Ally's back at the idea of herself on a podium. 'No. I should greatly dislike it. Really, Miss Forrest, I wish only to follow my own calling. We should dissipate our energies if we were to embark on some larger battle. There are true, brave fighters at work, and we serve best by proving ourselves equal in learning and healing.'

She thinks of her scholarship, of Mrs Lewis and Miss Johnson and the women of the Manchester Association and all the other associations in all the other towns and cities, of the women in America already running their own hospitals and clinics, the doctors training in Geneva, Paris and Dublin, other women campaigning for female suffrage, the women professors of Italy, the establishment of Girton College. Just occasionally, she feels herself on the crest of a wave, the weight of water bearing her along. She herself has only a small role, but the fellowship of women is a tide, and it cannot be turned.

'Must we not then use our position to claim full equality? Do you not wish to vote, if we are to graduate, to practise and to manage our own income? Are you not grateful that even if you marry you may now retain the use of your own salary?'

Only five years ago, a married woman, even if separated from her husband, could not receive the produce of her own labour. Mrs Gaskell's husband gave her a small allowance from the proceeds of her very successful novels. One of the most celebrated actresses in the land went hungry because her estranged husband declined to give her anything from the money she earned.

'Of course. Who could not be grateful, if indeed gratitude is the correct response to being given what is rightfully ours? But I repeat that we serve our sex best by showing our diligence and devotion to our own chosen work.'

Annie shrugs. Her hair is the same colour as the fallen beech leaves. Her smile lifts her arched eyebrows and shows white teeth as small and regular as a young child's. 'We are so serious! I am sure you are right. Come, shall we go to lunch? Though I fear it is mutton again.'

Who could care what is for lunch when she has just begun to be a doctor? Following Annie across the damp grass, Ally remembers again her own hands on the scalpel, the straight, bright incision running sure as water down the yellowed chest, the breasts, wrinkled as drying plums, lifted by her professional fingers, and this time she feels not nausea but triumph, ringing high and clear.

Dr Stratton tells them to walk the wards. You cannot begin to treat patients, she said, but you can observe those who do and it is never too early to learn how a hospital works, how patients communicate their maladies. Especially for you, whose opportunities have been of necessity curtailed and who must, for all of our sakes, excel. All eight do as they are asked, for at last Ally is among those who take things seriously. Although Annie brings flowers to the pauper ward, and feigns oblivion to the nurses' comments about finding jugs and wiping fallen pollen. They have not spent several years in training to act as parlour-maids to beggar women.

Ally brings nothing, though she knows that Mamma would think she should take the opportunity to distribute tracts. She is not there to save souls. She reads the patients' charts and notes, tracking the visible procedures of deterioration and sometimes healing that she is learning in the abstract. On the children's ward, number eleven's fractured femur is mending, the growing bone re-making itself once it had been realigned and splinted. On the surgical ward, number four has had an operation that hastens her end from the cancer they found tightening around her ileum. Ally has seen the parts of the tumour they were able to remove, a mass the size and approximate shape of her fist and darker, a bluer black, than the colour of congealed blood that she had always imagined when looking at the diagrams. Number four's surgical wound is barely healing at all from one day to the next and it is probable that her cancer will kill her before the skin closes. She has morphine for her pain, or at least for her whimpering which disturbs the other patients.

Ally goes also to the women's pauper ward, which is so much like the one at home that she has to look for differences. There is the same number of beds, placed at the same intervals, made of the same frames painted in the same black. There is the same placement of windows, with the same dimensions and opening mechanisms, in walls of the same height. It is the new design promoted by Miss Nightingale, fully ventilated, easily cleaned and the same from Edinburgh to Penzance. The patients' accents are different, so much that Ally does not understand many of the women here, but their bodies are the same, skin dragged by pregnancy and nursing, draped over bone or bloated by gin, hands marked by cooking and factory work, legs stippled with broken and bulging veins from years of standing. And their bodies do the same things, malfunction in the same ways: consumption, inflammation, infections of the kidneys, womb and appendix. Cancers of the breast, stomach and cervix, the failure of the heart to pump blood and the lungs to pump air. The mechanisms of the body are more finely balanced than those of any machine; the surprising thing is not that people die but that so many of them live as long as they do.

It is the hour when people die, the hour that used to be Ally's favourite when she studied curled on the window-sill with May's quiet breathing lapping like ripples on the shore. Few people sleep like that on this ward. Shapes shift, heads toss on white pillows in the low gaslight. Someone mutters, as if repeating a prayer or an urgent message, and there is the humming moan of a woman whose sleep has stolen her daytime stoicism. Someone snores, the rasping exhalations broken by murmurs of discomfort. The nurse sits at her table under the lamp, her cap and apron bright as a flag against her black dress. Ally passes between the beds, treading as softly as her heavy boots permit.

'All well?' she whispers.

The nurse looks up. Some of the nurses, it's said, dislike the women students, didn't come into nursing to take orders from a lady like any domestic servant.

'I don't like the sound of number three.'

To a man, she would say 'sir', but 'madam' degrades both of them. Ally counts beds.

'Pneumonia?' she asks. 'Shall I call Dr Garnet?'

This, really, is her role, a glorified messenger between the nurses who know when a doctor is required and the doctors who know what to do when they are called, and she learns from both.

'As you think best.'

Again, the unsaid 'sir'. It will be easier when they can call her 'doctor'. She wants to say no, nurse, you know the approach of death better than I do. She cannot say this. She turns from the nurse and approaches the patient. The woman lies on her side, dark hair spread across the pillow. Her face is hollowed by hunger, lips sunk into a toothless mouth. Ally watches the blanket intently, unsure if number three is still breathing. Pneumonia, May said, is the pauper's friend, an apparently peaceful departure even for the young, allowing time for goodbyes as a fever does not. She wonders how many deaths May witnessed, how many people saw May's face and heard her voice last of all. Envy of them pulses in her head. She steps nearer and touches the woman's hand flung out on the sheet. They have been dissecting hands, following the branching streams of vasculature and laying bare the cords of muscle and tendon. Hands – writing, cooking, cutting hands – are notoriously complicated.

The nurse steps forward and picks up the hand to check the woman's pulse at the wrist, gazing up at the railway clock on the wall. She shakes her head.

'She'll be gone by sunrise.'

The woman's neighbour turns over and says 'Elsie', her voice clear and ordinary as if she wants to tell Elsie that the washing is out and it may be about to rain.

'I'll go for Dr Garnet,' Ally says.

'As you please.'

She likes the hospital at night, the way patients and nurses are silenced by darkness, the chatter of meals and washing gone to leave the bare truths of sickness, pain and – sometimes – healing. Gas-lamps flicker, spaced like the stations of the cross along the corridors, and a breeze from the open windows brushes past her shoulder. She picks up her skirts for the steep stairs to the doctors' rooms and remembers to pray for number three. Mamma would say it is the chaplain and not the doctor to whom she should hasten.

She settles her skirts, tugs on her cuffs. Dr Garnet remarked last week that since there must be female students, it is a shame although no surprise that they are such grubby and unattractive creatures to find in the corridors. She raps on his door, insistence authorised by the imminence of death. Yes? he says, alert, as if he had been waiting to be called. Number three, she says, in ward seven, the nurse says she's dying. Pneumonia. He opens the door, although the protocol is that doctors speak from within when called by the female students. He's fully dressed, and behind him she sees a candle on the desk and a pen left on a half-written page. The room exhales pipe-smoke, tweed and sweat.

'Pneumonia, Miss Moberley?'

She stops herself bobbing a curtsey. She is not the house-maid. 'Yes, Dr Garnet. Nurse thinks she will be gone by sunrise.'

He regards her. 'Ward seven. A pauper patient.'

'Yes, Dr Garnet.'

'And what exactly, Miss Moberley, do you expect me to do about this?'

The candle-flame lurches, sending shadows skittering and tingeing his beard with red. She takes a breath, composes a full sentence.

'I thought you should be called.'

'Why did you think that, Miss Moberley?'

She is beginning to feel sick. 'Because she is dying.'

He puts his hands in his pockets. 'And what, Miss Moberley, do we do to prevent people dying of pneumonia?'

'Nothing. There is nothing we can do.'

'Indeed, Miss Moberley. You wish me, perhaps, to come and do nothing with you? And the nurse?'

'No, Dr Garnet.'

He leans back against the door jamb and crosses one foot over the other. He's looking at a point over her head.

'So you called me why exactly, Miss Moberley?'

Because the nurse suggested it, she thinks, realising how she has been tripped. Because someone is dying and you are a doctor.

'I'm sorry.'

'Quite. A lesson for you, Miss Moberley, since they tell me you are here to learn. Sometimes we can do nothing. Sometimes, in private practice, we may think it worth our while to rise from our beds and do nothing in order to please a patient or his family, and I will not deny that there is a skill to such inactivity. But you are not in private practice here, and nor am I. Kindly remember to ask yourself in future why you are calling a doctor before you do so. Good night, Miss Moberley.'

Still without meeting her eyes, he steps back into the room and closes the door. The click of the latch seems to echo down the corridor. Any of the other doctors who is awake will have heard their exchange. She stands, head bowed. She has behaved exactly as people expect women to behave, running for help without engaging her reason, making foolish demands of busy men. Allowing sentiment to rule action. Dr Garnet has been plain on the subject of his doubts about women doctors, or women in any capacity, and she has confirmed them. She has betrayed – stop it, she tells herself, tears now will only compound her idiocy – betrayed Miss Johnson, Mrs Lewis, Mamma. Behind the door, Dr Garnet scrapes his chair and coughs. She knew perfectly well that there was nothing to be done for number three, that the nurses are employed to care for patients and the doctors to treat them where treatment is possible. Fool. Idiot. She wants to bang her head on the wall until pain overwhelms her writhing self-accusation. Candle-burns to her arms, Mamma's blisters to her thighs. Her scalpel is back in her room, the gas jets too high to reach and anyway she must not be seen. She turns to the stairs and repeatedly swings her forearm, her radius, into the corner of the wall like someone practising a backhand tennis stroke. It hurts. Not enough.

Annie's mother has fulfilled her promise to invite Ally to tea. It is her At Home on Wednesdays and she hopes that one day Aunt Mary and Ally will call, but meanwhile she has asked Annie to invite her on their Saturday half-holiday. Don't worry, says Annie, she knows perfectly well that we have lectures on Wednesday afternoons, she just likes to keep up the etiquette. I don't want to go, Ally tells Aunt Mary. I have nothing to wear and no idea how to behave at a ladies' tea party. Well, says Aunt Mary, do you want to have friends? Do you want Annie for your friend? Come to that, do you want to be able to attend to ladies when you qualify? Because if so, you had better get used to the tea table. I won't see patients at the tea table, Ally replies, and people care much less about the cut of your bodice when they're whimpering with pain and afraid of death. I'm sure, says Aunt Mary, but they're not doing that when they pay you, I hope. Accept the invitation, Annie sounds like the kind of friend you need. As if Annie is a pre-scription for Ally's deficit.

She accepts, partly because she does not know how to decline, but wakes nervous, without appetite, and is not fully distracted by the morning's lecture on palsies of the hand. Edith is taking the one o'clock train down to Rochester, where her father is a Canon at the Cathedral. It will be the first time she's taken a train unescorted and she can't stop telling the others that she's not nervous, not like her sister who is afraid to cross the park alone and shudders if Edith mentions anything to do with medicine. Ally remembers what she heard of parks in Rochester during the campaign against the Contagious Diseases Act and reflects that Edith's sister shows reason. She puts her coat on carefully; the elbows are wearing and she knows she cannot be seen in patches. She would at this moment prefer to brave the dockers of Rochester and Chatham in one phalanx than Mrs Forrest's tea party.

The children, bound for a birthday party, are noisier than is their wont even on a Saturday. George spits the custard he dislikes into Freddie's bowl and is taken up to the nursery to be punished by Nanny, who keeps a large hairbrush for this purpose. Uncle James lays down his fork, grimaces as if some shadow of the smart that George is to suffer has fallen on his own skin, but says nothing. It is, Ally has observed, his rule not to interfere. I thought Grandmamma objected to corporal punishment, Ally said to Aunt Mary after hearing smacks and howls from the room below her own. Mamma has always said that violence breeds violence. As perhaps Elizabeth does, Aunt Mary replied, Grandmamma preferred slower and more painful methods; spanking is over and done with quickly and it works. If it worked, Ally thinks, you would do it – have it done – less often. She remembers the candle-flame. It is the practice of self-discipline that matters: a child learns nothing from being hurt by someone else. And at least Mamma had the courage to carry through her discipline her-self, to witness skin redden, blister, burst. She has never heard

Aunt Mary chide her own children, much less participate in punishment.

When the scuffle is over and the plates cleared, Uncle James leaves for his club. Aunt Mary dabs her lips and turns to Ally.

'So, my dear, shall we look at your clothes?'

Ally follows Aunt Mary's silk skirt up the stairs. It is the exact colour of the lily pads in Papa's most famous wallpaper. Orange fish, Ally thinks, it should have goldfish embroidered around the hem.

Ally's clothes, laid out on her counterpane in the filtered light of a winter afternoon, are unprepossessing. They look like the garments that people don't buy from barrows, already made over and darned, the skirts too wide for recent fashion and made for an unsupported waist, blouses cut to hang loose. Navy and grey have washed to the same indeterminate shade. She wonders for the first time why Papa, who cares so much for the touch of velvet, the fall of silk and the gleam of a rich dye reflected in firelight, never bought her a dress. Or at least May, for whom pretty clothes would be a better investment.

Aunt Mary folds her green silk arms, crushing the lace ruffles edging her sleeves.

'Evening dress?' she asks. 'Not for this afternoon, of course.'

Ally shakes her head. 'There has been no need.'

'Even your Mamma must give dinners.'

Ally leans against the bedpost. 'For friends who have known me since childhood. It is a long time since she entertained Papa's clients.'

Aunt Mary nods. 'I suppose so. But you know that I give dinners.'

Aunt Mary has given two dinners, occasions necessitating extra maids, the postponement of the week's washing and some distinctly sparse meals on trays for the children and Ally, who found that her studies precluded attendance.

'My work,' Ally suggests.

'Yes, my dear. Your work will eventually require you to be able to dine, you know. Patients of a certain rank expect it of their physicians. Events for hospital subscribers. I believe that there are hospital balls?'

'I am not interested in high society. I intend to run clinics for those who presently suffer and die unattended.'

Aunt Mary smiles at her. 'Very laudable. You will wish to make connections with those in a position to support your clinics. Come, my dear. Let your frivolous aunt play some small part in your success. All I can offer is a little polish.'

Ally shifts her weight. 'Truly, Aunt Mary, I am not fit for fine dinners. I hope only to avoid disgracing myself this afternoon.'

'We will attend to that first. Come, let us see what is in my wardrobe.'

There is, of course, little in Aunt Mary's wardrobe that does not require tight lacing underneath, and in any case Ally is four inches taller than Aunt Mary. She will not wear the vivid colours Aunt Mary favours. I would say, says Aunt Mary, that anyone brought up by my mother would want to wear nothing but magenta and scarlet, except that your Mamma belies me. Although who is to say what your Mamma really wants; what people do, you may observe, often bears surprisingly little witness to what they wish for. I should like to see Elizabeth in jade silk. She presses on Ally a fringed silk shawl the colour of pencil-lead, with the ghost of a feathered pattern in black, and a black skirt made when Aunt Mary was expecting George and in mourning for Grandmamma, which she has neglected to have made over because she so dislikes wearing black. The skirt is too big so Aunt Mary tells Ally to hold it around herself and summons Fanny to pin and stitch, work that will have to be undone before Ally can take it off again. Worn without hoops, it almost covers her worn-out shoes. She will remove her coat on arrival and there is nothing to be done about her hat. If it is afternoon tea and not merely a visit, Aunt Mary says, she will be invited to remove it. But in any case, this is a ridiculous position for the daughter of a prosperous man. It is time for new clothes and if Ally will not accept them from Uncle James, Aunt Mary will write to her Papa for money and take her to the shops herself.

She will not have Cripley, or even Fanny, to escort her. She will not take a hansom. It is taking too long to learn even this small area of London. According to Aunt Mary's directions, Annie lives closer than Ally expected. A grand address, Aunt Mary says. It's different from Manchester; here even the very rich live in the city itself, never more than a mile or so from the indigent in their courts. And Annie's street isn't the grandest, far from it. One day, Aunt Mary will take Ally to the new terraces by the Park and they will see unimaginable wealth, toddling children in the finest silks and feathers, carriages with six matched and gleaming horses, ladies' satin riding habits flowing like draped curtains over their mounts' muscled flanks.

'So if you find yourself nervous at the Forrests' house, remember that each of us has her place.'

'The rich man in his castle?' asks Ally. 'Goodbye, Aunt Mary. Thank you for the clothes.'

She checks the directions Aunt Mary noted for her and sets off along the street. Winter has come while she's been working and studying, walking her daily round of the flagged pavements taking her from Aunt Mary's house to the hospital and back, church on Sundays. Aunt Mary's church, because it is easy. Where she sits and thinks about the week gone and the week to come, whether George and Freddie are fidgeting and how much the lady in front paid for that hat, because it is easy. If she thinks hard enough about the branching of arteries in the abdomen, or the anatomy of the throat, she can get past the prayers for the departed without thinking of May. Who is not, of course, departed, not like that. Who is probably settled in for the winter on Colsay, sitting over a peat fire with her embroidery while the wind howls around the eaves, and not writing because there is no post until spring. Edith's family had no word from her cousin in Jamaica for almost a year, and then he walked into his father's house while they were in the middle of spring cleaning. It turns out that medicine, like Latin, provides a richness of lullabies for the troubled mind. *Amavi, amavisti, amavit.* Temporal, zygomatic, buccal, marginal, cervical: ten zebras bit my cat. The male students have ruder mnemonics.

The houses on Annie's street, like all the others she has seen in London, are identical to each other. There must, she supposes, be detached houses, made at different times to different plans, somewhere in the city. There must be people rich enough to want to live differently from other rich people. But not here. The numbers are painted in black enamel, all the same italic font, on the fluted pillars supporting porticos over the front doors. The pale stone looks porous, as if it would be soft to the touch. There are identical cast-iron boot-scrapers set like statues in low alcoves beside the doors, identical bells in circular bronze settings to the left, identical bronze doorknobs. Encaustic tiles in identical panels line the red-tiled front paths. Some of the brassware is less polished than others. The curtain-lining draped inside the sixteen-panelled sash windows falls in slightly different folds. Twenty-eight, thirty, thirty-two.

She adjusts her collar, twitches Aunt Mary's skirt around her feet.

There is a parlour-maid, who takes away her shabby coat and hat and leads her up stairs carpeted in thick-pile dark blue. Upstairs? Is Mrs Forrest an invalid? The walls of the hall are papered in three panels, a mode, Papa says, that can easily look like a half-blind maiden aunt's patchwork in inexpert hands. They circle a half-landing, the curved banister carved out of one piece of mahogany. The maid knocks at one of the panelled doors and then turns a china doorknob transfer-printed with a long-tailed bird and a spray of flowers.

'Miss Moberley, Madam.'

The room is full of light, and less full of objects than the décor of the hall led her to expect. There is a piano – does Annie play? – several sofas and chaises longues with finely turned ankles. The lady coming towards her is dressed – upholstered – in forest-green velvet with a beaded purple trimming, tightly laced above a bustle that rises like a fountain from below her bodice.

'Miss Moberley! Annie has told us so much about you. Thank you for sparing us your time. I know how busy you dear girls are on your Saturday afternoons. Come, sit down. You won't mind if I go on with my work, I know. My older daughter Harriet expects her child any day now and I have set my heart on finishing a shawl.'

Ally takes the Louis XIV armchair indicated, tucking her feet in and pulling the skirt down to cover her shoes.

'Your crochet is beautiful,' she says. 'I have not the patience.'

Mrs Forrest nods. 'Annie says such things are a shocking waste of time, that women are expected to waste their days in the painstaking manufacture of clutter that nobody wants. I dare say she is right, but I enjoy my crochet. I can't be comfortable with idle hands and it's not as if one can study physiology over tea. We cannot all be clever, after all.'

Steps run down the stairs and the door opens. Annie, in blue silk. Ally stands up, and then wonders if she should not have done. But Annie touches her shoulder and brushes her face against Ally's cheek. She is scented, something sweet and blossomy. Imagine a doctor wearing scent!

'You came! I'm so glad.'

Annie folds one foot under herself and curls against the end of the sofa by the fire. 'An idle afternoon, what bliss. There are crumpets for tea. With honey. And Molly's going to come down and toast them for us at the fire.'

'My youngest daughter,' puts in Mrs Forrest.

'She has hopes of Girton.' Annie stretches like a cat and rests her head on the sofa's buttoned velvet back. We are not animals, Mamma would say, without control of our sensual bodies. 'But she can't stop reading stories long enough to learn her arithmetic.'

Mrs Forrest stretches out her crochet across her knee and looks at it, head held bird-like. 'Molly has plenty of time, Annie. She may decide to be a doctor, or a teacher like Cousin Laura. And in all probability she will marry, anyway. Girls do, you know, even in these enlightened days.'

The firelight plays with Annie's russet hair. If Papa saw her so, he would want to paint her. She cannot imagine Annie taking tea at her house, talking to Mamma. May, who had friends, never once brought anyone home with her.

'Dr Garrett Anderson is married,' Annie points out. 'Mrs Leigh is married. Molly's headmistress,' she adds.

'I know, my dear. The world is all changed since I was a girl. Shall I ring for tea?'

8

THE BEACH AT INVERSAIGH

Alfred Moberley, 1879

Oil on canvas, 95 × 56

Signed and dated '78

Provenance: Moberley family; bequeathed to the Victoria Gallery by Alethea Moberley Cavendish, 1929

The sky hangs low, filling two thirds of the canvas with flat, grey cloud. The cold light comes from nowhere and the sea is dark as iron, lapping idly against a stony beach. Rocks puncture the surface of the water but cast no shadows. On the right, a low headland interrupts the meeting of grey sea and grey sky, but there are no houses, no animals, no people. Stone slabs lie on the beach like broken headstones. It is Alfred Moberley's only landscape painting.

*

'Number twelve wanted to speak to you, Miss Moberley. If you can spare a few minutes.'

She has begun to think that she will specialise in surgery, partly because these demands are fewer than in medicine. Always spare a moment, Dr Stratton tells them, and you will quickly learn to tell if you should spare two, but she sometimes thinks she would prefer hours in the operating theatre to these moments when what she is asked to cure is not sickness but fear. May would have been better at this. She turns back, although she has been hoping all day to leave in time to feel what may well be the last of this year's sunshine on her face. But number twelve, after all, will not feel the sun for some weeks. Number twelve is propped up on pillows that rise from each side of her head like wings. Persistent lower abdominal pain, irregular bleeding, nervous weakness. A palpable mass on the left ovary.

'Mrs Henderson. Nurse said you wanted to speak to me?'

Mrs Henderson's fingers pleat her sheet. Her eyes are fixed on the window over the head of the opposite bed. 'This operation. This cutting.'

Ally relinquishes the sunshine, pulls forward the chair that the nurses don't like anyone to sit on and sits beside number twelve. Beside Mrs Henderson.

'You are afraid?'

Mrs Henderson's gaze slides towards her and then back to the window.

'It's very natural to be afraid, Mrs Henderson. I think all patients feel like this before surgery. But afterwards, we hope you will be quite well again. Able to – to –'

What is it that Mrs Henderson's ailments prevent her from doing? She is a private patient.

'To see your friends and play with your children. Take care of your home again, go about just as you used to. And you know we have very good anaesthesia now. It will be just like dropping off to sleep. You will feel nothing at all of the procedure.'

Mrs Henderson nods slightly. She has heard all this before. It is not, probably, the pain that she fears, or at least not the pain that she fears most.

'Would you like me to ask Nurse to give you something to help you sleep tonight? It's best if you get a good rest.'

The nod again, as if she can't risk speech.

'I'll do that, Mrs Henderson. And I'll be back in the morning. I'll be assisting Dr Stratton, you know, so I'll be with you all the way through. By this time tomorrow, it will all be over.'

Mrs Henderson says nothing. Ally nods to numbers ten and eleven, also admitted for rest and feeding before surgery – one breast removal, one fistula repair – and goes to ask the nurse to give Mrs Henderson a draught. The other patients are probably better able to help than she is, knowing that they are walking the same road. Tomorrow will be Ally's first ovariotomy and only her third abdominal surgery; she, too, must try to get a good rest. She does not sleep well now, not since Papa wrote to her in January, his only letter. *Dearest Ally, you must brace yourself, for I am afraid that this letter is the one I have been hoping not to write and you not to receive.*

'He let me open and close,' says Annie. 'Even with the men there. But of course he had to make a joke about not using fancy stitching. If it were my scar, I think I'd like some daisy stitch.'

'What did you say?' asks Jane.

'Offered to put his monogram on the patient's abdomen. I was only surprised he didn't accept.'

The others laugh. It's true, Annie does say things no-one else would dare, and the doctors seem to like her better for her daring, but Ally's not sure every anecdote is entirely factual. And some of them are certainly in poor taste, as if she's competing, showing the men that women are just as capable of brutishness.

'Here they come,' says Edith.

The group rises and comes forward to the dais where the operating table awaits Mrs Henderson. A nurse holds each of her arms at the elbow, as if they are policemen and she a thief. Her pupils are wide and her nostrils flaring with each breath. Dr Stratton follows, poised as a dancer, and waits as the nurses help the patient onto the table and strap her wrists. The patient begins to mutter as the ether is applied. She falls silent. Her clenched hands uncurl as her breathing slows. Dr Stratton, Ally sometimes thinks, for all she speaks of the nervous strain of surgery upon the surgeon as well as the patient, likes her patients best in this state. Their conscious being is little more than an impediment to her true work. Perhaps surgery is the purest form of healing. The nurses raise the patient's gown over her sleeping face; she has already been shaved, ready for Dr Stratton's impatient blade.

The surgery appears to go well, and Mrs Henderson rallies enough to take some egg and brandy the following day, but on Wednesday her temperature begins to rise and by Thursday she is delirious. A messenger is sent for her husband, who brings two little daughters in time to see their mother die. Dr Stratton, pale, her blonde hair dropping from its coils, cancels her visits and spends the afternoon re-reading her notes and preparing a letter to the Board; since she declared herself ready to fulfil the hospital's mandate for female staff by operating alone and encouraged the Board not to replace Professor Dunstan as Visiting Chief Surgeon, she has carried out ten ovariotomies and lost four patients. It is only slightly above Professor Dunstan's mortality rate, and the sample is so small that the variation has probably no significance. Professor Dunstan himself used to say that surgeons learn only by experience and that the nation cannot have expert surgeons without first having inexpert surgeons. The very possibility of abdominal section is so new that almost all procedures are by definition experimental. Ovariotomy has relieved hundreds of women here and in America of symptoms that destroyed their lives, freed them from all the suffering that accompanies Eve's curse.

'Papa says he believes ovariotomies are unnecessary,' says Annie. 'He showed me an essay by an American doctor who cured five women of pain and hysteria by setting out the operating table, giving them ether, making an abdominal incision and then closing it.'

The others glance at each other. Things are different in America.

'Surely the women would realise that they still had monthly bleeding?' says Eliza.

'Apparently not. I suppose he told them, or let them think, that menstruation is independent of the ovaries.'

They all know, now, quite how little women know about bodies and reproductive function. Ally remembers May's story of a delivery where it became apparent as labour progressed that the mother had no idea how the child would leave her body.

'Mamma opposes it,' says Ally. 'Ovariotomy. She says it's another form of rape in scientific guise and that we experiment on animals and women without discrimination. She says that nervous women are in need of occupation, not further invalidism and indulgence. She says that boredom is at the root of most gentlewomen's troubles.'

And that Ally has betrayed her sex by collaborating with such treatment. Surgery, according to Mamma's letters, appears to cure sick women only because it satisfies doctors that there is a reason for their ill health, after the surgery if not before. Women's ailments provide the majority of doctors' income; the more often a physician attends a wealthy woman on her sofa, the more sick she believes herself to be and the more he is paid. Surgery makes her genuinely injured, a situation that gratifies both parties. May, Mamma thinks now, made the better choice, the more Christian choice, in giving herself to nursing, where her work was only to care. And Mamma has recently written a piece for the *Manchester Guardian* explaining why every Suffragist should also be an anti-vivisectionist. Mamma and her comrades see a continuance between the vivisection of animals and the theatre of surgery, the opening of a living body before an audience of men, prying into the secrets of life itself. Men, Mamma implied, are compelled to violate the bodies of women and animals out of envy of the female ability to bring forth new life. Male violence, a greater scourge of life on earth than famine or disease, is born of men's desire to own a womb by fair means – marriage – or foul – surgery. Ally feels increasingly sorry for Papa.

'Dearest Ally, I think there is little that your Mamma does not oppose. Would she rather we let everyone suffer and die?'

'She would say, I think, that suffering and death are part of the human condition and that we should approach them with dignity.'

Annie shrugs. 'And yet she wished you to be a doctor. Hardly a medical view. Papa says only that he is yet to be convinced that in most cases the risks of ovariotomy are justified by the benefits. Nothing about rape or animals.'

Edith looks up. 'I think she's right, actually. Your Mamma. Remember Dr Stanley's clitoridectomy?'

They do, all of them. The patient, already in the stirrups, had to be held down until sedation took effect. Dr Stanley, an established opponent of women doctors, plucked Annie from behind the male students and passed her the surgical scissors with an invitation to use them and a joke that none of them is likely to forget. Nevertheless, the operation went well, the patient made a good recovery and returned to a useful life cured of the symptoms that had troubled her to the point of suicide.

'But that is why we need women doctors,' says Ally. 'That is why we have so much support. We cannot both provide women with care equal to or better than that offered by our male colleagues and decline to participate in distasteful procedures. If you were to suffer a fistula, would you not rather be examined and treated by one of your own sex? And if you are to be so examined and treated, female doctors must be permitted to learn from experienced surgeons. Who, at this moment, are men. In some cases, men of indelicate disposition. We cannot demand equality and then pronounce ourselves too nice, too scrupulous, to learn as men do.'

Edith shakes her head. She's still gazing into the fire. 'No. We are supported partly because women expect us to reform medicine, not collaborate with cruelty in the name of equality. Do you want to be able to say that you can wield a speculum like a man? Spay a woman like a man? Joke like a man in the operating theatre?'

Ally shifts. She has, on occasion, smiled at Dr Stanley's quips. Women who do not are chaffed for their lack of humour, their feminine delicacy, and are not invited to assist in surgery. She looks up. 'Of course not. But I want to be in the operating theatre. I want to be entrusted with the speculum. And to reach that position, I accept that I will have to witness proceedings I cannot approve. And I accept that I will have to keep my disapproval to myself.'

239

'You are fortunate to have such an accommodating conscience.' Edith stands up. 'I find myself questioning, increasingly questioning, my willingness to continue to lend my presence and, tacitly, my sanction, to what is often little better than the torture of the poor for the sake of alleged scientific progress.'

'A doctor cannot afford to be sentimental,' says Ally.

'An immortal soul cannot afford to be cruel. To place ambition above humanity.'

All the ground and first-floor windows are lit, so that the house resembles one of the cut-out paper lampshades that Annie's married sister has taken to manufacturing in order to pass her time. The drawing-room sash is raised a few inches and the sound of a piano and a woman's voice, uncertain on the high notes, trickles across the wind in the plane trees and the rumble of carts from the main road. She had forgotten that Aunt Mary is having a dinner party tonight.

She unlocks the door with the key Uncle James presented on her twenty-first birthday, a gift well meant and well received although she had already, by then, attended several births and deaths and been entrusted with greater things than Uncle James's art collection. She will slip up to her room without encountering the party, which is a nuisance because she is hungry. Surgery always leaves her hungry, probably, she and Annie decided, because of the standing and the nervous energy required rather than any more esoteric reason to do with the assertion of the life-force. Nevertheless, a few hours' fast does no harm. She moves quietly up the side of the staircase, her black skirt brushing the new blue paint, and then as she crosses the landing Aunt Mary comes out of the drawing room. She's still looking back over her shoulder, laughing.

Ally curbs her childish desire to draw into the shadows and hide.

'Ally! Back so late, my dear? I dare say you have not dined, either. Let me send Fanny for a tray. I am sure there are still heaps of food in the kitchen. The beautiful ham was not half eaten. And there is creamed spinach and we did the potatoes a new way, a gratin, and the ices are gone but there is a splendid trifle. Come, let me ring for Fanny.'

She opens the drawing room door again.

Ally shakes her head. 'Truly, Aunt Mary, I couldn't. I have been in the operating theatre.'

Aunt Mary's forehead wrinkles. Her objections to surgery, Ally is sure, are merely aesthetic, but nonetheless she does not like to think of what Ally's hands have done before they come to her table.

'I suppose it does rather quell the appetite. But even so, you must eat something. I don't believe surgeons live on air any more than the rest of us! A little trifle? And a glass of wine, just as a restorative? I really think you might come and join us now, you know. No-one could call it attending a party just to sit down in your own home and take something on a tray. James was just saying that it is time you began to go about again, that it is a shame for a young girl to be so shut away. It has been almost a year.'

'Ten months,' Ally corrects her. Ten months, anyway, since May died. Nine months and ten days since Papa received the telegram asking him to go to Inversay and identify the body of a young woman washed up on the shore with the remains of a boat. Ally is aware of the difficulties of identification in such cases; it is not impossible, although not in the least likely, that it is not May whom they buried at St Margaret's on that frosty day in February.

'Anyway, long enough, surely, that you might enter the drawing room.'

Aunt Mary holds out her hand, an invitation. Ally shakes her head. At the best of times she cannot speak about the latest musical theatre, who has hopes of the Royal Academy, the difficulty of keeping a good cook, and now is not the best of times.

'You are kinder than I deserve, Aunt Mary. Just count me sullen and unsociable.'

Aunt Mary takes Ally's hand and strokes it, despite where it has been. 'I count you tired and still sad, my dear. I will have Fanny light the fire and bring you hot water and then a nice tray in your own room, and I'll stop pestering you to come and play with my silly butterflies. But later in the winter, you must begin to see people again. May would not want you to hide yourself away.'

Ally smiles. 'I believe May was quite resigned to my nature. Thank you, Aunt Mary. Please give my good night to Uncle James.'

Aunt Mary kisses her in a waft of powder and champagne. 'Good night, my dear. Rest well.'

She shuts the door of her bedroom and lights the lamp. Aunt Mary, arranging flowers for her party, has spared some amber and white chrysanthemums for Ally's dressing table, and left the latest *Englishwoman's Magazine* on her bedside table. Ally sits in her rocking-chair and unbuttons her boots. There is a splash of mud on her skirt. She stands up, unfastens the waistband and unbuttons her blouse, removing its ruffled collar. Mamma would not approve of the expense of her mourning clothes, but Mamma is not obliged to prove herself against some of the most confident professional men in the land on a daily basis. Ally unfastens her stays, sniffs them and returns them to the drawer. They are not tight, certainly not tight enough to set a bad example to any wealthy patients who might take a doctor's comportment as a model of wholesomeness – not that the hospital has any wealthy patients – nor to give anyone the impression that the doctor cares more for her appearance than her health, but they are a kind of armour. She is more comfortable with them than without, and if it is a moral compromise – well, it is not the most difficult compromise she will make to become a doctor. *If thine eye be single, thy whole body shall be full of light*: sometimes, as the rest of that verse makes clear, the need to demonstrate one's own moral supremacy is a distraction from true purpose, a form of showing off that gets in the way of vocation. In the name of a cause, when one's eye is single, pragmatism can be a moral principle. She picks up the grey silk dressing gown Aunt Mary gave her for Christmas and fastens its ivory buttons. I know silk is not practical for your work, Aunt Mary said, but I like to think of you enjoying it as a private pleasure. There's no sin that I know of, my dear, in the rustle of silk about your limbs.

Fanny knocks on the door and exchanges a jug of hot water for the muddy skirt. Ally washes her hands and face – one shouldn't care about Aunt Mary's jasmine soap, but the smell is soothing – and sits down. There is a hysterectomy on Friday, the vaginal method which Professor Dunstan is convinced is safer than the abdominal route coming into fashion, and she should study the procedure, but it's not worth starting to study when she will be interrupted when Fanny brings the tray. She touches a chrysanthemum and releases a drift of yellow pollen onto the embroidered white cloth on the dressing table. There were no flowers at home when she and May were growing up, not even when Mamma gave a dinner, although it would have been easy enough to cut roses in the garden. No flowers at May's funeral; many friends sent wreaths but Mamma gave them away, to people who have scarcely seen a blade of grass these five years, much less such hothouse blooms. It is not, said Mamma, as if flowers can do May any good now. She gave her life in the service of the needy; let us not mar her funeral with our own indulgence. In spring, they will lay the foundation stone of the May Moberley Mother and Infant Welfare Centre in Rusholme. She died, Mamma says, as she lived, in the service of the poor. Mamma never saw May's cashmere shawl, never, so far as Ally knows, wondered why May accepted Aubrey's commission to the island. More to please Aubrey than to please God. Ally wonders sometimes if May was wearing the clothes Ally had mended and pressed for her, if her own seams filled with salt water and lay about her dead sister as she tossed in the cold sea, wrapped her white legs when she came at last to lie on the stones of the shore. Papa must know what May wore. She has not asked, and does not know, what became of the shawl. It is more likely that May kept it hoarded in tissue in her room than that she wore it for a stormy crossing on a small boat.

Fanny knocks on the door again, bringing the tray with the wine, the trifle and the ham. Ally tries to take it from her, but Fanny insists; Madam told her to arrange things nicely for Miss Moberley. Fanny brings a side table to Ally's rocker, lays a tray cloth over it at such an angle that the lace points hang evenly and sets out her collation on Aunt Mary's best china. She adds a small crystal vase holding a single tea rosebud, one of the pale apricot ones that Aunt Mary likes best.

'Madam said since we had the best things out for the dinner to give them to you as well. She took the rose out of the arrangement herself.'

'She is most kind. Thank you, Fanny. I know these evenings are a strain for you.'

Fanny sniffs. 'Just so it all goes off properly in the end. Not like last time when the ices didn't come in time. Will there be anything else, Miss?'

'What more could I want? Good night, Fanny.'

She is hungry, but she takes a little wine first, to feel it quickening through her tired wrists and her stiff neck. She sips again and lets her head rest against the chair-back as the wine hums in her brain, holding off the pleasure of the salt-sweet ham and the vanilla and sherry scent of the trifle. Soon, but not yet. Papa stayed in Scotland for the inquest, where the Procurator Fiscal recorded a verdict of death by misadventure. Most of the evidence, Papa said, came from the Cassinghams' housekeeper, with whom May had shared the big house on the island. May had settled down well enough, she'd said, although of course any city girl would find island life very different from what she was used to. As it happened, there had been no confinements during the autumn so May had not had the opportunity to deliver a child, but she had taught the women a great deal about their own health and that of their children. The island men usually enjoy excellent health, being occupied for the main part about the fields and the shore and subsisting on plain but ample fare, but the father of a young family had been suddenly struck by the most acute abdominal pains and May, suspecting appendicitis, had insisted that the man's life was at stake and that he must be taken across the sea to the doctor in Inversay. She had been told that the seas were too rough and a storm brewing, but when she explained their friend's immediate peril several of the men volunteered to undertake the journey. It had been impossible to dissuade her from accompanying them. The loss of three strong young men was a grave thing for such a small community so far from all succour. The islanders had particularly asked the housekeeper to express their gratitude for May's presence and appreciation of her work. Sorrow presses like a tumour under Ally's breastbone. She is less hungry than she thought. She stands up, returns the laden side table to its place against the wall and takes up her surgery book.

Ally stands at the patient's covered face, holding her wrist. Blood has splashed out of the basin under the hole in the table and lies in shining pools on the tiled floor, reflecting the electric lights overhead. There are drops of sweat on Dr Stratton's pale face, although the only visible work is in the turning of her elbow and the rippling of the patient's abdomen, as if the thin body sustains a frantic foetus. With her sleeves rolled high, Dr Stratton's arms look thin and soft as a child's. The undulations cease and Dr Stratton withdraws her reddened hand holding a shred of dripping tissue, which she deposits in the bucket.

'The pulse quickens. One hundred and thirty. Weak and thready.'

Dr Stratton nods. They all know, have known for some minutes, how this will end. She pulls out more gauze, dripping as if with something less precious than blood.

'I cannot identify the source,' she says. 'There is too much bleeding. More light, please.'

From the patient's point of view, this is almost certainly better than allowing the disease to take its course. Uterine cancer patients typically suffer months of extreme pain exacerbated by dual incontinence that makes them ashamed to be in the presence of even their most intimate relatives and friends. The lower abdomen and the pelvic area simply

246

disintegrate over the course of many weeks, during which the cruellest thing is the patient's perfect consciousness and unimpaired mental function. From the surgeon's point of view, the established argument is that abdominal surgery is a new field and cannot develop without experimental procedures, especially where those procedures give the patient several additional years of usefulness if successful and offer a quick and painless end in place of a long-drawn-out agony if not. From Dr Stratton's point of view at this moment, the long-drawn-out agony might have been preferable. There are no survivors of her surgery this month. Bad luck, of course. But regrettable. The nurses push the patient's legs further apart and Dr Stratton, holding her scalpel, plunges back in. Ally finds the word 'evisceration' in her mind. It is as if the body slung from the stirrups is a bucket for pelvic organs, as if the surgery is a matter of transferring meat from one container to another. The pulse is slowing. Annie, standing at the other side, meets her eyes and looks away. Breathing is slow, and very shallow. The patient's face goes grey. Edith, standing behind Dr Stratton at the patient's feet, moves her lips in prayer.

Dr Stratton writes to the Board. She believes, truly believes, that the recent series of deaths during and after surgery are simply coincidental misfortune. Even if the last month is included in her tally, over the year she has lost almost exactly the same proportion of surgical patients as Professor Dunstan and rather fewer than Dr Stanley. Almost all her patients are women and so, allowing for the inferior health and nutrition of women in general which is known to compromise their strength and powers of recovery, one could argue that she is in fact a very successful surgeon. Nevertheless, as the only woman qualified to lead surgical operations in Britain at this moment, Dr Stratton is well aware, only too acutely aware, that her every error or ill fortune is seen to represent the capacities of women in general, that on her success or failure hangs the future of potential surgeons as yet unborn as well as those of her students, colleagues and indeed patients. She asks that from now until Christmas the Board will have her performance assessed and reviewed by Professor Dunstan, or any other senior surgeon of their choosing. Should this process raise concerns about her practice, she will cease to operate and return to training.

'I think I can do this no longer,' says Edith. She stands before them, like a child forced to apologise for something he does not regret in the least. 'I think I must leave.'

'After so long?' asks Annie. 'Having come so far? It is not as if you will have to practise surgery after this year.'

Edith shakes her head. 'It is not just the surgery. It is the need to excel, the requirement to prove ourselves better than men only to earn our place in the competition. And I cannot any more countenance unnecessary suffering, of humans or animals. That poor woman. And at least the poor are granted anaesthesia. I saw one of Dr Stanley's dogs . . .

They have all seen Dr Stanley's dogs. It is no trouble, to procure a stray dog, and if you have a scalpel there are perfectly straightforward ways of ensuring that a dog cannot make a distracting noise while you learn from its living body.

'That woman,' says Ally, 'suffered far less than she would have done had the surgery not taken place. And Dr Stratton gave her the only chance of survival.'

'We harm more than we heal. And I cannot do it. I cannot silence my conscience.'

'Then you have no choice,' says Annie. 'If you cannot. There it is.'

'If you would only qualify, you could open a clinic in the East End,' says Ally. 'God knows, there is need. You could join the Medical Missions. No need to cut up dogs.'

There have been women doctors in India for several years, because the Queen herself understands that Muslim women will not open their bodies to a male doctor as she cannot, apparently, understand that her own countrywomen might feel the same delicacy.

'No. I cannot. My soul accuses me.'

Annie, child of a cheerful house in which souls are less mentionable than parts of the body for which many well-brought-up young ladies have no vocabulary at all, bites her lip.

'I have found,' says Ally, 'that it can be hard to distinguish the urgings of our souls from our own internal longings. That there is a tendency for people to confuse desire with moral imperative, especially perhaps where we do not wish to own the desire. Edith, you risk acting on mere feeling. It is disastrous to confuse instinct and reason.'

Mamma hurting, burning, scorning her. Mamma saying how much she sorrows that Ally's weakness requires her to be disciplined. The policemen rounding up women on the street in order to strap them down, strip them and watch another man force a steel instrument between their parted legs, for their own good, to heal them from disease. The gentlemen who buy the compliance of hungry women for their most depraved imaginings, to spare their own wives the knowledge of their dark souls. The teachers, male and female, and nannies who find that in the course of communicating mathematics, manners and morals it is their unhappy obligation to hit children with canes, hairbrushes and belts. The hangman with his noose, and the crowds drawn – perhaps against their conscious will – to watch. Dr Stanley with his flayed, muted dogs and yes, why not, perhaps also Dr Stratton with her scalpel. Violence, the delight of violence, of power crudely wielded, is in our nature: how can we trust to any inner urging? Instinct guides us to perdition. No, the only protection from our bloodthirsty selves is principle, a rule adopted in the cold light of day and held against our strongest inclinations. First – last – she thinks, do no harm.

'You suggest, then, that I should violate my conscience on the grounds that being my conscience, it must be wrong?'

'I suggest that you should reflect long and hard, perhaps longer than it will take for us to qualify, before giving up all that for which you have worked on what may be a whim. I suggest that your immortal soul will accumulate little further jeopardy over the next six months, and by then you will at least have shown that another woman can stay this course.'

'I knew it,' says Edith. 'I knew this was all about the cause. In the name of womankind, you would have Dr Stratton continue to operate when you know, *you know*, she is beyond her competence and causing unnecessary deaths. You would have me, like you, keep my mouth shut and go along with acts I know in my heart to be wrong. Because you think it worth any cost, any number of souls and lives, to prove that women are equal to men.'

Ally's pulse is rising. She feels her face redden. 'Yes,' she says. 'Yes, I do. And I believe that generations of our sisters yet to be born will thank us for what we give. And indeed what we take from others. There is no principle worth having that does not exact a price. We must recognise the cost of our principles and take responsibility for that cost. We must not deny the consequences of our own actions. And if you cannot do this, perhaps you are right that medicine is not your true calling. Goodbye, Edith.'

She finds herself in the corridor, her breathing fast against her stays as her gaze fastens on the dusty floor. It is falling dark and the fire in the sitting room was dying down, but her face is hot. She feels ill. She leans on the wall, cold even through her jacket and blouse. And she thinks, perhaps Edith is right, or at least not as utterly wrong as Ally thought when she was in that room. Even in the name of the Hippocratic oath we hurt, in order to heal. Mamma believed, truly believed, that Ally needed on principle to be hurt, that hurting Ally was the way to heal her morals and her mind. Even if, as Ally has begun to understand, Mamma needs to hurt people for her own reasons. And Ally cannot say at this point that she regrets her pain, that she wishes Mamma had allowed her to grow up in bovine contentment, without ambition or self-discipline. Edith is right that the purpose of a moral imperative is to justify harm. If it is sometimes necessary to suffer, it must also sometimes be necessary to cause suffering. This, it seems to Ally, is the condition of human agency; our very lives cause harm to others and it is wilful blindness to pretend otherwise. We are all of us, every mortal soul, damaging persons. Our best hope, for salvation and for medicine – the thing, she thinks, that Mamma cannot do – is to own the damage we do. And to live with it. Edith is right to leave medicine. Her need to be perfect, to be above harm, set in sanctity above all others, would make her a dangerous healer. Holy, whole, hale, healthy: Aubrey told her once that these are all the same word. None of those states is the human condition. The healers are not whole. Ally's breathing tightens. These thoughts are like opening her own skin, peering under the muscle to the glistening organs of vitality.

The door opens again, a shaft of light swinging across the floor and walls, and in it, Annie's shadow. Annie starts.

'Ally! I thought you would have stormed out into the night. You were rather magnificent.'

Ally shivers. 'Don't. Annie, I don't feel well. Feverish.'

Annie touches her forehead. 'You're warm. Pain?'

Ally shakes her head. 'Just – unwell. Shaky.'

'Could be nervous,' says Annie cheerfully. 'Excitement, you know. A fever brought on by high principle. I prescribe a brisk walk and a quiet evening in the company of calming influences. Come home with me?'

Ally feels frozen, as if she can't leave the wall on which she leans. Something in her mind, something that has been coiled tight, is unwinding. The healers are not whole. The healers do not have to be whole because wholeness, holiness, are not human qualities. Humanity's greatest gift is love and not reason – St Paul is not usually among her prophets but this, for the first time, seems true – and Mamma, for all her time in church, does not know this. If she is to be a doctor – as she is to be a doctor – she will be a broken doctor, her own hurt as much part of her practice as her healing. A doctor who can see her own damage and not run away to hide. She shakes her head, wanting Annie both to go away and not witness the shame of her weakness, and to stay and lift her back into strength. Shaking begins in her shoulders and runs through her ribs and skull. Nervousness. Hysteria. Or ordinary human weakness?

'Are you really unwell?'

She shakes her head. Nothing a little principle, a little firmness of mind, won't cure. But just now, she seems to have neither. It's getting hard to breathe.

'My dear Ally. Come, take some tea with me. Or wine. Papa will be home. I can't leave you so, here.'

Spots whirl before Ally's eyes. She must stop this, here in the hospital. Stop it at once. She's risking everything Edith is throwing away.

She nods. 'One moment.'

Her ribs can't open to let in air. She pushes the air out, steps away from the wall. 'Yes, please, Annie.'

Annie takes her arm, leads her to the cloakroom where Ally pokes her arms obediently into the coat Annie holds out for her and ducks her head for her hat and scarf. There is nothing really the matter with her, but at this moment it's taking all she can muster to keep moving and breathing.

There are footsteps coming up the stairs, someone faster and heavier than Fanny, and then a pause. She puts down her book and goes to the door.

'George?'

'Cousin Ally. Are you very busy?' He looks uncomfortable, as if his collar pinches. She can't remember the last time he came up here to find her. Some concern about his health, or the changes of adolescence? He is, after all, well into the awkward age.

She smiles at him and holds the door open. 'Not so very busy. Come in?'

He nods, comes to a standstill in the middle of the rug, suddenly bulkier and darker among the embroidered whitenesses of her room, a figure in oils superimposed on a watercolour interior. She pulls forward the bow-legged tapestry stool from her dressing table and sits on it.

'Have the rocker. Is something troubling you, George?'

The rocker tips him backward. He's begun to sit like a man, legs thrown wide as if his manhood requires a seat of its own. She remembers how he used to leap into the air from the garden wall, from inside the carriage and from far too far up the stairs, confiding himself to the air like a gull. If she were a painter, she would have tried to paint him so, in that moment of rising, before the fall begins.

Frowning, he rolls the edging of a cushion-cover between his fingers. 'I went to a lecture. Three lectures.'

She nods, waits. Lectures on prostitution? On spiritualism? There are flyers, she recalls, advertising talks about gold-mining in Australia, and George is just the person, just the age, to be seized by the idea of a long voyage and a treasure-trove under a hot sun.

He looks up. 'About engineering. Lighthouses. He, the lecturer, he works for the Penvenicks.'

Not, then, a discussion of physiology or the joys of married love. 'The Penvenicks?'

'It's a Cornish firm. They build lighthouses. Richard Penvenick used to work for the Stevensons.'

Her gaze wanders towards her medical book. There is a fever patient causing concern, and she has a hunch that the fever is incidental to the real problem, that the tremors are not rigor but some disorder of the motor functions.

'And Richard Penvenick gave the lecture?'

He looks shocked, as if she's asked if St Peter gave last Sunday's sermon. She has not been to church for some weeks.

'Oh, no. Not himself. No, an assistant. He's called Tom Cavendish. He worked on the Longships Lighthouse!'

'The Longships?'

He nods, smiling.

'It's a rock off Land's End. Thousands – well, hundreds – of ships wrecked there. Some of them had come all the way from Australia, all those weeks, just to smash at the very entrance to the Channel. I mean, there was a light but it was old. And the waves broke right over it.'

Bodies washing on the waves, hair floating out from drowned heads. Those are pearls that were his eyes. She shivers.

'Oh my word, Cousin Ally, I forgot. I mean, not forgot, of course. I'm so sorry.'

He squirms, five years younger than when he sat down.

'Never mind, George. You didn't know her well. Keep telling me about the lecture.'

She wants to say that it's what May would have wanted, for his life to unroll as if she had never been, but she doesn't know. There was no reason to discuss forgetting. And what May might or might not have wanted is now quite irrelevant.

He swallows. 'All right. Sorry. Anyway, so he built a lighthouse. James Douglass did. And Tom Cavendish worked on it. They were there every day, just out on the rock. They couldn't even build a cabin, they had to go out every morning, whatever the weather. They shaped every stone, interlocking all the way up. I'll show you the designs, Cousin Ally, it's an amazing thing. Amazing that you can do it. You can't imagine the waves it withstands now. I mean – sorry.'

'Go on, George. I know that the sea is still there. Am I to take it that you want to be a lighthouse builder?'

He looks up, older again. 'It's all I want to do. I can do it. I've always liked maths. And I'm strong, you know that, I'm never ill.'

This, certainly, is true. With measles and a temperature of 104, George was trying to balance along the footboard of his bed and eventually had to be – Aunt Mary said – punished to stop him sliding down the banisters and getting chilled when he should have been resting. Ally's view is that a child knows when he is well enough to slide down the banisters. He has not even caught a cold for several years.

'What does your Papa say?'

He looks down. 'That's the thing. He says it's probably just a fad and last year I wanted to join the Navy and anyway I can do it after Cambridge if I still want to. But I can't. Cambridge would just waste three years and then I'd be too old for an apprenticeship. And I could study engineering here or in Edinburgh or Aberdeen and actually learn something useful. He says Engineering isn't a scholarly subject and I would regret Cambridge all my life, but I wouldn't. He means he would have regretted Cambridge if he hadn't gone. But honestly, Aunt Al, I've never been much interested in Art, and I'm no good at Latin and all that. I mean, I can get by, but you know I've always liked real things more than books. It's my life, not his.'

Ally nods. Either of them may be right, as far as she can see, but people learn more from their own mistakes than those of others.

'You know I can't interfere between you and your father. What does your Mamma say?'

His face brightens. 'Let the dear child be happy, mostly. Like the ending of a romantic novel.'

They both smile. Aunt Mary's novel habit has spread into a second bookcase.

He sits forward, coming to the crux. 'I just thought, you know what it's like to have – well, a calling. Because you wanted to be a doctor when you were young, didn't you? And that must have been much harder than me wanting to be an engineer.'

'Not, though, as hard as if I'd wanted to be an engineer,' she points out. 'And you know that there are girls who would give everything for the choice between Cambridge and engineering?'

'I know. Really, Cousin Ally, I do. Anyway, the thing is, I invited him, Tom Cavendish, to dinner. I mean, I asked Mamma first, if I might. And I know you're not going out yet, but I thought maybe, please, you might join us? I said Thursday because that's your day off at the moment, isn't it? I checked with Fanny.'

Dear George. She remembers herself at fifteen, the strength of her longings and the dread of the god-like powers of the grown-ups. George, plainly, has no idea how much easier these things are for him than for a girl with similar ambitions, but he has, still, his own passion and fear.

'Very well, George. My "day off" is in no way guaranteed, but if I can I will come to your dinner, and meet this Mr Cavendish, and if he asks me I'll tell Uncle James that work one loves is a rare gift not to be lightly discarded. Though I think he knows that. But I ask you something in return.'

'Anything you like, Cousin Ally.'

'Promise me that you will remember that there are girls all over Britain with just such capacities and ambition as yours, who might, given the opportunity, design just such buildings as you marvel over. And that they are denied not only the apprenticeship and training that is in your father's gift to you, but the education that would fit them for it, the freedom even to attend public lectures unescorted, much less to scale rocks at sea, and indeed the clothes that would make it physically possible for them to undertake such work. Promise me that however far you travel and however high you climb, you will keep these wasted intellects and forbidden dreams in your mind.'

He promises. She wishes she could make every professional

man in Britain make the same promise, add it to the articles signed at matriculation to the great universities.

They hear the front door bang as Fanny brings tea, and sounds of a scuffle in the hall.

'Boys?' calls Aunt Mary. 'Freddie? Did you have a good day at school?'

'Ow. You bully.' Freddie opens the door, rubbing his shoulder. 'He hit me.'

'He tripped me on the stairs.' George speaks from the hall.

'That's because he said his class heard me howling when I got the cane. I don't howl.'

Aunt Mary lays her book aside. 'Enough. We will have neither hitting nor insults. Why were you caned, Freddie?'

Freddie shrugs. 'Insolence. I didn't think he'd hear me.'

'Oh, Freddie. How did you do in your Latin?'

Freddie sits on his mother's footstool. 'I came second. Shall I pour you some tea?'

'Dear Freddie. Thank you.'

George stands in the doorway, shifting from foot to foot as if he requires the lavatory. 'What's for dinner? Cousin Ally, you will dress, won't you?'

Ally accepts a cup of tea. 'I am not in the habit of appearing unclothed at dinner. Yes, George, I will dress. Does my grey velveteen meet with your approval?'

He reddens. 'Sorry, Cousin Al.'

Aunt Mary replaces her cup in its saucer. 'I should hope so. Really, George. There is pheasant, from one of Papa's clients. Sole, a clear soup and I believe an apple charlotte. You could go down and discuss the menu in detail with Mrs Grant, if you like.'

'I know. Sorry, Mamma.'

Aunt Mary holds out her hand to him. 'Come and have some tea, darling. I have given dinners before, you know. And I doubt this Mr Carpenter is accustomed to the most elevated London circles. Weren't you telling me they lived on barley-bread and beer while building on some remote rock?'

George comes in as far as the fireplace and stands prodding the fire, which is burning very nicely already, with the poker. 'Cavendish, Mamma, not Carpenter. Things like beer and bread, anyway. I wouldn't mind, though. Think of people sailing past for a hundred years relying on something I'd built.'

'I know. It's an exciting idea. Leave the fire be, darling. Tea?'

George tries to replace the poker on the firestand, drops it and burns his fingers picking it up. Freddie sniggers.

'Bog off, Freddie.'

'George!'

'Sorry, Ma. Is Papa home?'

'In the study.'

He leaves the door open, the fire flickering in the draught.

Aunt Mary does not usually withdraw to leave Uncle James to his port unless there is a formal dinner party, for he likes to say that unlike most men, he prefers his wife's company to that of the bottle. But today, catching Ally's eye as Fanny removes the dessert, Aunt Mary makes an unannounced exception for Mr Cavendish.

Ally takes the blue armchair. 'I feel as if we have thrown Mr Cavendish to the lions.'

Aunt Mary picks up her cross-stitch. It has crossed Ally's mind that Aunt Mary, like May, does cross-stitch as a private snub to Mamma and indeed to Grandmamma. She wonders what happened to May's unfinished embroidery, presumably left on the island.

259

'I thought the point about throwing people to the lions was that other people stayed to watch. Anyway, James won't devour him. But he certainly won't trust him until they have talked it through.'

'Man to man,' says Ally. She doesn't want to do cross-stitch, but she does, sometimes, see the point of having something to do with your hands.

'Man to man.' The needle flashes across Aunt Mary's lap. 'I like him. He was polite to Fanny.'

There was trouble, a few weeks ago, when one of Uncle James's clients took too much wine and followed Fanny onto the back stairs where he was impolite.

'I had the impression he is unaccustomed to servants.'

Mr Cavendish's father, he told them in response to Uncle James's not especially subtle enquiries, died when Mr Cavendish was a child. His mother has not remarried, and gives music lessons in Harrogate. It seems a long time since she last heard her own northern vowels on another person's tongue.

Aunt Mary holds her cross-stitch away to see the effect of the new colour. She ought to have spectacles. 'I don't know. I dare say his mother cannot keep much of a house but he handled the silver with perfect aplomb.'

'Oh, Aunt Mary.'

She looks up, innocent. 'What?'

'I wondered why the fish-forks and grape-scissors. You were testing him.'

'I? No such thing. Anyway, if I were, he would have passed. But my dear, whatever one's children may choose or find themselves obliged to do in later life, you must see that training them for the best company opens the way for any ambition they may hold. Even Grandmamma taught us

260

to behave before she sent us into the slums. And George is still very young; naturally I don't wish to send him into rough company. Especially not when it's plain that he worships the man. Do you know, in some ways it was much less worrying when they were small and one's greatest anxieties concerned chicken pox and whether they would eat their meat?'

Ally crosses her feet. Her new shoes hurt. 'Chicken pox can be a very real anxiety. They are both strong, fine boys, Aunt Mary.'

'I know, my dear. I am unfairly blessed. Your poor Mamma.'

The dining room door opens, but only one set of footsteps crosses the hall. George stands in the doorway. He seems, Ally thinks, to stand in doorways rather a lot at the moment.

'Did they send you away?' asks Aunt Mary. What is it in Aunt Mary's life that has given her such placidity? Not anything that Mamma shared.

'Papa said one glass of port was more than enough and run along now. Don't you like Mr Cavendish, Mamma? The story about Godrevy?'

'He is not a natural storyteller.' Aunt Mary peels a scarlet thread from her basket, snips it with her silver snake-scissors, wets the end in her mouth and re-threads the needle. George's face falls. 'And so one believes what he says. My dear, he seems perfectly pleasant and personable. Perhaps a little too inclined to speak of his calling but that is most excusable in one of his age.'

George leans on the door frame. 'You see why I want to work with him?'

The red begins to make its trail across the canvas. 'Dear boy. Yes, I see why you want to go off to wild places and build towers on the waves. And I see why Mr Cavendish's enthusiasm is contagious. I also see why your Papa will say that this new vocation must stand the test of a little time before we change our plans for you.'

'But, Mamma –'

'I know. You want it now. But you are barely sixteen and it is our role, darling, to prevent you from making hasty decisions now that curtail your future in ways you will regret when it is too late.'

George looks at Ally. 'You chose medicine, didn't you, when you were younger than I am.'

The fire pops, sending a cinder onto the hearth. Yes, she did. Or had it chosen for her. Aunt Mary has stopped stitching.

'I chose to study more seriously than other girls. And I chose to attend extension lectures as well as my school lessons. It is not as if I had the opportunities open to you, George. We were not even sure it would be possible for a woman to graduate when I was sixteen.' She looks at Aunt Mary, Aunt Mary who has not only housed and fed but also cosseted her these five years, whom she will not betray now. 'And remember also all the men and boys for whom university is only a painful longing. You are prosperous and male, George. The world is yours. Don't waste your choices by acting like someone who doesn't have them.'

Aunt Mary nods, sends Ally a quick smile, and bends to her work. What she has said is not untrue, and after all if George really has found his vocation nothing his cousin has to say will turn him from it, and – at least as long as he refrains from marrying – nothing likely to happen in the next few years will prevent him returning to engineering after Cambridge. Papa and Aubrey developed their practice as artists while taking degrees. The dining room door opens again and the two men come through, laughing together. Good.

Mr Cavendish calls again, once while Ally is out, when, George says, he and Uncle James had a long conversation about Mr Turner's shipwreck paintings, and then one day when Ally returns from the hospital at tea-time, having been there since eight o'clock the previous evening. She walks home through a slow winter sunset, the bare branches of the plane trees black against a glowing sky. She and Dr Stratton lost the patient, a maternity case who haemorrhaged after a long breech labour. The baby lives, for the moment, as, it turns out, do three of its siblings, now in all probability cases for the Children's Home. She drops her shoulders, allows her arms to swing a little as she walks, and draws deep breaths of the cold. Good doctors can set aside both triumph and defeat. It took her half an hour to coax a cry from the baby and she is far from sure that her work was in its best interest.

She hears his voice in the drawing room as she closes the front door, and almost decides to slip straight to the kitchen and coax tea and toast from the new cook, who shows signs of being impressed by her work where the others have tended to see a poor relation. She can't hear the words, but Mr Cavendish is speaking fast, energetically, the way Papa and Aubrey used to talk about painting and design. The way people talk about work when it's going well. She finds herself walking, not creeping, up the stairs.

He's sitting on the ottoman in the bay window, his red hair extravagantly back-lit by the pink sky. Horizontal sunbeams pick out each droplet in the steam twisting from his teacup.

He stands up, holds out his hand. 'Miss Moberley! Mrs Dunne told me you were at the hospital.'

Ally hopes he doesn't have damp palms. She dislikes shaking hands. 'I was at the hospital.' He doesn't. 'I stayed on to see through a maternity case.'

'A happy ending?'

'No.' She sits down. By this time of day, she usually prefers to keep going until after dinner following a night's work, but she's too tired now. She must sleep very soon. Aunt Mary pours a cup of tea for her. 'People say working women give birth easily, that it's the rich who make a fuss, but it's not true. Poor diet and overwork make nothing easier.'

'Ally,' murmurs Aunt Mary.

Ally frowns. Is there blood on her skirt, is her collar awry?

'Oh. Forgive me, Mr Cavendish. I spend too much time at the hospital and forget what subjects are considered proper for polite conversation. It is a very pretty sunset, is it not?'

He sits forward. 'Indeed, Miss Moberley, it would be better for all of us were there more overlap between what is correct and what is important. Do you find that maternity cases do better in the hospital than at home?'

She sips her tea, comforting and too hot, glances at Aunt Mary.

'Go ahead, my dear. Consider me your antediluvian aunt.'

'The charity cases do, of course. At the very least we offer rest and cleanliness. Otherwise, the mother and infant may share a bed with other children from almost the very moment of birth. And where it is necessary, we can make a case to the Foundling Hospital for infants who would in all probability face a brief and uncomfortable future.'

'Really, Ally.'

She sits back. 'I am sure Mr Cavendish knows that babies are not found under gooseberry bushes, Aunt Mary.'

Amusement plays about his eyes. 'I believe I do, yes. And

that they do not always appear at correct moments, or indeed in correct arms. George tells me you have contributed also to rescue work, Miss Moberley?'

'Ally, what have you told the boy?'

Ally tries to remember. 'Very little, Aunt Mary. But he hears things at school and he is at an age to be curious. I told him to ask Uncle James. It is my mother's work, Mr Cavendish. I do not try to combine medicine with any other calling. And you? Surely your work leaves little time for charitable concerns?'

'Little time for organised philanthropy. I try to be mindful of the needs around me, and mindful also that my mindfulness does not in itself help anyone and indeed denies me the excuse of ignorance for my inaction.'

They smile at each other.

'Ally, have a sandwich,' says Aunt Mary. 'I am sure you did not eat lunch.'

9

BEE

Alfred Moberley, 1880

Carved in yew, 6 × 2

Signed 'AGM', no date

Provenance: Moberley family; bequeathed to the Victoria
Gallery by Alethea Moberley Cavendish, 1929

*This is the only reliably attributed example of Moberley's carving, a craft
he appears to have practised in later life as a kind of hobby and to develop
designs for furniture at the beginning of his career. The bee is the length
of a finger, big enough to allow him to model every detail; it is thought that
he may have used the insects in Street's collection as a model. The wood
is yew, perhaps from the tree in the graveyard of St Margaret's Church
which is known to have fallen during the winter of 1879, and the rings
in the wood darken towards the bee's sting. The initials AGM are visible with a magnifying glass under the thorax; a testament to Moberley's
skill and precision even in late middle age.*

*

It is, she has found, possible to mistake other men for him. He
has a type, a genus, that makes it hard to be sure until she can
see his face that the compact body, red hair and bobbing stride
are Tom. Half the men in London, this part of London, carry

a briefcase and wear a black coat and hat. He is, as ever, exactly to time; crowds dissolve before the omnibuses Tom rides, shoe-laces untangle themselves, verbose suppliers remember important appointments. If a thing won't work, he says – keys, the lid of Aunt Mary's sewing box – there is a reason, and then it is his practice to find the reason and resolve the difficulty, but in most cases, things do work for him, not only the tools and machines that realise his calling but the small intricacies of daily life. His clothes do not get lost at the laundry, his letters do not miss the post. *Dear Miss Moberley, I hope to call on you this afternoon and thought that as the sun seems likely to shine you might enjoy a walk in the Park.* He takes the weather seriously. She moves back, behind the curtain, just as he glances up before bounding under the portico and onto the step. She pauses before the mirror as the doorbell rings, pushes strands of hair back into her chignon and tugs her waistband smooth, merely ritual adjustments that undo themselves as she walks through the room.

He offers his elbow as they cross the road, where the first open carriages of the season jostle among the hansom cabs and carts. She finds that she has taken his arm, and also that she feels no objection when he does not release her as they enter the park. The plane trees have come into full leaf since she last thought about them, a rich blue-green too dense to paint in watercolour, and ducklings hurry behind their mothers around the fountains in the square pond.

He tucks her hand against his coat. 'This time last year, I was trying to stop myself blowing into the North Sea. I suppose there were tulips here then too.'

She tries to remember. April. The fever ward. 'I cannot say. I am sure I did go outdoors by daylight but the experience has left no impression.'

He does not reply. Perhaps she sounded repressive. 'You were building a lighthouse?' she asks.

His hair is even brighter in the sun, a metallic, inorganic colour. 'Unbuilding, this time. A strange place. The sea is in retreat, and the land so low that the channels shift from one year to the next. There had been a tower there for three hundred years, perhaps as much of a mark for those travelling by land as by sea, for in those parts the fields are flatter than the water. But there was a navigable channel when Richard Penvenick was first commissioned to put in a new light twenty years ago, and two years after that there was a great storm. Even the greatest towers, you know, can be moved by the waves, but on this occasion it was not the building but the water that moved. On the morning after the storm, the channel was no more than a trickle through the sand, something a boy could cross without wetting his short trousers. We waited, of course, to see if the whim that moved the water would return it, but after maintaining a redundant light for eighteen years Mr Penvenick sent me to remove the mechanism and lens.'

A child in a blue dress and white pinafore runs across their path, pursued by a smaller child in a sailor suit much impeded by a fit of giggles.

'I have always thought of the coast as static. As it is on a map. But of course it is not.'

'No. Quite apart from the movement of the land, the falls of the cliffs on the south coast and the shifting sands to the east, the tides are always in motion. I should say that the nation gains and loses some dozens of square miles of sand and rock with each revolution of the planet.'

Her steps check, as though dizzied by his extra-terrestrial vantage-point. She sees the Earth in its stately waltz through dark and light, each landmass expanding and contracting as though breathing.

'But your lighthouses stand firm.'

He turns to smile, a slight pressure on her arm. 'We hope so. It is my job, our jobs, to make sure that they do. But it is a constant battle against wind and sea, fought at least as much by mathematics and physics at Mr Penvenick's desk in Falmouth as by stone and mortar on the shore. We do not always win. Mr Penvenick encourages us to believe that failure is as useful to our science as success, but that is an old man's philosophy.' He frowns, looses her arm. 'I cannot say that I have learnt to love my mistakes.'

She wants to take off her gloves, feel his tweed sleeve under her bare hands. 'The same is said of surgery. And that most of those who die on the operating table are saved from a slower and more painful end. But there are lives in our hands. As in yours.'

More lives, in some ways, in his, since ships carry many hundreds of souls. She sees again May's hair rippling like weed in the water. Her hair would have come unpinned, surely, in the waves.

His other hand pats hers. 'We are too solemn for this bright day. Tell me, Miss Moberley, shall you take a holiday this summer? Celebrate your graduation? Or will you be returning to your family?'

The cold breath of the hall at home yawns around her. 'I hope to find work, and will go where it takes me. It is still difficult for a woman, you know, in private practice, and few hospitals welcome us. There may be an opening here. I am not eager to return to my parents.'

Although Annie wants it, wants to go on living with her cheerful family in their cheerful home. Ally feels, when she thinks of the summer, of the future opening before her, like a fledgling. After a certain age, most of them can land well enough. It is taking off again that is the problem. She pauses.

'I will be returning to Cornwall,' he says. 'Mr Penvenick has just won a new colonial contract. He did not communicate the details but he wants me to assist him with a new set of designs. I have hopes – well, he is sixty-five. And his son is a railway engineer who shows no interest in the lights.'

'Oh.' Something else that is changing. She should not have allowed herself to come to depend on his calls, which have bejewelled her winter's work. He comes, probably, mostly for George's sake.

'But I do not leave for another month. So we must make the most of the springtime, must we not?'

He meets her gaze. She blushes, and then blushes again for the blushing of a spinster and a professional woman, a woman who made an open-eyed decision to have a career, to be unentangled, single in vision. He nods, and looks charitably at the river, at the fat stone colonnades on the bridge where two small boys sit precariously fishing.

'Doctor!' Nurse Johnson's voice is high and sharp.

Dr Stratton puts down her needle. 'Please excuse us one moment. Miss Moberley?'

Ally hands the patient a pad of gauze. 'Hold this firmly on your arm. We will be back very soon, but please ring this bell for a nurse if you are concerned or feel unwell.'

The woman, who has said nothing, not even explained what appears to be a knife-wound on her arm, nods, her gaze not quite focused.

'Good.' Is it good? She hurries after Dr Stratton.

There's a policeman whose uniform is dripping onto the

271

floor, muddy smears and footprints across the tiles, as if someone has dragged a bag of earth through the room. A crowd of
people around the nurses' table, someone sobbing, a child left
to itself cruising determinedly along a row of chairs.

'Dr Stratton?' she says. 'Do you need assistance?'

Muttering, the crowd parts. There's a bundle of wet cloth
on the table, more water – sepia-tinged water – pooling
around it, around Dr Stratton's neatly shod feet. The bundle
contains a white hand, a thrown-back face over which Dr
Stratton bends.

'Roll her,' says Dr Stratton.

Hands reach from the crowd and push at the bundle, resolv-
ing it into human form. It contracts and spews more brown
water onto the front row, coughs. The policeman sits down as
if someone has cut his strings. Dr Stratton waits, her fingers on
the wrist. The patient gasps, retches again.

'She will do now,' says Dr Stratton.

Under their gaze, life resumes.

It is Ally who is called when the patient awakes. The sky is
paling, and from the doctor's bedroom she can hear the first
birdsong. The policeman did not see the young lady jump,
only heard the splash and a cry, but the stones in her pockets
tell a story that will be hard to belie. Ally follows the nurse
down the corridor, where the gas jets flicker like ghosts in the
brightening day. The patient nearest the door stirs, mutters as
they pass. The nurse, standing at the end of the bed, seems
disposed to stay, to harvest a story for the tea-table.

'If she's in trouble, it's not showing,' she says. 'And nobody's
hurt her that we could see.'

'Thank you, Nurse, that will do.'

The patient lies on her back, her head propped at an

uncomfortable angle against a pillow. Her hair, which looked dark as Ally's own when wet, has dried to a honey colour. She is slim, her collar-bones prominent as handles in the wide-necked gown, but the wrists are rounded and the hands pale, without obvious marks of labour. She looks young, but also like the sort of woman who will always look young. The patient gazes at the square of white sky above the bed opposite her own. Lifting it carefully, not to wake anyone else who might also have a taste for grisly detail, Ally sets a chair beside the bed and sits down. Love before reason; none of us is whole. She dismisses an urge to take the patient's hand.

'You are in the London Women's Hospital,' she says, as if making some observation about the weather. 'You were pulled out of the Hanborough Ditch yesterday and brought here. You were not breathing. One of the doctors revived you. You have pains in your ribs and chest because she had to push the water out of your lungs. Your throat is probably sore because you vomited several times. You may have a headache or feel sick.'

She stops. The patient has not moved, her eyes have not wavered.

Ally tries again. 'We don't know your name,' she says. 'Would you like to tell me your name? I am Miss Moberley and I am finishing my medical training.'

There is no response.

'You will need to stay here for a little while. Sometimes people catch a fever from water like that, and it will take time for us to be sure that you are quite well. Would you like to send a message to anyone? Family, or friends? We can write if you have no-one in London.'

The woman does not blink. Her brain, of course, may be affected by the drowning, or she may have been an idiot before she jumped into the water. Is it true, Ally wants to ask her, that drowning doesn't hurt? Did you come up three times before you sank, despite the stones? The stones are at the police station: where did she find stones in central London? Bricks would be easy enough to come by. Ally can, she finds, imagine perfectly well what it would be like to prowl the newly made streets where clay-red terraces spring up overnight, in search of bricks to hold herself down. The sun has risen and the rumble of the streets, of London, has begun. Soon, she will go home, have breakfast, allow herself a couple of hours' sleep before Tom calls. She wants to take him to the new Kensington Museum, which has just bought one of Papa's stained glass windows, and then perhaps there will be time for a walk in the Park before he must give his lecture. She should attend one of his lectures, while there is still opportunity. It would be good for her to think about mathematics again.

After all, she pats the woman's arm, lying inert in a hospital sleeve on the blanket.

'Very well. Try to rest. I will come back to see you again before I go home.'

She wonders whether to bother returning to the woman's bedside. She must have lain down seven or eight times in the night, always to be called again just as her mind quietened towards sleep. Dr Stratton was delayed in coming back onto duty and it is already past the hour when she had promised herself she would be washed and brushed in her own clean bed. Even so, who knows what betrayals, what discarded promises, brought this woman to gather her stones. She will keep her word.

The ward is awake now, some of the women talking to each other, an almost-recovered pneumonia knitting. Behind screens, the nurses are working their way along the row with bed-baths and hot water. There is a moment's silence as Ally passes through.

'She ain't said nothing,' volunteers the woman in the next bed. 'Didn't eat no breakfast neither. Not even her tea. She's maybe trying to starve since the drowning didn't work.'

Ally sits again, leans forward so the others can't hear. 'I'm sorry you don't feel inclined to talk. We might be able to help you. Please try to eat and drink.'

She sits back. A yawn washes over her.

'Excuse me. I'm very tired. I'm going to go home now and take some rest myself, but I'll be back later and I'll come and see you again.'

'Tell you what,' says the neighbour. 'If one of my girls behaved like that my husband'd give her a proper hiding. Downright rude when the doctor comes specially to talk to her.'

'I'm not a doctor,' says Ally. Does not say that hitting people cures nothing, that the failure or reluctance to control the urge to hurt is a more serious derangement than keeping silence. That sickness of the mind is as troublesome, as painful, as pneumonia or gallstones, even that there are events and encounters, family situations, that would leave any sane person filling her pockets with stones.

She returns with the glories of the museum still buoyant in her mind, and the solidity of Tom's muscled arm under her gloved hand. She has dreamt of Tom, dark, tumbling dreams for which she has a perfectly adequate vocabulary. The freckles on his wrists probably extend across his back and shoulders, the firmness of his arms means a taut belly and open chest. She sees that chest, those shoulders, moving over her own and

275

catches her breath right there in the corridor. You would think that knowing the human body as she does, knowing the layers of skin, fat, muscle and bone, the pathways of blood, mucus, urine and faeces, would diminish enchantment. Apparently it does not, and considering the numbers of married doctors and, come to that, nurses, this should be less surprising than she finds it. Of all the forms of learning, this should have protected her. And has not. She shakes her head, as if lust could be swatted like a fly.

The east-facing ward darkens early. The gas has not been lit, although dusk softens the lines of the metal beds and high walls. She passes her days, she thinks for the first time, in geometric spaces, her learning cradled by the perpendicular. Remembers again Tom's vertiginous perspective. May's mind must have been changed by the shape of her island, the sheerness of cliffs and the sweeps of hills. There are, surely, hills in that place?

The patient appears not to have moved. Catatonia, the first time she has seen it. She approaches the nurse first; the patient wet her bed but has not soiled herself. She has not responded to any approach. She has not taken food or drink, even when Nurse Selwyn tried spoon-feeding. Dr Stratton instructed them not to hold her nose, a technique occasionally used – not by Ally – to medicate children and the delirious. There has been some coughing, to which the patient appeared oblivious. The nurse turns to light the lamps as Ally walks back down the ward. The earth turns, the lights come on. Soon it will be bedtime.

She draws the chair forward again, seats herself. Of course the patient has been washed, but she wonders if there is a riverine odour, a ghost of water-weed and bubbles. Good night, sweet ladies. The patient's pulse is strong and regular, her breathing slow.

'You see, I have come back. I will be here, in the hospital, for the rest of the night and I'll ask the nurses to call me if you want to say anything, if you begin to respond. We are able to keep you safe here. We will keep you warm and clean even if you don't acknowledge us.'

She wants to go on and say that the patient can stay here for as long as she likes and that no-one will force anything on her, but it isn't true. The patient cannot be allowed to endanger herself by starvation. The hospital is not an asylum: once it is clear that the physical after-effects of her drowning have resolved, they will need to consider the girl's sanity. It is beyond doubt that she has committed the crime of attempting self-murder, witnessed by a police constable, and unless the police decide to pretend that she fell in while carrying stones for some other reason, there is no protection from the consequences of that crime. At the very least, enquiries will have to be made so that her relatives can be contacted or the appropriate parish billed for her admission to the lunatic asylum. Very soon, there will be considerable pressure, probably some coercion, to respond.

It is a quieter night. The crisis of a patient on the fever ward: there is nothing she can do that would not be better done by the nurses, but she stands, anyway, at the foot of the bed, watching and waiting until the woman's temperature turns, her muttering quiets and she falls into a natural sleep. A surgical patient wakes sobbing with pain: laudanum, and a more authoritative reassurance than the same words uttered by a nurse. Back to bed, pacing the corridors that will confine her dreams for years, through a building that will stand longer in her mind than on the ground. She will, she thinks, look in on the drowning girl. What is unspeakable by day can often find utterance now, in the hours of darkness and the place of sickness, both more and less real than the ordinary world.

She can see from the door that the patient has moved, and as she walks down the ward the nurse comes to meet her. The catatonia must have broken; now, then, the story can be told. There is no love worth dying for, she will say, or at least no love that grows from death. Shame can be redeemed, sin pardoned: even for extreme poverty, on an individual level there are possible resolutions, and in her experience those who feel most alarm at their destitution are also those most deserving of assistance. The patient can be sent to Mamma's Home, to Canada, even, should she wish to confess any truly criminal act, to prison, where she can expiate her wrongdoing. There is no life, Ally will tell her, that cannot be changed, no-one beyond redemption. We can outlast sadness and despair. Whatever damage has been done to this girl, whoever has harmed her, she is, is she not, still here? Still able to begin again? Ally has neglected her Bible these last months – years, even. She will perhaps read with the patient as her spirits – her spirit – recovers.

Nurse Sedley touches her arm. 'It's fever, Miss Moberley. Set in these two hours. We were about to call you.'

She hurries to the bedside, still careful to tread quietly past the uneasy sleepers under the gaslights. Nurse raises her candle. The patient's eyes are open but unfocused, her face flushed. Her breathing is fast and audible. Ally touches her forehead.

'One hundred and three,' says Nurse Sedley. 'Going up. I've sponged her.'

'Has she taken any fluids? Eaten anything?'

'No. I spooned in brandy but she let it run out of her mouth.'

'Bring some clear soup, please. And a spoon.'

The woman in the next bed, not, after all, asleep, sits up to watch. 'Throw it in her face, I would. Soon wake her up.'

'And a screen, please, Nurse.'

Ally strokes her patient's arm, folded, now, protectively across her breast. 'You're running a slight temperature. I expect you're feeling hot and your limbs ache, maybe as if there's a heavy weight on your chest. It's important that you drink something. We also need to keep your strength up so I'm going to offer you some broth.'

She wants to say that without it, her patient will become sicker, faster, but this may be exactly what the patient wants. She holds her cold hand and listens to the shallow breaths until Nurse Sedley returns. For Ally, the patient closes her mouth and turns her head away – acknowledgement, perhaps, of a kind – but she does not eat, and as the night passes, her fever continues to rise as her breathing becomes laboured.

'I can't, Al,' says Annie. 'Really. We've only got three weeks. It's not the time. It won't make any difference if we go after the exams.'

Annie's right, she knows. Now she should be concentrating on her preparation, tending to the exact balance of study, exercise and rest required for success. There will be six hours of examinations on each of four consecutive days, and then vivas the following week. One must train as a horse for a race, and all else must wait, must be put aside until afterwards. But what if something distracts, if there is such a persistent slipping of the mind that it would be perhaps more efficient to address one's distraction in order to return, single in mind, to revision? She has made it her business to find out what might happen to the next suicidal patient. Two doctor's signatures are required – and sufficient – to confine a patient to an insane asylum, to suspend, in most cases permanently, a citizen's most basic rights. The mad have no freedom of movement, no right of habeas corpus. Lunatics, like women, may not vote; may not control money, may not marry, cease as the doctor writes his name to be the guardians of their own children and the owners of their own houses. It is widely acknowledged that there is no clear border between madness and sanity, and widely known that sane people are and have been confined as mad for spurious reasons. It is, then, not the least important aspect of a doctor's calling to make this distinction, deciding who in this nation of eccentrics may safely be left to practise unusual habits and extraordinary ideas and who poses a danger to him or her self and others. Or perhaps who cannot be entrusted with an estate, or a child, or who is so lost in fear and despair that confinement in a place of safety and routine is an act of charity. One would think that the ability to recognise such states and distinguish one from another would be as important as the ability to tell pneumonia from a cold or a twisted ankle from a compound fracture.

Annie closes her toxicology book, her finger squashed in the later pages. 'You are quite right, Ally. Papa would agree with you. You should write to the authorities and suggest a change in the curriculum. And I will willingly accompany you to the asylum after the exams. But exactly because the treatment of the insane is not part of our syllabus, I see no need to address it now.'

Ally, leaning against the chair beside Annie's, stops fingering the brass rivets securing the back of the green leather upholstery. There is blue sky outside and the garden will be full of sunlight and rustling leaves.

'I know. But it seems wrong to graduate without having visited one. To accept the responsibility without understanding

280

the consequences. Without at least having seen where we're sending our patients. Asylums are surely not as bad as people imagine.' And if they are, all the more reason to go, to know what damage is being done before and while doing it.

Annie takes her hand, soothes the bitten fingertips. 'I will go with you. I promise I will sign no confinement orders until I have visited an asylum. But not now.'

She is late. A quarter of an hour late. Of course he has gone. He is a busy man, his days in London already short, and if she cannot show him the fundamental courtesy of valuing his time, if she has not even the professional competence that requires punctuality – He is down there, on the quay below the bridge, talking to the man with the boats. She lifts her skirts, too high, and hurries down the stone stairs.

'Mr Cavendish, I am so sorry. I was at the asylum and underestimated the time for the omnibus, and by the time I had understood how late I might be there were no cabs to be seen. I hope you will forgive me. I did not intend to waste your time.'

The boatman is gazing at her. Hysterical female. She must stop.

'Please believe that I do understand the claims on a busy man's day. You would have been perfectly in the right had you given me up; you are most kind to wait.' Stop, she thinks, be quiet. You reveal too much.

'Miss Moberley, please. Do not say another word on the subject. It is a pleasant day to dally at the riverside. So much so that, instead of walking, I thought we might hire a boat. I have been missing the water. Could you trust yourself to me on the river?'

She has not been in a boat since Aubrey rowed her and

May across the lake in Albert Park. Certainly not since May –
The river at her feet flows to the sea, out into the Channel,
which is a backwater of the Atlantic Ocean. It runs brown and
silent here, the colour of milky tea, and it is hard to imagine
fish or even weeds below the surface.

'Of course. Anywhere.'

The boatman smiles, raises his eyebrows. She must not be
obvious. She does not know the correct way to accept such an
invitation; perhaps it is not correct to accept. She draws aside
and stands watching the brown water absorb sunlight and
carry it out to sea while Tom pays the man.

'Let me help you,' he says, taking her hand, and she does let
him. The boat wobbles under her as she steps in, as she stands
with her feet below the water-level. She has to tuck her legs
under her to give him space to row. The tide is turning, he
says, and they will go upstream first. He likes to see the Houses
of Parliament from the river; she will have quite a new view of
London. He has removed his jacket and she can see the muscles bulging and flexing under his shirt sleeves. He rows
energetically, as if there is haste, and soon his face reddens
under the freckles.

She should say something. The least she can do is make
conversation for him. She clears her throat. 'Do you row in
Falmouth?'

He nods as he bends forward. 'Sometimes. Up the river.
Penvenick keeps boats.' The oars trail a moment. 'Easiest way
of getting around down there.'

She rubs the lace on her cuff between her fingers. The
shadow of her straw hat makes an ellipse on her grey linen
skirt. Water drips from the oars. She should think of something else to say.

He glances at her. 'There are some places where the trees

grow right out over the water. You can row under them, into the woods. Inlets without paths. Jungle, I sometimes think, though I've never seen a jungle.'

She looks up. 'Should you like to?'

'Maybe. I'd like to see more of the world. The empire. And you?'

The river swirls around the bridge pilings, making whirlpools and eddies of foam. The water is still silent and she can hear the oars dip and drip. Even from so close, she can't see into the river at all, as if it's really only two-dimensional.

'I hope only to be a doctor. It is ambition enough, for a woman.'

He pauses. 'Look up. You can see Westminster. St Paul's. But you have almost achieved that ambition. Surely there are more to succeed it?'

She shakes her head. She should be working, should have stayed in her room with her books. 'It is sufficient. More than sufficient. Many would say that I already expect too much.'

He leans to his oars again. 'And I say they are wrong. Your degree is only the beginning. Tell me then, how did you find the asylum?'

Wind comes over the water to ruffle her hair and tug her hat. 'It was both better and worse than I expected. The inmates seem safe enough. It was not dirty. Many of those I saw are encouraged to occupy themselves, or perhaps even compelled to do so, though I am aware that there are certainly others I did not see.' The 'back wards', the places where dirty and refractory patients are kept. She clasps her hands around her knees. 'But it was quite without hope. There is no treatment. Some cases seem to resolve with time, but for the great majority their incarceration is permanent and their condition can only worsen in the unrelieved company of the mad. The

283

asylum exists only to pass their time. Until death. A kind of warehouse.'

He stops rowing. The boat begins to drift, sideways. Stone sidings loom above them, as if she and he are ducks or frogs, creatures on a smaller scale than the surrounding edifices. 'But that is dreadful. An appalling thought. There is a resident doctor?'

She nods. It seems less dreadful here, floating in the sunlight. 'He conducted me around. Although he cannot approve of women doctors. He conceives his role as being to treat the inmates' physical disorders, where they exist and where the patients are able to give any reasonable account of their symptoms. In many cases, it is hard to distinguish delusion from sickness. He told me for example of a patient who believes that there are maggots inside her skull, feeding on her brain. She complains also of headaches and odd sensations in her ears, and it seems to me not impossible that there is some physical cause of these discomforts from which a disordered mind might deduce the presence of maggots; that in such a case the physical symptoms may precede the mental disturbance. But the doctor sees only difficult patients, constitutionally incapable of truth. And of course I had no speech with the woman herself. I am sure that if I were called upon to treat such patients I should find many difficulties not apparent in the abstract.'

'But you would like to try?'

She would like to pass her examinations, to earn her title. 'I cannot say. I must first qualify.'

'We should turn around,' he says. 'Perhaps you would like to try rowing? It will be easier, going downstream.'

She is afraid to stand on the water, afraid of the rocking and tipping under her feet and the pull beneath the slick surface.

*

They walk through the Park, although the sun has set and there is only the last stain of red in the western sky, against which the skeleton trees stand black. The leaves are gone and there is no scent of flowers but it is not cold. Her dress is damp under the arms and perspiration prickles in the small of her back. She seems to be bare-headed. Tom is talking about ceramics, about a new pigment used in a glaze that comes out deep, strong turquoise but deadly poisonous if used inside dining ware. It is for flower vases only, he says, and she is about to argue that people prefer white china or glass to display flowers when she sees May, tightly laced and wearing her violet dress that Mamma gave away, running over the bridge. And then he is behind her, his hands over her breasts, his lips and tongue on the nape of her neck, and a flock of birds, starlings, rises from the trees in the dusk and whirls over their heads in a scrabble of wing-beats and scaly feet.

She wakes, mouth dry and pulse bounding. Her hands move to her breasts. Will he, will anyone, touch her there, ungloved fingers on bare skin? Scalpels, she thinks, the surgeon's pen, the blade working over exposed ribs. She will not have a child, will not suckle. Mothers do too much harm. Aubrey, once, unbuttoned her dress, untied her chemise and shift, helped her to pull them down and arranged her, nubile, a nymph, on the dais in his studio, holding uncomfortably high a lily from the arrangement in his hall. He touched only to guide the pose and although she shivered at each brush of his fingers he did not offer, and she could not ask, for more. Although perhaps May –

She sits up. Grey light seeps around the curtains. Her stomach turns. Today the final results will be posted. You may look, Dr Stratton said, on the noticeboard outside the Committee Room from noon. And I am sure that none of you have cause

285

for anxiety. But people – men – do fail here, at the end. The results are not exactly final in that it is permitted to repeat the year, sometimes more than once, but for men this is a merely individual shame; no-one is likely to conclude that one student's, or even several students', low marks mean that men are unfit to practise as physicians. To betray the cause now – her throat closes. How can she walk down that corridor, approach that board, knowing that her final failure may be pinned up for all to see? To have to tell Miss Johnson, Mrs Lewis, Mamma – She pulls up her legs, bows her head on her knees. She could be sick, unable to leave her bed, and wait for Annie to send word. Could be weak. She hears a whimper from her own chest. It is all right for Annie. Annie's brother-in-law, she says, failed two of his qualifying exams because his mother's final illness disrupted his preparations. A good son, who has made a good doctor and a good husband. The light is strong enough to read her wrist-watch waiting on the bedside table. Seven hours to wait.

She discovers when she goes down to breakfast that she cannot speak. Bacon, offers Uncle James, and when she opens her mouth to say no thank you, just a cup of tea this morning, no sound comes out, not even the whisper of someone with a bad cold. Her lips move, she can pass air over her vocal cords, but she cannot make a sound.

'Cousin Ally needs to see the doctor,' says Freddie. Scrambled egg bounces off his tie.

The sudden onset, she wants to say, is strongly indicative of a psychosomatic symptom resulting from considerable nervous strain, the kind of phenomenon to which the strongest minds may, given sufficient anxiety, find themselves prone. She can say nothing.

'Perhaps,' says George, 'Cousin Ally, unlike some people, keeps silence when she has nothing to say.'

Uncle James lowers *The Times*. 'Are you quite well, my dear?'

She nods, gestures and mouths towards the teapot.

'Tea? Perhaps a drink will help you?'

Perhaps it will, perhaps the heat will relax the cords. George passes her cup.

'It's Mr Cavendish's last lecture today,' he says. 'Will you go, Cousin Ally?'

She had forgotten. It is possible that by this evening she will be gathering stones of her own. I may be detained at the hospital, she wants to say, but no words emerge. This will pass, she thinks. Panic pulses under her sternum. She will speak. There is no organic trouble, no physiological reason for her muteness. A dumb doctor would be no use. Dumb and female, doubly crippled. She tries to ask for the milk jug although her tea already has milk in it. This is a hysterical complaint, a nervous ailment, the kind of trouble that her detractors expect of women. Tom, who thinks her strong, must not know of her weakness. Three and a half hours until the results will appear.

She has no memory of turning from the board, walking across the red and black tiles, past the shiny apple-green walls, for what may be the last time. She is on the doorstep, dazzled by sunlight, damp with sweat, hearing as if for the first time the roar and pulse of the city around her; wheels, horses, trains, machines, humans. The plane trees sough below the sky, white sunshine sparkling from their leaves as if from ruffled water. Someone seizes her shoulders, a face moves in towards hers.

'You did it, darling! I knew you would. Oh, well done. I'm so pleased.'

Annie, in a halo of jasmine scent and tendrils of hair and

unsuitable tulle-trimmed hat. Cool hands take hers, as if inviting her to the dance.

'Are you happy? You must be happy. All your work, darling, all those years. Such triumph. We must send a telegram to your parents. Lots of telegrams, to everyone! And there is a prize, did you know that? You could take a holiday or – oh, anything you like.'

Ally looks at her. She may be about to cry. Jubilant, yes, she should be jubilant. But is not. She wants to turn and run through the streets to – somewhere, to hide herself. She has indeed done it, but nothing has changed, nothing feels different. And qualifying, even at the top of her class, is only permission to move on to the next thing to do, which is to find a job, to avoid returning to Manchester.

'Dearest Ally, are you not pleased? How can you not be happy? Come, Papa has champagne on ice in readiness.'

She must speak. 'Congratulations, Annie. We have all done well.'

Annie shakes her head. 'Yes, yes, of course. And thank you. I am very happy. But you –'

'Don't, please.'

'You don't wish to be congratulated?'

She twists away. Annie drops her hands.

'I'm sorry, Annie. I can't do this. Celebration. Best leave me. Honestly, go. Drink your champagne and dance and be happy. And I congratulate you.'

She lifts her hands to Annie's shoulders, not, she knows, as someone accustomed to embracing, to affection, would do, misses Annie's cheek with her lips, touches her face and turns to go, almost running, her footsteps a panicky staccato across the flagstones.

She finds herself in the Park, her hair sticking to her damp face and itchy under her hat. There are children paddling barefoot, little girls with their skirts tucked high into their knickers. She could unfasten the boots that press her stocking seams into her toes and leave the imprints of their bindings on her hot feet, lift her skirts to unbutton her suspenders and roll down her black wool stockings. She remembers May in the river with Aubrey, and Papa balanced before his easel under the willow, a painting bought by a railway magnate and now somewhere in the warren of Bowden Park Hall. Does the magnate know what happened to the girl in his picture? There are no girls in pictures, of course, only arrangements of light and line, colour and shape. If she sits on this bench, she will be taken for a prostitute. She walks on, slow as a lady. Her feet ache. She is thirsty. She leans on the parapet, the stone flesh-warm in the sun and abrasive on her forearms. Doctor Moberley. Dr Alethea Moberley. She has done it. And she is not going to telegraph anyone, nor take someone else's champagne, but stand here by the water in the sun, hot and thirsty, and call herself by her new name.

'Darling! We were worried about you.' Aunt Mary, in a swirl of kingfisher silk. 'And congratulations, my dear girl. Such a triumph. James says it will be in the newspapers! Such a splendid return for all your work. We are all so proud and pleased for you.'

She accepts Aunt Mary's kiss. 'Thank you. And thank you for all your help, Aunt Mary. It would have been a very different thing if I had had to live in lodgings and pay my board.'

'Nonsense, darling, you would prevail over any adversity. And we love having you here. Come, we have made a little party for you. It is not every day someone makes history in the house!'

We are all making history, Ally thinks, future becoming present becoming past moment by moment as the planet spins.

Tom is there, holding a sandwich on a plate and standing in the bay with George, and Uncle James poised like a bird beside the silver ice-bucket usually saved for dinner parties but now beaded with condensation at half-past four in the afternoon, and the boys washed and brushed since school.

'Hurray!' shouts Freddie. 'Three cheers for Cousin Al. Hip hip!'

The men cheer foolishly, self-conscious as someone singing to a child before other adults, and Aunt Mary, a tear sliding down her cheek, holds Ally's gaze, beaming. Uncle James passes the champagne to Tom and comes to kiss Ally.

'Congratulations, my dear. We are all very proud of you.'

Ally swallows, fights down the urge to run again.

'Thank you, Uncle James. It would have been so much harder without your patronage.'

Tom, who has been struggling, vanquishes the champagne. It runs over his fingers, across the coppery hairs on the backs of his hands.

He hands her a glass. 'Champagne, Dr Moberley?'

'I will see you to the door,' she says. It feels as if the champagne's bubbles are drifting and bursting in her head, and she doesn't care that the others exchange glances.

The hall is dark and she almost stumbles over the umbrella-stand as she reaches for his coat. He steadies her, a hand on her arm.

'Careful, Miss Moberley.'

'Dr Moberley,' she says. 'Ally. Call me Ally.'

He is still touching her. He reaches up the other hand and

strokes her cheek. 'Ally. Listen, Ally, I need to speak to you before I leave for Cornwall.'

She looks up. Really? Will he really, now?

He shakes his head. 'Not now. You are – this conversation requires the cold light of day. Things are complicated.'

She clings to his arm. 'I have taken champagne. I am unaccustomed.'

'I know. So we will say good night now, and if I may, I will call in the morning?'

She rubs her cheek on his shoulder. 'Of course you may, Mr Cavendish. Tom. Whenever you choose.'

'Look for me at ten.'

She leans on him. She could go to sleep here and now, his jacket smooth under her cheek in the darkened hall. Except that she has to keep standing up.

'Ally? I need to go now. And you should perhaps go to bed.'

'I like it here.'

'Good.' He takes her hands from his arm, guides her head back to the vertical. 'Good night, Ally. Sleep well.'

The stairs tilt as she climbs them and the bedroom floor does not seem to be at quite the customary level. Undressing would be much too complicated. Despite her corset, despite the knobbly seams in her stockings and the suspender-buttons pressing into her thighs, she sleeps dreamlessly until Fanny opens the curtains and another bright day stabs her eyes.

Aunt Mary has sent breakfast in bed, and there is a parcel on the tray, something oddly shaped and heavy with a Manchester postmark.

'She said you would need a tray, Miss Ally. She said to tell you not to stir until you've eaten it. And a parcel came for you. And congratulations, Miss Ally.'

She sits up. A headache, naturally, and the smell of bacon

is not appetising. She prods the parcel, something hard in a soft wrapping. Papa has not forgotten her after all.

Fanny brushes something from Ally's skirt, tangled around her legs. 'Shall I help with your clothes? Perhaps something more comfortable for you?'

'I will undress in a moment, thank you, Fanny. I was somewhat indisposed last night.'

Fanny smiles. 'Yes, Miss Ally. Your coffee.'

She always drinks tea, but Fanny is right, coffee will help. What did she say to Tom? She remembers holding him. When he was trying to leave. Fanny has just put the tray in her lap so she cannot curl back under the blankets. Were they all laughing at her?

'Thank you, Fanny.'

The breakfast-tray is a good preventative for hysteria; one cannot writhe in embarrassment with a tray across one's lap. At least he is going away. She will not have to see him again. And they have no acquaintance in common. Did he say that he would call before or after she disgraced herself? She can apologise, of course, but he will not forget. He is not, surely, a man to mock a woman's affections, but even if he is not laughing at her, astonished by her forwardness, he may be dismayed that she has misunderstood his intentions. How could she think any man would want to marry a professional woman? She made her choice a long time ago. Drink your coffee, she thinks, and as she takes a sip she remembers Elizabeth Garrett Anderson's marriage, Dr Mary Scharlieb who is a wife and mother as well as an excellent surgeon. But Elizabeth Garrett Anderson does not take too much champagne and embrace reluctant gentlemen. Dr Scharlieb's husband, for that matter, is either dead or in India, she cannot remember which. What has she done? She must not expect him this morning. Whatever would have happened will not now. She must devote herself to finding work. She cannot expect to stay here indefinitely, contributing nothing. She is as much relieved as ashamed to find that it is already past nine o'clock, three hours beyond her usual rising time. By the time she has eaten what she can, washed and dressed there will be no more than a few minutes to wait until she can be sure that he is not coming and concentrate on the pages of the *British Medical Journal* listing vacant situations, or perhaps visit Dr Stratton who suggested that there might be a position of the sort that she seeks under Dr Alan Haigh at the Birmingham Asylum. She would be the first woman mad-doctor, the first to take a special interest in nervous cases.

She dresses in her old grey skirt and blouse, as if she is not expecting him, and bundles her hair into a lopsided knot, as if she believed that behaving as if he were coming would make him less likely to do so. She does not open the parcel, which is probably nothing, probably some silk Papa wishes her to match at Liberty's. She is learning, trying to learn, to stop expecting Mamma and Papa to take notice of her success, pronounce her whole and sane as they believe themselves to be.

In the dining room, Aunt Mary is talking to the new cook, making lists of what is to be bought, cooked and eaten for the next seven days. Green peas, Aunt Mary says, so look out for a pair of nice plump ducks. She favours the butcher on Parthenon Street. And she will send out for Friday's dessert; Stone and Son sell such excellent candied fruits that there is really little point in making them at home.

'As long as you are sure he doesn't colour them with copper and lead,' says Ally. 'Some of those grocers were very high-class.'

'I've known Stone these twenty years, my dear. He would do nothing of the sort. And anyway, I am sure James would know if he did.'

Uncle James claims to be able to tell what plants the cows ate before producing the milk that made his butter.

'Thank you for sending up my breakfast, Aunt Mary. I am sorry – I regret any impropriety yesterday evening.'

Aunt Mary glances at the new cook, as if every detail has not already been discussed in the kitchen. 'Thank you, Mrs Bridge. I will come down and finish this later.' They wait; Mrs Bridge crosses the rug, the bow of her white apron swinging over a firmly upholstered navy behind. 'Nonsense, my dear. It was a pleasure to see you at ease for once. And I should say you are due months of breakfasts in bed after these last three years, but I dare say you will not take them.'

Ally shakes her head. 'I must earn my bread, you know, now that I am qualified. I should betray all my friends if I adopted a life of ease.'

But that sounds like begging, or like a reproach to Aunt Mary's own ease. 'I beg your pardon, Aunt Mary, I did not mean anything. I am a little dazed still.'

Aunt Mary puts down her pen. 'You must not fancy that you owe your friends any particular course of life. They did not, and did not intend to, buy your future in supporting your present. You have made all of us very proud, Ally. And now you must do what will make you happy and healthy and keep you that way. You have proved everything already. And I hope it goes without saying that you are warmly welcome to make your home here for as long as you like.'

The sky behind the lace curtains is grey, one of those days when the tentative progress of the English summer falters. 'Has there been any telegram for me, Aunt Mary? Any letter?'

'No, my dear. Perhaps your parents are away from home.'

She nods. She was foolish to hope. She believes she has ceased to look for approbation and is yet repeatedly surprised, hurt, by Mamma's lack of interest. But Aubrey would like to know, and she must write this morning to Mrs Lewis and Miss Johnson. And then call on Dr Stratton to discuss her future.

The doorbell rings.

10

FAN

Aubrey West, 1879

Gouache on white wove paper, 19 × 25

Signed 'ABW', no date

Provenance: Alethea Moberley Cavendish, bequeathed to
the Falmouth Polytechnic Institute, 1929

It is not a real fan. It was not the function that interested West. A semi-circular banner, an outline inked as if with compasses on the watercolour paper that he used throughout this year, purchased from an art supplier in Glasgow on his second Hebridean trip. Most of the surviving works from 1879 explore the people and landscapes of the west coast of Scotland, but this shows an obvious Japanese influence, albeit with some reference to some of the more abstract oils painted during this phase. A dark filigree shape extends tendrils from the left-hand side, its branching severed by the edge of the fan. They end in bulbous curves towards the right-hand side – roots? Deformed fingers, or some kind of mould? Fine veins of red run behind them, exact as fennel-fronds, and on the right edge is part of a white curve speckled like an egg with freckle-coloured dots, the white blushing flesh into an open orifice. The background is a pinkish-brown shade that is not part of his usual palette and the plant shape a darker brown, tinged with green at the edges. Seaweed. A shell. Sand.

The woman with the maggots in her head is not here. She has been moved to the back ward, Dr Camberwell explains, after attempting to remove the maggots via her ear with a crochet hook. There is a new young doctor, someone Ally might like to meet, who is keen to provide occupation even for the private female patients. He believes that they would be less intent on self-destruction had they other ways of passing the time, but of course – as Dr Camberwell himself predicted – providing further pastimes only provides more opportunities for ingenious self-harm. It is all very well for the pauper patients, who are accustomed to labour and would doubtless be quite unmanageable if they were not allowed to wash and scrub. It is strangely difficult, is it not, to conceive of a ladies' occupation that does not entail the use of some sharp or pointed implement? Almost inclines one to see the drawing room in quite a new light, what, all those pretty little weapons in fine white hands? No, it is quite impossible for Miss Moberley – oh, but she is far too pretty to be called Doctor – to see the back wards. A distressing sight, most unfit for fair eyes, and in any case the presence of strangers only upsets patients who are already *in extremis*. Allow him instead to conduct her through the women's parlour, and then perhaps into the gardens? The roses, if he does say so himself, are really rather delightful at the moment.

Most of the patients stand as Dr Camberwell and Dr Moberley enter the room. It reminds Ally more of school than of the hospital, with a dulled parquet floor, wooden chairs set against the walls and an occasional table before each of the two windows, although there are no plants here, no pictures or bookshelves. There is an odour as the patients gather around, as how indeed, she thinks, in this weather should there not be, from those denied clean linen and a daily bath? Their clothes are ill-fitting, in some cases so much so that dresses cannot be fastened and feet shuffle, and she wonders how much more sane these women might feel and appear to be were they allowed their own clothes and shoes.

'Dr Camberwell –'

'Excuse me, doctor –'

'Please, sir, when am I to be released?'

'Doctor, I must speak to you. I cannot sleep.'

Dr Camberwell steps back. 'Now, now, ladies. See, I have brought you a visitor. Are you not lucky? This is Miss Moberley. She is taking an interest in establishments such as this.'

A tall woman, standing behind the others and wearing a skirt made for a short one, laughs. 'Lunatic asylums, Dr Camberwell. Establishments such as this are lunatic asylums.'

'Monomania,' murmurs Dr Camberwell to Ally. 'Seems as sane as you or me until she starts to think she's shedding her skin like a snake.'

An older woman in a stained jersey, too hot for the time of year, plucks his sleeve with a grimy hand. There is a crescent of dirt under each fingernail. 'Please, doctor. Please.'

Please what? He pushes her hand off. 'This way, Miss Moberley, this way. A sad case, episodes of terrible profanity and the most violent rages.'

She has been devoting herself to the literature of insanity these last weeks. She knows there are other doctors in Britain at this moment also wondering about the relationships between madness and incarceration. There are those, writes Professor Matthews, who, despite appearing sane while within the asylum, are quite unable to function when returned to the

299

world outside, but there are almost certainly also some whose temporary madness is made permanent by confinement to a madhouse. It is a problem for physicians that the risks of testing this hypothesis are intolerable.

Mamma does not come to the wedding. She writes: she cannot leave the Home, the Hospital, and if Ally will insist on marrying in London instead of from her own home, she must accept that her friends and family may decline the inconvenience of attending. And Ally deludes herself if she imagines that any hospital will employ a married woman, if she has really convinced herself that she is not throwing away all the gifts and opportunities that others have laboured to offer her. Mamma is ashamed to have to tell Miss Johnson that Ally has chosen, after all those years of work, to marry. Perhaps, Ally says, the letter in her hands, they should after all postpone the wedding, rearrange so it can take place in Mamma's church when Tom returns from his journey. A few months, after all, taken from a lifetime together? Aunt Mary takes the letter from her; no, she says, Ally, your loyalty will belong to Tom now. Elizabeth has always been hard to please and you must not sacrifice your marriage, your husband's interests, to your mother's urging. You are not a child, in whom obedience is in principle laudable, but an adult who must, and does, take the most serious decisions on a daily basis. Begin as you mean to go on; if you have real doubts about your marriage, address them with the utmost attention. If not, do not allow the concerns of a person who has never met Tom to trifle with his and your happiness. Of course you will find work; I am sure that many women would much rather be attended by a married woman than a virgin, and certainly male patients are more likely to find your attendance acceptable. Is there not a crying need for a female nervous doctor, when so many of women's mental troubles begin with experiences unique to our sex? There is, after all, a modesty of the mind as well as the body. There are many things it will be perfectly proper for you to know as a married woman. It is not, she adds, in the least unnatural that you should marry from the establishment that has been your home these past years. And I believe that Alfred will come, whatever Elizabeth does.

And on one count, at least, it seems that Aunt Mary is right. Ally has written to the Chief Medical Officer of the Truro Asylum, who has recently published an essay on the diagnosis and treatment of religious melancholy, asking if she might study with him with a view to developing a specialism in nervous and mental cases. There is a letter with a Truro postmark at her place at breakfast; yes, he would welcome her, and is pleased to see that some of the best new graduates take a serious interest in mad-doctoring. With the expansion of the great asylums, he believes there will be many opportunities for new research and employment in this area, and some women patients will doubtless respond better to a female physician. It is not a paid position. They will depend on Tom's salary, for now, and will live in the cottage he rents, with a daily girl to help Ally with the rough cleaning. You should perhaps, says Aunt Mary doubtfully, ask Mrs Bridge to teach you to cook. Aunt Mary, who has not stirred a pan or sliced an onion these twenty years, has forgotten Mamma's methods.

They decide that she is too old for orange blossom and tulle, that it would be ridiculous to see a doctor blushing under white lace and a veil. In years to come, Aunt Mary says, I suppose there will be so many doctor-brides that their dress will not seem a problem in the least. I suppose professional women will find ways of doing these things. Ally will not promise to obey; it seems a bad idea, says Tom, to begin a marriage with an undertaking made in bad faith. Not being a parcel, she declines to be given away. They are making new rituals, building the road under their feet. There will be no honeymoon, for Tom, already back in Cornwall and barely able to spare time to come to London for the wedding, is required at work. It will all, he writes, be worth it in the end, when their ship comes in. Penvenick has won the big colonial contract and he is being sent to make the preliminary reports. Mr Penvenick will not tell him where he is going; the whole project is of the utmost commercial sensitivity, and while naturally he has complete faith in Tom or he would not be sending him, it is possible that even the nature of Tom's preparations would betray his destination if he knew what it is. And so Tom must trust him, as he trusts Tom, and if all goes well they will both be rewarded.

Presents arrive. Annie's Mamma sends a tea-service, white bone china patterned with yellow and blue tulips, with pointed handles and octagonal saucers and plates. Tom's mother passes on her own silver coffee-pot, sugar bowl and cream-jug on a silver tray engraved with roses, which will require constant polishing. When Papa sends a Persian carpet, flickering with purple and blue, she knows he will not come. A post-card comes a few days later: Papa has been honoured by the inclusion of one of his pictures in the grand exhibition in Paris, and he and Aubrey are passing the remainder of the summer in France. There is a revolving bookcase from Miss Johnson and a hand-made kidskin doctor's bag from the Manchester Women's Education Association. And Aubrey, who has not acknowledged her graduation, has written only once since May's funeral, sends a framed design for a fan, a drowned fan. Seaweed creeps and reaches. And of her bones are coral made.

*

Aunt Mary will not countenance Tom staying at the house the night before the wedding, but she divorces tradition so far as to invite him to dinner. A cold collation, she says, the kind of dinner one might expect in a house whose daughter marries in the morning. He arrives earlier than expected, and leaves Fanny protesting in his wake as he runs up the stairs. Ally and Aunt Mary, hands full of tissue paper and underwear, hear his steps and stop as if they are about to be photographed. What if she doesn't like him any more, what if the man to whom she has been writing all summer is not quite the same as the man about to come through the door? She bites her lip. Aunt Mary folds the paper around Ally's drawers and goes to the door.

'My dear Tom.' She takes his hands. 'And so you could not wait to see your bride! Shall we go downstairs?'

Ally drops the petticoat she is folding. Why, anyway, are they trying to protect hidden garments from creasing? No-one will know if her chemise shows folds. His hair is bright even here, in the dusk of the attic corridor. He looks tired, travel-stained. And he is indeed himself, no figment of paper and imagination but bone, flesh, skin, freckles.

'Ally.' With a glance towards Aunt Mary, he kisses her cheek, stands back.

'Did you –' Ally clears her throat. 'Did you have a good journey?'

'No. But it doesn't matter. You are well?' He looks her up and down, as if her grey skirt and untidy hair will tell him any of the things she is failing to say.

'Nervous. But well.'

Should she enquire reciprocally after his health, as if they have only just met, as if they will not in the morning promise to love and cherish each other until death and in the evening ... become intimate? She feels a prickle of defensiveness, as if they

303

are two cats in one room, opposing magnets attempting to touch.

He looks up. 'I missed you. I am happy to be here.'

Aunt Mary coughs. 'Oh, very well. I will expect you both in the drawing room for tea in ten minutes.'

Her skirts flow down the stairs behind her, like water over stones. Everything pauses.

'Yes,' says Ally. Downstairs, the drawing room door closes. 'I also.'

She swallows. 'I had a letter. Yesterday. From Dr Crosswyn. He says I will be welcome to study with him. He appears to have no objection to women doctors.'

Tom reaches towards her, touches her hair. And then changes his mind and drops his hand. 'I am so glad. I have been speaking to the people at the cottage hospital for you, but that will be much better. And they have often need of an extra pair of hands if you should find yourself at a loose end. At liberty.'

'Or if we should need the income. Thank you, Tom. You will not object, then, if I do not earn at the beginning? While I study?'

'My dear. I thought we had established this. If you do not object to cooking for yourself, to living in a small cottage and keeping no conveyance, how could I object to your studying? And perhaps one day, you will be a famous physician and I content to entertain your aristocratic patients and fend off elegant ladies who would demand your attentions and waste your time.'

'Ah, but you forget. It is the women accused of wasting time in whom I interest myself. Invalids and nervous cases.'

'Then perhaps I shall fend off gentlemen with broken backs. In any case, I promise again: I would no more prevent you following your calling than you would have me resign from this journey. And I have been told, by the way, to prepare for a temperate climate not unlike our own.'

'Canada?' she asks. The west coast, they have thought, from where a Trinity House Committee has recently returned with a set of recommendations that someone will need to implement.

'Perhaps. But then what need for secrecy? And anyway, in some regards the Canadians are in our vanguard in lighthouse improvements.'

They reflect again, standing at the top of the attic stairs in Bloomsbury, on the globe, the spread of pink across the map. The Chinese treaty ports can surely not be described as temperate. The Stevensons are already at work in India. No-one would try to survey the Canadian east coast in autumn and winter. Australia, especially in this season, is hot. New Zealand?

Tom shrugs, looking at her, still, as if she might be about to do something, as if she has omitted some necessary act.

'We should go downstairs,' she says. 'Aunt Mary –'

'Aunt Mary fears that we will offend the proprieties. Or perhaps only that we will offend the proprieties in her house. Just tell me, Ally – you are happy? You look forward to tomorrow?'

Her shoes are scuffed, must be polished before tomorrow. Her mind stretches towards the words he asks to hear, towards the speaking of affection and desire. If she did not know better, she would say that there was a physical change in her, that her heart rests more comfortably under her breastbone for his faith. She would like to tell him that she sleeps more easily and wakes without the life-long start of dread at another day. That his importance to her is frightening. Without looking at him, she nods.

*

Annie arrives while they are still at breakfast, accompanied by a maid who carries a rustling dress bag over her arms as if about to present it at the altar. Uncle James and the boys half-rise, a kind of reverse bow.

'Good morning! Eggs, Ally? You are not too nervous, too refined, to eat at such a moment? Dear me, where are your bridal sensibilities?'

'Somewhere in the schoolroom with my white veil and obedience,' says Ally. 'Have a sausage. Have two.'

Aunt Mary dabs her lips and folds her napkin. 'Really, girls. Please. Fanny, another cup for Miss Forrest, please. And you might help – Jane, is it? – with the dress. Annie, would you care for some eggs?'

Fanny and Annie's Jane murmur and Jane retreats, her tread heavy on the stairs. Annie sits down. 'Thank you, Mrs Dunne, but I have breakfasted. A cup of tea would be most welcome, if Ally is not in haste to dress.'

Ally butters toast. She will not play the blushing bride, will not slip into the role waiting at her feet like a hole in the road.

'I do not see why it would take me longer to put on a dress today than any other day. George is the slow dresser in this house.'

George has recently progressed from combing his hair without being asked to using a pomade whose turpentine smell always flashes Papa's studio into Ally's mind. He checks his collar in the hall mirror before leaving the house and fusses over the crease in his trousers.

'He's started talking to girls,' says Freddie.

'Because it's more interesting than talking to little boys who can't open their mouths without trading insults.'

'Stop it, boys. Today of all days.'

*

They stand together before the mirror, Annie in her copper-green evening dress, made suitable for a morning wedding by the addition of an embroidered velvet bolero, Ally in cloudy blue that will take her to Penvenick's Christmas party or hospital dances in Cornwall. Annie has pinned Ally's hair for her and secured a gravity-defying hat that Ally will never be able to pin properly when she wants to wear the outfit again. Annie has dabbed Ally's nose with powder and her cheeks with rouge, instructed her to pout and then grimace while Annie paints her lips the colour they are anyway. Mamma would not approve. Masked, costumed: she does not look herself.

'I feel like taking it all off,' she says.

'I am sure Tom would be delighted.' Annie hands her her bouquet, irises and baby's breath. 'You are beautiful. Come along.'

She holds the flowers, from whose stamens Annie has thought to snip the egg-yolk pollen. Annie sweeps the door open before her, drops a mocking curtsey.

'Hold up your skirt on the stairs,' Annie says. 'There will be a loop under the flounce.'

There is.

'Annie,' she asks. 'Annie, do you think Dr Moberley Cavendish is too much?'

They reach the landing. Annie dusts something from Ally's shoulder.

'I think Dr Moberley Cavendish is splendid. And very pretty. Come.' She crooks her elbow, and arm-in-arm Dr Forrest and Dr Moberley Cavendish proceed down the main staircase to the portico where their carriage awaits.

Everyone comes to the station to see them off, the boys piled together in the carriage with Uncle James and Tom facing

Aunt Mary, Ally and Annie in a clutter of feet and a froth of skirts. They lower the windows to let in the sunshine and the susurrations of London in summer, of the children shouting in the parks and the street-sellers crying their wares, machines humming in factories and workshops. She thinks of the voices of London, all the people speaking at this moment: the chatter of shop-girls, the oratory of barristers and the hectoring of bus-conductors. Behind the voices, there are the sounds Londoners no longer notice, the background noise that constitutes city-dwellers' idea of silence, the pistons, whistles and steam bringing people, letters, milk from the lowlands and wool from the hills, fish travelling on ice from the seaside and polished cherries from the orchards of Kent and Herefordshire. And drowned in those sounds, the silence of the river bearing ships freighted with spices and silks – cashmere shawls – from the outermost reaches of Empire to the grocers of English high streets. From how far up in the sky, she wonders, could one hear London? How do birds, winging the Channel, understand the city? Falmouth is a long way away. Tom says it is not a quiet place, but bustling with as many tongues, as many trades, as the City itself. There are parks and public gardens there too, though it seems unlikely that children living by the sea would choose to play in parks. You cannot hear the sea from the cottage, he says, but he sometimes wakes at night to hear fog-horns and ships' bells and knows that a fog has crept up the estuary in the night. Rivers on the map usually remind Ally of vasculature, roots and branches, but in West Cornwall it seems to be the other way around, as if the sea reaches its tentacles far into the land, as if this place where they will live, this peninsula off a peninsula, may at any moment become an island.

There was champagne at the wedding breakfast, with the cold chicken and ham and asparagus, the wine jellies and strawberries, and the boys are boisterous, nudging each other and giggling. Annie and Aunt Mary talk of weddings past, of Annie's sister's wedding where the bridal bouquet was delivered only after Annie's despairing mother had dispatched the younger girls to pick every flower blooming in the September garden, of Aunt Mary's own wedding at which Grandmamma wore black and arrived late. Tom is opposite her, his black shoes polished to marmoreal brightness, for her. He has new grey trousers with braid running up the seams, for her. He is leaning forward, elbows on his parted knees to brace his weight against the movement of the carriage, a masculine pose. He's talking, smiling. His jacket sleeves have ridden up to expose starched white cuffs, their opening held by barred silver cuff-links over muscle, tanned skin and golden fur. Later, she thinks, later – Uncle James smiles at her and then she meets Tom's gaze, answers the question in his raised eyebrows without a word.

Yes. She is happy; she looks forward to tomorrow.

ACKNOWLEDGEMENTS

Most of this book was written in two cafes in West Cornwall and on the Cornish Riviera trains between Paddington and Truro. I thank the people at Earth and Water in Penryn and at Espressini in Falmouth for letting me write there for hours, and I thank the staff on First Great Western trains for insisting on the quietness of the Quiet Carriage (an insufficiently acknowledged contribution to English letters and scholarship). Thank you to Katy at the Falmouth Bookseller who not only met but foresaw my research needs.

My colleagues in the Writing Programme and the English Department at Warwick University give me a supportive writing community.

I thank Sharon Dixon for conversations about women, medicine and nineteenth-century surgery, Sinead Mooney for late-night discussions of historical fiction and Margaret MacDonald for advice on research in art history. Errors of fact or probability remain, as ever, my own.

Thank you, as always, to Anna Webber at United Agents, my first reader and voice of reason.

It is always a delight to work with Granta Books. I thank my editor Max Porter, Anne Meadows and everyone else there for looking after me and my books with such intelligent assiduity.

COLD EARTH

'Moss is such a master at evoking suspense . . . a rich treat'
Jane Smiley, *Guardian*

'Full of burial pits, strange happenings and the cries of the dead . . . an
apocalyptic take on *Lord of the Flies* meets *The Secret History*'
Metro

On the west coast of Greenland, a team of six archaeologists has assembled to unearth traces of the lost Viking settlements. But while they
settle into uneasy domesticity, camping between the ruined farmstead
and the burnt-out chapel, there is news of a pandemic back home. As
the Arctic winter approaches, their communications with the outside
world fall away. Utterly gripping, *Cold Earth* is an exceptional and
haunting first novel about the possibility of survival and the traces we
leave behind.

'An unnerving, ambitious debut . . . utterly absorbing and – appropri-
ately enough – very chilling' *Daily Mail*

'A thought-provoking, suspenseful work that leaves the reader in no
doubt about the fragility of the human condition: not just of the individual struggling to survive a hostile environment, but of a species that
is changing its home planet in potentially deadly ways' *Observer*

'Moss's stark writing delivers stinging splashes of cold water. Every
element of the novel is distilled for purity of purpose' *The Times*

NIGHT WAKING

'Moss writes marvellously (and often hilariously) about the clash between career and motherhood' *The Times*

'Highly enjoyable' *Daily Telegraph*

Anna Bennett hasn't slept in months. Overwhelmed by the needs of her two young boys and opposed on principle to domesticity, Anna is a historian struggling to write without a room of her own. Stranded on a Hebridean island where her husband is researching the puffins, Anna's work changes when her son finds a baby's skeleton buried in the garden. As an investigation begins, Anna must confront the island's past while finding a way to live with the competing demands of the present.

'Tartly humourous, sad and clever' *Sunday Times*

'A brilliantly observed comedy of twenty-first century manners . . . a tightly plotted mystery that keeps the reader wondering, and hoping, until the final page' *Financial Times*

'The trials of family life are comically and stylishly depicted . . . [an] original and accomplished novel' *Daily Mail*

'I read *Night Waking* with avid enjoyment and no small amount of recognition' Maggie O'Farrell, *Scotsman*

Also by Sarah Moss and available from Granta Books
www.grantabooks.com

NAMES FOR THE SEA
Strangers in Iceland

'Hilarious . . . one of the most enjoyable travel books I've read'
The Times

'Honest, funny, frank and insightful, it is a reassuring guide to the strangeness of being a stranger. An enviable experience beautifully described' Gavin Francis, author of *Empire Antarctica*

At the height of the financial crisis in 2009, Sarah Moss and her husband moved with their two small children to Iceland. From their makeshift home among the half-finished skyscrapers of Reykjavik, Moss travelled to hillsides of boiling mud and volcanic craters, and the remote farms and fishing villages of the far north. As the weeks and months went by, she and her family found new ways to live.

'Beautifully written . . . Moss grapples with new foods, customs and landscapes that are both oddly familiar and wildly alien'
Financial Times

'An entertaining, insightful book [and] a refreshing antidote to wrestling-with-the-landscape travel writing . . . Moss is a very good companion' Kathleen Jamie, *Guardian*